SERRA ROSE

Consumed

Contents

Content Warning

This book is intended for readers who are 18+. It contains detailed scenes of consensual sexual intimacy. It also includes themes and scenes that may be triggering for some readers.

Dubious consent
Decapitation
Acts of war
Abusive parental figures
Death by fire
Bondage/use of restraints
Violence
Loss of parent
Organ removal
Deaths
Murders
De-fanging
Risk of breath restriction

This is a dark romance, and Carlos sees no need to soften his language. He is gruesome and bloodthirsty.

Be kind to yourself; your mental health matters.

Translations

Spanish/Castellano

Cazadora - Huntress
Mi Reina - My Queen
Mi Rey - My King
Mi Tigre - My Tiger
Helado - Ice cream
Padre - Father
Estúpida - Stupid

Italian

Fondamenta - Sidewalk on a canal
Calli - Streets
Calle - Street
Grazie - Thank you
Piazza San Marco - St Mark's Square
Ponte di Rialto - Rialto Bridge
Sestieri - Six neighbourhoods of Venice: Castello, Cannaregio, San Polo, San Marco, Santa Croce, and Dorsoduro (each is a Sestiere).

French
Ma chérie - My Darling

Vampire Clans

Carlos's clan: La Voz (The Voice)
Giuseppe's clan: Famiglia di Sammarinese (Family of San Marino)
Roman clan: Legione (Legion)
Gabriela's clan: La Primera Familia (The First Clan)

Previously in Bloodsong

After grieving the loss of her sister, and recovering from the breakup of a toxic relationship, Quinn returns to her halted music career. She and her bandmates and best friends, a romantic couple named Mia and Lilith, are invited to play at the local bar, where she meets Matteo - a mysterious and hot stranger mesmerised by her voice. Instantly drawn to him, she is unaware that he is a vampire.

On her way home after the gig, Quinn is confronted by an unknown man, relieved when Matteo appears, saving her from a gruesome attack. Once she has gone, Matteo, already feeling possessive and protective of her, kills the attacker.

The murder of a human draws the anger of his vampire Queen, who punishes Matteo with starvation. During this time, he paints Quinn, finding that focusing on her has helped calm his feral nature.

Quinn and her friends attend the opening of a new art gallery, only to find that Matteo is not only an artist, but the gallery owner. He shows her his art; however, she is shocked to discover that he has painted her. She reacts badly, which wounds Matteo. After being spoken to by a friend of Matteo's, Carlos, she realises that she has been rude, and she attempts to find him to apologise. She finds him in mid-feed, discovering that not only are vampires real, but she is attracted to one.

Quinn struggles to accept her new reality, and her attraction to Matteo. In the meantime, her first concert has been booked, and she tries to focus on her band's dream. However, Matteo's persistence soon weakens her resolve, and she agrees to give him a chance to prove himself to her.

She soon finds herself falling for Matteo, and hiding his secret from her friends. After an evening at a masquerade, they give in to their desire for each other, only for him to drink from her and lose control. To save her life, he shares his blood with her, which awakens a blood-fuelled sex frenzy for both of them. She soon faces a vampirelike bloodlust, which he helps her through to ensure she remains human.

Matteo's blood leaves her system and Quinn returns to normal, needing space from him. He gives in to his feral nature, going on a rampage throughout Melbourne, and burning down his art gallery before his Queen has him caged.

Quinn discovers that one of her friends is a vampire hunter, and Matteo is given to the Hunters. Seeking advice from her parents, she learns that she is a siren, and her connection with the vampire is due to her Calling him; the one worthy of her heart. She learns the effects Matteo's death would have on her.

Quinn allies with Carlos to rescue Matteo, taking an arrow to her chest, and Matteo shares his blood with her, turning her into a vampire.

Her first feeding results in one friend's death, the other declaring her an enemy. She and Matteo join a new clan, with Carlos as their King.

The clan soon decide to leave Melbourne, to claim Venice, Italy, as their territory.

Map

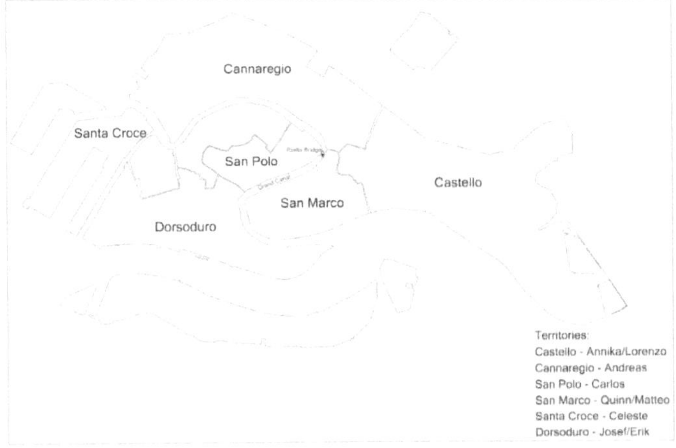

Map of Venice and territories of La Voz Clan

Chapter 1

Kingdom of Aragon (Spain) - 1107

On the night of my wedding, we gathered around a large fire in the centre of the village. Sounds of celebration echoed into the night, and the heat of the flames, combined with the ale I'd been drinking, wrapped me in happy fog. The aroma of cooked meat filled the air, along with burning wood. People nearby played music while others danced. I took another sip of sweet ale from my vessel and watched my new wife on the other side of the fire. She caught sight of me watching her and smiled before lowering her eyes, tucking hair behind her ear.

I wished I could smile back. She didn't deserve my iciness. My bride was a beautiful woman, with deep brown eyes and brown hair. She was olive-skinned, and her face lit up when she smiled. I'd have to have been blind not to notice her beauty. But the marriage had been forced on me, on us. Arranged by my father. In his words, at twenty-three, I was to behave like an adult and cease my shameful ways. To be a responsible member of society.

My younger brother, Jullian, stood next to me. His hair was straight and black, and he had the same olive colour as the rest of us, his eyes grey, like our mother's. He was already almost as tall as me, despite the five years between us.

"You're avoiding her," he commented.

"Don't be stupid," I snapped.

I glanced around the fire, catching the gazes of those I'd seduced recently. Men and women, I loved them all. I smiled at each of them, disappointment weighing on my heart. As a married man, I was to commit to one person. I'd managed to avoid marriage longer than most people my age.

Jullian's words rang true, though. I was avoiding her. But then, so was she. We both knew we'd soon have to return to my home as husband and wife. I figured she was a virgin, and would likely be afraid of being alone with me. I'd have to be gentle and comfort her. I was not accustomed to being gentle, so I dreaded it as much as she did.

"Don't you like her?" my brother asked. "Most grooms wouldn't leave their bride's side."

"She is beautiful," I agreed. "I think I frighten her."

"She's not afraid of you, but what's in your trousers!" Jullian elbowed me. "You're known for your rough habits."

I couldn't hold back the grin then, raising my eyebrows. Both of us laughed.

"Carlos!" my older brother, Patro interrupted me. "This is a joyous event. Shouldn't you be dancing with your bride? Drink and dance. It'll keep our father happy. Then afterwards, take your new wife, and hopefully put a son inside her."

Patro looked more like me than our younger brother, our curly brown hair that of our mother's while we'd inherited our father's blue eyes. The main differences between us were the four-year age gap, and that I was smaller in build than him.

I raised my tankard. "I am drinking!" I grinned at him, swaying on my feet.

Patro was already married with sons. The idea of fatherhood did not appeal to me in any way.

"Is he drunk?" Patro asked Jullian.

Jullian chuckled. "He's been that way since the ceremony."

I finished my drink. "I need to take a piss."

"I wouldn't go too far into the forest. The wolves are hungry. Someone else was found with their throat ripped out." Patro warned.

"I heard that it's just one wolf, dragging people from the village whenever it gets hungry," Jullian said.

I'd heard the talk of wolves and the rising hysteria that was coming from it. The last three weeks had resulted in people being afraid to leave the safety of the village. "I have my dagger," I reassured my brothers.

They laughed. "Is it actually sharp?" Patro asked. "Isn't it just ceremonial?"

I glared as I left them. Wandering through the village, I considered pissing in my father's bed. The idea made me laugh as I pictured his reaction. I turned my thoughts to the wedding. I'd met my new wife only once, and she'd barely said anything. I'd got the impression she wanted to be married even less than I did. She did look somewhat younger than me. I let out a frustrated sigh.

"Why aren't you enjoying yourself, like everyone else?" a woman's voice came from the dark.

I couldn't see anyone. "Who's there?" I demanded. It was not a voice I knew, and fear tingled down my spine.

She stepped forward. Firelight of a nearby torch reflected off her face. The light seemed to be playing a trick on my eyes. Her eyes didn't look normal.

She had long dark hair, with a small, secretive smile. The way she walked seemed wrong, more animal than human. I couldn't look away from her, as if hypnotised. I'd never seen her before.

"Are you here for the wedding?" I asked. "Everyone's by the fire."

"A wedding?" Her smile widened. "That's what drew me here. It's quite the celebration."

I glanced over my shoulder towards the fire with the urge to return, where people could see me. I was both drawn to this woman and afraid of her. Something about her presence screamed, 'Run.' In my state, I hoped I wouldn't have to. When I turned back to her, she had moved closer, without a sound. I stepped back, fear flooding me. This close, her eyes looked red. She breathed in deep.

"You smell delicious," she remarked, her smile widening.

"You're afraid. Good. I do love my food to have flavour."

Food? I caught sight of long, sharp fangs lengthening in her mouth.

"What …?" The sight of her fangs sent my heart pounding, and my terror held me in place, unable to look away. I wished I had stayed by the fire, with my brothers.

"Run," she whispered. "That scent of your fear is irresistible." A low growl rose from her.

Finally, my feet regained the ability to move. I turned and ran. But I didn't make it far, before she blocked my path, amusement and hunger reflected in her eyes. Behind her, my wedding celebration continued, no one looking for me. She took a step towards me.

"You're afraid, but not as much as you should be," she noted. "That's disappointing. You've been drinking, haven't you? That always numbs the fear."

Had I been sober, I'd probably have been pissing myself at the sight of such a creature.

"D-Demon," I muttered, and reached for my dagger. It should not be a sharp blade, but I'd ignored that rule when I'd had the dagger made.

She smiled again. "Oh, poor little human, I am *so* much worse. I am hungry, though, so you'll probably die."

I tried to run again, but she caught me easily. Again and again. Laughing at my attempts. I'd tried to make it to the celebration. The two of us faced each other just beyond the glow of the fire. I held my dagger up in front of me.

She laughed again. "Oh, you're delightful!" She advanced on me. "It won't hurt," she whispered. "You'll enjoy my bite. You might even be begging for more. I am first-generation, so my venom is a little more potent than others of my kind."

First generation, venom, her kind? I had no idea what she was talking about. But before I could say anything, she lunged at me, and we hit the ground hard. She leaned in, forcing my head back, and her fangs pierced my throat.

Oh! I was filled with heat and want. The feeling spread out, and I let out a moan. Another surge flooded me, and I started to grind against her. She was somewhat older, but I didn't care. I only wanted. Writhing with desire, lust fogged my mind. Somehow, I knew she was drinking from me, my blood. I didn't fight her, letting the waves of pleasure wash over me. The world started to fade, laughter and music from the fire growing faint. I moaned again.

"You *dare* lay with another woman on your wedding night?" My father's furious voice broke through my bliss.

The woman lifted herself from me, blood dripping from her mouth, and she turned around, hissing. I'd never heard a person hiss like that before. She crouched, keeping herself between me and my father. I squirmed on the ground, wanting more. Whatever she'd done to me, I wanted more. It was intoxicating. I couldn't move, struggling to remain awake.

"Demon!" My father shouted. and drew his sword.

Others responded to him, drawing their own swords. No longer able to hold on to consciousness, I let myself fall into a pleasure-filled sleep. The sounds of growls and shouting were the last things I heard.

I passed in and out of consciousness many times. Mostly with the woman's mouth to my throat, waves of heat and pleasure pulsing through me. If she wasn't drinking from me, she was watching me, her red eyes on my face.

Finally, I awoke to silence. The woman who'd attacked me crouched nearby, watching. Blood dripped from her mouth, down her chin.

"You're a fighter, aren't you?" she laughed. "I've been feeding off you throughout the day, and you keep begging me for more."

I sat up with a groan, light-headed as I glanced around us. "How did I get in the stable?" I asked. Daylight seeped in through the gaps in the boards of the stable.

She smiled, flashing her fangs. "I was wounded, and hungry. So I brought you here to feed in peace." She pointed around the stable. "Unfortunately, I'm stuck here until the sun sets. Half your village is outside, and they're a little unhappy."

"You bit me," I accused.

She laughed. "Many times. You enjoyed it, too. You were grinding yourself against me. I *did* warn you my venom was potent."

I frowned at her, but I recalled the effects her bite had had on me. My cock twitched at the memory.

"I can smell your arousal." She shook her head in amusement. "You're practically on Death's door, but you'd happily bare your throat to me again."

Need flooded through my body. I didn't want her, just what her bite did for me. "Did you bring me in here to kill me?" I asked.

"I did," she admitted. "But I also hoped having you with me would hold your people off. It seems to be working so far: otherwise, they would have burned this stable down by now. I don't know for how much longer though."

"I've never known such pleasure," I murmured. "I want more."

"You'd welcome your own death," she marvelled. Before I could say anything, she struck, sinking her fangs in again.

Yes! I closed my eyes. If this was death, I'd die happy.

Disappointment surged through me when she pulled back.

"You'd be more concerned about dying if it weren't for the effects of my bite," she informed me. "That heat surging through you, that's the venom. The pleasure, the desire you feel. That stops you fighting as I feed from you. I give you a pleasurable death that you embrace. Without that effect, my bite would be immensely painful."

She smiled at me with a dripping red mouth.

"Who are you?" I asked. "*What* are you? Are you a demon?"

She laughed. "Yes, you humans do like to use that word a lot. I've seen a lot of non-human people, but I can't say I've seen any demons." She eyed me. "Knowing what I am isn't going to change the outcome of the situation we're in. I will take my fill from you, leave your body here for your people to find as soon as I can leave. But since you asked, my name is Gabriela. I am a vampire. An immortal being who survives by drinking human blood."

Raised voices outside the stable drew my attention. Hers, too, and she hissed at the door, baring her fangs. I recognised my father's voice.

"My father isn't known for his patience," I told her. "It's likely that he'll assume I'm dead soon, and they'll try to bust their way in here. Or burn it."

The amusement dropped from her face for a moment as she eyed the door. "Then protect me," she commanded. "And I'll give you more of what you want."

She rose to her feet, pulling me up. I swayed on unsteady feet, feeling weak and shaky. Despite the severity of the moment, I laughed. "This is one way to get out of married life, and having children," I muttered.

"Oh, yes, your wedding," she said. "Where I caught you wandering in the dark instead of enjoying the presence of your new wife. I'm sure you would have made a great husband and father."

I said nothing as I moved towards the door. I had no idea how to protect her, but I needed to try, to get what I wanted. When I reached the door, I leaned on it heavily. The edges of my vision darkened, and I wondered if I was going to pass out.

"Don't die on me yet," her voice was right next to my ear. I glanced at her. She held up my dagger. "Here, maybe this will help you. They may not welcome your presence. I can smell their fear. Humans do stupid things when they're afraid." She lifted my arm and bit into my wrist but released it without drinking. Once again, I was overcome by heat and the need for her bite. "Here's a taste of what you want. If you want more, find a way to get rid of them. Convince them I've left, if you must. Don't let them burn me."

I caught a glint of fear as she stepped away from me, taking shelter in the most shadowed corner of the stable. I tightened my grip on the dagger, and it took effort to pull open the door. The bright sunlight poured over me, and I let my eyes adjust. It was low in the sky, nearing the western horizon. Twenty men stood at the door, five with bows raised. Many villagers stood behind them, watching.

"Step aside," my father demanded. When I didn't move, he glared. "Get him out of the way."

As someone reached for me, I struck out with my dagger, slicing across his throat. Blood sprayed over my face and I stared in horror as he fell. I'd never killed anyone before. *I'm a murderer.*

"Move!" my father said. "Or die with the demon."

"She's not a demon," I corrected. "She's a—"

I stopped. My father raised his bow and drew back the string, releasing an arrow. It hit the ground at my feet. A warning shot.

"My idiot son," he said. "An embarrassment. He deserves to die with her."

"No! Father, what are you doing?" Patro asked. He stepped forward, only to be pulled back. He struggled against the hold on him. "Stop!"

My entire life had been about expectations and disapproval. I glanced over my shoulder, meeting the eyes of a being who offered me pleasure and death. I didn't know what to do. Neither option made sense to me.

"I don't want to die," I admitted.

"Then get out of the way," my father said again.

I couldn't move. I'd killed someone, which meant my village would soon demand my own death. I took a step back, into the stable. "I'd rather take my chances in here," I admitted.

"Then you're choosing to die with her." My father fired another arrow, this one hitting me in the stomach. "Burn it down."

I stared down at the arrow sticking out of me. Pain started to spread out from where the wooden shaft had pierced my gut. *He shot me.*

"No!" Patro called out in fear. "You'll kill him. Carlos!"

"Your brother is already dead." My father released a third arrow, this one striking my chest. And another, piercing my side. Then a flaming arrow flew past me. The fire spread quickly.

"Let him die." My father turned his back and started to walk away.

I cursed and tried to speak. No words came out as I gasped to breathe. *Coward. You turned your back. Don't you have the stomach to watch your own son die, by your hand?* I wished I could say the words. To curse him. I wished he would die slowly, my only regret that I wouldn't see it. The rest of the villagers looked down at me and walked away. Patro stared at our father in horror, and back to me.

Unable to stand, I fell. Everyone I ever knew had turned their back on me and left me to die in a burning stable. I silently cursed them all. They'd all stood by as my father shot arrows into me. *Feel my wrath from the grave: I wish a painful death on you all.*

Patro's face was full of anguish, fighting to get to me as

men pushed the doors closed. The vampire stood over me.

"Well, this isn't exactly what I had in mind," she admitted. "Now we both die." She smiled. "Although, I also didn't expect you to kill someone. That was a waste of blood."

Knowledge that I was going to die flooded through me, a cold truth that made me want to roar in anger. I stared at the spreading flames. This was going to be painful. I closed my eyes, letting darkness claim me.

"Wake up, little killer," Gabriela whispered. "The sun has set." She lifted me in her arms.

I had no strength, and a tear slid down my cheek. I was going to die, and I hoped her bite would take away the pain.

"Don't worry, brave killer, I've got you." she said, her voice suddenly soothing. She lowered her head, her tongue sliding over my throat.

A splintering sound, followed by alarmed shouts filled my head. The fire and the stable were gone, and she carried me deep into the forest, far from my father and those who wanted me dead. I could feel myself fading, pain filling my entire body as I struggled to breathe.

"What are you doing?" I choked, my voice barely audible.

"Do you want to live, Little Killer?" she asked me.

I didn't understand her question. I was dying. I opened my mouth, but instead of speaking, I coughed. My entire body convulsed as pain overwhelmed me

She entered a house that I knew. A house I had played in as a child, with my brothers. It was long since abandoned when the old man in it had died. My grandfather had been a kinder man than my father. I caught sight of others watching us, their eyes red. I whimpered.

She lowered me to the ground and stroked my face. "I

know, you are dying. And it hurts. But what you did impressed me. You will not die today. I'm giving you life."

Her words made no sense. I could only stare at her in confusion, my breaths pained. Those watching us remained silent.

She glanced up. "The villagers may come searching. I have to remain with him as he slumbers. You don't have to stay."

I coughed again, groaning in pain. One by one, the others left. Only one stayed, his hair and beard blond, his grey eyes on my face. He was a large man with bulky shoulders. "I will stay," he offered. "You need protection, too. Are you sure about him?"

"Thank you, Erik. Yes. I like him, he's got *fight* in him, with a killer's instinct. He killed a man simply to get more of my venom." Gabriela smiled at him, then down at me again. "This is not your end." Her soft voice was all I could focus on.

She crouched over me. Fingers stroked through my hair, soothing. My heart spasmed. I groaned again. Pain punched through me, radiating across my chest, as she pulled the arrows free. A scream broke free.

I knew I was dying, and instead of giving in to fear, anger churned my thoughts, images of revenge and wrath that I knew I would never be able to carry out. I closed my eyes, unable to hold back my inevitable death. She cupped the back of my neck and I felt myself lifted, as she embraced me.

Warm liquid gushed over my lips and into my mouth. My eyes opened, and I found I was pressed against her neck. I licked my lips, need flooding me. I tasted the very essence of life and death. Fire roared through me as I took more, and I realised it was her blood she was feeding me. Pain, confusion, and fear overwhelmed me, and I let out a groan. But then all I knew was hunger, and I latched on to her throat.

"Don't be afraid, Little Killer. You are dying, but you will awaken to a new life. A better life. You will be fearsome! For all time!"

A tear slid down my cheek, leaving a warm trail. I was too young to die, and fear grasped my heart. I let out a whimper, trying to pull away from her.

"Keep drinking," she whispered, holding me tight so I couldn't move. More blood spilled into my mouth, and I wanted more. "Don't fight me, just keep drinking. This will give you a strength you could never have imagined."

Chapter 2

Venice - 2045

I'd been hunting the human woman for half an hour before she finally noticed me. I wasn't trying all that hard to avoid being seen. Like those around her, she appeared taken in by the magic and glamour of Venice. Once she caught sight of me, her eyes shifted down the length of my body, widening. I smirked, ensnaring her gaze just long enough to indicate that she also had my attention. She had skin with warm brown tones, and her black curly hair sat past her shoulders. There was a grace about her, and confidence in the way she walked.

The familiar Sestieri of San Polo was full of tourists awed by masks, jewellery, blown glass, lace, art supplies, and souvenirs in the well-lit shop fronts. Their chatter and warm bodies brushed past me as I approached the woman. This was my territory, I was on the hunt, and many were drawn towards me. But there was only one I wanted to draw in.

"You're allowed to look," I whispered in Italian into her ear. I delighted in the way her heart started to race. "Are you not here to enjoy yourself? You're in Venice; live a little." I touched her back, causing her to shiver.

"I'm sorry, I don't speak Italian," she said in English.

I was momentarily thrown off that she hadn't melted at my words, my closeness, like other men and women. Speaking in Italian should have had her swooning. I recognised her accent, though, which made me smile.

"You are Spanish," I acknowledged in English.

I hadn't thought of my home country in a long time. I'd left it many centuries ago and found amusement that I'd picked Spanish for dinner that night. A taste of home, while unexpected, was a delight that made my canines ache. I could already taste how sweet she'd be, pressed against me, moaning under my venom's effects with her head thrown back. My cock twitched and I fought to keep my fangs from emerging. I was hungry, and it had awoken my other need.

She nodded. "I am."

I stepped back and held out my arm and lowered my voice. "You are too beautiful to be alone. Please honour me with your company," I murmured in the modern dialect, Castellano. "We can watch the gondolas. The Grand Canal is quite a sight under the full moon. Or if you prefer, we can go to Ponte de Rialto."

She stared at my arm and hesitated.

"I won't bite," I told her, continuing to speak in Castellano. "Unless you want me to." I gave her my most dazzling smile, holding her gaze again.

She finally gave in. "Okay," she said at last, her deep brown eyes lighting up. "I can't refuse that smile."

Her full lips were inviting, I wanted to kiss them before I fed. Hear her whisper my name as I growled in her ear. The desire to caress her throat before I bit into it overcame me. Unsure where such a yearning came from, I mentally shook myself. She took my arm. I led her away from the well-lit shops, towards less-populated, narrower streets, to my favourite alleyway that would give me privacy as I took what I needed. She'd take pleasure in my bite, then I'd send her back to continue her evening, whatever she was doing.

"You're fluent in Castellano," she continued to speak as we walked.

I laughed. "I would hope so, I *am* from Spain." It dawned on me how hungry I was as I listened to her heartbeat. Her scent washed over me, apples and vanilla.

"You're Spanish, but you speak Italian. How long have you been here?" she asked.

Only for hundreds of years, as opposed to the small number of decades I was in Spain.

I took a right turn. "I've lived here most of my life," I told her. "I did live in Australia for a while, too," I added, in an Australian accent that would have made Quinn proud.

"Australia? What was that like? Don't they have deadly spiders?" she laughed nervously.

"They do," I replied. "Drop bears too."

"Drop bears?" I had her attention. "What are they?"

I suppressed the urge to smile. Quinn had told me about drop bears years ago, and I enjoyed telling this story just as much as she did. "A cousin to the koala, they like to drop out of trees on the unsuspecting."

Her eyes widened as she stared at me in shock. "That sounds terrifying."

I chuckled.

We crossed a small bridge, and she'd gone silent.

"What's on your mind?" I asked, turning another corner. We were almost there. "Scared of the drop bears?"

"Where are we going?" she asked, glancing over her shoulder.

"It's okay, just for some privacy," I murmured. "Cosier, for just the two of us. Then we can watch the gondolas, I promise."

I pushed my will, using compulsion to keep her calm. In recent years, it had become more difficult to lure women into the shadows to feed, as they had become wary. Not that I could blame them. For a moment, I wondered why she was so trusting. Pangs of hunger burned their way through me, removing such concerns. No one could resist my vampire charm. Man or woman.

I longed for the taste of her blood. It was hours later than when I usually fed. In the alleyway, I stopped, pulling her to me, our bodies pressed together, and lifted her chin to bring her gaze to mine. I caressed her cheek, pushing her further into the shadows until her back hit a wall.

Her heart skipped as her eyes focused on my lips. I leaned toward her throat, my fangs lengthening. I was so close I could practically taste her, my mouth watering as I longed for the bliss that came with feeding. I licked her throat, coating her neck with my venom. It would quicken the healing process, hiding evidence of my fangs. She shivered, and I realised the distinct scent of arousal was missing.

I barely registered the click before pain pierced my gut. I pulled away with a growl, staring down at an arrow.

Her eyes hardened, blazing with hatred, and she raised her arm, a second arrow released from under her sleeve, and I moved fast. Not fast enough. It hit my right shoulder. She fired again, this one hitting my chest, just missing my heart. Her hand lifted, rubbing at her neck, and she glanced at it.

Fucking hunters. How had I managed to almost feed from one? I'd been too distracted, thinking about kissing her, too hungry, to notice anything amiss about her. Her willingness to follow a stranger should have tipped me off.

'Matteo. Get here. Now.' I commanded my second, while summoning the rest of my clan. I couldn't communicate with them like I could with Matteo, but they would have picked up on my sense of urgency.

"You missed, *Cazadora.*" I pulled the arrow from my chest and threw it to the ground. "This was my favourite jacket, a gift."

"Filthy bloodsucker," she fumed in Castellano and fired again. This time I caught the arrow.

"You've now tried four times and failed to kill me; you should make your next shot count." I moved too fast for her to see, stopping just before her. "Here, you can have this back." I jabbed the arrow into her shoulder, eliciting a delicious scream from her. I pulled the arrow out and licked her blood from the arrowhead. "Mmmm, it's been awhile since I've had the blood of a Hunter. You're sweet. Could do with a little fear, though." I pushed her against the wall. She struggled against my hold as I dragged my tongue over the blood that seeped from the wound. I growled in satisfaction.

A white-hot pain pierced my gut. I glanced down to find she'd stabbed me with a knife. Dark laughter rumbled from me. "You're a determined one, aren't you?" She pulled the knife out and stabbed me again. "Oh, poor Huntress, you're all alone. That was your first mistake." I'd never seen a solo Hunter try to take on a vampire before. "The knife play is quite alluring, though."

"You talk too much," she snapped before jamming her knife upward into soft flesh from below my jaw. Pain flared as the tip of the blade hit the roof of my mouth. She twisted it.

I stumbled back, my amusement gone. A slow wave of fury and pain rolled through me. I tried to speak, but the blade held my tongue in place. The sensation unsettled me, and I growled again, putting warning into the sound.

"What? No more taunts?" She flashed a cold smile and raised her arm again, aiming for my heart.

I moved, the arrow impaling me in my back, just missing my heart. I ran straight into a wall. My vision went dark, and when it cleared, my second, Matteo, stood before me.

"Carlos." he held me up. "What happened?"

I pulled the knife out, a low growl vibrating in my chest.

"I'll kill her." I muttered when I could talk again. "I'll drink her dry and throw her in the canal." My body was trying to stitch itself together. "Get this fucking arrow out of me."

Matteo pulled the arrow from my back, as others from my clan arrived. I almost collapsed. but he grabbed me.

"You're hurt," Matteo declared, and he turned his attention

to my clan. "Lorenzo, get him a human," he commanded. "He needs to feed."

Lorenzo left without a word.

"She caught me by surprise." I grumbled as my hunger surged, mixed in with rage.

"Who?" Quinn asked.

"The Huntress," I grunted.

"There's a Hunter here?" Josef asked, him and Erik shifting into high alert. They stepped in front of me, watchful. The rest of the clan closed in, too.

"You let a Hunter get the better of you?" Matteo frowned. "Carlos, how?"

I tore my jacket off, annoyed by the arrow holes in it. My tee-shirt was no better, now more red than white.

"I spent half an hour hunting her," I said. "She was hunting me, too. She picked the wrong vampire. I have a taste for her blood, and I will make her beg for me to kill her." Shaking with fury, I resisted the urge to growl again, clenching my jaw.

"You tasted her blood?" Quinn asked. "Was she...?" She left her sentence unfinished.

I knew why she was asking but wasn't ready to let go of my anger at being hunted by what should have been my meal. "I stabbed her with her own arrow." I smirked. "She was young, sweet, with a taste of home."

Quinn cast a look over at Matteo.

"A taste of home," Matteo repeated. "So, Spanish."

Relief showed in Quinn's eyes. Her concern for her friend bothered me. After twenty years, she still refused to let go. "Relax, young siren. We fooled your Australian friend already. She left believing Venice was a wasted trip." I rubbed at my jaw. "Besides, she'd be, what, close to fifty by now?" I replayed the whole thing. "This one counted on the surprise attack right before I could bite her. I was so close, my fangs were at her throat!"

Lorenzo, a vampire who was only slightly older than Matteo returned with a human male, who stared straight ahead, not blinking. I preferred the taste of fear but couldn't be fussy with my hunger blazing through me. As I fed, Matteo and Quinn drew in close, protectively, the rest of the clan watchful.

'This one won't make it.' I told Matteo. *'Too hungry.'*

"Everyone, leave." Matteo said. "Quinn and I have this. Be on watch for the Hunter. Young Spanish woman, she's bleeding. If you locate her, keep your distance. No one takes her on alone."

'I want the pleasure of killing her,' I told him. *'She ruined my fucking jacket.'*

Quinn had gifted the jacket, and I was rather fond of it.

"Quinn can always get you a new jacket," he replied with a laugh.

Quinn scoffed. "Of course I will." She moved closer to me, her hand on my arm as I drank from the human. "I know how much you like your leather jackets."

The clan left us. Consumed by hunger, I drank down the sweet blood. I growled from within my chest, letting the red haze wash over me. Killing him was against the accords, but I was too hungry to care.

I pulled away from the human only when the blood stopped. Matteo stepped in, using his knife on the corpse's throat to disguise what my fangs had done. As he carried the body to the canal, I let Quinn lick the blood from my face. I had made a mess but didn't care.

I enjoyed having others clean me. The act was incredibly arousing. I occasionally shared a bed with most members of my clan, and I held affection for them all. Erik liked to watch me with others; sometimes his need to touch grew too much for him to resist. He and Josef had a closeness that hinted that the two of them shared more than just territory.

Quinn's hand pressed against my chest, warmth seeping through my tee-shirt, and I held her by the waist. Her licking my chin was enough to soothe my anger. I kept my attention on our surroundings. Before she finished, I rubbed my cheek back and forth against hers, blood smearing on her face. She mirrored the motion, then tilted her head.

I pressed my lips to the side of her exposed throat. "Tonight," I said. "I want you and Matteo to come to me tonight." Instead of biting her, I kissed her neck. She let out a soft sound, yearning in her eyes.

'Police.' Matteo's voice reached both me and Quinn, and she glanced up at me, the yearning in her eyes turning to concern.

'Which direction?' I asked through our bond.

'Yours. Quinn...' His protectiveness of her merged with his desire to protect me. 'Carlos, the Hunter is with them.'

I swore under my breath. 'Matteo, get to safety. I won't let anything happen to her.' I pulled away from Quinn. "Grab my jacket, then follow me. The Huntress is bleeding, so don't let yourself be distracted by her blood. That's what she's hoping for." I quickly grabbed the arrows and knife I'd discarded. With Quinn next to me, I leapt to the top of the building. From the roof, we watched as the police followed the Hunter into the alley. I couldn't hold back the growl as I stared at her.

"You're afraid," Quinn said in a low voice. "In these twenty years, I've never seen you fear anything."

I hated to admit it, but she was right. "Even Kings feel fear occasionally," I said. "You've never known me to fear anything, because I've never had reason to fear anything while you've known me. There are very few things in this world that scare me, beautiful siren." I nodded to the Huntress below us, knowing I would have to give up my favourite alley. "But a Hunter that attacks as I'm about to feed from her is close to the top of that list. She came very close to killing me tonight."

Only one other Hunter had ever come that close to killing me, and I didn't like that I had almost met my end. The vampire/Hunter war had ended centuries ago, and I'd become accustomed to humans not fighting back, nor shooting arrows at me as I was about to feed from them.

Chapter 3

The Huntress had led police to my favourite feeding spot, and as I stood on the roof watching them, her eyes darted upwards. The scent of her blood would have sent me into a frenzy if I hadn't just drained a human.

"She knows we're here," I told Quinn. "Or, at least, she knows *I'm* here."

"Is this where you saw the attacker, miss?" one of the police officers asked.

"It is. He had a knife." She held her hand to her wounded arm.

"You should probably get that seen to," the other officer

said. "You're lucky you got away."

"I will," she promised. "It's not as bad as it looks."

I knew she'd be taking care of it herself. Hunters tended to avoid hospitals as much as possible. In the modern day, explaining wounds raised too many questions.

Quinn glanced at me. "Why is she with the police? I thought they preferred to hunt us in secret. Not to expose themselves."

Quinn had been lucky to not have come across any hunters, other than her friend. She'd unfortunately been killed when the very same friend shot at Matteo with an arrow, hitting Quinn instead. Her human life had ended that night, only for her vampire life to begin. The two of them had become almost inseparable.

"They do. She's skating close to the line by getting the police involved. Perhaps she ran into them and had to explain why she was bleeding." I took in a deep breath, taking pleasure in the scent of her blood.

"Why is she alone?" Quinn asked.

"I don't know, but that's a problem for another day," I replied, ready to leave. I wasn't entirely sure the Huntress was alone. One chance meeting didn't mean her family wasn't here, too.

"I know you can hear me, filthy bloodsucker," the Huntress's voice was low, but reached us easily.

Quinn met my eyes, and we turned our attention back to the scene below. The police were making calls, and the Huntress had her back to us.

"You have my knife, and it's of sentimental value. I want it back."

"She can't be serious!" Quinn muttered.

"I'll give it back, alright," I replied. "I'll plunge it deep into her heart, where it belongs."

"Isn't that a waste of blood?" Quinn smirked at me.

Quinn's words brought a smile to my face. I laughed. "You're right, I'm going to make her enjoy it, as much as I will. I will draw it out, and she'll be begging for more. Either that, or I'll make her live her worst nightmare while I give chase. Oh, that delicious scent of fear! I can already taste it!"

"We will meet again, and next time my arrow will fly true," the Huntress continued her communication with us. "There will be one less vampire in the world, and it will be all the more safe for it."

I growled, fighting against the urge to leap from the roof and sink my fangs into her throat, biting deep.

"You have your clan —" Quinn started.

"So did Gabriela," I reminded her. "She still died."

The memory of my maker's death washed over me.

I watched over Venice from the roof of Matteo's family home, making sure my clan was safe. The low hum that had been Gabriela's presence for the last five years became a roar of anger and pain. Despite breaking from her clan, she was the one who'd made me a vampire, and our blood bond was still intact.

Something was happening, so I listened. Even across the distance, we could communicate. I'd tuned out of the bond when I left her in Melbourne and was convinced she'd done the same. Now, anger, protectiveness, and a sliver of fear came through. Had I still been in Melbourne, I would have sought her out to help her.

"What's wrong?" Matteo asked, coming up behind me. "I feel your worry."

"It's Gabriela," I explained. "I think she's wounded." I pressed my hand to my left rib, where it felt like I'd been stabbed, or shot. 'Gabriela? What's happening?'

Matteo said nothing. He had his reason for anger at Gabriela. She and I hadn't parted on friendly terms, either. But he saw no need to speak ill of her. She was still my maker, and we never turned our backs on other vampires, especially when Hunters were involved.

'Carlos...' Her voice was faint. 'Luis,' her call for her maker only worried me more. It was our instinct to reach for our makers in moments of desperation. For her to be desperate enough to call Luis, I knew something was terribly wrong.

Another stabbing pain, this time in my back. "Hunters have found her," I muttered. "She's been shot, twice."

Fear flooded me through our bond. I fell to my knees as another arrow pierced her chest. It missed her heart, but through our bond I still felt her pain. 'Gabriela, please..no...run! Get away!' Gabriela would never run, though, and that knowledge hurt more.

Matteo grabbed my shoulder, offering what comfort he could. He'd killed his maker and told me the agony it caused him the moment she died. Josef and Lorenzo had endured the same pain with the loss of their makers.

"What's happening?" Matteo asked in a low voice.

"She's in a lot of pain," I rasped. "She's angry, and afraid."

My stomach was tied in knots. Gabriela was **never** afraid. Whatever was happening was dire. She was about to die, and that fear soaked into me. I struggled to breathe, feeling like I was fighting for my life. Pain licked at me like flames, and I groaned. Matteo put his hand on my shoulder, his presence calming.

Screams filled my head. Gabriela's screams, of anger and

agony.

"*Matteo!*" *I groaned. Was I dying?* "*Gabriela!*"

He knelt beside me, and I knew he could feel my pain. "*Carlos, you'll be okay. I survived it; you will, too.*"

'*Gabriela?' I reached out to her, tears sliding down my cheeks.*

'*Carlos,' her voice came through our blood bond. It had been five years since we'd spoken. There was none of the hostility she'd shown when we last saw each other, just pain and fear.*

I thought I heard the roar of flames, a reminder of a stable I'd lain in, long ago. Heat licked over my arms, and my heart skipped a beat.

'*Gabriela?' I reached out to her again, unsure what to say. The time we'd spent together washed over me. She was my maker, and it hurt that I could not protect her.*

Her laughter echoed through my head. 'You do not have a gentle bite.' Her response was completely in old Castilian, the older dialect of what was now Castellano.

I knew those words! I'd been human, she'd said them as she fed me her blood.

'*I never did,' I admitted.*

'*Don't be afraid, Little Killer. You are dying, but you will awaken to a new life. A better life. You will be fearsome! For all time!'*

I knew those words too, she'd spoken them to me as I lay dying, the last thing I'd heard as a human.

'*It's called a blood bond,' she said, her voice inside my head. 'We'll always be able to sense each other. Sleep now, my brave Little Killer. I'll pull you from slumber when it's time. You'll hear my voice in the dark, and you'll awaken powerful and immortal.'*

My heart broke. In her pain, she was reliving my last moments as a human.

I tried to comfort her, murmuring to her in old Castilian that she would be alright.

"Not this time, Little Killer," she said. "They found my den."

I knew then why she hadn't run. She hadn't wanted to leave her den.

'No, Gabriela.' Another tear slid down my cheek. 'Gabriela, I'm sorry,'

'Carlos, I'm sorry,' her words pierced my heart. "Forgive me."

Her presence was ripped from me, and I blacked out.

When I came to, the entire clan huddled around me. The blood bond was gone, leaving me empty.

'Carlos, we're here. Your whole clan is here. We mourn with you.' Matteo's silent communication contained his sympathy. "We broke away from Gabriela's clan, and she might not have been a perfect Queen, but she was our King's maker, so tonight, to honour Carlos in his loss, we honour Gabriela," he said to the clan.

"My maker had been killed by a Hunter," Lorenzo said. "Gabriela saved me from meeting the same fate."

"She came to Venice where she found a feral vampire and gave me a family," Matteo said. "She forced a blood bond on me and Carlos, and I couldn't ask for a better person to be bonded to." He grabbed Quinn's hand. "Along with my little cantante, of course."

Each of the members of my clan spoke a small memory of Gabriela, and I had been there for most of those moments. Fond memories.

"I didn't know her very well, and I'm not sure the two of us would have been anything other than hostile. But I would never have met Matteo if not for her." Quinn murmured. "Nor Carlos. As frightening as he was when I was human." There was no hiding the smile in her voice.

I held back laughter. 'She was my favourite human,' I told Matteo quietly. He must have repeated my words to Quinn, as her body shook.

"She gave me this life." I said and met Erik's eyes. He'd been there. "I was nothing special as a human, and she promised that I could have whatever I wanted. All I had to do was take it. I accepted her gift, and never looked back."

Being their King, I had inherited the ability to sense my vampires' emotions, as well as their thoughts. While many of them had despised the way Gabriela had commanded us, I didn't sense any hatred for her. They cared that I was in pain, and their priority was me. I had never needed my clan as I did at that moment. She had died calling out to me; and in her absence, I held on to my clan as if my life depended on it.

The memories left me grieving once again, and wondering whether I was about to meet the same fate.

"Come on, let's go home," I suggested to Quinn. "If we don't leave now, I'm going to do something that will only bring more Hunters. Besides, I have plans."

I had a lot to do before she and Matteo came to my room that night.

Chapter 4

I kicked the door closed behind me, my hands shaking. I pressed my back against the door, leaning my head back, closing my eyes. He'd shoved my own arrow into me, yet somehow I lived. I'd never faced a vampire as strong as he was and swallowed my own fear. When he'd used his vampire speed and stood in front of me, I thought for sure I was dead. I lifted my head and let it thud back against the door again. *Estúpida.*

I sent a message to my father. *<Engaged enemy; failed to eliminate.>*

It didn't take long for his response. *<Report.>*

<Male vampire, caught by surprise during feeding. Fired three shots, unable to pierce heart. Vampire escaped.> I downplayed how many times I'd shot at the vampire. The fact that he'd stabbed me with my own arrow was humiliating. I left that out. As well as that I'd almost become his dinner. I shuddered in revulsion at the memory of him licking my arm. And my throat.

<Describe vampire.> My father replied. I sighed. No questions about how I was after fighting a vampire by myself. I recalled the vampire. It had been dark, but I'd seen enough under the lamp lights.

<Early to mid-twenties. Dark brown curly hair. Spanish, but has resided in Italy for a long time. Strong.> The second before I worked out what he was, there had been a moment of attraction. I suppressed another shudder. To be attracted to a vampire was unthinkable.

I stopped leaning on the door and moved towards my bedroom. Opening my laptop, I wrote my own entry in the Hunter records as I waited for my father's response. He'd sent me to Venice under suspicion that at least one vampire was here. It had taken me three months of watching, and I'd noticed his hunting me. I'd let him lead me away so I could kill him without witnesses.

<Report when eliminated.> My father replied.

I wouldn't be able to go home until I had killed the vamp. I wasn't sure even after that my father would allow me to return. Not after what had happened in Spain. I put my phone on the table and paced my room, replaying the events. He'd come so close to feeding from me, and had actually tasted my blood. There was a danger to that, and it scared me that he might be able to find me, and was probably hunting me at that very moment. I'd had a perfect shot of him, and he'd moved at the last second. His chattiness had disturbed me. They didn't usually talk to Hunters while they were trying to kill us.

I could have died tonight but didn't. That thought wasn't any comfort at all. I had lost my one chance to catch him by surprise and kill him. *How am I going to do this?* It wasn't as if I could catch him by surprise again. I'd announced my presence; he'd be more prepared next time.

I studied my weapons laid out on the table. My mini crossbow was my go-to weapon, and I was glad I had the hidden one up my sleeve, though the bolts were smaller, but I also had two swords, knives, as well as a few wooden stakes. The vampire had taken the knife my mother had given me for my eighteenth birthday. The only thing I had left of her. I sat down, grabbing a needle and thread. I clenched my teeth as I pushed the needle into my shoulder.

Chapter 5

I'd just finished showering and had a towel wrapped around my waist, rubbing my hair dry. Two humans were chained up, one to my bed, the other to the wall. Matteo, already shirtless, entered my bedroom with Quinn. On his chest, the words "La Voz," had been tattooed. The two of them knelt before me, their heads bowed. I smiled, the sight of them on their knees already stirring lust within me. I reached for Quinn's chin, lifting it. Her eyes, already red, met my gaze. She gave me a hungry smile, showing off her fangs.

Matteo had taught her control over her vampirism long

ago. But she was young, and every now and again, her control slipped. I preferred my clan to show their true selves anyway, so I always encouraged it within the den. We had no need to hide what we were from each other.

The sweet aroma of arousal rose from both of them as they ran their eyes over my body. As Matteo let out a low rumble, his eyes, shifting to crimson, darted to the humans chained up. His feral nature was always close to the surface, and it looked like he wasn't trying to hold it back.

"Soon," I told him, and his eyes lifted to meet mine. "Both of you, stand," I commanded.

Matteo and Quinn rose to their feet. I advanced on Quinn, and she bared her throat, her eyes closing.

Matteo and I struck at the same time, sinking our fangs into her throat. My bite was not as gentle as Matteo's, but deep and savage. The fire in her blood and her growl only added to my own lust. I opened my mouth and bit down again, deeper, my fangs tearing into flesh. Blood gushed onto my face, and she leaned against Matteo, his arms sliding around her waist. She moaned, wrapping one arm around my back, her other hand holding my head to her.

I licked the blood from her neck. The moment I finished, she cleaned my face while Matteo watched us, his eyes full of hunger. Her tongue slid over my chin, and I was already hard. I reached out to Matteo, stroking his face, smeared with Quinn's blood. There was a savageness in him that Quinn had calmed, but tonight that feral beast wanted to play.

Quinn turned to Matteo, her tongue on his face eliciting a low rumble from his chest. I moved around, drinking from him, Quinn doing the same a moment later. Through the blood bond with Matteo, his deep love for Quinn and satisfaction at having us feed from him flooded in.

Without a word, we turned, as one, to the human male tied to my bed.

I put one hand to Matteo's back, and the other to Quinn's waist. "My anniversary gift to you both. A vampire wedding anniversary should have more humans, but this will have to do."

I lowered my head to whisper into Quinn's ear. "This is for you, a delicacy I know you enjoy. All you need to do is sing to him." I indicated the other human. "Both of them are waiting for you, Quinn." I smiled, turning to Matteo. "And you, my feral. But you must share."

Dark joy crossed Quinn's face, a ferocious smile as she licked her lips, looking at the human on my bed, the other in the corner of my room, shackled to my wall. We were breaking the accords, but tonight was special. Tonight, I'd make an allowance. The Hunters would never find out. Neither would the Barones.

As King, I made an effort to give all my vampires acknowledgement on the day they became vampires, and other celebrations. Matteo and Quinn had married twenty years before, an event that was civil, combined with his living descendants, and her parents. But tonight, I wanted this night to be special. For both of them.

Matteo kissed the back of her neck. "It's been over twenty years since you died for me. Since you chose my world." His voice became guttural, indicating his approach to his feral nature.

"*Our* world," she corrected him.

"Our world," he agreed. "But twenty years ago today, we

swore ourselves together, forever. You took on my name. Humans marry to grow old together; we marry to bind ourselves to each other for eternity."

"Tonight is special." I agreed. "I couldn't let the night go without a couple of drinks. They're under my sway, waiting for you, sweet siren."

Matteo grabbed her, their kiss wild as deep growls rose from both of them.

I'd planned this with Matteo, the two of us selecting the humans a day earlier. I moved to the table, picking up a jug. A rich, chocolatey aroma rose from the jug in my hands. "Perhaps you'd like this for more flavour." I gave her the once-over. "You should undress. Chocolate and blood can be quite messy."

"I want her to be messy," Matteo said. "That way, I get to clean her."

"Mmmm, that does have appeal," I teased her.

She laughed and pulled away from Matteo, delight shining in her eyes as she reached for the jug. I let her take it from my hands. She snapped at my jaw in a playful manner before moving towards my bed.

She began to hum. By now I'd grown used to her alluring siren powers. I gave in to her voice, the desire a pleasure. The human on my bed opened his eyes, looking around at all of us, before his gaze stopped on Quinn. Under her thrall, he struggled against the bonds in an attempt to rise to her, an erection tight against his trousers. She handed Matteo the jug before removing her tee-shirt and jeans. On her back was the tattoo she'd gotten as a human, a rose inside a music staff. As she turned to face me, I traced my fingers over the tattoo over her heart. The same as Matteo's: *La Voz.*

Each member of my clan had gotten the same tattoo, at her suggestion.

Standing in her undergarments, she approached the bed. The human couldn't look away from her. Quinn lowered herself to the bed, crawling towards the human. I stood at the foot, as she ripped the human's tee-shirt in half down the front. I smiled as she kissed his body before reaching his mouth. The human moaned into her kiss.

Finally, she took the jug back, pouring chocolate sauce over the human's torso, chest and throat. She cast the two of us a joyous smile. "It's perfect," she said and started to lick chocolate from the human. He squirmed under her tongue, moaning, still trying to reach for her. As she reached his throat, lying flat on top of him, she sank her fangs in.

Matteo took the other side of the throat, and I took the wrist. I preferred the spice of fear; his blood had more of a sweet taste to it. A warmth spread across my chest, an effect of the lust-filled blood. Quinn's hand rested on my back as she fed.

One from my clan chose that moment to walk in, and I lifted my head and turned to glare, a threatening growl erupting from me. Lorenzo froze, lowering himself to his knees, head bowed. He'd been drawn by the call of the siren.

"Get out." I used the power of my command, something I didn't often do. "I will tear your throat out and feed your heart to Matteo. Do not interrupt without good reason."

He quickly left, and I returned to the feed. I let the red haze wash over me, and the three of us fell into a feeding frenzy. The scent of blood filled the air, low grumbles of contentment rising from Matteo and Quinn.

It wasn't long before the blood flow stopped, and we

all lifted our heads, turning towards the other human. A woman, under my trance. Quinn barely moved before she was in front of the captive, humming again.

Quinn's chin was absolutely dripping, as was Matteo's. She pulled him into a kiss, the two of them pressing themselves hard against each other, their need overwhelming. I circled them until Quinn grabbed me, turning around to kiss me. Her lips tasted of blood and chocolate. She pressed her tongue against my fang, her blood in my mouth. I groaned into her kiss and sucked on her tongue.

Matteo removed Quinn's bra, peeling it from her, his hands sliding over her body. He leaned down and nipped on her earlobe. She pulled out of our kiss and reached up, one hand on my cheek. She half turned, reaching for Matteo.

"*Ti amo*," she whispered to both of us. "My feral, and my King."

Matteo's pride pushed through our bond at her speaking Italian.

Finally, she pulled herself away from us, and yanked the woman's head to the side. "Help yourself, my sweet feral," she told Matteo.

He buried his fangs in the human's throat, and she claimed the other side. I took my time, to appreciate the sight of their feeding, breathing in the rich scent of blood and desire. Matteo had one arm draped around Quinn's waist, his deep growls showing he'd given in, buried under his own feral nature. Something I'd seen him do many times over the centuries.

Quinn's hand caressed the back of his head, her own satisfied sounds pleasing me.

I dropped to my knees, pushing my way between Matteo

and Quinn, to bite the human's inner thigh. As her blood flooded into my mouth, I let out my own growls, taking pleasure in the feed.

I was flying, intoxicated. Letting go of the human, I rose to my feet and stumbled to the bed. We'd overfed, and I could barely stand. I discarded the corpse from my bed and lay down, resting one hand under my head, the other on my chest, a wide smile on my face.

As Quinn lay down next to me, the entire bottom half of her face showed her meal. Matteo lay on the other side of me, just as bloody. Both of them rested their heads on my chest, and I stroked their hair.

She reached across, her hand sliding across the blood on his chest, and then licked her own fingers. "You're sexy covered in blood like that; you know that, right?" Her eyes moved to mine. "So are you," she whispered and licked my face. The two of them cleaned me, then each other before curling into me. Quinn was Matteo's, and he was hers. But they both belonged to me. My cock pushed at the towel, which somehow I hadn't lost. As if sensing its movement, Quinn's hand reached down and pulled the towel away, stroking me. I groaned.

Matteo rubbed his cheek across mine, his affection for both me and Quinn coming through our bond in waves. The two of them drew together in a kiss.

"Mine." Matteo murmured, pushing her hair from her face. "Forever."

Even in his feral state, his possessiveness of her shone through.

I grabbed the knife from my bedside table. He climbed to position himself over me.

I gave the knife to Quinn, and she sliced it deep down my chest without hesitation. It stung, and then Matteo's mouth was against my flesh, licking my blood away. Quinn bent down to kiss me. I grasped the back of her neck with force, our kiss savage, hungry.

The cut on my chest closed, and Matteo watched us in silence. I let Quinn go, and the two of them kissed again. When they pulled apart, I grabbed Quinn's throat in a tight grip, forcing her to her back. She gazed up at me with a smile, eyes filled with longing. Matteo grabbed the knife from me. He sliced a long, deep line into her abdomen. As I lowered my head, licking the cut, Matteo pulled her panties from her with ease. He shifted, placing his head between her legs.

She squirmed beneath us. Her hand pulled my hair, her other grasping Matteo's head. I let out a sound of approval and lifted myself up. Matteo wasn't done, and long, agonised moans came from Quinn. I watched her rise higher towards an orgasm under Matteo's tongue. Her head tilted back, and her back arched. I couldn't resist her bared throat and bit deep. She let out one long moan as her climax rocked her. Tremors passed through her body. I released her.

When Matteo lifted his head, I licked both human blood and Quinn's wetness from his face. Finally, he lay back, grabbing Quinn's hand, bringing it to his mouth to kiss her palm. Still quivering, she sat up and helped Matteo remove his trousers. The moment I cut into Matteo, she straddled his body, rubbing herself against his cock as she licked his chest. The two of them growled, hers almost as feral as his.

She pushed herself up from his chest, licking her lips. He wrapped his arms around her back in a bear hug, pulling her hard against his body. I lay down next to them, intoxicated and blissed out from overfeeding. Matteo rolled over on to his side, locking her in between the two of us. With us both embracing her, Quinn reached back, pulling my arm over her. She and Matteo faced each other while she leaned into me. Matteo shifted his arm, letting it drop over my hip.

I nipped at Quinn's shoulder, before closing my eyes, a low, content rumble vibrating within my chest. Their own happiness sounded, echoing mine as we fell into a blissful slumber.

Chapter 6

The three of us lay on my bed in a naked, tangled mess of bodies and limbs. After feeding from the humans and each other, blood drunk, we'd passed out. I kept my eyes closed, listening to the two of them kissing. My bed shifted as they moved away from me, and I knew Matteo had pinned Quinn underneath him.

"You still have chocolate on you," he whispered to her.

"I want you to bite me," Quinn pleaded. "Matteo, please."

He growled softly. "You know I love to hear you beg. Perhaps we should take this to *our* bed. The things I want to do to you. I want to let the feral out."

"Then what are we waiting for?" she laughed. "I want the feral."

They left quickly, but I could still hear them in their room. With my bed to myself I stretched out, listening. It was difficult not to hear all that went on in my den. My entire clan belonged to me, and while I knew they each held great affection for me, I also knew when to let vampires go, to love each other.

As I listened, I picked up the fast heartbeat of a human, and the unmistakable venom- induced moan of a man. I smiled. Celeste had a habit of bringing her food home when she felt the need for more than just their blood. She was very particular about not fucking out in the open. The humans she took to her bed had a tendency to be very loud. Since the sun was up, she would likely spend the day with him and release him that night, with any memory of Celeste, and the den safely compelled away.

I left my bed to have a shower, then returned to my bedroom to find Josef in the doorway with Erik.

"My King," Josef said, him and Erik bowing their heads. "Perhaps you'd like us to discard last night's fun before they start to stink?"

I glanced over at the dead humans. "Erik, you and Lorenzo get rid of them. As soon as the sun sets, take the boat, drop them deep." I dried myself. "Josef, I have another job for you, and Andreas." I pulled on boxer briefs and jeans.

Lorenzo appeared. He and Erik each lifted a body in their arms easily and left.

"What do you require?" Josef asked.

"I want you to look through the Hunter records. See

what you can find on Spanish Hunters. I want to know all the families, and if there are any independent Hunters," I ordered him.

"Finally putting their own records to good use." Josef grinned. "We won't have anything up-to-date, since they locked us out. But I'll see what we *can* find."

I laughed. "Well, after what you went through to get them, I figured it was time to use the Hunters' biggest asset against them. Our situation calls for it. A Hunter announced her presence rather loudly last night, and I intend to find out who she and her family are before they can discover who I am, and how small of a clan we have here." I pulled on a black tee-shirt. "They never hunt us solo. It's likely her family is here, too, and last night was as unexpected to her as it was to me. They'll make sure no one's caught unprepared or alone again. We need to be careful." I grabbed my jacket and let out a sigh. "If somehow she is here alone, I'll make sure to send her to her family in pieces."

Josef smirked. "You still haven't decided how you're going to kill her yet, have you?"

I shrugged. "Every time I think I've decided, a new idea comes to me. I can't decide whether I prefer to make it hurt, or make her enjoy it."

"You could always hunt her, make her run. Work for the kill. That enticing fear that you love so much will be your reward at the end," Andreas added from the door.

"I'll keep that in mind," I agreed. The idea did have appeal.

Andreas was our technology expert, but he had a creative side to him that had always impressed me. In Austria, during the sixteen hundreds, he'd fought in a war and discovered the existence of vampires on the battlefield. Hungry for the strength they'd displayed, he had convinced one to turn him, and they had become a trio of terror until two were killed, leaving Andreas to find a new clan. That search had brought him to us. The two of us had become good friends in our early days.

"We'll find all we can about Spanish Hunters," Josef promised. "From your description, I'd say she is from a family. She's too young to have become a Hunter herself and trained for it. She's likely been trained for years."

A loud thud distracted me from the topic at hand momentarily. Growls followed, and I chuckled. It seemed the things Matteo had wanted to do to Quinn had escalated beyond their bed. A quiet hum began, and Matteo's growls rose, becoming feral. Another thud, as if someone had been shoved into the wall.

Her siren voice gripped us all. Josef's eyes turned red as he forced himself to resist it. Any other time I'd have given myself into it and barged into their bedroom. While we'd all learned that Quinn had an appreciation for what she insisted on calling vampire orgies, neither she nor Matteo would welcome us entering their room uninvited. She was using her voice on the feral part of Matteo, which likely meant it would get very rough in their bedroom before long.

"Perhaps anything within the den can wait a few hours?" Andreas suggested with a grin. "I don't think we're going to get a lot done while she's singing."

I wanted to march into their bedroom and make them kneel before me. To let my rough side out as I claimed first Quinn, then Matteo. To make them both scream my name, to mark them and fuck her against the wall as he watched. I shook myself out of it and cast a look around my bedroom.

As I reached for my sunglasses, I nodded in agreement.

"Perhaps some fresh air," I suggested.

The siren voice only affected the males of the clan. I had seen our siren pull women under her sway before, but neither Celeste nor Annika had ever been affected by her song. I had also seen other effects of what Quinn could do. I'd made the right decision in keeping her existence quiet. No other in our world knew the power she had as a vampire siren, and I planned to keep it that way.

Chapter 7

I left my den, the others following me outside with their own sunglasses over their eyes. Each went their own way, though. A slight breeze ruffled my hair and clothes, the heat of the sun irritating. Magic Wielders in Australia had found a way for vampires to be in the sunlight without being blinded. The enhancement had become popular amongst the vampire community once that blessing went global. I'd found their magic-infused sunglasses useful over the years, but I still had a preference for the night. I'd gone too long accepting my life in the shadows. The warmth of the sun on my face had become strange, unfamiliar.

As I walked through Venice, I watched the humans around me. Drawn here from all across the world, they came for the gondola rides and the Venetian masks. This time of year was busier, though, with *Carnevale* coming up. My clan's favourite time of year. People were already parading around the city wearing masks they'd bought just for the event.

Cries echoed out as humans' excitement over masks became too much for them. Children screamed, and I regretted my decision to walk through the crowd. As I scanned those around me, I met dark brown eyes through a mask. It was a long stare, unflinching. The human heartbeat indicated she wasn't a vampire, so I approached her, curious. Before I could reach her, she turned around, walking away, her steps sharp in heels. She stopped quickly, and she cast a glance over her shoulder towards me. Her message was clear: she wanted me to follow. I frowned. When humans were drawn to me, they didn't walk away. She didn't walk like the Huntress. I considered perhaps she was another Hunter. I let my curiosity win and followed at a distance, keeping my eye on those around me.

She led me across Venice, stopping occasionally to turn in my direction. When she turned down an empty street, I took in my surroundings. No one was around. This had become a game, and as I advanced on her I contemplated feeding. She'd clearly wanted my attention, and now she had it.

The woman stopped, her back to me, waiting.

"That was quite a walk you took me on," I said, taking a step forward. "Did you have something you wanted to say to me, or was it just about the chase? I do enjoy the chase."

No sooner had the words left my mouth that I found myself no longer on the ground. Flung through the air without her lifting a finger. I smashed into the wall. Hard. Every bone in my body felt that impact. I groaned when I hit the ground. I glanced up at her to find she'd turned around, her hand held out, the grip of magic still vibrating through me.

"So, not human then," I managed, wincing through the pain. "Entering a vampire's territory uninvited is just plain rude." I didn't get up. She'd likely fling me against another wall. "But attacking a King, you're *declaring war.* You better have a good reason for being here."

"I don't need an invitation," she replied. "Not when I am here on behalf of another."

I laughed. "I don't care who you're here on behalf of. This is my territory. I don't take too kindly towards intruders." Unwilling to disturb Matteo, instead I used my connection to my clan, summoning Erik and Josef. I gave them a nudge, showing them where I was.

"But you haven't heard who I'm here on behalf of." She took her mask off, eyes burning into mine as she smiled at me. Her black hair swept over her shoulders in waves. She was warm brown, Egyptian, with high cheekbones, full lips, and heavily lined eyes. A face I knew. The last time I'd seen her, she'd declared herself leader of all Magic Wielders. She'd allied with King Luis, declaring that vampires and Magic Wielders had a common cause.

"Maya, I didn't recognise you. My apologies," I said.

"King Carlos, get on your feet," she demanded.

I climbed to my feet. "What was your reason for the follow-me eyes?"

"You are summoned," she said, ignoring my question. "The Bloodking requests your presence, and that of your second. You've had twenty years to formally announce your new clan and request your claim to this territory. Did you think he would overlook or just not notice your presence here?"

Shit. "I humbly accept the Bloodking's summons," I replied, taking a knee in front of Maya

Josef and Erik arrived and saw me kneeling before Maya.

"My King?" Erik asked, his eyes on Maya "You kneel before a human? Is this what you called us for? Is she the Hunter?"

Maya turned her attention to them. I needed to stop them from attacking her. She could hurt them easily.

"No, Erik, I was mistaken. I bow before the Bloodking's Magic Wielder. Please show her the same respect you would show King Luis."

"My apologies, Lady Maya." Erik knelt without hesitation. Josef followed him.

I smiled at the title. She'd once gone by that name, but not in a long time.

Maya looked down at the three of us. "You haven't changed one bit," she said to me. "Still chasing the unsuspecting victim into dead-end streets for the sake of frightening them."

I grinned at her. "While I do want to maintain a respectful tone, you are incorrect. It was you who led me here. Disguised. I did not recognise your scent."

She laughed. "Yet you still gave chase, just as I knew you would. I must admit, though, that I was surprised to find you outside during daylight hours. What business forces a King from his den in the middle of the day?"

I shot Erik and Josef a look, smirking. We rose to our feet, the formal aspect of the conversation now more relaxed. "That, dear Maya, would be a King's business. When will the Elders be here?"

She reached out her hand, holding a card between her fingers. I took it, glancing at the address on the front. A villa on the mainland. "Two nights from now," she said, and her eyes darted to Erik and Josef. "Which one of you is his second? You are also expected to be there."

"Neither of them," I said.

She frowned, still watching Erik and Josef. "You did not summon your second? Unusual for a King."

"Erik and Josef are my most experienced warriors. My second, Matteo, might have attempted to rip you apart. But I will make sure he is there when I meet with King Luis," I accepted.

Her eyes widened at the name. "Matteo Barone? The feral? He still lives?"

There wasn't a vampire who hadn't heard of Matteo, so it was no surprise that Maya had, too. Her question irritated me. "He does. I am blood bonded with him, and I have seen an improvement in his nature. He is important to everyone in our *La Voz* clan." I met her eyes, making my message clear: do not talk of Matteo's life.

She shrugged. "I suppose that will be a discussion you'll have with the Elders. Don't be late. You may be a King to your clan, but you still have to answer to King Luis."

I watched her walk away.

"You knew this day would come," Josef said. "That he let twenty years pass without seeking you out was unusual."

"It's likely he was waiting for you to approach him?" Erik contemplated.

I weighed their words. I'd avoided contacting King Luis. At first it was because of how Gabriela and I had parted ways, and the fact that I had a known feral and killer in my clan. Then after Gabriela's death, the last person I'd wanted to see was her maker. But as a King who had claimed territory, I should have made a formal request the moment we arrived in Venice. I should have declared my clan. I had personal hurts I held against King Luis, but Josef was right. I had known this day was coming.

"Perhaps," I agreed with Erik. "I can only hope that my blood bond with Matteo will be enough to prevent King Luis from forfeiting his life."

It bothered me that Maya had entered Venice without my knowing. My clan and I guarded my territory fiercely, always aware of an uninvited presence. I'd defended Venice, including from a female vampire who had attempted numerous times to enter. I'd sent her bleeding back to wherever she came from each time. Had I a Magic Wielder of my own, I would have been alerted the moment Maya entered the city. "I need a Magic Wielder." I muttered. I would have to reach out to their community to ask for assistance.

We stopped near the Grand Canal, watching *Ponte di Rialto*.

Erik faced me. "Why did you call us? You didn't look like you needed us for a summons."

"She didn't reveal herself to me immediately, and she threw me against a wall," I admitted. "I wasn't sure if it was another clan trying to claim Venice, but I thought it best to have warriors with me should a battle break out."

"Instead, you have a summons from the Bloodking," Erik noted. "Is this something we should all be present for?"

"No." I replied. "The order was for me and my second to

present ourselves. That's what we'll do. Had he wanted the whole clan there, he would have stated as such."

"While you're attending to their summons?" Josef asked.

"As I said back at the den. Find the Huntress and her family. Find something I can use to my advantage," I commanded. "I will kill her, and her family."

Chapter 8

I was on the prowl. I wanted something different and knew where to find what I desired. I'd hunted there before, but with Matteo and Quinn. Friday nights were about musicians, and usually our sweet siren sang, drawing humans out with her voice. But Saturday nights they pumped up the music, and every person in that club would already be drunk.

Admiring my new leather jacket, I left the shadows. I could never resist feeding in bars. No one around ever noticed when I took my fill. The only thing they saw was what they wanted. Lovers wrapped in a passionate embrace. No one would ever believe or suspect vampire feedings were happening around them.

Inside the club, music pounded against me, the smell of humans and alcohol heavy. I searched the room for anyone who might be by themselves. Man or woman. One dancer with her back to me caught my attention, and I watched her. She was there to attract attention; that much was obvious in the way she moved. Her curly hair was dark, the red top sat off her shoulders, revealing a tattoo of a butterfly, and I caught sight of a red flower on her wrist. A bandage was wrapped around her arm. Her lower back was bare. Tight black jeans revealed a perfect ass.

She definitely had the focus of human males on the floor, who couldn't keep their eyes off her. I smiled. Apart from those admiring her, she seemed to be alone. She chose that moment to turn around. The pulse in her neck made my canines ache, bare, inviting. I lifted my eyes to her face and bit back a growl. *Huntress!* I cast my eyes over her again and moved towards the dance floor, seeing the perfect opportunity to catch her off-guard. I'd kill her eventually, but for now, I wanted to have fun.

From behind the Huntress, I slid one hand on to her waist, the other resting on her bare stomach. I moved in time with her, swaying as she did, pressing against her back. Humans danced in a strange way these days. She didn't stop. One hand came up, pressing against the back of my head, her other over my fingers on her stomach, and she leaned into me as we danced. I was close enough to lean down and bite her. The contact sent sparks along my skin, and I suppressed small shivers.

The scent of arousal rose from her, and I grinned. Her ass

pressed hard against my cock, which responded immediately to the contact. In the middle of the dance floor, with an erection poking into her back, I clenched my jaw. *Traitor*, I cursed. She practically rubbed herself against me. Damn, this woman was more than a Huntress. She was a temptress. A seductress. I could feel the warmth of her body through my tee-shirt.

I gave a soft kiss to the spot under her ear and growled. "You look good enough to eat, little *Cazadora*." I breathed in deep. "And you smell delicious."

The only indication that she'd heard me over the loud music was a slight tensing of the muscles in her body. Her heart skipped a beat but remained steady, her lack of fear disappointing. We continued dancing, her body and mine pressed together.

"What do you think you're doing?" she seethed.

I tightened my grip as a reminder of my strength. "What? Vampires can't have fun?" I lowered my head to kiss her throat.

Her fury was unmistakable, and she tried to pull away. "Get your fucking hands off me," she ground out through gritted teeth.

I smirked.

"I could sink my fangs into your soft little throat," I asserted, overwhelmed by her scent of apples and vanilla. Her fear did spike, and I smiled against her neck. "No one around us would blink." I was enjoying this, a show of my power. "They would see nothing but lovers in an embrace, caught by passion." I kissed her neck again, letting her feel my fangs. "If only they knew the deadly dance we were in." I pressed my lips against her skin. "*Vampiro and Cazadora.*"

Her body went rigid. "Get your hands off me."

"Struggle, and I may tear your throat out, which would be a waste of all that delicious blood." I rubbed my cheek against hers. "Or I may kill everyone in here and leave you alive to explain yourself out of this." She stilled, the fight leaving her. "Good girl." I licked her throat. "Mmmm, I remember your taste." The temptation to bite her flickered through me.

"I'll kill you," she promised, her body trembling as her delicious fury rolled over me.

"What is it that you're angry about?" I whispered into her ear. "The fact that a vampire has you trapped while surrounded by people, or is it that you enjoyed the feel of my body against yours before you realised it was me?" I pushed against her, hard. "That you enjoyed the feel of my cock on your ass. It made you think *you* had the power, and it turned you on." I lifted my hand from her waist, wrapping my arm around her chest. "Tell me, sweet *Cazadora*, who has the power now?"

Her silence, and the way she shook with rage, only widened my smile.

"I asked, who has the power?" I repeated tightening my embrace.

"Fuck off," she grunted in pain, her anger deep in her voice.

I let out a low, threatening growl. Her body sagged a little, the surrender a subtle admission of my power over her.

"Good choice," I told her with menace in my voice. "You're a smart little Huntress, aren't you?"

"Let me go." Her soft words were not of fear, and I detected a slight increase in her lust. She hated me but was unable to resist the feel of my body against her. No human could.

"Say please," I commanded.

"You'll have to compel me if you want a fucking please, *diablo.*"

"Now there's a thought." Satisfied that I'd gotten under her skin, I released her. "*Adios.*"

I saw no need to hurry and glanced back at her once. She hadn't moved.

I spotted a man by himself at the door. Good. Time to eat.

Chapter 9

The heat of the bar suffocated me as I struggled to calm my temper. *That fucking vampire.* He'd held me close, and I'd enjoyed the contact, and the firmness of his body pressed against mine, not realising who, or what he was. I should have known. I should have recognised that his body temperature was cooler than that of a human. My skin still blazed from his touch, and I wasn't completely sure it was in repulsion. He'd had his fangs against my throat, and I didn't know why he hadn't bitten me.

I took a deep, shuddering breath and let it out slowly. *I'm still alive.* He could have killed me and left my body on the floor before anyone realised what happened. I finally turned around in time to see him approach a man by the door. Regretting having no weapons, I struggled to let them go. I'd been careless and could only hope he'd stick to the accords. To follow him would be suicide. *I can't stay here, though.* Night ruined, I went out the same door the vampire had.

Outside, the night was cool, and a lot of people were around. I caught the shadow of the vampire and his victim, retreating down an alleyway. In the same direction he'd taken me.

Don't try, Camila. I clenched my hands into fists. The pulsing pain from my shoulder served as a reminder of my earlier brush with death. I forced myself to walk away. Guilt washed over me, and a tear fell down my cheek. As I walked down towards where I was living, I took in my surroundings. People were happy, shopping, discussing gondola rides, and taking photos. I couldn't deny Venice was a beautiful city, and wished I had better reasons to be here.

I let the charm of the city pull me in, hoping to shift my mood. Like other visitors to the city, I found it hard to ignore the beauty and history of Venice. The buildings had that old feel to them, with tall, arched windows and brightly coloured shutters. There was nothing that didn't leave me appreciating the city. I always found myself admiring bridges, cathedrals, and museums. Gondolas carried people through the canals, sometimes with Italians singing. I'd found a chocolate shop with a chocolate fountain, and I could never look away from the blown glass and beautiful masks.

I'd spent most of my time in San Polo and San Marco. The Rialto Bridge connected the two, and I always paused on the bridge to look out over the Grand Canal, wishing I could ride in a gondola. I even had a photo of me next to the canal with the bridge behind me. I enjoyed that there were no cars in Venice with their noisy engines, nor people pushing their horns in road rage. I had watched the sunset, and I wished I could do half of what the tourists did.

Tonight had been a mistake. I'd forced down the guilt that came with anything I did that wasn't hunting -related. Such as to change my usual Hunter wear for something that I knew looked good, and felt a little flirty. Buying the clothes in Venice had been difficult. I'd used cash so my father wouldn't see where I was shopping. For once, I'd wanted to have fun before I had to "work." But work had found me.

I needed to establish the boundaries of his feeding ground and would have to wait until the following night to attempt to hunt him. I silently apologised to the man who would be his meal. I could think of nothing worse than being fed on by a vampire. The very idea horrified me.

On my way home, I passed an art gallery with 'Grand Opening' signs hanging from the front. I had no interest in art, but it might be nice to attend an event. Wear a nice dress, sample wine and food. I took note of the date, in a couple of weeks. I knew what I was in Venice for, and it was not routine to go beyond duty, but I couldn't resist.

It was a romantic city, and I was there alone, hunting vampires. Not for the first time, I considered hanging up my crossbow and just walking away. My father had sent me here, without support, and I was terrified. I wandered the streets watching those around me. Simple lives, without fear, without the weight of a duty cast on them by their ancestors. They knew nothing of vampires, nor of any other paranormals, and I envied them.

I'd been so lost in my thoughts that I was surprised to find myself in an outdoor cafe, the smell of coffee in the air. I took a seat, deciding that an espresso would be good to help keep me focused. I had set aside time to train later that night before I went on a patrol. Although the vampire had already fed, so it was unlikely I'd find him that night.

My espresso arrived, and I had a view of one of the smaller canals. Watching couples go by in gondolas, I smiled when one had someone serenading them. The sound of Italians singing really made me realise I was in Italy. I didn't speak much of their language, but I enjoyed listening to it. After three months here, I picked up on words that weren't Italian and had learned Venetians had their own dialect.

A man watching me caught my attention. He had dark hair and blue eyes, and I didn't miss the unmistakable recognition in his face. I realised he looked familiar. He smiled at me slightly, a friendly smile. *Where have I seen him before?* He wasn't someone I'd seen in Venice, but I'd definitely seen him before. *Is it possible he's another Hunter?*

My Father had not told me other Hunters would be here, that he'd included in the Hunter network that the potential vampire in Venice was being taken care of. After the two run-ins with the vampire, maybe help from another Hunter wasn't a bad thing. Hunters were extremely suspicious, though, so before I spoke to him, I needed to identify who he was. I needed to know which family he was from, so he'd trust me enough when I approached him.

Every Hunter had a record, so we could identify each other. I grabbed my phone and logged into the network, pulling up the search page. I paused. I needed a faster way to identify him. So I opened the camera and lifted my phone higher. I smiled brightly at my phone, as if taking a photo of myself. Through the screen, the amusement in his eyes was unmistakable and he shook with laughter. I uploaded his photo into the search function.

His picture brought up a record, but not one I expected. A drawing of him showed on my screen. His hair had been longer, with more facial hair. I recognised the drawing style from an artist who had recorded all those of the First Hunters. With a frown I clicked open on the record and started to read.

Josef Alfaro was among the First Hunters in the thirteenth century. When faced with the loss of his entire family, he joined others who sought to take down the plague of vampires. Like many, he was tired of cowering from the monsters that came from the dark. The vampires' weakness to wood was discovered, and his skill with a crossbow took down many before they started to wear armour blessed by wielders of magic. The First Hunters soon discovered that fire and beheading were just as successful.

He led a group of more than twenty Hunters deep into the forests of Italy to track vampires. One of those he hunted was Carlos Rivera, a vicious vampire and known to be a general to King Luis himself.

My heart pounded as I read the record, trying hard not to raise my eyes.

Josef's group were found in camp, their throats ripped open, no survivors. Josef was not found among them. There were unconfirmed reports that he was sighted before three massacres in which vampires knew where to attack. Some statements show that vampires used signals known to Hunters, allowing them through defences, decimating many factions of Hunters.

While present at the fire that declared the Vampire War, it was regrettable that he was not among his fellow Hunters during the signing of the accords. Many recognised him at the head of the opposing army, alongside The Original Three, and many other well-known vampires. It is unknown who turned him, but he became just as ruthless a killer as those he once hunted.

I was right in my evaluation that he was a Hunter, but I couldn't have guessed he was one of the First Hunters.

"Josef Alfaro," I muttered under my breath.

I winced, realising he would have heard that. When I glanced up, he was gone.

Chapter 10

I walked the streets of Venice breathing in the scent of humans, coffee, hot food, and wine. Humans, dazed by the beauty of the city, caught in excitement, stopped when they saw me. Some were drawn to me; others seemed to sense something off about me. My presence sent chills down their spines, and they gave me a wide berth, careful to not get too close. Their very instincts told them, without their knowing it, that I was dangerous. I enjoyed the effect my presence had on them.

I was in a cheerful mood, and when one did get too close, I hissed, showing fang. A man stopped dead in his tracks, the scent of fear enticing. He stared at me in disbelief and horror.

"Run," I whispered. "I'm hungry."

He turned and ran the other way, pushing past people. Those he ran by glared after him with annoyance on their faces. I resisted the urge to give chase, chuckling as I continued in the direction I was walking. I'd already fed, but he wasn't to know that. I missed the days where I'd been free to reveal myself and drink until intoxicated. Laws had been put in place and enforced by the oldest of vampires. The Original Three.

I made my way towards a boat that waited to take me to the mainland, where Matteo would meet me. This would be a difficult meeting, for the both of us. I didn't know how Gabriela had avoided the Bloodking's wrath in keeping a feral alive. I knew her reasons to do so, but had King Luis known? Many knew of his soft spot towards Gabriela, the first human to be turned, centuries before my own existence.

I approached the boat and paused as Matteo caressed Quinn's cheek.

"I'll be alright," he murmured. "Carlos is with me."

"I should come with you," she whispered.

I approached them. "No, you shouldn't. Your presence wasn't requested, so they'd see that as defiance." I cast her a gentle look, hiding my own shame. "Also, I haven't exactly been forthcoming about having a siren in my clan. They might recognise what you are."

Confusion filtered through her eyes. "Why don't you want them to know?"

I tucked a lock of hair over her ear. "The Elders like to believe they're the most powerful among us. We saw what your mother did to Gabriela. I myself felt the strength of her voice. If they were to learn of you, they might not take that very well. I can't protect you if they decide your existence is a problem."

Matteo growled his disapproval. I glared at him. "They barely tolerate your existence. You weren't around when ferals ran free, hundreds of them."

I tried not to sound too pleased with myself. I'd been the one to create the first Ferals, releasing them on humanity. Without taking their blood during the turning process, and creating a blood bond to help stabilise them, they'd been creatures solely focused on their hunger, unable to control it, stuck in permanent frenzy. It had been a delight to hunt with such creatures, spilling blood at will. When the accords had been set, every last feral was hunted down and killed. While not bonded to them, it had still pained me to see those I'd created reduced to nothing.

"They would have killed you the moment they knew about you if not for our blood bond," I told him. "You're lucky Gabriela got to you before they did." *Or the Hunters.*

Quinn frowned. "We all know why she sought him out."

I lifted her chin. "I will not expose you to them and risk you. They think your kind died out, and I'd have them continue to believe that." The desire to protect my clan included any potential threat from the Elders. I turned to Matteo. "We need to go."

He kissed Quinn before we climbed aboard the boat. The boat's engine roared to life, and the driver steered us away. Matteo glanced back at Quinn with a smile, and I suspected he was talking to her through their bond.

I'd been to plenty of meetings with the Elders as Gabriela's second and knew what to expect. A part of me was exhilarated for the offered drinks that awaited us, while also curious as to how Matteo would respond to that.

It was a short boat ride to the Mainland, where we met The Original Three outside a villa they'd taken control of. King Luis, Nico and Sia; The Original Three. Every vampire made was from their bloodlines.

King Luis had long black hair and a narrow face, with a shadow of facial hair. He exuded a power like no other. It seeped from his very being, making it hard for any vampire who came across him to not know who he was. Once known as The Shadow King in his world, we'd named him The Bloodking. A name he accepted with honour. No matter what name he went by, he was the King of all vampires. He matched Matteo in height and build.

Next to him was Sia, with blonde hair and delicate features, but a sly smile. Her husband, Nico, was almost as tall as Luis, a warrior whose job it was to protect and advise our King.

I knelt before King Luis, Matteo beside me.

"My King," I said. "I am in your service, as always, as is my second." Words I'd heard Gabriela say many times.

He grasped my chin, lifting it. I met his eyes. Unlike those of us who'd once been human, his eyes were always crimson. As were Nico's and Sia's. King Luis had once explained to me that they'd been born as vampires, in a different world where they walked freely as themselves. No one knew what had made them leave that world, and they hadn't offered us information.

"Thank you for answering my summons. Rise, Carlos. We have much to discuss."

I rose to my feet. "This is my second, Matteo Barone."

He stood, taking his place beside me.

King Luis, Nico, and Sia's eyes remained on him for a long time.

"You brought a feral?" Nico's eyes narrowed. "You dare bring a feral in the Bloodking's presence?"

King Luis put his hand on Nico's shoulder to silence him. "I'm sure Carlos did not mean such an offence. I will let him explain. Perhaps we should move our conversation inside."

They led us into a large room. A crystal chandelier hung from the ceiling, throwing light and reflections onto the walls. Heavy blue curtains covered the windows, and I glanced up at what looked to be marble, with artwork carved into the walls. It was a spacious room with five lounge chairs in the centre. Three facing two.

"Please, sit." King Luis indicated to the chairs.

Before we could take a seat, Sia's eyes moved over Matteo, and she flashed her fangs at him. "You are from my bloodline, I can smell it. I can feel our blood connection." She moved fast, and grabbed him by the jaw, licking his face. He tensed. "Our blood connection is strong. Who is your maker?"

"Bianca," he said. "I killed her for it."

Her smile slipped, her hand tightening on Matteo. Until that moment, it hadn't occurred to me that Matteo's maker was the very same as the first Sia had turned. I'd never met her, as she had been banished long before my time. His discomfort flowed through our blood bond.

"I didn't realise she was the maker of the feral," she said. "I remember her death. She didn't reach out for me, but I felt the emptiness the moment our bond ceased."

I watched her with worry. She had just discovered who'd killed her daughter. Would she hurt him over it? Matteo said nothing in response, and he knew enough to not try to pull out of her grasp.

"I always loved the nature of the ferals. To have my very own…" She pressed her face into his neck, breathing in deep. "You are delicious." She turned to King Luis and Nico. "I want him."

"Matteo belongs to another," I told her. "The newest of my clan is rather protective of him. As am I, as a maker would be to his fledgling."

"Let him go," King Luis ordered. "Everyone, sit."

She released him, disappointment glinting in her eyes. We sat in the chairs, the Elders opposite us.

Nico watched Matteo. "You were the Vampire of Venice," he growled. "A feral, you should have been killed." He turned his eyes to me. "Why was he allowed to live? You and Gabriela were there for the elimination of his kind. I know how much their destruction hurt you. Why did she spare him? Why would you name him as your second?"

I had expected this. "Matteo is bonded with me. To hurt him is to hurt me," I told him and glanced at King Luis. "Gabriela had reasons for her actions, none of which I understand. Matteo is not the risk to us that she was. He is not completely feral. Not like those the Hunters eliminated. He's different." I put my hand to Matteo's arm. "He's mine."

Sia let out a low growl. I realised my mistake. I had just claimed one from her line that she wanted. But I met her eyes without flinching. I was not about to let her take a member of my clan.

"Sia," King Luis warned. He nodded thoughtfully. "Yes, Gabriela was very blood-thirsty, as I remember you were. You, however, buried that more easily than she did. I understand her inability to adhere to the accords was what got her killed. I felt and mourned her death, as I know you did, my boy."

I hated being called 'my boy.' I pushed down my annoyance. I also fought against anger at his words. All I'd endured and he spoke as if it were easy for me.

"It was not so easy," I acknowledged. "I often reminisce about those days. All of us had primal natures that we were forced to suppress. I lost many friends in that war. Like many others, I struggled to rein in my hunger, to not kill," I shifted my gaze to Sia, who was still enraptured by Matteo, then back to King Luis. "I endured torture every time a human died at my hands, as you'll remember." Memories of the last time I'd suffered at his hands washed over me. It was hard to forget the pain he'd forced onto me. I forced down my anger.

"Does he kill still?" Nico spoke of Matteo as if he weren't there, his eyes hardening.

"There are still vampires across the globe who make the occasional mistake, just as he does. But he does not do so purposely. It has been years since he has taken a life." I forced the two we had killed together with Quinn from my mind. "Since turning his beloved, he has gained more control."

"She helped you gain control of your nature?" Nico asked.

Matteo glanced at me and nodded. "She did."

Sia smiled. "You found your hunting partner."

Matteo lifted his eyes to her, his hesitance melting away. "I did." He returned her smile.

King Luis eyed Matteo, then me, his expression hard to read. Likely he was speaking with Nico and Sia through their bond. I waited, hoping he wasn't about to decide to eliminate Matteo.

"Let's begin the meeting, then," King Luis said at last. "You come here with your second, and I thank you. The last time we met, you were the second. Now, you claim the title King, over Venice. We've heard of a few missing humans, but that happens everywhere. You've left no signs of the existence of vampires and done nothing to attract attention."

I clenched my jaw. The fact that a Hunter was in Venice indicated that *something* had attracted attention.

"All those we feed from are compelled to forget they saw us. We are a clan of nine, and I have had to defend my territory only a few times in twenty years."

"Your territory?" Sia laughed, and I tried not to flinch. I hadn't asked any of them for permission before we claimed Venice as ours. That alone could be considered an offence.

"Venice was empty when we arrived," I told the Elders. "We do not touch the locals, only tourists." An agreement I had made with the Barones. Descendants of Matteo and his brother.

"You still did not seek approval from *us*." King Luis rarely got angry, but I caught a flash of it as he raised his voice and his eyes hardened.

I bowed my head. "Then I seek it now."

Nico's scorn of Matteo was apparent. "So, why did you bring the vampire of Venice back here?"

"I missed my home," Matteo said. "After we separated from Gabriela, it became clear we needed to leave."

"You speak when spoken to, feral," Nico snapped. "You are the second; you do not speak for your King." he glared at me. "Did you let your second choose the territory you claimed because he 'missed his home'?"

'Matteo, perhaps it's wise you let me speak,' I told him through our bond. *'He's already taken issue with you. While any action is the decision of King Luis, Nico is his advisor.'* I met Nico's eyes. "He merely suggested Venice. It was my decision to come here. We needed to leave Australia in a hurry. I knew the territory we once had in Rome had been claimed by another."

King Luis frowned. "Yes, your presence in Australia was not un-noticed. Explain."

Matteo's eyes burned into mine, and I felt his fear. He'd attacked many, and he had done so willingly in one night of bad decisions.

"There were unfortunate deaths. None that my second is responsible for." I paused, grateful for the first time that Gabriela was dead. I was about to lay responsibility on her. "My maker's inability to control herself led to part of the clan breaking away and accepting me as their king." They didn't need to know that it was a siren who had given us that ability.

Sia leaned forward. "You separated from your maker, for the first time in how long?"

"Almost a thousand years," I replied. "I'd been loyal to her. She'd given me this life, and I will be eternally grateful for such an existence, to experience lifetimes no human could imagine. But she came to abuse her power, forcing many in her clan into obedience." I shot a glance at Matteo. "Something I will not do with my own clan."

"I can't say I've ever seen a vampire willingly separate from their maker," Sia pondered. "Especially one who'd stuck by them as long as you did."

Is she impressed?

"I imagine she challenged you for that," King Luis grinned at me.

I nodded, recalling how she'd taken me by surprise, and attacked me before leaving me bloody on the floor of our temporary den. At that point she was no longer my Queen, but was still my maker, and it had hurt. "She tried to rip out my throat."

King Luis leaned forward. "Had you still been there with her, you'd all be dead alongside the rest of her clan. Only her Magic Wielder managed to escape."

This was news to me. "They all died?" His revelation was like a punch to the gut.

"You didn't know?" There was sadness in his eyes. "The Hunters took out her entire clan. I've seen with my own eyes the remains of her den after they torched it."

I absorbed this in silence. We may have left the clan, but I didn't wish them dead. I'd been with many of them for centuries. Clans tended to have a closeness that human families never would. Matteo's grief echoed my own. Humans have beliefs as to where they go when they die, a wide variety. Vampires have no such beliefs. We believe we just cease to be. My thoughts turned to Celeste. I had tried to convince a few into leaving with us, but Celeste was the only who did. She'd fallen to her knees, bared her throat, and sworn loyalty to me the moment I asked. In that moment, I appreciated that I still had her.

"This saddens you." Sia said. "Even though you left them."

I nodded. "They were still my clan. To learn of their death…I had thought in Gabriela's death, her new second would take her place." I forced down the pain that rose, determined to not show weakness in front of the Elders.

King Luis watched me thoughtfully. "Tell me who you took into your clan," he commanded.

I listed off my clan's names. "Erik and Josef you will remember from the war," I added. "The others are younger, having joined us over the years. Quinn is our most recent, from Australia."

King Luis gave me a tight-lipped smile. "Maya told me you named yourselves Clan La Voz. Until you make a formal request to declare a new clan, territory, and the title of King, none of you exist. Many who knew you were part of la Primera Familia thought you died with your former clan."

I blinked. "That did not occur to me," I said. "I never sought to be a king until it happened." I rose from my chair, once more kneeling before Luis, bowing my head. "I ask that whatever you decide, that you do not punish my clan. They merely followed me."

The silence stretched out. I resisted the urge to raise my eyes.

"You care for your clan," King Luis remarked in a low voice. "To offer yourself, and beg for them to be spared from punishment. You have shown yourself to be a true leader."

I glanced up then. Resolution glinted in his eyes. He had come to a decision.

"I grant you sole territory of Venice, King Carlos," King Luis said. "Next time, try to remember that *I* am still *your* King."

"You have claimed such a small territory. The smallest for any clan." Nico added. "That you have lived here as long as you have without drawing attention is impressive."

"In fairness, they are a small clan," Sia laughed. "Can you

imagine a full-size clan living here? No wonder no one else has claimed this territory."

King Luis glanced across at her, his face softening as he did. As the two of them gazed at each other, it was easy to notice their bond. It was not unlike my own affection for all of my clan.

"This concludes the meeting," King Luis's eyes lit up with joy. "Time to drink in celebration."

Chapter 11

They led us to another room, almost as large as the one we'd left. As expected, there were at least fifty humans laying on couches, watching us. My mouth watered, having remembered the last time I had been involved in this. Already I yearned to bite down, to let blood flow down my throat.

Next to me, Matteo tensed. *'You never told me...'* he stopped and took a deep breath slowly. *'Carlos, I cannot lose control. Not here, not with the Elders to witness it. Please, if you have to, use our bond to pull me back.'* Even in his silent voice, I caught the tremor. He was afraid. His thoughts turned to Quinn

'I will not need to,' I told him. *'They will instruct us in a way that the command takes hold. Similar to what Gabriela used to do to us, only more, harder to break.'*

King Luis put a hand on my shoulder. "If I remember correctly, you have certain preferences. Instead of quiet and compliant, you enjoy the spice of fear. Is that still the case?"

I nodded, unable to shift my gaze from the humans. Their heartbeats pounded in my ears; the smell of their blood washed over me. I was barely holding myself together. To have this many humans to feed on was reminiscent of the old days, and the vampire part of my brain was delighted.

Sia laughed. "A man with good taste."

"What of your second," King Luis glanced at Matteo. "Are you of similar taste?"

Matteo shifted his gaze with effort to King Luis, a slow smile spreading across his face, eyes red. "I do like to hear them scream," he admitted. "It is music to my ears."

King Luis's laughter boomed from him, his eyes lighting up. "Fear and screaming. You two are alike. Gabriela chose well in that bond. Is it about the chase, too? Do you like to draw it out?"

My own smile widened. "It does add pleasure to the hunt."

Sia moved fast, standing in front of Matteo, King Luis taking my gaze in his. I felt his mind take hold.

"Don't fight us," Sia whispered.

I hated the compelling voice of another being used against me, but I let myself relax.

"There will be no killing here," they said in unison. "The accords will not be broken here today. You have many to choose from. Take pleasure in the feed, and move on to the next. If you kill, you will forfeit your own life."

The command reverberated through my entire being. As they'd been talking, Nico had retrieved a woman from one of the couches. "You have use of the entire villa," King Luis said.

The woman's eyes widened as she saw me and Matteo. I was in front of her in an instant, showing her my fangs and red eyes. As Matteo joined me, she smiled. *Damn, a volunteer, likely addicted to the venom of the Elders.*

I lifted her hair, my fingers brushing against her throat. Matteo let out a growl from deep within his chest. His feral nature had taken over.

'*Matteo, are you still with us?*' I asked.

He nodded, not taking his eyes from the human woman. '*I am, Sia's command holds strong. Release her, let her run. I'm ready to give chase.*'

I turned back to the woman. "Run," I told her. "Be afraid. Scream for my friend."

The fragrance of fear almost sent me into a frenzy as she ran from the room, a scream spilling from her. Laughter came from the Elders. My body quivered as I held myself still, waiting. Next to me, Matteo did the same. I tore off my jacket and tee-shirt, not wanting to ruin them. This was a feeding in which it was expected to be messy. Matteo took his tee-shirt off, and he gave me a savage smile.

"Ready?" I asked him.

At the scent of blood, I glanced over my shoulder. The Elders had started already, Sia's body pressed against that of the man she'd chosen, rubbing herself against him. King Luis and Nico growled, drawn into their own feeding, their shirts removed.

Panicked gasps came from the woman who'd run from us,

and I couldn't hold back any more. We gave chase.

Matteo quickly cut off her escape. "Scream for me," he whispered.

A second scream split the air, and I laughed at the gleeful glint in Matteo's eyes.

I grabbed her chin, lifting it to bare her throat to us, and I let out a growl and licked her throat slowly. Matteo mirrored my movements.

'*She smells delicious,*' I said silently.

He smiled in agreement. We struck at the same time. Releasing venom into my bite, I wrapped an arm around her waist, my other grasping the hair on the back of Matteo's head. Her blood had the spice of fear that I loved so much, with the hint of desire from our venom. She moaned, her hands dropping as her body relaxed completely, so we were holding her up.

I lifted my head a second before Matteo did.

"It's all-you-can-eat," I told him as I carried the human back to the room we'd left. "Sex is allowed, if they want it. Many will expect it, so you have to let it be known if you only want their blood. You can bite them anywhere, just don't mark them. You mark any, you have to take them when we leave." We stopped at the doorway, and I laughed at the wonder as he looked around the room. "Welcome to an Elder summit. Now that I've officially been recognised as King of Venice, we'll be invited to one every ten years. Sometimes with other clans. Drink, and move on to the next."

"I feel blood drunk just looking at this," he whispered.

He left my side, moving into the room, only to be surrounded by humans. I lay our first human of the occasion on a couch and sought out my next. The Elders were already on their second, King Luis and Nico bare-chested, while Sia had stripped completely, taking space on a couch with her prey, a male. He was removing his jeans hurriedly as her mouth latched onto his neck.

I fell into feeding, taking enough of their blood before moving on. Some tasted sweet, while others had a richer flavour. The equivalent of a steak and a dessert. Around me, humans moaned from being bitten. The Elders took pleasure from the humans who wanted it.

I caught sight of Matteo gently removing a woman's hands from his belt. "No," he told her firmly, and let out a growl. "Bare your throat."

I was blood drunk when I searched the room. I wanted someone who'd be willing to offer their body as well as their blood. A woman with black hair and blue eyes approached me and put her hand to my chest. A sign that she wanted whatever I asked of her. Without a word, she tilted her head back, exposing her throat. I pulled her into my arms and ran my tongue over her neck, before biting her. As I fed, another body pushed in against mine, and I lifted my head. The black haired woman's eyes shone with lust, while the second human, a blond man with his shirt off, reached up to touch my face.

I looked at them with a grin. "Perhaps we should move to a couch," I suggested.

They both followed me and sat, looking up at me. Both of them were aroused, wanting. I removed my jeans and advanced on the woman. Once again, she bared her neck to me and I pinned her body beneath mine. Her legs wrapped around my waist, and I sunk my fangs into her throat.

The man's hands slid over my leg and ass, his lips touched my shoulder, and he trailed kisses over to my back. I eased myself into the woman, her soft moans encouraging me. The red haze closed around me, and the room blurred.

I stopped at the sound of a growl. Matteo had locked on to a human, the animalistic gleam in his eye a sign he was all but gone. His gaze was on Sia as she advanced on him, a predatory smile on her face. I pulled myself from the woman.

"Enjoy each other," I told them. "I will return." I moved to put myself between Matteo and Sia. "I wouldn't do that, if I were you," I warned, unsure I was speaking clearly, or why I was challenging an Elder. If she so desired, she could tear me apart.

"He belongs to another, I know." She pointed around the room. "She's not here. I want a taste."

"Sia, leave the feral alone," Nico said from the other side of the room, his voice husky as he thrust into the human woman in his grasp, her lust so thick I could almost taste it.

Sia glared at me. "Command him to come here, or I will," she ordered.

'Matteo?' I hoped a part of him held on.

'She wants my human,' his voice was still his and he clung to the person, meeting my gaze.

A low growl grumbled from him again.

'No, Amico, she wants you. Come here.'

He released his human and moved to stand next to me. I could tell he was as intoxicated as I was, and I grasped his shoulder. *'It's alright, she just wants a taste.'* I didn't like it, but Sia was a woman who wouldn't be refused, so we didn't have a choice.

She moved towards him like stalking prey. Matteo's eyes dropped to her body, and he quickly diverted his gaze, looking at me instead. Sia's lips curved, and she circled the two of us before planting her hand on Matteo's chest.

"I will not betray my beloved," he told her.

She lowered her head to his chest, licking the blood, moving up to his chin. "I'm not asking you to," she murmured. "I just want to taste you." she lifted her eyes to meet mine. "Both of you."

Before I could react, she had her hand on my abdomen, waiting. She wanted me to deny her, so she could force me. I could tell by her smile, by the wicked glint in her eye. In response, I grabbed her jaw, tasting the blood, and she growled in contentment. Matteo followed my lead, and the two of us lapped the blood from her face. Nico was beside me, then King Luis, circling the three of us, hunger and lust mixing in their gazes.

Sia reached out, her hands closing around our throats. She pulled me to her mouth first, and her fangs sunk in. My whole body tensed as her venom was released, and I could have come there and then. I groaned, the potency of Elder venom stronger than I remembered.

Our venom awakened desire, pleasure, lust. But theirs was pure euphoria, often unleashing bloodlust.

"Mmmm," she said against my throat

She released me, only for two more sets of fangs to sink into my flesh. I shuddered, my mind clouded, and I clamped down on my own tongue, tasting blood. I couldn't stand, so the three of them held me up. I needed something to bite down on, and Nico pushed a human at me. Drunk from both my feeding and their venom, I couldn't see straight, but saw enough to clamp onto the human. I was aware enough to know they were doing the same to Matteo. Then the red haze buried me completely. I gave in to both hungers, returning to the two humans waiting on the couch for me.

Chapter 12

I woke naked, with the human woman in my arms. Warmth against my side revealed the man. On the other side of me was Matteo, with a human woman in his arms. Their throats bore mostly healed bite marks. Powered by the large quantities of blood I'd ingested, I laughed, my head still fuzzy from overfeeding and Elder venom. I lifted my head, finding the Elders naked and curled up together on the other side of the room, humans with them. The rest of the humans were asleep.

"That was interesting," Matteo's voice was husky. "I don't remember ever having that much, even before Gabriela found me. And when they bit me…" he took in a deep breath and let it out in a rush. "Much stronger than Gabriela's. More enjoyable than her bite."

I chuckled, understanding his reaction.

"Their venom is hard to resist." I spoke in a low tone. "It really has a kick with the potency." I could only imagine what their venom did to humans. It made sense then why so many were there willingly. Likely they were addicted. Not that I could blame them. The room was heavy with blood and arousal, with the sweet remnants of orgasms.

"Do the meetings always end like this?" He sat up, his red eyes on my face. "I don't remember much."

"You went into a feeding frenzy; we both did. That's part of what their venom does to us." I glanced around the room. "However, having what humans call an 'all-you-can-eat buffet' does tend to be quite the temptation no vampire can resist."

Unlike Matteo, I remembered my feeding frenzies, and I enjoyed every moment of them. I stretched, satisfied with myself. Panic filtered across Matteo's face, and we both searched the room, looking for the telltale sign that his frenzy had led to a death. Every human remained alive, their chests rising and falling as they breathed.

"They told us not to kill; naturally, it would reach that part of you." I finally sat up. "You even kept your pants on," I noted with amusement. He was shirtless, but had not given in to the need to fuck as he fed. "I think Quinn would have enjoyed this. Perhaps I should bring in my own volunteers, have some fun with the two of you. And anyone else in the clan who wants to take part. I always did enjoy this part of an Elder summit. It really makes a man hard, when they're that eager for my cock and as intoxicated on my venom as I am on their blood. Mmmm."

Matteo laughed. "You're making me hard, just thinking about it."

I moved towards Matteo, fangs extended. "If only we were at the den right now," I growled, pinning him beneath me. I licked his throat, contentment rumbling from my chest. Still partially drunk from overfeeding, I was pushing my boundaries. Matteo had made it clear that I could only take them to my bed as a pair. But in my post-feeding high, I wanted to claim him, with the humans right next to us. He tilted his head, baring his throat. I bit down. *Your feral half enjoyed last night,*' I told him through our bond as I drank from him. *'I want your siren to release that feral side as I take you both to my bed. I want her to unleash the rougher side in me. You know what her voice does.*' I released his throat, capturing his gaze. "Tell her what awaits her when we get home." I commanded.

I could smell his arousal, and his breathing had become ragged, but I climbed off him.

"You're drunk," he said, adjusting himself through his jeans.

"This was once a constant state for me." I laughed. "We could feed freely, and I would drink until I couldn't see straight, almost every night." There was a power, a strength that came from that amount of feeding, and a wave of nostalgia washed over me. I recalled last night's feeding frenzy. I'd cleaned Matteo, then he'd licked the blood from my face. "Your feral half certainly enjoyed himself. How do you feel?"

His wide smile was answer enough. He was as high as I

was.

I grinned back at him. "It was quite a night." I nuzzled the neck of the human next to me. She opened her eyes and tilted her head back. "We can go home tonight. Back to your Quinn. There will be more on offer before then, but not to the extent that there was last night." I bit into the woman's throat.

"Carlos," King Luis's voice echoed across the room. "Come with me."

I lifted my head, annoyed at my breakfast being interrupted, but I climbed off the couch. A human brought me my jeans, which I pulled on, and I followed Luis from the room.

He led me to an indoor garden. Many varieties of flowers grew, of many colours, the air thick with their floral scent

"Let us create a blood bond," Luis commanded.

I frowned, not understanding why.

"I have made many children, but there was no bond like I had with my first, Gabriela." He put a hand on my shoulder, his grip strong. "That broken bond created an emptiness that I know you feel, too. The absence of your maker can be filled by another. I will take her place, be as your maker, as you are to Matteo."

I could not deny that Gabriela's death still haunted me, the absence of her presence leaving a hollow ache deep inside me. "We did not part on good terms," I admitted. "But in her final moments, she called out to me across the distance. I felt her death, her pain, and her fear."

He nodded. "She reached out to me, too. She told me she was going to die, and that you would be the one to end the life of her killer. Drink from me, Carlos, and we will be joined in our grief for her and bonded by blood."

I hesitated. "What will this do to me?" I asked. "I know the potency of your venom; what of your blood?"

"It will enhance everything, as it did when you turned. Your senses, and your hunger. I will be beside you as you adjust," he encouraged.

I hesitated. He tilted his head, slicing across his throat with a blade I hadn't noticed earlier. Only a shallow cut, but his blood welled up, and the scent of it sung to me. I couldn't resist. I lunged at him and bit in. Burrowing in deeper, I bit hard, groaning against his throat. His blood was rich, powerful, and I wanted more. I'd never tasted such power in blood before, not even when Gabriela gave me hers as I lay dying when I was human.

King Luis bit into my wrist. I shuddered, echoes of Gabriela's voice fading.

'*Let her go,*' King Luis's voice was in my head as the blood bond kicked in. '*Accept me.*'

I could feel his pain and sadness as my own, releasing tears for her death. He'd loved her. In a way, I had too, grateful for what she'd given me. His fangs tore at my wrist, and we fed from each other.

'*Let her go, my son,*' he said again.

My body was in overdrive, hunger wrapping around me like I'd never experienced before. I didn't know when I'd fallen to my knees, King Luis with me. Energy blazed within, my dark nature intensified. I pulled away, and he let me. Every sound filtered in, fifty human heartbeats nearby no longer a low thrum, but thunderous. People were talking in low voices, and the sound of a boat roared as if it were right next to me. I swayed.

"You're okay," his voice was both in my head and spoken. "Come. You need to feed." His own hunger flared, mirroring mine. Even though I'd fed plenty last night, I needed more.

Three strong vampire heartbeats approached with the gentle and quicker beats of a human. My fangs lengthened, slicing into my own lip.

'Carlos?' Matteo's voice sounded worried. He met my eyes as he entered the garden. 'Are you okay?'

Sia and Nico walked in after him, a human following behind.

King Luis motioned to the human woman, and she went to him willingly. 'Share her with me,' he told me, and I found myself moving forward. 'I want to enjoy her fear as you do,' he said in my head. 'Make her afraid.'

I usually only shared with members of my own clan, but I was eager, hungry. I reached for the human, guiding her chin to bring her gaze to me. I took her mind in mine.

"Be afraid," I whispered.

As she trembled, her eyes wide with horror, I struck, King Luis taking the other side of her throat. Sia caressed the back of my neck, her breath warm before her fangs pierced my shoulder. Her venom moved through me just as Nico joined in. A low, savage grumble rose from me, and I struggled against the desire to tear into the flesh in my mouth.

Sia stroked the back of my head.

'Invite Matteo to drink,' King Luis instructed.

I reached down for the human's hand, holding her wrist out towards Matteo. 'Drink.'

As Matteo, King Luis, and I fed, it dawned on me too slowly that we were taking too much. I released her at the same time the others did.

Sia picked up the human, and I heard the heart racing. I watched them leave.

"Don't worry, she'll live," King Luis said. "She'll have Sia's blood and be good as new."

"Won't that create a feral?" Matteo asked.

"Only if she feeds. We have a separate room. She'll be restrained until she is no longer Bestowed." Nico smirked. "All laws are upheld; accords are not broken. In a week or two, after she's rested, she'll be ready to return to her kind, and she won't remember a thing."

I stared from Nico to King Luis. I had been there during the creation of the accords and personally knew how serious the Elders had been in ensuring no one broke them. To break them meant death or starvation, either at the Elders' hands, or Hunters'. But they'd found a loophole, and I couldn't help but wonder how long they'd been doing this. A wide smile crept across my face as I considered the possibilities this could open up for me and my clan.

Chapter 13

King Luis's blood had sent a jolt through me, which turned everything up. I burned with hunger and need in a way I never had before.

"It will take a few days before you adjust to what I've given you. It won't be so overwhelming. You have to get yourself under control before I can put you back into the world." King Luis smiled, the presence of his mind replacing where Gabriela's once was.

I didn't want Matteo to stay, though. The looks Sia gave him were enough to worry me. "I need you to go home," I instructed him. "With the visitor from out of town, I trust you to keep everyone safe. Tell them I chose to stay with the Elders for a while longer. You're my second; they'll listen to you."

"Will you be okay here?" he asked.

I nodded, trying to reassure him.

He studied me. "You feel different through our bond," he said. "What do you feel?"

I considered it for a moment. "It's a rush. Everything is more." I didn't tell him that I also craved vampire blood. That the very scent of his blood so close had me clenching my jaw so hard my teeth hurt.

As soon as Matteo left, I wandered the villa. King Luis, Sia, and Nico were feeding again. I could smell the blood from the other side of the grounds. But I hadn't been invited, so I could not just enter the room unless they wanted me there. Before long, I heard sounds of them fucking.

The sun rose, and with it, humans around us. Needing to rest, I took the bedroom they'd given me and stripped before falling into a deep sleep.

I awoke from dreams about my early days as a vampire, fangs extended as the last of the screams of my dream faded. Breathing hard, I tried to calm down, when I noticed the three warm bodies of the Elders wrapped around me, as naked as I was. King Luis lifted his head when I tried to move.

He pulled me into his gaze. "Stay," he commanded.

Unable to escape, the other two lifted their heads, looking at me the way vampires regarded humans. I barely had time to notice their hungry smiles before all three of them bit into me. King Luis's and Sia's fangs were in my throat, Nico taking my wrist. My apprehension faded as their venom took hold in time for King Luis to offer me his wrist. I knew what they were doing: they were getting me hooked on Elder blood and venom. I just didn't know why. But with their venom overwhelming my system, I didn't care. I *couldn't.*

Sia ground herself against my cock. "Mmm, you're already hard," she purred in my ear. "I know you take many to your bed, Carlos. You love so generously. Do you think you could handle me?" I couldn't answer, could only growl as a red haze rose up.

There was a human in my room. The effects of venom combined with the scent of blood and the drum of a heartbeat sent me into a frenzy. I couldn't hold myself back. With a savage growl, I left the bed and launched myself at the human, the motion knocking the woman to the floor as I tore into her throat.

"His nature has always been just below the surface; all he needs is a nudge. He was a killer, and he will always be one." The words were spoken far away, unimportant as I let the blood carry me through the red haze into bliss.

The fog cleared, and I looked down at the human woman beneath me. I had not been gentle with my bite. I'd ripped her delicate throat and let her blood gush, it now dripping from my jaw down my chest. Her glassy eyes stared at nothing, her heart stilled forever. Not even vampire blood would help her. Panicked, I lifted myself from her and turned, to find Sia, Nico, and King Luis watching me from my bed.

Sia's eyes gleamed with delight. Nico and King Luis mirrored each other's satisfied smiles. Not yet able to think straight, I growled and started to back away.

"Stop," King Luis's command became restraints that I couldn't break.

I had killed. Right in front of them. As they advanced, surrounding me, I considered reaching out to Matteo, but decided against it. He would march in here with the clan at his back, and all of them would die.

"We're not going to kill you," Nico said.

Before I could say anything, Sia closed the distance and started to lick my chest, cleaning me. The feeling of being cornered had my mind pleading with my body to run, to attack, anything. But I could only stand there, naked, as the three of them licked the blood from me. I closed my eyes, fighting my growing lust.

When they were done, they stepped back, watching me.

What is happening right now? Surely I had to be hallucinating. I turned my gaze to the dead human again.

"He's not ready," Sia murmured, disappointment heavy in her voice. "This isn't the wild, rebellious Carlos I remember."

Ready for what?

"What I did may have broken him," King Luis admitted. "Give him time. He'll be ready when it counts."

"I hope so, if you're relying on him to be at your right hand, with the others," Nico muttered.

Confused, I could only stare at the human I'd killed. I knew the consequences, had lived it. *Why are they not killing me?*

Nico left with the body, and I faced the remaining two Elders.

"Tell me, did you at least enjoy that?" King Luis asked.

There was no denying that I had. Everything I'd done, all

I had been came rushing back. But I wanted more. I could not give in to that. I could not break the accords.

"Ah yes, the accords," King Luis murmured, as if he'd heard my thoughts. "Wouldn't life be easier if we didn't have them? Live like we used to?"

"The Hunters will never permit that." I replied.

King Luis's grin grew wide, Sia's too.

"Carlos, don't tell me you're afraid of humans? They need numbers to take us on, and if we were so inclined, it would be an unfair fight."

My muddled thoughts zeroed in on the Huntress who had almost killed me mid-feed. And that Gabriela and the others had been wiped out.

"Oh, she's lovely." King Luis had seen the Huntress from my mind. "Her death will bring more Hunters."

"Why do I feel like that's what you want?" I frowned. "You let me break the accords. You knew what your venom and blood would do." My mind was in chaos over what had just happened.

"I have much I would like to discuss with you, but not yet," King Luis said. "Sia's right, you're not ready. But you will be."

They walked from my room together, leaving me to wonder how I had just survived after killing a human in front of them, and why the very people who enforced the accords were bent on breaking them.

Chapter 14

I scoured through records in an attempt to find the vampire I'd faced. I now knew that he wasn't alone, so it was likely there was a clan here. I searched for vampires in Venice, Spanish vampires, and even vampires in Australia. The one name that came up in two searches was Matteo Barone. However, there was an old drawing of him, and his facial features didn't match. I skimmed through the article until I read '**known accomplice of Gabriela Ramirez and Carlos Rivera.**'

There were no pictures of them, though, and Gabriela had

been killed along with her clan in Melbourne. Matteo had turned a human. But none of that interested me; he was not the vampire I hunted. I glanced at the name 'Carlos'. I'd seen his name in Josef's record.

'Among the most dangerous vampires still alive from the war. Known by three names: The Father of Ferals, The Killer, and The Immortal Wolf, Carlos is a vicious, bloodthirsty vampire that will snap your neck for fun. Has a known hatred for Hunters and has torn out the throat of many for daring to enter his territory. Whereabouts unknown. Unlikely to have died in the fire that took out Gabriela and her clan. Might be with Matteo Barone and Quinn Bailey.'

I shuddered, hoping the vampire I hunted was not Carlos. Surely, if it was, I would not have survived. This one, while I didn't for a moment think he wasn't dangerous, was more smug and arrogant than anything. He wanted to kill me, but he also wanted to play mind games, and had shown me that at the bar.

I searched through the list of Spanish vampires, and the name 'King Luis' came up. *'King of vampires, one of the Original Three. The Elders are easily recognised by their permanently red eyes and have no humanity. No Hunter has seen them for around three hundred years. Earliest records of the Elders originate in Spain, where the plague of vampires began. It is thought that these three were born as vampires, but that all others were turned.'*

I sighed. The vampire had blue eyes, so he was not one of the Elders. There was the possibility that the vampire was no one noteworthy. Just a filthy bloodsucker that needed putting down. Now that I knew there was more than one vampire there, I considered calling for help. One was already too much, but two, likely more, would see me dead.

Almost midnight. I closed my laptop and prepared myself for the hunt. First I attached the hidden crossbow to my arm and pulled my jacket on before loading myself with knives and wooden stakes. Last, I picked up my mini crossbow and tucked it into my holster, which I concealed with my jacket. If anyone saw me, it would just look like I was walking the streets of Venice. They wouldn't see that I was armed to the teeth, out to kill a vampire. Vampires. I still didn't know how many there were there.

I took a route different from the one I usually took. He'd been at the bar, so I decided to check if he'd returned. As I rounded a corner, I caught the sound of someone humming. It was a beautiful sound that drew me forward. Unable to resist, I needed to follow its pull.

The humming stopped, and I glanced around. Unsure how I had gotten where I was, I caught sight of a red-haired woman watching me with amusement.

"It looks like I caught something unexpected with my Siren Song," she said with an accent that might be Australian.

I examined my surroundings again, my mind foggy. "I'm sorry, I . . ."

She appeared in front of me, her eyes red, and I reached for my knife.

"Vampire," I grunted.

My heart pounded and I tried to clear my head. I backed away from her.

"It might take a while for the effects of my song to wear off," she said with laughter. "Not that it will matter."

She advanced and I drew my crossbow. Her eyes dropped to my weapon and met my gaze with a wide smile, her fangs emerging.

"Back up," I warned her.

When she took another step towards me, I fired the crossbow. The first arrow hit her shoulder, and she growled. The second pierced her throat and she froze, eyes wide. She started to choke, reaching for the arrow. A pained whimper escaped her, and I prepared to fire again, aiming for her heart. Something hit me hard and I landed twenty feet away, on my back. Pain crashed over me, and I fought against the urge to groan. I lifted my head, trying to regain my senses.

"Quinn," a male voice I didn't recognise said. "You're okay, *mi amore*."

She whimpered again, and there was a loud snap. He murmured something to her, then he stood over me, his face in shadow. He gripped two broken arrows. But instead of attacking, he dropped the arrow pieces. "I would feed you to my beloved, but our King wants to deal with you himself when he returns. It is taking all my self-control not to rip you apart where you lie. Count yourself lucky, *Hunter*." He sneered at the word Hunter.

My body hurt too much to move, and I'd lost grip on my crossbow. I pulled out a knife, fearful that he'd still attempt something. The growls coming from him spoke to a deep fear inside me.

"My sweet feral, come to me," the woman vampire said. "I need blood, but he's made it clear to leave *her* for *him*. I need to feed."

He took a moment longer to react to her words than I would have liked. Then, finally, he turned, returning to her side, and the two of them disappeared. I let out a sigh of relief and lowered my head on the ground. It started to rain, drenching me in seconds, but I lay where I was, letting the cool water wash over my skin.

My relief was short-lived when I went over what he'd said. *King.* Somehow, I was sure he was talking about the vampire I'd already faced. Cold fear rolled through me. A King. I was in trouble.

Chapter 15

By the time I left the Elder's villa, not much had changed. My senses were still overwhelmed, and as my clan welcomed me back, I just wanted to be left alone. I still hungered for vampire blood as much as human blood, and I did not want to put my clan through that. Reminded of Gabriela's habits, I now had more of an understanding of her. In my bedroom, I locked the door and lay down on my bed. But sleep wouldn't come. Instead, memories of the beginning of the war forced their way into my mind.

Flames of the village glowed against the night sky, and screams rose from within. I marched forward, only to be held back by Gabriela.

"What are you doing?" I demanded. "Those aren't just humans in there. Our people are dying, too."

We'd taken shelter in a human village to hide and heal, keeping the humans alive in an effort to hold the Hunters at bay.

"They're already dead," she said. "If you go in there, you'll die, too."

The screams tore at me. "They've declared war on us," I searched the forest behind us. "I'll kill every last one of them."

Sia ran from the village, covered in burns and blood. Her eyes flashed with fury. "They came out of nowhere," she said as her burns started to heal. "They don't care that this is a human village." She glanced at Gabriela. "Can you still sense King Luis?"

Gabriela nodded. "He's with Nico; they're safe."

"What about Amara?" I asked.

Sia shook her head. "She's not in there. Maybe she went after the Hunters."

I heard the drawback of a bow string and searched the forest again. Ten Hunters advanced, raining arrows on us.

"Tell King Luis we'll meet him by the river," Sia instructed.

Enraged by losing vampires, and that we no longer had a food source, I wanted to kill the Hunters. My fangs extended.

"No." Sia glared at me. "We've lost enough vampires tonight. We get to the river."

So instead of taking on the very Hunters who'd burned the village, we sped past them, arriving at the river. King Luis and Nico were crouched down. Other vampires started to join us.

Sia let out a roar of anguish as she fell to her knees beside King Luis. Nico covered her mouth to silence her. He whispered words to her in a language I had heard them speak before. Their language from another world. Muffled cries and gasps drew my curiosity. I walked over and clamped down on my own horrified gasp. King Luis and Nico had been crouching over the body of Amara, the fourth Original. In King Luis's arms, her head had been separated from her body. Red eyes open but unseeing, fangs bared.

A knock at the door tore me from my thoughts. I sat up, the echoes of the past making me restless. Emotion clawed at the back of my throat, the warmth of tears threatening to overflow. I could already tell it was Matteo at the door.

"What?" I demanded.

"Let me in, Carlos. You can hide from the rest of the clan, but not from me. I can feel your pain."

I considered ignoring him but knew he wouldn't go away. I unlocked the door and let him in, backing away as he entered.

"You're thinking about the war again," he said. "You haven't done that for at least a couple of centuries."

Damn that blood bond of ours. While I didn't usually dislike having the connection we had, there were times it was a nuisance to have someone else inside my head.

As I looked at Matteo, hunger washed over me, and I clenched my teeth.

"You're hungry." He frowned. "Quinn's getting ready to sing. Join us."

I shook my head, afraid I'd be just as likely to drink from them. "How is she?" I asked.

It worried me that the Huntress was becoming more of a problem after attacking Quinn. I'd not quite accepted the human death at the villa before Matteo's voice had come through rageful and on the verge of his feral rising up over Quinn being hurt. It had taken a lot of talking to convince him to leave the Huntress for me.

"Mostly shaken up," he said. "The Hunter almost killed her. If I hadn't arrived when I did, I could have lost her." Fear glinted through his eyes. "I almost turned feral right then and there," he muttered. "I wish you'd let me kill her. She was in our territory."

"I have a score to settle with her," I said. "If anyone is going to kill her, I have that pleasure." I didn't want to admit to him how much it worried me. I'd been in the Elders' villa and wouldn't have been able to do anything. If she had killed Quinn, Matteo would have torn out the Hunter's throat and lost himself in his feral nature. There was also the matter of their connection and what that would do to him. I had been in no position to protect Matteo or Quinn from my Hunter problem. I needed to take care of it, and soon.

Hunger flooded through me again, and I gritted my teeth.

"I'll get Lorenzo to bring you someone." Matteo's watchful eyes missed nothing. "Something happened, didn't it?"

I couldn't tell him what I'd done. No one in my clan should know. It wasn't just that I'd killed a human, it was that I'd enjoyed it and wanted to do it again. That the blood gushing down my throat had awakened my bloodlust. It occurred to me that if anyone would be sympathetic, he was the one vampire who would. The one who struggled with his own feral nature.

"Was there something you wanted?" I asked instead, burying all thoughts of what had happened.

A line formed in his forehead. "You've shut me out. What are you hiding? You came back in a mood, you're thinking about the war, and now this. You've not spoken to me that way since we were first bonded." Quinn's voice calling his name drew his attention. "I'm going with Quinn. When you're ready to be our King again instead of a human teenager, you know where to find us." He turned around. "Should I slam the door, or will you do that yourself?"

His anger was enough to knock me from my mood.

"Wait." I stopped him.

He faced me, arms crossed over his chest.

'I can't risk the others overhearing us,' I used our bond to speak with him. *'Go with Quinn. I'll go hunting; we can talk after.'*

'Come with us,' he urged. *'You always love watching Quinn sing. I can talk to Quinn to let you pick who she draws out.'*

His willingness to accept my moodiness and pull me into his and Quinn's hunt broke down my defence. *'I killed someone, Matteo. Right in front of the Elders.'*

He stared. *'They didn't try to kill you? Are we in danger? Are you? Why did they let you go?'*

'They're the ones who orchestrated it.' I frowned. *'It felt like a test, for some reason. I'm not sure if I failed or passed.'*

His eyes narrowed. *'Why?'*

I told him through our bond what had happened.

'I don't like it,' he said as Quinn entered the room.

'Neither do I. They're up to something, and until I know what it is, I think we should all be careful.'

"This looks serious." Quinn said. "Should I come back?"

I smiled at her. "No, your beloved is ready to go."

I shot a look at Matteo, warning him: *this is not for the clan to know.* As they left, I locked the door again, pushing down the desire to follow them, to feed off them both.

Chapter 16

After two days of the ever-growing hunger, which I knew could only be satisfied by vampire blood, I started to avoid my clan. I could feel that King Luis had left Venice, but his presence still remained. Our bond had been made, and I would never be free of it.

It was the second time I'd hunted that night, trying to satisfy my hunger with human blood. I wandered the streets of Venice, not really paying attention. Dark clouds hung in the sky, and the air had a chill to it. I wasn't affected by cooler weather, but my warm breath still came out white.

I picked up the Hunter's familiar scent and moved towards

it. The trail led me through streets as if she were weaving.

"Where are you?" I muttered. Tonight, I would kill her and leave her face down in the canal. My plans for how I would accomplish this were ever-changing. I was yet to decide on what I would enjoy the most.

I stopped at the alley where she'd almost killed me and found her looking around.

"You have to know I don't come here any more," I said. Her heart jumped, sending a spike of fear through her. The prospect of a fight brought a smile to my face, lifting my mood. "Are you stalking me?" I asked with laughter. "I don't know if I should be flattered or concerned by your obsession with me." She held a crossbow, with a knife shoved into a holster at her hip, and an angry silence vibrated from her. "How's the shoulder?"

Her scowl deepened. "Why do you talk so much?"

"Not used to us talking, are you?" I chuckled. "You prefer the savage monster, instead? Does it make us easier to kill? I can growl, if it'll help?"

I moved too fast for her to see, standing in front of her, and I let out a deep growl, showing fangs. Her eyes widened, but she had good control of her fear. She glanced at my mouth, where I knew signs of my recent meal showed. She averted her gaze, her lip curling in disgust.

"You have been well-trained, haven't you?" I noted. "Clearly, you know what fear does to us. You're locking yours down nice and tight. I'm impressed."

"I don't need you to be impressed, *diablo*, I need you to shut up." She raised her crossbow level to my chest.

"*Diablo*? Is that what I am?" She fired an arrow, and I caught it. "You missed," I laughed. "If you could please stop doing that, I just had the first jacket you ruined, replaced."

I caught the twitch of her finger and grabbed the crossbow, pushing it off to the side as another bolt was released. I stepped in closer, breathing in her scent of apples and vanilla. Once again her eyes darted to my mouth.

I glanced around, expecting her family to appear. But each time I'd seen her, she'd been alone. Even Josef and Quinn had caught her by herself. Just as she was now. There was no family here. Just her. A wide smile spread across my face.

"You Hunters usually descend in large numbers; it takes entire families to hunt us." The scent of her spike of fear had me leaning forward to breathe her in. "Why are you here all by yourself?" I asked.

"That's none of your business, *diablo*." Her eyes widened as she realised her mistake.

She tried to back away.

"There's that word again. Tell me, sweet *Cazadora*, if I'm *Diablo*, why are you looking at my mouth?" I licked my lips, anticipating what sound she would make as I sunk my fangs into her neck. *Should I make her scream in pain, or moan with pleasure?*

I pushed forward, until her back hit the wall. With hands on either side of her, I leaned towards her. "I'm going to enjoy this," I growled.

Her body tensed, and she struggled under me, pushing at my chest. I ignored her feeble attempts and ran my tongue over her throat. She gasped and her struggle stopped. I paused with a slow smile and licked her throat again. Her heart skipped and her breathing hitched.

"Oh, sweet *Cazadora*, I do believe you enjoyed that." I pulled away, eyes darting over her face.

Her fear kicked in then, flickering through her eyes. And disgust. She'd enjoyed my licking her throat, then been disgusted by it. By me, because I was a vampire. I rubbed my cheek against hers, feeling the shudder tear through her. I leaned in again, this time towards her mouth. Her lips parted, possibly an unconscious movement. But I closed the gap, pressing my lips to hers, my tongue slipping into her mouth.

The crossbow shook as she tried to aim it towards me. Our bodies were tight against one another, and a deep shudder passed through hers. The sound of the crossbow being fired and a thud off to the side only brought a smile to my face. Another shiver moved through her before she yielded completely to my kiss. Her tongue pushed against mine and she let out a slight moan that made my cock hard.

I stepped back, licking my lips. "Mmmm, you do taste good. So what does the devil taste like?"

Her eyes hardened again, burning with an intense fury and hatred. She fought against my hold on the crossbow. Wiping at her mouth, she spat at my face.

I smirked, wiping her spit away. "You show disgust now, but I felt you kiss me back, little *Cazadora*. I'd say you enjoyed that. I know *I* did."

Pulling the crossbow from her hand, I threw it away.

"Stop calling me that." She reached for her knife.

"Please don't do that," I requested.

"You like that jacket. Yeah, I heard." She cast a look down at my chest. "I imagine you'd have to replace clothes, since blood's hard to wash out."

"Aww, your concern is touching —" my words cut off as she brought the knife up, and I gripped the blade to stop her attempt to stab me in the chest. As it sliced into my hand, the sting was enough to let my humour slip. "Now you're just pissing me off." I warned, my voice dropping to a threatening tone. "Drop the knife, before I snap your wrist."

She didn't move, instead fought my grip, pushing the knife. I brought my other hand up and gripped her wrist before breaking it with a loud crack. A pained scream erupted from her mouth.

"I did warn you." I said, letting her go.

A tear slid from her eye, and she whimpered in pain. The knife clattered to the ground, and she cradled her arm. The pain was enough for her mask of fury to drop, softening her features. I saw her for her youth and wondered again what had happened for her to come to Venice to take me on alone. *Who would send her here without any sort of support? Is it possible she's not from a family of Hunters, but someone who recognised us another way? Someone who was lucky enough to already have training somehow?*

Her body started to shake, a possible indication that she would be going into shock. I sighed. "You're just too lovely to leave here like this. You're likely to wander into the canal or something. I can't have something as simple as drowning take my kill from me."

"You're letting this drag out," she observed, her voice weak. "Why?"

"I suppose I do have a darkened sense of fun," I mused. "After that kiss, and what we shared at the bar, I cannot help myself. What is it you humans say? 'Don't play with your food'? What can I say? I like to play."

Her eyes were wide as she stared at me in horror, and she let out another whimper of pain.

Damn Carlos, bleeding heart. Before I could think it through, I tore into my own wrist and pressed it hard against her mouth. She fought against it, but the second my blood hit her tongue there was no fight. Humans could not resist our blood — not even seasoned Hunters had that ability. I wrapped one arm around her lower back, and she relaxed against me, groaning and closing her eyes. After taking King Luis's blood, mine would probably have a stronger effect over her.

To avoid accidentally making a feral if she did turn, I'd need her blood, too. For a few days, I'd be bonded to her, and it would likely overwhelm me. But if she fed, her mind wouldn't cope with the change, and she'd likely tear through Venice before any of my clan found her. While her tongue slid across my wrist, I lifted hers to my mouth, taking just enough. My venom hit her system, and she moaned again.

I stepped away, her broken bone healing itself. She opened her eyes, now bright red, terror and realisation lit up in their depths. "That colour looks good on you." I laughed. "I expect you know what this means. This will be fun. Maybe not so much for you. Come find me if you give in. All you need to do is ask for Carlos Rivera. No vampire in this city will hurt you while you're Bestowed."

I left her there, no longer wanting to play with her. Chances are she was trained in resisting the hunger that our blood put on humans, but if she did give in, she would seek me out. Only if she tasted human blood would she turn. My jovial mood was over. Taking pity on her was unlike me, and I needed to get away. The only human I'd softened on in my long existence had been Quinn before she turned.

"You're getting soft in your old age, Carlos." I grumbled.

Chapter 17

He'd called himself 'Carlos'. Not only was he the King of his clan, but extremely dangerous. Yet, instead of killing me, while I waited for my death to come, he'd fed me his blood, and left me there. The hunger was something I'd never experienced. Not only that, but he'd taken mine, connecting the two of us. His smug presence was already on my nerves. I wiped my mouth with the back of a trembling hand. I was all too aware of what vampire blood did, and my father had trained us how to resist. But I hadn't expected it to be this powerful.

I ran my tongue over my teeth, relieved that there were

no signs of any fangs. I stared at my wrist in shock. He'd broken it, but now there was no sign that the breakage had happened. The cut on my arm was also gone. *Get home. Now!* I was ten minutes away, but it meant walking through the middle of a populated square. I could already smell people, and hear their heartbeats, and my mouth watered. I would have to take the longer way, sticking to side streets. I clenched my fists tight, not failing to see the irony of sticking to the shadows like a vampire. My eyes would be red, not something I would be able to hide.

I forced myself to move. It would take me twice as long to get home this way, but it was better than the alternative. I'd walked these streets for three months, so I was more than familiar with the layout. *Avoid people. Stay in the shadows. Don't get seen. Don't feed.* I repeated the words in my head over and over again as if they were a lifeline.

I clung to the wall as a couple rounded the corner, and my hand tightened around the knife handle. I didn't even remember grabbing it. *Don't move. Don't move.* I watched them walk past, the hunger for their blood so overwhelming that I had to press my face against the side of the building, holding down a growl. They passed, and I forced myself to walk again. I stepped onto a bridge and dropped my knife and crossbow into the canal. It was better that I didn't have weapons on me that could cut and draw blood.

At one point Carlos's presence pushed against my mind. *'Are you having fun yet?'* he asked, his voice and laughter in my head.

'Fuck off,' I thought back to him, releasing a string of curse words in Castellano.

His laughter boomed in my mind, but he pulled back, his

presence returning to a quiet hum.

Somehow, I made it home. Locking the door, I headed towards my bedroom and grabbed my laptop, placing it on the bed. Then I moved towards the restraints I'd set up in case something like this happened. Closing the leather cuffs around my wrists, I grabbed my phone.

<Compromised, vampire blood ingested.> I waited for my father to respond. This was the last thing I wanted to tell him, but he'd told me to report everything of importance. I left out the kiss, but that wasn't important. He didn't need to know that the vampire had kissed me. Or that I'd kissed back, with his warm body pressed hard against mine, and I'd wanted more. I shuddered, forcing down the memory. Overwhelmed with desire, I hoped it was just a side effect of his blood. Hunger for blood mixed with yearning for sex, heat twisting around my core. I whimpered.

"I'm in over my head," I muttered, pulling on the restraints.

'Oh, you're a little heated, I can feel it from here.' came Carlos's voice again in Castellano, filled with arrogant amusement. *'My blood and venom really are potent at the moment, aren't they?'* Fury surged in me at his laughter. *'Tell me where you live, sweet Huntress, let me take care of one need.'*

I didn't respond. He was taunting me. I wouldn't grant him the reaction he wanted.

<Have you fed?> My father's text showed no sympathy.

<No. Restrained.> I replied.

<Record process. Send daily.> He responded, again with no questions about whether I was okay. I sighed, and I sat cross-legged on my bed, pulling my laptop towards me.

I started to write.

Engaged vampire. Fight ensued, leading to an injury. Vampire force-fed me his blood and left. Day one of being afflicted. Hearing impacted, and sense of smell. Hunger for blood powerful.

As I entered the record, I knew my father would read it the moment he got it. I could almost see him at his desk, waiting. There was very little detail, and I was holding back a lot of information.

As expected, he sent me a text message.

<Please include more information than that next time, Camila. You know this.>

I growled in frustration and almost slammed the laptop closed. Instead, I typed in *Carlos Rivera* into the search. I'd already seen enough in other records to know who he was and how dangerous, but curiosity got the best of me.

A few hits came up. I opened one and started to read.

'Carlos Rivera.

Also known by: Father of Ferals. The Killer. The Immortal Wolf.

It's estimated that he was turned by Gabriela Ramirez in the early eleven hundreds in Spain. The pair of them left many villages in ruins, possibly his own among them. He tore apart his victims so much, it was thought a pack of wolves was responsible for the deaths, until they started to collect stories from the survivors, of which he left very few.

They soon left the country and joined other vampires. Alongside the Original Four, they took part in the longest and most savage killing spree recorded in history. They held no value for human lives, as is typical for their kind. Over the course of a hundred and fifty years, the violence and blood they spilled ended more lives than we have an accurate record of.

Their darkness spread like a plague. But it was the ferals set loose on the world that are mostly attributed to Carlos. Ferals are created when blood is shared but not taken in return. The blood exchange creates a blood bond, giving stability to the newly turned. Without this, the young vampire loses themselves in a permanent bloodlust.'

I stopped reading, glancing down at the already faint twin marks on my wrist. He'd taken my blood while he gave me his. Careful to not create a feral in case I gave in. I shuddered at the thought and returned to the record.

'Men, tired of the bloodshed, started to fight back. They established how to kill vampires, starting a Hunter army, responsible for protecting humanity from their kind. This duty still lives on in their descendants today. In the late twelve hundreds, war broke out between vampires and Hunters. Many lives on both sides were lost, until the remaining Original Three agreed to laws that ended open killing of humans. The First Hunters created the accords, in which Hunters were forced to agree to only hunt vampires who took a human life, starting an uneasy truce between vampires and Hunters. Ferals were eliminated, and their creation was banned.'

Terror flooded through me. I had come to Venice under the impression it would be easier and less dangerous than Greece. Already I had come across four. A King, one of the First Hunters, and whoever the others were. I sent a message to Sofia. *<I am hunting Carlos Rivera, and he is the King of a clan. I've already come across three others, so I don't know how many there are.>*

Her reply came back quickly. *<Millie, you need to call for help somehow. This is too big for you. Diego said our ancestor faced him in the war and it was a brutal confrontation. Diego has a new weapon that he will try to send to you. It emits sound that will incapacitate vampires momentarily.>*

<*I'm scared, Sof.*> I typed back.

<*I know. Please be careful. We will do what we can, but our Father is watchful of us both.*>

I returned to the record.

'*Carlos is known to instigate rebellions against accords, by killing humans. Hunters intervened, demanding those involved to be killed. King Luis forced the end of the rebellion with severe punishments.*'

I couldn't help but wonder what that meant. What was a severe punishment to a vampire? Starvation? Why was that not in the records? Did the Hunters not know, or was it too brutal for them to want it recorded?

Last sighting of Carlos was in Melbourne, Australia with another vampire just as brutal, with a feral nature: Matteo Barone.

I returned to the search and typed in Matteo Barone, Carlos Rivera, Melbourne

There was an entry from twenty years ago.

August 2024: Matteo Barone, identified in Melbourne, Australia by the De Micheli family, descendants of Hunters, who called for his elimination in Venice. Gabriela Ramirez and Carlos Rivera among associates. Matteo targeted Quinn Bailey, singer of Roses and Thorns, fellow band member to Lilith De Micheli.

After a night of vampire attacks, Queen Gabriela agreed to hand over Matteo to Hunters for execution. Quinn Bailey arrived in a possible alliance with Carlos, leading to Matteo's escape. Many Hunters were killed in the fight that ensued, including Richard De Micheli. Lilith shot Quinn. Romantic Partner to Lilith and fellow bandmate, Mia Wallace, killed upon Quinn's awakening as a vampire. Quinn and Matteo left Australia late 2024. Gabriela remains in the city. Unknown if Carlos left or remains in Melbourne. Other vampires identified: Erik Haraldson and Josef Alfaro.

I quickly looked up Quinn. In public records she had been missing, assumed dead. Her parents had lost a daughter a year before. Promising singer, with their first tour booked before everything happened. I stared at her photo. It was her! Quinn was in Venice. Could the male vampire who'd shown up be Matteo? She had referred to him as her feral. I had to tell someone they were here.

I returned to the Hunters' records.

In August 2029. Gabriela and her clan were eliminated. Kill organised by Lilith De Micheli, who claimed Gabriela's life. If Carlos, Quinn, or Matteo are located, contact Lilith immediately. After Quinn Bailey's parents made sudden trips to Venice, it is thought they are there. Unable to confirm upon visit to the city. **Do not engage without support. Extremely dangerous.**

Sofia had told me to call for help. I couldn't ask anyone from my family; perhaps Lilith would be the support I needed. There was no record of her death. I added a note to the records.

In February 2045, Carlos Rivera sighted and engaged twice. First interaction caught the vampire by surprise. Vampire escaped after inflicting non-lethal wound. Second interaction, force-fed vampire blood, self-restrained during period of vampire bloodlust. Lilith, if you get this, I need your help.

I didn't know what time it was in Australia. I typed in her name to see her record.

Lilith De Micheli trained from an early age but didn't come across her first vampire until she encountered Matteo Barone in her twenty-ninth year. Lost her brother and much of her family in the fight. Human civilian Quinn Bailey was on site and shot with an arrow. Barone turned her before she died. Mia Wallace, romantic partner to Lilith, and third member of Roses and Thorns was killed by Quinn.

Lilith went on to lead her family on hunts, focused on eliminating any remaining clan after Gabriela was caught killing humans, thus breaking the accords. Attempted to locate vampires in Venice unsuccessfully in late 2026.

In 2027, Lilith's father was turned, becoming feral, and Lilith was forced to kill him. Lilith declared war on the vampire clan. The war lasted three years until she finally took down Gabriela, one of the oldest vampires we have record of outside of Elders. Den located and razed.

I'd just reached the end when a message popped up. *<Message received. Location?>*

<Venice.> I replied back.

I waited for her reply, realising she was probably skimming through my recent reports.

A wave of hunger surged through me. Nearby I picked up the sound of heartbeats, only adding to my need for blood. Grateful for the restraints, I reached for the water bottle by my bed. I gulped back half the bottle. Finally, A response popped up. *<Have you sighted Matteo and Quinn?>*

Damn, she really wanted those two.

<I faced Quinn. Male vampire, possibly Matteo, showed up. Quinn wounded; both escaped.> The more I thought about it, the more I believed it had been Matteo.

The next response took longer. *<Hold tight. Tracking a den in New Zealand, training new Hunters. I'll be there in a month.>*

I wasn't sure I'd last that long.

Chapter 18

Through my connection I'd created to the Hunter, I taunted her, finding amusement in the hunger and her desperation that flowed through our bond.

'Are you having fun yet?' I laughed as I returned to the den. The resounding *'fuck off,'* followed by her cursing at me in Castellano, only made me laugh harder.

It was likely she'd restrain herself while under the effects of my blood, so she'd be out of my way for the next three days. I still wasn't sure why I hadn't killed her, instead of giving her my blood. I'd need to tell my clan to not harm her in the meantime. We had a rule, to not harm The Bestowed while under the effects of our blood.

Back at my den, the rest of the clan prepared for *Carnevale.* Their excitement echoed through the villa. It was our favourite time of year, as we walked among the humans, feeding to the point of intoxication. They were trying on their masks and costumes. I stepped into my room, reaching for my own mask. Black with red and gold. I'd taken a liking to it a few years ago. Everyone else bought a new costume and mask every year, but I liked my mask. I usually wore a black suit and shirt with it.

A wave of desire surged through me, and I laughed again. The Huntress was experiencing the best part of being Bestowed. The intensity of her need was so strong my cock hardened. I pushed my mind into hers again, her reaction surprising.

'Oh, you're a little heated, I can feel it from here.' I spoke to her in Castellano , *'My blood and venom really are potent at the moment, aren't they?'* Her fury set me laughing again. *'Tell me where you live, sweet Huntress. Let me take care of one need.'*

I had no intention of putting my cock into a Hunter, but it amused me when her disgust pressed against me.

I'd never been bonded to three people before. The Elders had told us it could not be done. Only they could form blood bonds with more than two. The presence of three minds was a strange sensation. Unfamiliar, but not the pain I expected. Just a little crowded. If I focused on them too much, it would likely become too loud; but for now, it was manageable.

"My King? I have something to tell you," Josef said, pulling me from my thoughts.

"Why do you all get different costumes every year?" I

asked him. "It's very human to go through that process." I lifted my mask to my face, inspecting it in the mirror with satisfaction. "Do you not like the costumes and masks you pick?"

He stared at me in confusion. "Do you not want to go to *Carnevale*?" he asked.

I resisted the urge to let out an impatient sigh. "I enjoy the festivities of *Carnevale* as much as everyone else does." I flashed a smile. "Especially when we feed."

"Your line of questioning isn't quite…you." Josef admitted. "It's rather…human."

I did sigh then. It was possible that my bond to the Huntress had her humanity pushing in on my mind. "Damn humanity," I grumbled. "I should have known better than to give her my blood."

Josef met my eyes. "You shared your blood? With a human?"

I put my mask down. "She is Bestowed, so no one can harm her while she is under the effects of my blood."

"We will respect the law of The Bestowed," Josef said. "But who did you share your blood with?"

I glanced at him, trying to decide how to admit I'd done it to the Huntress out of kindness. Realisation dawned on him, his eyes widening. "The Hunter?" he asked in shock. "You Bestowed *a Hunter*? Do you intend to turn her?" A slow smile spread across his face. "This is a cruel form of torment, My King. Even for you. What do you plan to do? Will you track her through the bond? Kill her when she is no longer Bestowed?"

I considered his words. I could do that, but it didn't seem right to use a blood bond in that way.

"Was there something you came to say?" I reminded him, changing the subject.

"She knows my name," he said.

I waited, but he offered no more. "Who?" I demanded, letting impatience slip into my voice.

"The Hunter," he said. "She saw me watching her. I'm certain she took a photo of me and accessed the Hunter records from her phone. I didn't know they could do that. She knew my name."

"What were you doing watching her?" I demanded. "Why would you let a human take a picture of you?"

"You told me to find out who she is," he reminded me. "I caught sight of her, and she looked familiar. I think I've come across her record before, but there are a lot of Spanish families. I was trying to place where in the records I'd seen her. Unfortunately she took my photo and identified me before I could. I left."

I glared at him. "Where did you happen to come across her? I have only seen her in my territory, as well as Matteo and Quinn's." Had she expanded her hunting grounds? I thought it was unlikely. Once they found vampires, Hunters didn't tend to stray from that area.

"I was in your territory," he admitted. "I wasn't hunting. I just hoped to catch sight of her."

I launched myself at him, wrapping a hand around his throat, and I slammed his back against the wall. "You know how I feel about my territory," I growled. "I divided Venice up so we don't cross into each other's feeding grounds. You may cross boundaries, but not for hunting."

"I *wasn't* hunting," he choked out. "Please, Carlos. You wanted to find out who she was, I was following your orders."

I released his throat but didn't move away. "And where did that get you? She now knows I have you in my clan. You know Hunters have been looking for you for centuries. One of their own, turned vampire? They despise your existence. She already knows of Matteo and Quinn. If we're not careful, we're going to have Hunters descend on Venice. With *Carnevale* so close, I'd rather not have to handle that."

He lowered his gaze. "I'm sorry, I thought to—"

I held a hand up to silence him. "Let me handle the Huntress. You've done enough."

"I can still identify her, now that I know what she looks like," he pushed.

"What did I just say?" I raised my voice.

He hung his head. "Let you handle the Hunter. As you command, my King."

"Leave," I ordered him. "I want you gone from my sight. Don't let me catch you in my territory again."

His eyes flashed red, anger glinting in them. He'd always had a temper, and I needed to put him in his place. I bared my fangs, showing him my own red eyes as I let out the most menacing growl I could.

"Is that a challenge?" I asked. "I'd be happy to accept, just voice it."

He dropped to his knee, eyes returning to their usual blue. "No, my King, forgive my temper." He tilted his head, exposing his throat to me.

With a bared throat before me, hunger blazed, so strong my fangs ached. The urge to take the invitation he was offering was strong enough that I took a step forward before I stopped myself.

I stepped back. "Go," I commanded again. "Leave the Huntress to me. Identify her through the records, that is all I require of you. Come to me when you have the information I asked for."

He didn't move, but lifted his eyes. "You won't drink?" he asked.

"That's not necessary," I told him, forcing my gaze from his exposed throat. "I think I've made my point. You've submitted. That's enough. Now go. Don't make me ask again."

He rose slowly, his eyes meeting mine. His shoulders slumped. I'd hurt him by not feeding from him when he offered up his throat. I had never denied that invitation. But then, I had never hungered for their blood, either.

Chapter 19

The morning neared and I lay on my bed. I closed my eyes and images of the war rose up once again. *Ten days had passed since the start of the war. Hunters had established that fire and beheading were as good as wood to the heart to kill us. King Luis quietly absorbed the death of Amara, his Beloved. Sia had gone mad with grief over losing her sister, and Nico and King Luis had become very protective of her. I took eight vampires to find a village that the Hunters weren't already in. Hunger flared as I caught the whiff of blood.*

I led the others to the outskirts and listened. Satisfied that the village was Hunter-free, I moved forward.

'We're clear,' I called to Gabriela, who had stayed back. 'Bring the others.'

We had planned to take the village, and I needed to check that they wouldn't fight us before everyone else arrived. I hadn't counted on my hunger getting the best of me. I'd torn through several humans before Gabriela pulled me out of my frenzy. The eight with me had done the same. To the humans that saw us, I would have resembled something horrific, covered in blood and laughing, intoxicated from overfeeding. Many had run from the sight of us, only for us to give chase. By the time we were done, half the village was dead, the rest rounded up into a stable

"This didn't quite go the way it was supposed to," Gabriela commented. "We needed this village to last."

I bowed my head. "I should have had more control. I didn't realise I was so hungry."

"We're all hungry," Gabriela said. "But we've lost too many vampires. The trap they set, drawing us out with their own blood, took down twelve of us."

"The Hunters are catching up," King Luis grumbled. "They're only about a day behind us. We need to slow them down. At least to put enough distance between us to not feel the arrows at our backs."

I grinned. "Then we send ferals after them."

Nico glared. "You would turn our food into ferals. Half the village. We have starving vampires on the verge of madness, and you want them to remain hungry?

"Then let them feed," I said. "Have someone else turn them. There are still at least fifty humans here. Enough for a small army to hold back theirs while we —"

"Flee like cowards." It was the first time Sia had taken part in our conversation. "After what they did to Amara, you would have us run? We should be tearing them apart." She glared at me. "They call you The Killer; go kill them."

King Luis was the King, so he always had final say. "Drink," he told everyone and met my eyes. "You, and the ones you came with, you've fed, so you get the privilege of turning them."

So when everyone had fed, we shared our blood with the humans. Then we waited for the sun to set before most of the vampires left. Those of us who turned the ferals had to wait behind to awaken them. It would be a massacre on both sides: feral and Hunter.

'Carlos,' Matteo's voice interrupted my thoughts.

I sat up, glancing at the door to find him standing there, and forced a smile.

'Why are you reliving the war all of a sudden? Ever since you met with the Elders.'

The war was a couple of hundred years before his time, but he knew enough about it. Every vampire knew of our history.

'Don't worry about me,' I told him.

'The humans have a name for this. They call it PTSD. I don't think you are okay. You killed a human, and suffered no consequences, which you think the Elders pushed you to do. Now all of a sudden you're reminiscing about your time when you fought armies of Hunters. I don't like this.'

I scoffed at the idea of PTSD. That was a human condition; it should not apply to us. We were bringers of death, made for killing and bloodlust. We lacked the humanity to experience such a thing.

"I feel your hunger, all the time," he said out loud. "But I know you're feeding. What aren't you telling me?" Matteo entered my bedroom. "What else did the Bloodking's blood do to you?"

I growled at him, a threat to back off. His eyes flashed back at me. If anyone else behaved towards me in this manner, I would not have allowed it. But I'd chosen Matteo as my second. It was his job to question me. To push me.

"You're our King, Carlos, and we need you strong. Fucking talk. *Now*." He glared. "You haven't taken any of the clan into your bed since you returned. And you refused Josef when he bared his throat. Don't think I haven't noticed. What is it you're avoiding?"

I gave in. Matteo wouldn't stop until he got the answer he wanted.

"I crave vampire blood as well as human blood," I confessed.

"Like Gabriela, that makes sense now." Understanding flickered in Matteo's eyes. "Then drink from us. It's never worried you before."

"Because I've never been *hungry* for it before," I shot back.

In a flash, Matteo was in front of me. He towered over me, his body wider than mine, whereas I was leaner. We'd fought plenty, and he often used his size to his advantage.

"Then drink." Matteo bared his throat. "Or I will hold you down until you do."

I couldn't hold back any more. I latched on. As I fed, the relief of having my hunger sated worried me. I still hungered for human blood, but to hunger for that of my clan, too, was going to take an adjustment. After all Gabriela had done, I did not want to be like her.

'It's alright,' Matteo told me. *'We're your clan, we understand.'*

I pulled away to realise everyone else had walked in, and they were on their knees, baring their throats. They had heard our conversation.

"I cannot," I shook my head.

Erik gave me a small smile. "Had I known you had exchanged blood with the Bloodking, I would have explained this side effect to you."

I frowned. "You knew?"

He nodded. "Gabriela, and those of the first generation, all hungered for vampire blood. It's what made them so powerful."

Lorenzo stood, approaching me. "I know you fear following in Gabriela's footsteps, but you've proven to be a better leader than she was. This isn't you being like her. This is you needing us as much as we need you. Let us feed you, Carlos."

No one disagreed. I sighed, the hunger fulfilled. "Thank you," I said. "I am sated for now, but I'll be sure to let you know when I'm hungry again."

Chapter 20

I stood in the shadows opposite Matteo's new gallery. He was hosting an opening, and he had drawn a large crowd. I smiled, remembering his first attempt. It hadn't gone the way he'd hoped. Excitement buzzed as people lining up were let in. Tourists and Italians alike, the human scent wafting towards me.

I could sense Quinn's approach to where I stood. Her slow heart was thunderous. Her footsteps, even for a vampire, were loud to my new, sensitive hearing.

"Stop," I told her, and she paused mid-step.

She took a cautious step forward. "It would mean a lot to

him if you were there," she said.

She was wearing a green dress, her red hair up, strands framing her face. "Is that the one from the masquerade ball in Melbourne?" I asked.

Amusement filtered through her eyes. "Um, no; Matteo tore that one in half to get it off me."

I smirked. "Of course he did. What's a night of passion without the tearing of clothes? That was likely the best sex you'd ever had. He'd had a long time to perfect his methods." I winked. "No mortal man would have matched after, had you remained human."

"It was definitely mind-blowing," she agreed. "The exchange of blood may have had something to do with it. We went at it all night."

I chuckled. "I knew you'd be one of us before long. I'd never seen him so interested in a human before. He and I spoke of you the day he gave you his painting. He wanted you, he wanted to turn you, and it was never going to end any other way."

She smiled. "Vampire and siren, neither of us stood a chance of resisting the other. Are you hungry?" she asked.

I growled low, my eyes on her throat. My fangs felt large in my mouth.

She stepped towards me. "It's okay," she encouraged.

I grabbed the back of her neck, pulling her towards my mouth. As my fangs pierced her flesh, she tensed, groaning. Something tasted different about her blood. It still had the same fiery taste of vampire blood, but there was something else to it, sending a burst of desire through me. I wondered if I was tasting her siren blood.

"Wow, Matteo's not wrong about your venom being

more potent," she murmured, her hand sliding around my lower back. She pressed herself against me. "That's really something."

I released her, satisfied. "Your blood tastes different." I told her, licking my lips.

"Different how?" she asked with a frown.

"I think with Elder blood, I can taste the siren," I admitted. "It's subtle, but there's a sweetness, one of desire."

She ran her tongue over my chin. "Come inside," she insisted. "Matteo will be happy to see you. A fun night of playing the part of a human."

She held her arm out for me to take.

I grabbed her hand and tucked it under my arm. "I at least know that you should be on my arm, not the other way around." I glanced down at my leather jacket, white tee-shirt, and black jeans. Not a drop of blood in sight. "Am I not under-dressed?"

"Yeah, nah, you're fine. People will just think you're an artist." She winked. "An incredibly hot biker type of artist."

"Okay, lead the way then, Lady Barone," I said.

She shook her head in amusement and led me towards the gallery.

Inside, humans were dressed in formal clothing. Food and wine were being passed around. Quinn quickly reached for two glasses of red wine, handing one to me.

"Why are you bothering to drink?" I asked, glancing around us, dropping my voice. "It's a different type of wine that we get drunk on, not this."

She took a sip. "I like the taste. I know you don't have value in human food or drink, but maybe you should try it. You might find you like it. This is a good wine."

I glanced down at her with a small smile. "I see you're in a sassy mood."

She grinned back. "I see you're using modern words. I'm impressed."

"I suppose I've picked up some newer words our youngest vampire has taught me." I chuckled. "Being smart with your King is ill-advised," I said lightly.

She took another sip of wine and her eyes glinted with mischief. "Then perhaps you'd like to punish me later, with Matteo watching."

"The thought appeals," I admitted and looked around the room. Humans filled the gallery, examining art. The lights were dim, but I could see everything as if it were brightly lit. Every shadowed corner was not dark enough. I caught sight of the rest of the clan, milling around. They had separated, but spoke to each other across the room.."Speaking of your beloved, where is he?" I asked.

"He's talking with the Barones." She shook her head, laughing. "That's still weird. He'll make an appearance soon." She put her hand on my arm. " I know you only go to events like this to feed. Thank you for being here."

I shot her a look of disappointment. "You mean I can't feed?" I made a show of looking around the room. "But they all look so delicious."

Her laugh brought a smile to my face.

"They're not for biting!" she said.

I faced her so no one else could see, and showed fang. "What about chasing? You know I do love a good chase. That scent of fear? Mmm!" I took a sip of wine. It was smooth, sweet, with the flavour of fruit. "You're right, by the way."

"About what?" she asked.

I raised my glass. "Italians do make excellent wine," I commented.

The humans around us stopped talking then, and a man approached the microphone. Pietro Barone. One of Matteo, or his brother's living descendants. The family's typical dark hair and brown eyes were there. If I stared enough, I could almost see a faint resemblance. Quinn had said it herself, it was odd. Vampires didn't usually have any relationships with their children or descendants after turning. But Matteo had missed his daughter growing up, and said that despite her being dead for centuries, it helped him feel closer to her. He believed that killing her mother, and what he'd become, he'd taken her childhood from her. Fatherhood was a foreign concept to me, so I couldn't relate to his wanting to be part of his family still. But I'd allowed it.

"Welcome, everyone, and thank you for coming tonight. Our benefactor thanks you, as well. He asks that you show the new artists appreciation. Feel free to buy anything that appeals to you. The older Barone Collection, however, is not for sale. It belongs in my family, and that's where it will remain."

"He's not selling Matteo's older work?" I asked Quinn as Pietro continued speaking. It seemed strange that the human descendant would prevent art being sold.

"He's purchased it all himself," Quinn replied. "A few paintings are being moved to his villa, and Lenora's. As well as the rest of the family's. Seeing as their ancestor painted the work, they see it as valuable and want it to remain in the family's possession." She gave me her biggest grin. "Except the ones in the private exhibition, of course."

"The private exhibition?" I laughed. "You mean Matteo's ancestors didn't want to buy the naked artwork of us that he painted? I'm offended."

Quinn turned towards the room that had been built at the back of the gallery, and she shook her head. "The first time I posed naked for him, he promised no one would see it. Now I'm willingly on display for all to see. I really don't recognise myself at times. I'm so glad my parents don't know about this."

"Ah yes, shame. A foreign concept to vampires. Now, you pose nude, let Erik watch you fuck your beloved, and walk around the den naked." I put my hand to her waist. "Will you take part in the sampling?"

As we watched, Josef lifted the curtain to the room, walking in. A moment later, Erik followed. He stopped at the door, cast a quick look around the room, and met my gaze, his eyes dancing with amusement and hunger. He quickly stepped through the curtain.

"I think I will," Quinn replied. "The fact that there are humans who paid extra to allow vampires to feed from them just blows my mind."

'I'm more surprised that it's Venetians, and that the Barones organised it," I commented. "Rich humans really will throw money at anything, as long as it's exclusive to them. Even if it means being food."

I turned my focus to Pietro. He was still talking.

"The benefactor's generosity has been felt in the art community. He will not present himself, but watching the enjoyment of art is enough for him."

"Why is he not presenting himself to the public?" I asked.

"Because he hopes the gallery will be around for a long

time." Quinn said. "It'll be hard to explain to people in twenty years why he hasn't aged." She glanced at people approaching the speaker.

Matteo made his way across the room towards us. He was dressed in a suit, his hair parted on one side.

"Carlos, you're here." He smiled at me, with gratitude in his eyes, and he grasped my shoulder. "Thank you, old friend."

Quinn gave Matteo a kiss. "I remember your first opening. That was an unforgettable night."

"Isn't that when she caught you mid-feed?" I laughed.

"It was." Matteo grinned at Quinn. "You fainted."

"Well in my defence, you were the hot gallery owner, with the sexy Italian accent, and you had blood dripping from your chin, with red eyes and fangs. It was a lot for a human to take."

"Sexy Italian accent?" I asked.

"It's that thing she has for accents." His eyes lit up. "Mi.. Her friend told me that she loved Italian, and I thought she meant food. So I took her to an Italian restaurant."

Quinn beamed up at him, the two clearly sharing a cherished memory.

He'd avoided the name, so I took that to mean the friend she'd killed when she first awoke. While vampires didn't usually hold remorse over such things, she'd never forgiven herself for her first kill being that of her closest friend.

"Oh really? Accents?" I stepped up to Quinn trying to lighten the mood. "So if you'd met me first…" I switched to Spanish. "You are a rare beauty that brought light to my endless nights, and had you not been meant for another, I would have pursued you myself."

Matteo narrowed his eyes at me, but then smirked.

As Quinn grinned, the scent of lust rolled off her. "I have no idea what you said, but it sounds hot as fuck." She shook her head in laughter. "If I'd met you first, I might have been drawn to you. But our interactions when I was human terrified me, so I probably would have run screaming."

I growled low. "What a chase that would have been."

Matteo frowned. "Okay, okay. That's enough. She's *mine*."

Quinn leaned into his chest. "I love when you get all possessive like that."

I clapped him on the back. "Worry not, *amigo*, she is yours." I took in our surroundings. Paintings that I recognised were hanging from the walls. Art that Matteo had worked on in the time I'd known him. Only a fraction of his collection but still impressive. The work of other artists hung alongside it. "Please don't burn this one down." I told him. "I do find that I quite like your art. Especially your earlier work. Art has changed over the years. I really liked what came out of the Renaissance."

Quinn stared. "Carlos, you surprise me."

I shrugged. "When you have a long life as I have, you find things to pass the time. I had an appreciation for art, and music."

I'd piqued her interest. "Music?"

"Mozart and Beethoven were among my favourites, their concerts were —"

She gasped. "You saw them? Live? I want all of the details." She eyed me. "For someone who doesn't like to live in human society, you certainly have an appreciation for the finer things humanity produces."

"I fed at their concerts, too," I told her. "No one was paying attention to me." I watched Matteo's descendants speak with an artist, before shaking her hand. Obviously they'd purchased her art, the excitement clear in her eyes. "I played the piano for at least a hundred years. Maybe more."

Her eyes lit up. "Carlos, you and I are going to have a serious talk. Twenty years I've known you, and you know I'm a musician. You never thought to tell me any of this?"

I put a hand on her arm. "I didn't think you'd want to hear it, after losing your career."

She lifted Matteo's hand to her mouth, kissing it, love shining between the two. "I have time to follow that path again. Maybe we can start our own band."

I laughed. "No, I couldn't play in front of people."

"Carlos, she's here,' Josef said from the back of the gallery, before disappearing behind the curtain again.

Matteo growled, his eyes focused behind me. I turned, suppressing my own growl. The Huntress had arrived.

Chapter 21

While afflicted with the hunger Carlos had forced on me, and enduring his taunts, I almost unlocked myself many times. I used the time to read about him, as well as Matteo, Quinn, and Josef.

The only vampire not of vicious reputation was Quinn, who'd only been a vampire for twenty years. I had no doubt she was just as dangerous, and I started to research sirens.

Sirens were a supernatural species with connections to the sea, from which the mermaid myth arose. Their voices had the power to draw a human to them, or force him to his knees. Sirens can control the effect of their power with what they call Intention.

Their voice can be alluring or a weapon, depending on their Intention. Humming is at a lower strength; however, be warned that when they sing, they have less control over the impact of their voice, no matter their Intention. When they sing, the strength of a Siren's Song is magnified in comparison to when they hum. Creatures of desire, but highly aggressive when threatened. Will always seek out the sea. It is thought there was once an Island, near Ireland that they called home. No siren has been seen since the late seventeen hundreds. If ever crossbred with vampires, Magic Wielders, shifters, or any other paranormals tied to the night, it is likely they will become extremely powerful, and should be eliminated.

While it is thought they have died out, there have been the occasional stories of an enchanting song.

I frowned. She had referred to a Siren Song, so they *had* to be alive. She had been humming when I'd been drawn to her. *Could she be both vampire and siren?*

I returned to researching Matteo. It was then that I'd found he had owned an art gallery in Australia which had burned down. He'd disappeared that night, and many thought he'd perished in the fire. I looked at the gallery that would be opening in Venice. There were articles about the mysterious owner, and that the Barones had also contributed towards the gallery and its opening. I'd already learned they were an old family that had held high esteem in Venice for hundreds of years. Likely descendants of Matteo or his family. I wondered if they knew about him. So I made plans to go to the opening, hoping the bloodlust would be gone by then.

Three days of torment, and I was finally free. I couldn't help but feel a small twinge of sympathy for vampires. To live with hunger like that would be enough to drive anyone insane. I had only endured three days of it, in comparison to the centuries most vampires did.

I prepared for the opening of the art gallery. If Matteo was the mysterious owner, he'd probably be there. So I would be too, in the hopes that Carlos would be as well.

With only a few hours to spare, I hid ten speakers that my brother had delivered, near the gallery. In broad daylight, it wasn't easy to hide something with so many people around.

I dressed for the event, wearing a red dress, and loving the feel of the material on my skin as it clung to me. I took the time to hide an arrow in my bag. I was about to go into enemy territory. I needed to drive them outside to watch me kill their King. I didn't know how many there were, but hoped I was right about Carlos being the one that led them. To think that there was someone worse as their leader was unbearable.

As I made my way to the gallery, my heart pounded hard. I had no idea how many vampires were in Venice, and I hoped I wouldn't come across any on my way. I didn't know if they knew what I looked like, but after tonight, they would. What I was doing verged on insanity, and I had a very small window within which to use my new weapon.

I walked into the gallery, doing a quick scan of the spacious room. Classical music played quietly in the background. A woman holding a tray filled with wine glasses approached me, and I took one, watching the way she moved as she walked. Unless she was putting it on, she definitely moved like a human. My heart pounded as I took a sip. It was a dry wine, with a fruity flavour. I had only ever tasted Merlot or Pinot Noir, but still didn't know which wine I was drinking. The hunger was gone, but the memory of it remained. As did the nightmares about blood.

I glanced around the gallery, noticing paintings of sunsets, castles, and beaches. I recognised art of Venice, Rome, and Florence. Amongst them was a combination of sketched portraits. I wandered around, trying to be discreet in searching the room for vampires. There was a separate room attracting a small crowd, and as I was trying to walk past, I got ushered into it.

Inside, the room was dark, with spotlights on eight large framed paintings of people. In between each pair of paintings was a black curtain. They were naked portraits, painted realistically, with nothing hidden but their faces. Covered by Venetian masks, the models posed without shame, especially the males. I stopped, studying the painting of a man who had shoulder length blond hair. His grey eyes burned into mine. His pure white mask, with gold designs painted over it, covered his entire face.

"These are life-size," came a male voice I didn't recognise

over my shoulder. "Have you inspected the goods yet?"

I jerked in surprise, not realising someone was standing so close to me. My eyes were instantly drawn to the model's penis. I'd seen my fair share of cocks, but found I couldn't look away. The pose in the painting was as if the model were daring people to look. His entire torso was covered in tattoos that may have been Scandinavian. I walked away from the owner of the voice, and glanced up at the next painting. I allowed my eyes to graze down the body, towards the length between his legs.

"Did you want to pay for a private viewing?" a woman asked.

I turned around, my eyes straining in the dark. "Excuse me?"

"A private viewing," she repeated. "With the models. It's very intimate. Thirty thousand for half an hour. If you want more time, It will be fifty thousand."

Thirty thousand Euros?! I almost gasped out loud. *What are they selling here?* "All the models are putting themselves on show at the gallery?" I asked.

"Think of it as an interactive display," the same male voice from before sounded from close by. "See any you like?"

I turned my attention to the other paintings, as if subconsciously. Three women, Five men. My gaze stopped on one that seemed to be held in importance. He sat in what looked like a throne, relaxed, his cock at eye level. A wolf tattoo covered one side of his chest, one eye blue, the other red. As my eyes trailed up his body, the image of kissing the abs and chest filled my mind. A spark of heat flickered in me, and I forced my eyes away. His mask was black, with red and gold painted over it.

The eyes followed me from the artwork, and I shivered, as if the models truly were watching me. All of them.

The male laughed. "Oh, I think she sees something she likes. He's out in the main gallery." Cool breath brushed against the back of my neck, and I suppressed a shiver. "I did see you admiring me first, though. Perhaps you'd like to share some with me first." A curtain lifted, the figure standing with his face in shadow. "Step inside, I'll give you what you're looking for."

What is going on here? Foggy-minded and almost panting with need, I mentally shook myself. If I didn't know better, I could have sworn I was under the sway of a vampire, on the verge of following this stranger through the curtain into darkness.

"Not her, Erik," someone else spoke up, walking from behind another curtain. "It's *her.* I think she wandered into the wrong room." A hand gripped my arm tightly. "Are you lost? Or just stupid? You have no idea what you stepped into. You're not welcome here."

The grip tightened, and I was pulled towards the exit, and pushed roughly into the main gallery, relieved to be able to see again. I glanced over my shoulder, making eye contact with Josef.

Shit!

"Carlos, she's here," he said, and he returned to the dark room.

So Carlos *was* here. As I met the eyes of two people staring at me, one looked away. The way the other person moved hinted that she was not human. I scanned the room again, moving away from the curtain before Josef could grab me.

"I was hoping you'd be here," I spoke in a quiet voice, but

someone walking past looked at me in shock and moved away quickly. Human. "I've already spotted three of your kind in here, one of whom is openly staring at me. Are you hiding?"

Josef left the private room with another, and started to move towards the exit, along with the other two I'd already noticed. Two others followed. Vampires. All of them. My heart pounded, and I took a deep breath to calm myself. I assumed they'd been given the command to leave and would be waiting outside. The red-haired vampire, Quinn, walked in my direction. I didn't immediately turn my focus directly on her, watching her movements.

Finally, I lifted my eyes to her. Red hair, a green dress, and deep emerald eyes. Quinn Bailey looked the same as the photos I'd seen from twenty years ago. Only now that she was a vampire, there were differences. The permanent hunger in those eyes, especially in the way she eyed me up. She was a little pale, but not as much as the movies made vampires out to be. She'd been pale in her human photos too.

"Hello, Hunter," she gave me a cold smile. "You shouldn't be here — you know that, right?"

I noticed her accent again, the Australian twang softened with signs that she'd been in Italy for a long time.

"Hello, Quinn." I kept my tone light. "I heard this was an open event."

"So, do you know any of the artists?" she asked.

"I know of one," I replied. Quinn's presence wasn't as terrifying as Carlos's, but it was still chilling. "Perhaps you know him, too. Matteo Barone. Is he here?"

Her eyes flashed red, and she glanced over her shoulder.

I assumed towards Matteo or even Carlos. They were possibly talking to her. "I don't think you realise the trouble you've put yourself into. You walked into our territory. You're lucky Matteo didn't leave you in pieces the other day. By the way, that really hurt."

She was putting on a friendly tone for the sake of anyone in the room who might watch, but the anger in her eyes was unmistakable. "You would have killed me," I told her, matching her friendly smile. "So don't give me the anger, when I was only doing what you would have."

Amusement filled her eyes.

"Where is he?" I asked. "I saw your friends leave, and I'm guessing Matteo is here too. After all, this is his opening."

"Oh, they're here." Quinn said without an ounce of worry in her voice. "Is this really what you want? To confront either of them while you're alone?"

I took a sip of wine to calm my nerves, and as I lowered my head again, I caught Quinn staring at my throat. She quickly averted her eyes.

"What do you want, Hunter?" Quinn's voice dropped, low, threatening. "You're uninvited. This is a night of celebration for us."

"I want a world free of vampires," I offered, again searching the room. "Matteo Barone is a known killer; therefore, he has broken the accords. So have you, when you killed your own friend." I caught the flash of pain in her eyes. So she *did* still have a conscience. "Remember Lilith?" Now I couldn't stop taunting her. "I'm sure she'd love to know you're here. I know you two used to be friends." I searched the gallery again, catching two shadows in the darkest corner. "She's made quite a reputation for herself. She took down Gabriela and her entire clan. Maybe she can help me finish off those she missed. Starting with *you*."

A low growl rumbled from Quinn, and Matteo came out of nowhere. Using his vampire speed right in front of the humans. I'd succeeded in pissing them off. *Good.* Another growl, more guttural came from the dark corner, loud enough for everyone to hear. People looked around, not finding the source. I knew that sound all too well.

"I recognise that growl. Carlos, are you watching me from over there?" I turned my attention to where I thought he was, ignoring the large vampire standing in front of me. The records had not mentioned how massive he was, and as he towered over me, fear fluttered in the pit of my stomach. "You have two killers in your clan, Carlos. That you have allowed them both to live means that you have also broken the accords. The three of you will die; then I'll see to the rest of your clan."

Matteo glanced around to check that no one was watching and bared his fangs at me. Finally, Carlos revealed himself, taking his time to walk over to us. His lips moved as if he said something, and Matteo stepped back. I took in his leather jacket and white tee-shirt. Even when everyone else was in formal wear, all he had was the same thing I'd seen him in every other time. The tee-shirt was tight, and it was hard to not notice his muscles underneath. He was lean, and everything about him screamed *vampire* at me. But despite that, I couldn't help but notice, he had a certain appeal. Despite what he was, he was pleasing to the eye. *Camila, stop!* I forced down my thoughts.

He smiled at me. "Hello, sweet *Cazadora*."

The three of them surrounded me, and for the first time, I

questioned my plan.

"You should leave," Carlos told me. "Challenging us on our territory is a little foolish. Even for a Hunter."

"You won't do anything," I said. "Not here, in the light, where people can see you."

Carlos laughed.

"Why did you come here?" Matteo asked. "What are you hoping to achieve here?"

I flickered my eyes towards him, but back to Carlos. "You told me to seek you out," I forced a smile, hoping it looked like a smirk. "Here I am, I found you."

The four of us, locked in a deadly stance, were starting to attract attention.

"I didn't tell you to ruin his gallery opening," Carlos put a threat into his tone. "You *really* should leave *now*. While you still can."

His usual smug attitude was gone, revealing the animal underneath the anger. He wanted to rip me apart, and I wondered if my revelation about who'd killed his maker had been too far. He stepped towards me, our faces inches apart. I tried to step back, but Matteo blocked me. I hadn't even seen him move.

"You're really going to do this *here*?" I asked, not taking my eyes from Carlos. "In front of so many witnesses?"

Quinn started to hum, a beautiful sound that echoed around the gallery. Only, it seemed to be coming from within her. I recalled what I had read about sirens, and noticed, everyone in the gallery turned towards us. They moved as one, stopping in a circle. My heart thundered. I didn't know what she was doing. Vampires could compel, but this was something different. The record had mentioned crossbreeding. *A vampire and a siren, how powerful would that make her?*

"Witnesses that answer to *me*," she said and glared at Carlos. "Why aren't you doing anything? She came into our territory." Her eyes flashed red.

He pointed to the people around us. "Do they know what's happening right now?"

Quinn shook her head.

"Outside, now," he ordered her and Matteo. Then he grabbed me and took me outside using his vampire speed.

He used enough strength in his grip to remove my urge to struggle. He could easily crush my bones, and we both knew it. The second we were outside, his clan closed in. I couldn't contain my fear, and they reacted, their fangs flashing in the light. I was cornered, and I only had one hope of escape.

"I will kill your entire clan," I promised Carlos.

He laughed. "Good luck with that." He glanced up at Matteo, releasing my arm. "Maybe I'll turn her and send her home." Despite his laughter, the intimidation and fury were still there. His eyes were crimson, and he was ready to kill me.

Now was my chance. I dipped my hand into my bag, grasping my phone.

"Do you not hear that?" I asked.

As expected, they all lifted their heads as if listening. Good. I pressed the button. Ten speakers started playing. The sound was too low for human hearing, and I could only imagine how bad it was to those with sensitive vampire hearing.

Every vampire surrounding me fell to their knees, with their hands against their ears. I pulled the arrow from my bag, glaring down at Carlos.

"Carlos!" Matteo cried out, his voice filled with fear.

As I raised my hand high, Carlos hissed at me, a savage sound, baring his fangs. The glint of fear shone from his eyes, and I rammed the arrow straight for his heart. He caught my wrist at the last second, the tip against his chest. I turned the end up towards his throat and pushed it in with everything I could.

When his hand released my wrist, he started to choke. I kicked off my shoes and ran, like my life depended on it. I'd kicked a very angry hornets' nest and once again failed to take him out.

Chapter 22

I slowly became aware that someone was licking the blood from my throat. Freshly healed, I groaned. My entire clan curled in around me, in my bed, their heartbeats' rhythm soothing. Matteo's tongue dragged over the blood again, the roughness of his chin scratching. Quinn's body was pressed in behind mine as she wrapped me in a hug.

"I'm getting really tired of being stabbed," I grumbled. "Please tell me someone at least killed her. Or has her chained up so I can."

No one moved. Matteo's eyes met mine. I glanced around

at each of them, noticing they had been bleeding from their ears. I reached up, finding blood outside my own ear.

"None of us could move until that sound stopped," he said. "No human reacted to it, either. It was as if only we could hear it. She used that to escape. It stopped after five minutes."

I caught the spark of fear in his eyes and reached out to him.

"You almost died," he revealed. "I couldn't move, and I thought I was about to watch her kill you."

Quinn tightened her arms around me, pressing her head against my back. Each of my clan reached out and touched me.

"I'm okay," I said to comfort them. The truth was I was as shaken as the rest of them. She had come damn close to killing me yet again, and I was afraid the next time we met she might succeed.

They curled in tighter around me, stroking any part of me they could, needing the connection. My hunger flared. As if sensing it, Matteo exposed his throat, and I gave in before I could stop myself. Flooded with our bond, I felt his fear and guilt. As I fed, I poured calm into him.

I pulled back, but I was still hungry as I turned onto my back. Quinn nuzzled into my neck, and others lifted their heads, meeting my gaze with red eyes. "I'm okay," I said again. Each member of my clan all wanted to protect me, to nourish me, to help me heal. But there was expectation in their eyes, as they watched me.

"The Huntress came into our territory and openly challenged us," I acknowledged. "She challenged me. But to challenge one, she challenges all of us. She has declared war on us, and I will respond. *Only me.*" My anger fuelled me. "She is alone, so I can handle her."

"I want to hear her screams as her blood drips from your lips and chin," Matteo growled.

I smiled at him, revealing my fangs. "And you shall," I promised.

"What if more come?" Quinn asked, sitting up to meet my eyes.

I sat up, too, taking her chin in my hand. "Then I'll kill them, too. I'll bathe in their blood to keep you all safe."

She smiled at my words, and crawled around me to curl into Matteo, stroking his chest. He wrapped an arm around her and reached for me. I lay on my back again, one hand behind my head, the other wrapped in Quinn and Matteo's grip. I could tell that they'd all fallen asleep, satisfied that I would do my job. They would all fight to protect each other, and me, but it was on me to protect them, too.

I closed my eyes, but the image of the Huntress ready to kill me jolted me awake. I had barely stopped her, in pain and weakened by that auditory weapon. I recalled what I'd heard. It had been at a frequency that drilled through my head and made it feel like my ears were being stabbed by hot pokers. I had never heard anything like it. Likely the Hunters had come up with something new; they were always getting creative in ways to bring us down. I clenched my jaw as I considered that. She had used it to help her escape, but it could have been worse.

The sun had risen, but sleep wouldn't come. What came, however, were images of war that I couldn't hold back.

War had raged for five long years. The Hunters had called to meet with the Elders. I'd been the one to receive the messenger before I tore him apart. But we'd agreed.

I stood in a field with Gabriela as the Elders faced off against Hunters who'd taken the mantle of their leaders. With our army at our backs, the Hunters had their own. They'd recruited more humans.

"We're here, Hunters; do you seek to surrender?" King Luis asked.

He'd taken Gabriela and me on as generals, Sia and Nico with their own.

"This war has cost us both," a Hunter with scars on his throat said. I growled, recalling the day I'd put them there. I had meant to kill him and had nearly been decapitated for it. Annoyance surged through me as I realised I'd failed to kill someone of importance. His eyes darted towards me, as if he were remembering, too. "We're here to propose a truce."

"You started this war," I accused. "By fire. Now you seek to finish it with talks of peace? Coward."

King Luis shot a glare at me meant to silence.

"We propose that we cease fighting. We won't kill your kind unless you take a human life."

I laughed, as did Gabriela next to me, only for us to be silenced again with a withering look from King Luis.

"You're in full armour with weapons that you've used to kill my people," King Luis said. "Why would you come to peace talks dressed for battle?"

"As are you," another Hunter said.

We'd taken to wearing magically enhanced armour to protect ourselves from arrows.

"We're still at war," a third Hunter spoke up, a woman with braided, white-blonde hair. "Until we make peace, you are still our enemy, and we would be stupid to not be in armour."

"What are your terms for peace?" King Luis asked, his tone calm, even though anger rose from him in waves. "Other than no killing."

"You separate and don't all live in one area. Assign some of your people to monitor all vampires who are adhering to the accords. If we find that a vampire breaks the agreement, we have all rights to take them down."

"How will you enforce this? We'll outlive you and your children," Sia said.

The rest of us laughed.

"Our children will take up our purpose, as will theirs. Our descendants will be Hunters for as long as there are vampires."

"Let me get this straight," King Luis said. "As General Carlos said, you started a war with us. You sought to destroy us because you hated us. Now you think we can coexist? Why?"

It pleased me that he was no more willing to trust them than I was.

"I am tired of this war. I am tired of losing people, as I'm sure you are."

King Luis cast a look over his shoulder at me, smirking. "We can make more, faster than you can," he said, returning his attention to the Hunters. "And without the blood bond, they tend to get a little feral."

I couldn't hold back my grin, making sure the Hunters saw my fangs.

"No more ferals," the woman said.

"All ferals must be eliminated." the scarred Hunter said.

I growled. "You would have us kill our own people?"

"Either you do, or we do," the leader said. "We'll make sure they hurt before they die."

I cast a look back at our army. Half of them were ferals. Most *of which I'd turned. Rabid and wanting to kill the humans, the only thing that held them in place was my command. Bonded or not, I was still their maker. "And you call us monsters," I grumbled.*

"We don't get much out of this," Sia said. "What will you give up?"

"We already gave up everything to take you down," the second Hunter spoke up. He resembled one of the ferals in our army. His left eye was missing. He pointed to me. "That one took my brother and turned him into a soulless, mindless rabid dog. Every one of our army has lost everything because of vampires. You want to know what we give up? We give up killing you. We let you feed from people, until you kill. You're unnatural and should not exist, but we're agreeing to leave you alone."

"Have your night, we'll return to the lives we're supposed to live in the light of day. We'll co-exist in different worlds."

"And you want us to enforce your terms to create peace?" King Luis asked. "We don't always have control; our hunger tends to get the best of us at times."

"Then punish those who lose that control. You can learn to feed without killing," the white-haired Hunter said.

"You want us to separate into smaller clans?" Nico asked. "Why? So we're easier for you to put down?"

The woman Hunter stepped forward. "Together you end entire villages in less than three days, your numbers are too great. If you separate, maybe people stand a chance against your kind."

'They fear extinction,' Gabriela laughed through our bond.

The idea struck me as to how much we needed humans to live, for our own survival. 'They have a point,' I replied. 'Without humans, we have nothing. What do we feed on then?'

Her eyes met mine and then King Luis turned, studying me.

"There are no winners in this," the Hunter with the missing eye said.

"We agree to your terms," King Luis said with reluctance. His tone indicated he wasn't happy. "We will punish those who can't learn to live by new rules." He turned, facing our army. "There will be no killing humans." he declared. "To maintain peace, we have agreed. I will pick vampires to lead smaller clans, and we shall follow the accords that the Hunters have laid out. Any vampire who breaks the accord will suffer the consequences." He turned to me. "We must follow all of their terms. That includes the ferals."

I searched our army, passing my gaze over the ferals. "I cannot do that," I told him. "I cannot kill other vampires. Especially ones I've turned. If they want to eliminate them, they will have to do it themselves."

I raised my eyes to Matteo, understanding then why Gabriela had bonded him with me. He opened his eyes, meeting mine over Quinn's head.

"It's the Hunter, isn't it?" he asked. "That's why you're reliving the war. Is she here because of me?"

I nodded. "I think she is. You and Quinn. By the accords, I'm supposed to let her do her job." I thought back to my time at the Elders' villa. "But I feel like the Elders are planning to start a new war. To them, we lost, and they don't accept defeat all that well. They held no fear of the hunters when I was worrying about the accords."

"You said you were a general or something back then. It makes sense that they'd try to recruit you. Especially with your history."

I frowned. "I'm not the only one here with history. They were just as interested in you."

"Because I'm a feral," he said.

I didn't say anything. If I was right, it would mean returning to as we once were. I couldn't deny that such a thought appealed.

"You want that," Matteo recognised.

Quinn turned towards me. The rest of the clan lifted their heads.

Lorenzo let out a deep growl. His loss had been great. "If the Elders start a war, we will follow you," he said.

"I too have suffered their senseless murder," Celeste said. "My clan had killed no one when they came for us. I will follow you."

Quinn and Matteo's silence hinted at them having a private conversation.

"You know I'm in," Josef said with a grin. "Hunters have been trying to take me down since I turned. I still feel what they did to Rowan."

Andreas and Erik also agreed that they would follow me. I waited.

"War is not something I want," Quinn said. "But I feel like the Hunters would look for any reason to kill us anyway. If it were to come to that, I would follow you, and defend our clan."

All our attention was on Matteo. As my second, they valued his say as much as mine.

"I think we should wait to see if the Elders do intend to start a war," he said slowly. "But if that is the case, I do not wish to go against them. If they want to claim back what was lost, then we shall show the Hunters that they will not win a second time." He paused and his eyes flashed red. "If war starts, I will make ferals and lead them myself."

Chapter 23

I reached for my mask. Throughout the den, vampires prepared for *Carnevale* with excitement. Erik and Josef joked about who they thought would get blood drunk first. Celeste, Lorenzo, and Annika discussed what they preferred, who would be an appetiser and who would be their main course. Andreas spoke to Quinn about whether she would draw her meal to her with her Siren Song.

It was a day that we had not missed since arriving in Venice. I glanced at my reflection, smiling at the black suit I'd worn the last few years. Matteo stood next to me, examining his own costume.

I admired the two of us in the mirror. "This event is almost as old as I am, and I am continually impressed by the effort humans put into this," I told him. "Yet here we are, year after year, going through the same motions as humans. Our excitement may be for different reasons." I showed fang. "But I have to admit, I wouldn't miss it."

"I attended *Carnevale* when I was human, with Giovanni, and with Marisa and our daughter, Aria," he said of his brother and wife, a wistful glint in his eyes. "Even when I was a child, it was something that I was drawn to. The excitement was hard to resist. We were expected to be quiet, to not let our excitement get the best of us in front of people. Our father would warn us that if we embarrassed him, we would not be able to attend the following year."

"Your father sounds like he was pleasant to be around," I remarked.

His eyes darkened. "I killed him," he reminded me.

He'd told me a long time ago that his father had found him hiding in the villa Matteo shared with his wife and daughter. That people whispered of the Vampire of Venice being one of the Barone brothers, and that Matteo's own twelve-year-old daughter had run screaming to Giovanni about her father being a monster and killing her mother. As talented an artist as Matteo, she'd drawn a picture of him, which we believed was used by the Hunters in their records. His father had been foolish to confront Matteo. He'd soon found himself face to face with his son in feral madness.

I grinned. "Humans always think they can approach inhuman beings without consequence."

He lifted his mask to his face. This year, he had chosen a black and gold mask with feathers, matching the black and gold of his costume. He had painted music notes into the mask. To allow for feeding, all our masks left the mouth uncovered. "My family was always heavily involved. They held the biggest, fanciest events, and everyone wanted to be part of them."

"Well, nothing's changed there," I laughed. His descendants still had heavy involvement, always holding a masquerade ball every night during the event. Which we of course attended. They knew us, what we were, and looked the other way. As long as we stayed away from the locals.

Chatter of the clan had died down as everyone moved to the foyer. "They're waiting," Matteo said. "It's time to go."

We walked to the foyer. The moment I entered the room, they dropped to their knees. Matteo moved to join them, and I grabbed his arm. "You are my second. There are times where you stand next to me, and I would have you next to me today. They bow to you too, Matteo."

Behind the mask, his eyes met mine in surprise. I'd shaken him with my words, but he stood tall, facing the clan. Had I a Queen, she would be at my side; but Matteo was in an important position in the clan, and he should be acknowledged as such.

"It is misty, just as you hoped," Celeste said to me. Her mask was gold and blue, complete with feathers. Her costume was deep blue, with gold trimmings. "Our gondoliers await."

I glanced around at my clan. Quinn wore a feathered mask that matched Matteo's in colour, with the same music notes painted on it. Her hair sat around her shoulders. She had chosen to wear a gold dress this year, with black lace and ribbons, a tight bodice and a wide skirt. Erik simply opted for a plain black suit similar to my own, and his mask was bone white with black Scandinavian symbols painted on it. Josef's costume was black and white, his mask black, lined with feathers. Annika and Lorenzo both wore green masks. Her dress was green and gold. Andreas had a black and blue mask, his costume gold and white.

I led the clan from our den to the waiting gondolas. We would make our appearance down the Grand Canal, and soon the festivities would begin. It pleased me that the opening ceremony always took place at night. This allowed for us to take part in the ceremony before blending with the crowd and attending the masquerade balls.

Venice was usually crowded, and I had to admit that I did find the atmosphere invigorating. It was especially thrilling that we could feed in the open, almost as we once had. No one noticed when we passed among them, often too caught up in everything around them to notice that vampires were feeding in the centre of activities.

I took the front gondola with Matteo, standing as we moved through the mist.

Behind us, Lorenzo helped Annika and Quinn into their gondola, Andreas and Celeste in another, and Erik in the fourth with Josef.

We arrived in time for the opening ceremony, the mist clinging to the water and either side of the canal. I watched the crowds with a smile, already anticipating the feeding that would take place.

"Get ready," I told my clan. "The show is about to begin."

We passed through the mist, joining the opening cere-mony. The occupants of vessels around us wore magnificent costumes of various colours. Dresses that the wearers would have taken months to hand-make with elaborate detail and historical accuracy. Others wore costumes that resembled those of the traditional theatre of Italy. The masks were a variety, from brightly coloured fantastical creatures, to sad clowns, jesters, harlequins, birds and cats, to the more morbid and grotesque devil masks, and those resembling plague doctors. Masks were lined with feathers and gems. It was a time we left our shadows while remaining anonymous, reveling in the celebrations as much as the humans did, while also taking enjoyment from feeding in the streets unnoticed.

The heavenly notes of violins drifted across the water. The voice of a soprano began, soon joined by that of a tenor, holding me spellbound. My clan around me were quiet as we listened. The singers were surrounded by dancers, some donning wings, some holding flames, all of them in brightly coloured costumes and masks. The procession was led by the Pantegana, a boat in the shape of a rat that would explode in front of Ponte di Rialto. Trailing behind it were rowboats, Venetian sailing boats, and gondolas. The mist that clung to the water really made the scene look mystical and otherworldly.

Humans on the boats around us danced and waved to the onlookers on either side of the canal. Those lining the sides of the canal were entranced.

"How about a little song from our siren?" I requested, glancing over my shoulder to Quinn.

Her eyes glowed green as she gave me her joyful smile. "Of course, my King."

She started to sing. A soft sound that rose from her and resonated across the canal. Her voice was at a low level that would merely draw people's attention to her. To us. Humans from other gondolas turned their attention to us.

"Sing, my siren!" Matteo encouraged his beloved, caught up in her power. "Bring them to their knees for our King! For us!"

The strength of her voice grew, and every human was caught in her power. It was a true gift to see her use her ability in this manner. We were irresistible to humans. What we were drew humans to us. I still didn't understand how it worked. Even when they were scared of me, they still couldn't look away. Like moths to the flame. But the voice of a siren, one such as Quinn — a vampire — they fell under her sway especially easily. Our ability to compel, mixed with her voice, gave her more of a hold over humans than I could hope for.

A few people in the crowd fell to their knees. I couldn't hold back the grin. The feeling was intoxicating. I longed to be among them, feeding.

"I do love to see them on their knees," I commented with glee.

"Kneel to your King, humans. Just as it used to be." Matteo laughed. "You're enjoying this too much, Carlos."

"No such thing," I used a phrase Quinn said a lot. "Come, I'm hungry, I've been savouring this all day."

Erik let out a growl, followed by Josef.

"What are they growling about?" I asked Matteo. "This is supposed to be fun."

"Hunter." Josef said. "It looks like Quinn's Siren Song has provided you with an opportunity."

I turned, following the direction towards which they were focused. She was amongst a small number of humans not in costume or mask. Under Quinn's influence, she wasn't moving, just staring from where she stood, closest to the canal. Clearly the festivities had drawn her.

"An opportunity indeed," Matteo noted with glee in his voice.

I grinned. "Then let's not keep her waiting."

I signalled to our gondoliers, and they moved us towards where the Hunter waited, fighting the urge to leap from the gondolas and land beside her. We left the gondolas and approached the Huntress. My clan stood around me as I grasped the Huntress' chin, tilting her head to expose her throat. She stared, unblinking, the same as those around us. Entranced by Quinn's Siren Song.

"Perhaps I should have our siren release her so she wakes in time for her death," I pondered.

Josef and Erik laughed. "Will you kill her here, out in the open, or take her to the shadows?" Erik asked.

"Can I suggest something?" Celeste placed her hand on my arm.

I caressed the Huntress's neck, and glanced at Celeste. Red eyes met mine with a wicked smile.

"Why do I feel like you have a delicious idea?" I grinned at her.

"I do." Her smile grew wider and she handed me a card. "Instead of leaving her body here, to frighten the humans, and attract unwanted attention, while also angering the Barones, give her this. Have her come to you at the masquerade tonight. She can be your main course."

Annoyance surged that Celeste was suggesting I not kill the Huntress where she stood.

Matteo started to chuckle. "She makes a good suggestion. You're in a mask; she won't recognise you. She'll show up seeking you out. The mysterious masked man who handed her an invitation to one of the most exclusive events in Venice."

I had to admit the idea had appeal, but again I was irritated that once again I was letting the Huntress live.

With a loud sigh, I stepped away from the Huntress. "Quinn, release the humans." I glanced at the Huntress. "She lives…for now. Leave. Except for Celeste. It was your idea; *you* present her with the card. I will stand behind you, so she knows you present it on my behalf."

I retracted my fangs, taking on the human appearance. I put on a warm smile, one that would set her at ease.

Quinn stopped singing, and my clan walked away. It took a while for the humans to emerge from their trance. The Huntress blinked at Celeste, staring at the invitation being offered to her. Then she caught sight of me. I stepped forward, and without a word, I bowed and lifted her hand to my mouth, kissing the back of her hand. A gesture Matteo had once told me had women swoon. As expected, a small smile lit up her eyes, and her heart fluttered.

"Who are you?" she asked.

Instead of replying, I pointed to the invitation to the Barone's party. She read the card without taking it.

"I'm a guest?" she asked, confusion clouding her eyes. "Who's guest?"

I lifted a hand to my chest and waited for her to take the card. She hesitated before taking it.

A man next to the Huntress glanced down at the invitation.

"*Signora*, you've received an invite that you cannot turn down. That is an exclusive event, to which it is an honor to be invited." He met my eyes with envy.

I kissed her hand again, gave her my most dazzling smile, and walked away.

"Who is he?" she asked the stranger next to her.

I glanced over my shoulder to find them both watching me.

"No one knows," came the reply. "Every year, he picks someone from the crowd to invite. I hope you have a dress and mask. The event is one everyone would love to be invited to. You are a lucky woman."

I turned my attention away from their conversation. This was the part of the evening I looked forward to. "Now, we feed," I told my clan.

Chapter 24

After the parade, I separated from my clan and wandered through the crowds. Thousands of people were there, and as the flight of the angel started, everyone's eyes were focused up. This was usually a day event, but *Piazza San Marco* was well lit up. I found a man and fed from him, quickly moving on. His scent of desire followed me as I sought out my next snack.

Cheers broke around me, and I stopped to take in the marvel that was the angel. A woman suspended above the square in a pink costume. Wings were strapped to her back. She waved at the crowd below, dropping rose petals, and her face lit up with delight. Music played, and as she was lowered I glimpsed Josef taking advantage of the distraction, occasionally glancing up to admire the angel.

"I'll never get tired of that," Celeste said from next to me, looking up at the angel.

"Neither will I," I admitted, as taken by the festivities as the humans around us. I hadn't noticed her approach. "Trying to sneak up on me?"

She lowered her gaze, giving me a coy smile. "Never."

"Your idea was a good one," I told her. "We can dance before she arrives."

She beamed at me, and I caressed her cheek. "Would you like to share a drink?" she asked me.

"Of course!" I held out my arm, waiting as she tucked her hand in.

We walked together through the crowd. Tourists stopped us, taking photos of anyone in costume. We usually avoided having our picture taken, but in full costume no one was likely to pick up a photo in fifty years time and recognise us. Technology had become a nuisance for those of us who didn't want to be seen. I smiled politely as we posed, Celeste gripping my arm.

"In a perfect world, we'd show what we were to them," I spoke quietly to Celeste. "They'd either bow to us, or run from us. Either would be most pleasant."

She laughed, then nodded to a man watching everything around him. "We have a new visitor."

It was clear on his face that this was the first time he had been to *Carnevale*. His eyes were wide with wonder, his jaw slack.

"I think we have a drink we can share," I whispered into

her ear.

The two of us approached him.

"Hello," I said. "Are you enjoying the sights?"

He nodded. "I am. Nice costumes." His accent was American.

"Perhaps you'd like to join us for a hot drink," Celeste offered. "It is a cold evening. There's an all-night cafe that allows you to rest, especially if you've been walking all night." She stroked his chin, gazing into his eyes.

I smiled at her compulsion. He followed us, not once asking where we were taking him. We left *Piazza San Marco*, leading him towards a dark alcove. Celeste struck first, and I took the other side of his throat. The two of us held him up, restraining ourselves enough to not put him in hospital. He was a little unsteady on his feet, so we leaned him against the wall, encouraging him to sit.

Celeste leaned towards me, her tongue lapping up blood from the corner of my mouth.

I stroked her hair. "*Ma chérie,* I am grateful that you are here with me," I said.

She didn't need to ask me questions to know what I meant. "As am I," she replied. "I miss them, though."

I gave her a soft kiss. "So do I." I pulled away. "I will enjoy our dance at the masquerade. Enjoy the feast."

She beamed up at me and moved back towards the festivities. I glanced down at the human we'd just fed from. He was staring up at me.

"Forget about what you just saw," I said to him. "You got overwhelmed and needed to sit down. Close your eyes for a bit, then return to *Piazza San Marco.*"

His eyes closed, and I left him there.

I came across a walking tour, finding myself surrounded by people wanting to pose with me. With a wide smile I pulled them in a one-armed embrace and grinned at the camera. The scent of blood wafted across the *Piazza*, and I glanced over in time to see a human woman walking from shadows, Erik wiping his thumb across his lips to remove blood. He met my eyes with a glint of amusement, and he stepped from his hiding place to continue the hunt. He was already blood drunk, and I chuckled to myself.

Chapter 25

I stared at my reflection, not recognising myself. I wore a red and black mask that only covered my eyes and nose, with feathers fanning out around my face. The red and black dress almost had a Spanish flair to it. I smiled. I definitely looked sexy. I hoped the masked stranger would think so too. I had one night. One night of fun and dancing, to forget about hunting vampires, and my reason for being in Venice. To be normal.

The invitation was a stiff card, black, with gold writing. There seemed to be a family emblem at the top. A single letter B. For a moment I put down the invitation and glanced over at my weapons. It occurred to me I should be more cautious and maybe take something in the chance that vampires were around. Unable to find a weapon that I could hide, I decided against it, hopeful I was making the right decision.

I felt less guilty than I would have when I arrived in Venice, about going to such an event. Since I was a child, I'd been taught that everything should be about the hunt. Focus on the hunt; everything else is a distraction. But in a different country, and far away from my father, I'd made up my mind to go. I wanted to go. To take in the sights and pleasures that Venice had. I grabbed the invitation again. It didn't have my name on it, but people around me had told me that to receive the invitation was an honour. The masked stranger was known to invite someone every year.

Happy with my dress, I walked towards the door and paused, glancing back at my weapons again, dread pressing into my chest. The last time I'd gone out without weapons, it had been a poor choice, when Carlos had shown up at the bar. I opened up my evening bag and dropped a wooden stake into it, next to my phone. Then with one last glance at my dress, I closed the door behind me.

I made my way towards the address on the card. The eerie mist that clung to the grand canal earlier remained, which added a mysterious feel to the city. People were still milling around, but there were fewer remaining. Many in evening wear seemed to be on their way to parties. Excitement burst within my chest as I approached the venue. The men stationed on the doors barely looked at the invitation I held before waving me inside.

I scanned the room, in awe of the variety of colours in

dresses and masks. The lighting was dim, and soft music played. Nearby, a couple were already kissing. I didn't see the masked man who'd invited me, so I approached the staff walking around with glasses of red wine on silver trays.

With a glass of wine in my hand, I watched the dance floor. There were at least thirty people already dancing. As they moved, I caught sight of the red and black mask on the other side of the room. He was looking right at me with a small smile on his lips. Kissable lips. My heart skipped a beat when his smile widened. He approached me slowly. In front of me, he bowed and held a hand out to me.

"*Ballare*," someone said, pushing me forward. "Dance."

I downed my glass and put it aside before stepping forward, reaching for his outstretched hand. Piercing blue eyes watched me. Not a word passed between us as we joined the dance. The music thrummed through me as we moved as one, my smile widening. This was more fun than I'd had before. His hands were warm and firm. One hand pressed against my lower back, holding me in place as we moved.

My heart thundered, and I noticed people watching us. I lifted my gaze to the piercing blue eyes of my dance partner. I didn't know why he had picked me, but I didn't care. For the first time in my life, I couldn't hear my father voicing his disapproval. I had a taste of sheer delight as his hand pressed harder against my lower back. Pulling me closer to him.

He gazed down at me, intensity burning in his eyes, with a slight unfocused glaze, as if he were intoxicated. I'd probably never see him again, but caught up in the moment it didn't matter. I started to yearn for his kiss. Those lips looked inviting. I wasn't one to take the lead, though, and could only wait to see what he would do. Would our dance lead to other things? The idea thrilled me.

He bent his head down, and I let my lips part as his pressed against mine. Elation soared, as did my heart. The heat of his kiss pushed aside all doubt and hesitance. His arms tightened around me, his tongue firm against mine. All too slowly did it dawn on me how familiar the kiss was. And that it tasted of blood. I stiffened. The masked stranger wasn't a stranger at all. The intensity in his eyes had been hunger. I pulled back from the kiss.

"Well, sweet *Cazadora*, don't you look ravishing," he commented.

"Carlos," I gasped.

He smiled down at me. "The one and only."

Chapter 26

"Carlos is a little intoxicated," Erik said in a low voice as he danced with a blonde human woman. "He just hissed at someone."

"It's Carlos; of course he is," Quinn laughed, her and Matteo surrounding a human male. "But you're one to talk, Erik; can you even walk straight?"

"Erik's always intoxicated," Lorenzo remarked, as he and Annika moved in time to the music. "I don't think I've seen him sober since I've known him."

I grinned down at Celeste as they talked to each other across the room. Her head rested on my shoulder. Clearly she'd had a little bit too much to drink too, and I was mostly holding her up.

"He was once, about a century ago," Matteo laughed. "I've never seen a vampire so miserable."

"I think tonight he's got some competition with Carlos," Annika said. "Who's going to babysit our King if the Huntress doesn't show up?"

Already blood drunk, I was in too good of a mood to worry about their remarks. They were correct. I'd spent the last two hours taking my fill of the crowd, and leaving behind humans panting for more, an effect of my venom. However, most of the clan were just as intoxicated.

The music paused, and Celeste pulled out of my arms. "She'll be here soon," she acknowledged. "Anyone else want to dance with him before the Hunter gets here?"

Annika was in my arms a second later, her eyes glazed as she stared into my face.

Lorenzo smiled. "Try not to fall over," he told me.

I wrapped my arms around Annika. "It's the drunk holding up the drunk," I joked.

Annika and I danced, a slow dance where we didn't have to move much. I was grateful. Annika's arms were tight around me. Half way through the dance, she leaned up, kissing my cheek. I pressed my lips to her forehead.

Quinn's laughter burst out. "That's how we know Annika's drunk; she's in her lovey-dovey mood."

"How do we know Quinn's had too much to drink? She starts talking about everyone else's intoxication," Matteo added with a chuckle.

"I think our King's main course has arrived," Josef noted from a dark corner of the room, where a woman had her head back, his lips at her throat.

I shifted my gaze from the dancers and caught sight of a woman in the doorway, looking around. She wore a black and red dress with a Spanish flair, her mask matching, with feathers fanning around her head. I was almost certain it was her. The red carnation tattoo on her wrist confirmed it. Lorenzo took Annika back into his arms; the two of them moving away.

"I was starting to think she wouldn't show," I replied. "Looks like I get my fun after all.

Andreas made his way past her. "Mmm, she smells delicious," he said once he was away from her. "Dinner is served, My King."

"Perhaps dinner and dessert," I replied.

I could already taste her blood, and as I watched her, my cock twitched. For a moment, there was no sign of Huntress in her movements. Just a woman. There was a grace to her, an allure, which was surprising for a human. I couldn't look away as she reached for a glass of wine from one of the servers. In that dress and mask she really was quite a draw.

"You match," Quinn joked, pulling me from my thoughts. "That's adorable."

"Adorable?" I challenged.

Quinn grinned at me from across the room. "Oh, Carlos, don't pout. You can be adorable and hot."

Finally the Huntress caught sight of me and stilled with a wine glass halfway to her mouth.

With my warmest smile, I approached her and bowed, holding my hand out, eyes meeting hers. Someone pushed her forward, telling her to dance. She finished her wine and took my hand. I pulled her into a slow dance. Her lips curved into a smile; her eyes shone with merriment. As we moved, I struggled to hold back my fangs from emerging. Her heartbeat and warmth awoke the urge to tear into her throat and bury my face in the gush of blood. Her attempts to kill me were challenges that I needed to answer in kind.

Her gaze lifted to my mouth, and I didn't try to hold back the smile. All she knew of me was that I was a masked man who'd handed her an invitation. I found myself curious as to whether she had known it was me, and if she had come armed. Or if she had been too caught up in the excitement of *Carnevale*. But when I leaned forward, her lips parted.

"He's going in for the irresistible Carlos Rivera special." Annika declared, and I held back my own laughter.

Naturally, the Huntress couldn't resist. I gave her a soft kiss, pressing my hand into the small of her back. Her eyes closed.

"I'll give my next meal if she bares her throat," Erik offered.

"Rip her open and leave her in a bloody heap," Josef suggested.

"Well, that would just be a waste," Celeste added.

The Huntress stiffened in my arms, and her eyes shot open. She now knew who I was, but in front of half of Venice, she was unable to react. Unfortunately, I was in the same position.

She pulled out of the kiss. Disgust and horror filled her eyes.

"Well, little *Cazadora*, don't you look ravishing," I commented.

"Carlos," she said.

I smiled down at her. "The one and only."

She tried again to pull out of my grasp, only to find my

arms locked around her, holding her to me.

"What are you doing?" she demanded.

"Dancing." I replied. "Aren't you having fun? You were a moment ago."

She glanced around the room, and the two of us continued to dance.

"Why all this? Inviting me to dance?" she asked.

I had to admit I was impressed by her lack of fear.

"Well, I saw you all by yourself, and you looked so lonely. No one should be by themselves during the biggest event of the year." I lost my smile, adding threat to my stare, lowering the tone of my voice to match. "I was going to kill you where you stood, but I thought this might be more fun. Our previous dances had you catching me unprepared. I thought I'd get the upper hand this time."

Her eyes darted around the room again, her entire body tense. "You're not going to kill me in front of all these people."

"That's exactly what I'm going to do. No one will notice. They're all too drunk. Although I did enjoy that kiss. Care for another?"

She shook with rage in my arms. Amused that my taunts were having their desired effect, I lowered my head, breathing in her familiar scent of apples and vanilla.

The sight of her standing over me with an arrow sent a chill through me. She'd come close to killing me, in front of my entire clan, and I could do nothing in the middle of the people. There were too many eyes on us. I tightened my grip. Fear flickered through her, and I fought to hold back my fangs.

"Let me go," she said through clenched teeth, yet she didn't try to pull away. She knew better.

I smiled down at her. "People are watching," I reminded her. "We're only halfway through the song."

She relaxed in my arms, only slightly, casting a glance around her. "You've been feeding. A little risky, don't you think?"

I chuckled. "Awww, are you worried about me being caught? Or did you enjoy the taste of it? I've heard that even after vampire blood is gone, some humans still crave it for a few weeks. Perhaps you'd like another taste?"

I dropped my mouth to hers again, letting my fangs emerge this time. She pressed her lips closed, so I shifted my kisses down her throat. I made sure she could feel my fangs. She suppressed another shudder.

"You know, it would be *so* easy," I whispered against her throat. "Have you ever been bitten by a vampire before? What our venom does to humans is quite remarkable. You might find you enjoy it."

'*What are you doing?*' Matteo asked me.

'*I'm in a playful mood,*' I told him.

I'd overfed, and the intoxication that came with it often brought out this mood in me. So in the middle of a masquerade ball, with soft music playing, I danced with a woman who'd tried more than once to kill me. The earlier kiss had sent pleasure blazing through me. Her lips were soft, and in that moment she'd kissed back, there had been a roughness to her kiss. A need. Our dance was one for show, and I was overcome by her scent, the closeness of our bodies.

"What's your game?" Her voice was low, filled with hatred. "I saw you during the opening ceremony, now here. You're feeding in both worlds? Weren't you supposed to keep to the shadows?"

I could feel the entire clan watching, just waiting for the command. *'Tell them, not here.'* I ordered Matteo. *'Let me have my fun. I want to see what she does. In front of everyone, I think it's safe to assume she won't attempt to kill me.'*

He relayed my words to the rest of the clan.

"She came looking for you at the gallery, I don't think she was expecting you here," Josef agreed.

"Game?" I repeated the Huntress's words. "We enjoy these social events as much as humans do. If you're trying to remind me of the accords, *Cazadora*, that was not a part of them. I'd know; I was there." I glanced around the room. "I could break your neck and be gone before you hit the floor."

"But you won't." she let out a shaky laugh. Nothing but bravado. "Because you want to remain hidden, and while we're here in the middle of this crowd, you'll do nothing."

Forcing down my own fury, I waited for the music to finish. Then we could stop dancing, and I could take her from the crowd.

When the music did finish, she didn't pull free. Just lifted her chin in defiance and met my eyes with a glint of challenge.

"What will you do now?" she asked, and I caught the tremor in her voice. Despite her attempt to hide her fear, it was pushing through. "What's the next move, King Carlos?" She put contempt into my title.

The music started up again, and we continued to dance.

For a Hunter on her own, she had bravery. I was slightly impressed that she was attempting to taunt me. I was also a little unsettled by her. I needed to get back on top, get under her skin. I forced a smile.

"You're afraid," I told her, speaking in Castellano. "That's why you won't let go. You're choosing to dance with a vampire, because you know that in this room, in front of all these people, this is the safest place for you." I chuckled. "We can dance all night if you like, sweet *Cazadora*, I don't mind. But eventually, you'll tire." I pointed around the room. "Do you remember all the faces of those you brought to their knees at the gallery? They're here. Which of the faces behind masks is human, and which is vampire?"

Her heartbeat picked up and I lowered my head, whispering into her ear. "You only know Josef, Quinn and Matteo, but they all know you. Your face, and your scent. You tried to kill their King; they're a little irritated."

"You still talk too much," she muttered, while scanning the room.

I smiled in triumph. She was shaken.

Chapter 27

I glanced around, wondering where the vampires were. From memory, there were a total of nine. A small clan by normal vampire standards, but still more than I wanted to face. It didn't help that everyone in the room was hidden behind a mask. Carlos and I were locked in a dance that I needed to keep going while I worked out my escape. The moment I left the room, his entire clan would be on me. I'd been trained to control my fear, but I had to admit I was terrified. Carlos would take longer than I would to tire, so he already had me at a disadvantage.

Being this close to a vampire was intimidating. He'd said it himself, that he could kill me and vanish before my body hit the floor. I was in the arms of a killer, and his touch made my skin crawl. As if sensing my discomfort, he shifted his hand from the small of my back, sliding it up. There was no way I could pull away. I'd chosen this play, and he had me trapped.

His warm breath brushed my ear. "To use your words, what's your next move?"

I'm going to die. No! Not like this! "I suppose we keep dancing." I said lightly.

"I suppose so." Amusement flickered in his eyes. "I could almost suspect you're enjoying our little dance. It is a delight, I must admit." His voice dropped. "Your body is so warm, and you do smell good enough to eat."

He was playing with me. "Didn't anyone tell you not to play with your food?" I muttered.

I didn't want to think about how much I'd yearned to kiss him before I'd known who he was. I should have recognised the effects vampires had on people. Their very presence, irresistible. I'd been so drawn up in the thrill of the evening. I'd felt so mysterious in my mask, and someone had chosen me to dance with. I'd stepped forward eagerly, unknowingly into the arms of a vampire.

I didn't want to think about how his hand felt on my back, or the firmness of his body against mine. The usual arrogant smirk had softened into a smile that someone who was slightly drunk gave, his lips just as appealing as they'd been when I'd kissed him. Heat flushed through me, and I frowned. He was a vampire, and to have such thoughts was abhorrent.

His smile flashed down at me, and a chuckle rumbled from him. "Food? Is that an offer?" he asked.

I realised I'd just referred to myself as food. "No!" I said quickly. No matter what I said, he would corner me every time.

"You're so tense," he laughed. "You'll only tire yourself out more. Why don't you relax? I get the feeling we're going to be here for a while."

I hated to admit it, but he was right. Every muscle in my body was resisting his touch, and I would not last long. I forced myself to relax.

"That's better." His hand on my back pressed me harder to him. "Let's have some fun."

Everything in me wanted to pull away, to escape. Instead, I raised my eyes to his in challenge. In their depths were amusement and hunger as he watched me. I wished I could kick myself. My nervousness, mixed with the glass of wine I'd had, was affecting me. He had me off-balance, and I didn't know how I was going to escape from this.

He dropped his head, his warm breath against my ear again. "You were to be my main course, but now you're making me work for it. I have to admit, you do look appealing in that dress. If you weren't a Hunter, I'd be tempted to unwrap you. To slowly peel that dress to reveal what lies beneath."

I didn't know what to say to that. A new song began, and many left the floor for a break. "That may have been flattering a thousand years ago, but now it's just creepy. Not at all what women want to hear." *What am I doing?*

His smirk returned. "Is that so?"

Don't talk. He's trying to trap you in some mind game. I glared at him.

He gazed into my eyes, and I could see that he was as unsettled as me. Once again I caught a slight glazed look in his eyes, his cheeks flushed. The sign of overfeeding. He was what vampires called blood drunk. I hoped those he'd fed from were alright. And that he wasn't about to go on a killing spree. It was known intoxicated vampires lacked control.

"You're drunk," I pointed out. "That makes you a danger to these people."

Laughter boomed from him. "I may have overfed a little," he admitted. "This is my favourite time of the year. You will be dinner, and dessert, you sweet little Huntress. Then I will continue on to the next human."

He spun me around and dipped me, our bodies pressed together.

"Then while you're here, I'm saving someone from such an atrocity, as is the duty of a Hunter," I shot back.

"And this is my Kingly duty," he replied, and his eyes swam before me. "Sleep, Huntress."

Shit! I'd been foolish to fall into that. I struggled against the words, but it was too late. Unable to fight his command, I fell into the embrace of black nothing.

Chapter 28

The Huntress's eyes widened as she realised what I was doing. But she quickly went limp in my arms.

"Finally," Matteo grounded out, and stalked towards me, scowling. "Now that you're done flirting with her—"

"No." A male voice drew both our attention. He spoke loud enough for us to hear him through the music, to know the word was directed at us.

I frowned at Matteo and glanced across the room into dark brown eyes glaring across at me. Pietro Barone stormed across the room, the crowd moving out of his way as he moved.

"I forget, is he yours or your brothers?" I asked Matteo's. I had never cared to learn the difference.

"Giovanni's," he replied. "She, however," he pointed, "Is mine."

I lifted my gaze to a woman who was not far behind Pietro. Lenora. Also a Barone descendant.

They'd both taken their masks off, and they did not look happy.

"Remove your masks." Pietro demanded in Italian. "I want to speak with your King."

Any other human would not have been able to speak to me in such a way without finding themselves surrounded by my entire clan. But the living descendants of a member of the clan were another matter entirely. For a human who knew what we were, he showed no fear. Only anger. My clan stayed back, but watched us.

I passed the Huntress over to Matteo, removing my mask. "You're speaking to him," I confirmed. "Would you like to explain why you barged across the room with such boldness?"

Lenora faced Matteo. "Release the girl. Remove your mask, too."

Barone security surrounded us, keeping humans away, and one man took the Huntress from Matteo. I nodded, and he removed his mask. Lenora and Pietro exchanged a glance.

"Brother of my ancestor," Pietro nodded his head respectfully to Matteo, then addressed me. "King Carlos, we had an agreement. We help cover any accidental deaths, pay for the silence of those who end up in hospital by your own or your clan's doing, and keep an eye out for anyone who may escape your compulsion. In return, you gave us your word that no Venetians would be fed from, and that during *Carnevale*, no one would get hurt on our grounds."

"She's not Venetian," I told him. "She's Spanish, so she's not under the protection of our agreement." I flashed him a cold smile. "You're no stranger to our activities, Pietro. Need I remind you? Just last week, you attended a gallery opening, in which your wealthy friends were paying to be fed from. Why do you interfere tonight?"

Lenora lifted her phone to face me. I stared at a video from outside the gallery, the Huntress standing over me, holding the arrow over my chest. She rammed it down and I barely stopped it. "It seems you have a Hunter on your hands. While we cannot interfere with her hunting activities, when she is defenceless and on our grounds, she is under our protection."

I growled, my face inches from Lenora's, baring my fangs. She didn't back down. Instead, her eyes narrowed as she glared back.

"It is on me to protect my clan and myself from her. We have not broken any accords; she has no authority here." I informed her.

Pietro chuckled. "You and I both know that's not the truth," he said.

I shot my death stare at him.

He let out a sigh. "Look, King Carlos, we respect you, and we turn the other way while you feed and fuck your way through the tourists. Whatever game you and the Hunter are in, keep that to the streets. Not while she is my guest, during *Carnevale,* nor while she is unarmed. Surely it's beneath you to go after one so defenceless?"

"But she is my guest," I pointed out. "She came at my invitation."

Lenora stepped forward. "Did she know who it was who invited her? That she'd be walking into her own death? Not here. Stand down. This is to be a night of celebration. For all."

Matteo put his hand on my shoulder. "My King. Perhaps we can keep peace tonight."

I knew what he was asking me. To not hurt his descendants.

'Let them have her. This was an opportunity that you took; but there will be another chance to kill her. The clan will not fault you for this,' he spoke through our bond. *'You have given her reason to fear you. Do not cause our peace with them to rift.'*

I met his eyes and nodded, letting my fangs retract. "My apologies," I said to Pietro and Lenora, glancing around the room. "I seem to have disturbed everyone's evening. Perhaps it's time I take my clan elsewhere."

Lenora was wary as she watched me. "You're welcome to stay."

"Agreed," Pietro confirmed with a smile. "I would rather know you're here, not stalking that poor girl. Perhaps you'd like to join us for a drink to cement our peace. I'm sure your clan will allow that."

"I accept your invitation," I said.

Lenora turned her attention to Matteo as we followed Pietro. The clan followed closely behind, as did the security team. One of them carried the Huntress. "It has been a pleasure to see you again. I would like to invite you to an event next week. Bring Lady Quinn. My son is to be married."

The Barones had a relationship with Matteo; they had welcomed him and Quinn into their family. It had allowed for an easier co-existence between my clan and Matteo's descendants.

"I would be honoured, thank you," Matteo agreed.

"Good, I'll have an invitation delivered to your den in the morning." Lenora smiled up at Matteo before focusing on me. "Thank you, King Carlos. We appreciate you allowing us to live in harmony."

The woman was well skilled in diplomacy. She had always addressed me respectfully, but without fear. Which I admired. Pietro too. They both knew Matteo's history, and mine, yet spoke to us as equals. In a way they were, politically. But they also had an understanding that we had an agreement because I wanted it as much as they did.

"Of course." I said. "There is no reason we cannot share Venice. You have certainly kept your side of our agreement, covering any signs of our feedings. Kept us in the dark. For that, I am grateful."

We arrived in a large room filled with couches and a bar. A chandelier hung above us, and the lighting was low. Pietro and Lenora took a seat.

"As have you, by feeding only on tourists and leaving Venetians alone. You've held other vampires from entering our city and becoming a threat. We give you our thanks," Pietro said.

"Our agreement has benefits for both of us," Matteo spoke up. "But remember, he is the King. Your approach tonight was a challenge. Perhaps rethink how you approach vampires. Especially one who is intoxicated and likely to take such a challenge badly."

My clan waited behind me. I took a couch, and they spread out, taking their places. Matteo sat next to me.

A human handed Pietro a whiskey, and Lenora a glass of wine.

"Thank you. Please, bring in our guests," Pietro instructed. The human left the room, and he glanced at his security team. "You can leave, you're not needed. Please, make sure the Hunter gets home safely."

The security left the room. I was disappointed that once again the Huntress had escaped her fate, but knew I would have another opportunity. I made up my mind to track her to her house, something I should have done earlier.

"I'd offer you a whiskey, but I've ordered something more suited to your tastes." Pietro said.

No sooner had he finished speaking, when more humans entered the room. Dressed in gowns and suits, I counted nine. Men and women. They glanced around at us in surprise.

I gave a slight nod, and each member of my clan moved too fast for the human eye to see. They each claimed a human, leaving one for me. I smiled at Pietro. Each of my vampires let out a low growl and sunk their fangs into exposed throats. The scent of blood filled the room.

"I do like our arrangement," I said. "However, does it not disturb you that you hand over your own kind to be food?" I rose from my seat, and claimed the human woman staring around at what was clearly a vampire feeding. Humans succumbed to the effects of vampire venom, moaning in pleasure.

"They came to this masquerade looking to have some fun.

I'm sure they get that and more from your bites," Pietro replied. "My main concern is that no one dies." He raised his glass. "A celebration. Another year of continued peace and coexistence."

I bit into the throat of the human. Already well intoxicated, it was likely I wouldn't be able to see straight.

I lifted my head. "Indeed," I agreed and went back to my drink.

Chapter 29

St Mark's Square was flooded from high tide as I walked by to get coffee. I walked into a cafe that had a view of the square that wasn't full of water, and I waited to be seated. I ordered an espresso, watching as people walked over raised platforms across the square. Some waded through the water in knee-high rubber boots, the sounds of splashing as they walked.

"May we join you?" a voice asked with an Italian accent.

I glanced up at the woman who'd spoken. In her late forties, she was tall, well dressed and gave me a warm smile. Her brown eyes crinkled at the corners. Lenora. Beside her was a man who I knew to be Pietro Barone.

I'd met them two nights prior at *Carnevale* Masquerade, after they rescued me from Carlos and his clan. They'd both come to my house to introduce themselves.

"Certainly," I replied.

They took a seat. The waiter brought my coffee and spoke in Italian to the Barones. Lenora shook her head.

"No," Pietro said in English. "But I will pay for her espresso."

"You keep poor company." I said when the waiter left.

Lenora smiled. "I'm the direct descendant of Matteo Barone, Pietro of his brother. We know what they are. We have an agreement with them. They don't kill, and they only feed from tourists."

I sipped my coffee. It tasted stronger than my usual cappuccino I was used to. Bitter. I had to admit I liked it. "So you allow them to feed from people?" I asked in disgust.

Lenora glanced around and lowered her voice. "It's not something that we feel great about. But twenty years ago, we had a choice. They compelled Pietro from what is now their den, and we realised Matteo had returned. So we came to an agreement to coexist. They only feed from tourists. No locals."

I couldn't believe what I was hearing. "So, why didn't you burn the place down?" I challenged, and met Pietro's eyes. "You let them push you from your home, and use people who are drawn to Venice, for food. How can you fail to see what's wrong with that?"

I owed these people gratitude; they'd saved me from Carlos and his clan. I still didn't want to think about what would have happened if they hadn't stepped in. But I couldn't understand why they'd willingly let vampires remain in their city. "You should have called in Hunters the moment they arrived. To allow them to remain is a betrayal."

Lenora's pleasantness faded. "We don't want your war here. It is unwelcome. Our family has known for generations about Matteo, and we knew he'd return. Vampire or human, he is family. All we want to do is keep the peace, and King Carlos was gracious enough to agree."

The only thing worse than vampires, was the idea that people existed like Lenora and Pietro. Who helped vampires. To accept vampires, to allow them to claim Venice was unnatural. "You look the other way," I accused. "That's why there have been no reports of vampires here. You protect them." I scowled. "You cover it up. And you charge people money to let vampires feed from them."

Pietro glared at me. "And they protect us. Their presence stops other vampires less willing to coexist from staking their claim. No other vampire clan would agree to spare the locals. Matteo and Carlos were more than willing to agree to that. He employs people and pays them extremely well."

I had no words and turned my head away. As I did, I caught sight of a dark silhouette on the roof of a nearby building, the full moon behind. I'd seen Carlos enough to know it was him. Watching me. Ice crawled down my spine, and I wondered if I was actually safe with Lenora and Pietro here.

"Would you protect me? Or would you cover up my death, too?" I asked. "Carlos intends to kill me; would you just look the other way?"

Lenora and Pietro glanced at each other and then up at

the roof from which Carlos was watching us.

"I think you should leave." Lenora suggested.

"Excuse me?" I asked. "Why?"

"For your own safety," she replied. "As I already said, we don't want your war in our city. We're rather protective of Venice. Either you're going to kill him, which would have his entire clan after your blood, or he'll kill you, which will bring more Hunters here. Neither outcome would suit us."

"You're protective of Venice?" I scoffed. "You're doing a poor job of showing it by allowing vampires to exist here."

I stared up at Carlos. I couldn't see his face, but it was clear he wasn't trying to hide. Memory washed over me of his body against mine and that kiss. I suppressed a shudder. I would keep that from my reports. No one needed to know that. Yet again, I wondered if it was time to put out a call for help.

Carlos leapt from the roof, landing without a sound, and approached.

Pietro rose. "King Carlos," he said with a warning in his voice. "This is not keeping the peace."

I was shocked at how he spoke to a vampire King. Men moved in, clearing the entire outdoor cafe.

Carlos stopped, his eyes on me, flashing red.

"You speak of peace," he said to Pietro. "She has made numerous attempts on me, and almost killed Lady Quinn," he met Lenora's eyes. "I know you welcomed Quinn into your family alongside Matteo. If he hadn't arrived in time, we'd all be grieving her loss. The Huntress arrived in a city we both wanted to remain peaceful, and she declared war." He turned his stare to me. "This will be your one and only warning. Leave, as Lenora said. If you choose to stay, then you best hope I don't find you first."

Lenora stood and approached Carlos. Again it surprised me how they were both unafraid of him. Vampires were often unpredictable, and he'd just as likely tear out their throats for daring to speak to him in such a way. The two of them spoke in low voices.

"I'm protecting my territory," Carlos declared loudly. "And my people. If any of my clan die at her hand, your peace *will* be broken. Because I will tear out her throat and leave her as a warning to any Hunters who think to enter my territory."

My heart pounded, fear squeezing against my chest. He advanced, putting his hands on the table and his face inches from mine. I saw nothing but open hostility in his eyes, and a dangerous glint that only added to my fear.

He took a deep breath in and let it out slowly. "I can smell your fear. You're right to be afraid. They've now assisted you twice. There won't be a third time."

"Please, King Carlos." Pietro said.

He glared at me once more, then without another word, he vanished.

"Please leave," Lenora said again. "We cannot protect you if you stay. You do not fall under our agreement."

I wanted to leave. More than anything, I wanted to leave. Unfortunately, under my father's orders, leaving wasn't an option. He had sent me to Venice for a reason. "I can't," I admitted. "I have no choice."

Chapter 30

I left the Huntress, the scent of her fear enticing. It was the first time her fear had peaked so high, and I found satisfaction in knowing she was afraid. Infuriated by the Barones' interference, I held back a growl. Every time I came across the Huntress, my need to kill her only increased. The night of the masquerade, I had kissed her as a way to play the game of seduction, to get her defences down. But it bothered me that the memory of it kept forcing its way to the surface.

I needed to feed. Hunger burned its way through me. I had been hunting when I caught the scent of the Huntress, only to find her once again protected by the Barones. I would need to have a word with Matteo.

As I fell into the hunt, I forced myself to calm down. In the bad mood I was in, I was likely to tear into throats and kill. I had been denied a kill, so I wanted one. A mental nudging from Josef and Erik caught my attention. They shared a territory, and I knew where the Huntress was, so there was nothing to suggest danger. But they wouldn't call for me if it wasn't important. Once again my hunt had been interrupted, but I made my way to their feeding ground and sought out their presence.

I found them at the water's edge. Before them was a boat. I recognised the vampire that faced them. A woman in her late twenties, black wavy hair, dark brown eyes with the olive tone of many Italians. Age reflected in her eyes; she was at least a few centuries old.

"You!" I growled.

She had made three attempts over twenty years to enter Venice.

"I ask that you let me enter. Please, I need to see—"

"No. Did I not make it clear the other times you tried to barge into my territory?" I demanded. "I have been a patient man with your foolish attempts. But tonight I am not in a patient mood."

She left the boat and knelt in front of me. Erik and Josef stood behind her. I caught the unmistakable scent of arousal and glanced at them. They were attracted to this female. I glared. Erik merely smirked and shrugged, while Josef focused on her, tips of his fangs showing.

She bowed her head. "Please King Carlos, I don't intend to take your territory from you. I am—"

"Leave or die," I said. "I will tear your heart from your chest and drop it and your body in the canal."

She rose from her knees and took a step back, only to find Erik and Josef blocking her way.

"What kind of a King doesn't hear out those trying to speak?" she challenged, her eyes red.

So, she had a temper. She'd be well suited to Josef. I almost laughed at the idea.

I growled. "One who has more important matters to attend to, over a stray vampire making continuous attempts to enter my city despite my forcibly removing her."

I wrapped a hand around her throat. "Leave. Go back to whichever clan you belong to. Tell them the Bloodking has named Venice mine. I have been lenient in allowing you to live. Defy me again and you'll find that leniency gone."

I released her and she swiftly returned to the boat. I watched as she left.

"She's insistent," Josef remarked. "I like it."

"Yes, I can smell your desire for her," I grumbled. That was all I needed, for my clan to grow smaller as a good friend chased another vampire.

"Well, she is a beauty," Erik agreed. "I always did love a stubborn woman."

I frowned. "You both want her? I don't want you two fighting over a woman."

Josef laughed. "My King, there would be no fight. We would happily share her."

The two of them had a close friendship, and that was unsurprising.

"You are not to let her into Venice," I reminded them. "Or you'll find yourselves sharing her boat."

"We can always find mutual ground," Josef noted with humour in his eyes. "And return in time for a pre-dawn breakfast." He grinned at me. "We would never leave you, Carlos. We're just admiring a beautiful woman. You are our King, and we'd never betray you."

They both lowered themselves to one knee before me.

"I know you wouldn't," I acknowledged. I knew their loyalty.

They rose to their feet.

Erik stared out across the water. The sound of the engine faded. His red eyes shifted to me. "We have so few women in our clan, all of which you have claimed. Now that we know Gabriela's entire clan died, I regret not talking more into leaving with us. Of course it was only natural that Annika would follow Lorenzo." He lowered his head. "I do miss Ingrid. She had quite the ferocious appetite."

"And it was a surprise to us all that Celeste was able to tear herself away from Gabriela's control," Josef added. "Much to Erik's pleasure, he does like to watch the two of you." Josef shot Erik a grin. "And he doesn't leave the den when Matteo and Quinn fuck. Those two really are like animals."

Amusement and lust filled Erik's eyes. I laughed. These two knew how to lift my mood.

"We share humans all the time, but it would be nice to have someone with equal…drive and stamina." Erik growled. "The two of us together are too much for humans, they tire out so quickly, and we would like to not have to worry about breaking someone. To not have to hold back."

I frowned. They had never voiced such thoughts with me before.

"Would you consider taking more into our clan?" Josef

asked.

"It might be a possibility," I agreed. "But we can't turn tourists; that would draw attention when they go missing. Turning locals would break our agreement with the Barones." I glanced across at the retreating boat. "Perhaps we need to make an alliance with another clan." Their eyes lit up with hope. "Why didn't you two tell me you were lonely?"

They exchanged a glance. The deep affection that passed between the two was unmistakable. The pair did more than share humans; they shared a bed. I'd been right in my evaluation. That was plain as day. "Oh, we're not lonely," Josef told me. "We just desire…more. Someone to share. To claim, as you have."

I nodded. "Alright. If you find someone willing to be claimed, I would welcome her into my clan." I smiled. "The entire clan would need to accept her, too. Now, I'm hungry. My hunt has continuously been interrupted tonight."

Josef bared his throat to me. My fangs lengthened and I bit hard with a growl. One hand grasped the back of his neck, while my other wrapped around his arm. His hand pressed against the small of my back as I fed from him. The fire of his blood warmed me, and my hunger lessened. I'd bitten deep, and blood spilled, dripping from my chin. I released his throat and rubbed my cheek against his, rumbling deep in my chest. Josef's own growl reverberated through me.

"Are you satisfied, my King, or do you need more?" Erik asked. I turned, and he licked Josef's blood from me before tilting his head to the side. As I nuzzled into Erik's throat, drinking, I was aware of Josef's body against my back. When I lifted my mouth from Erik's neck, Josef licked my jaw. The two had just taken each other's blood.

"You two have blood bonded," I said.

Josef met my eyes. "We have."

"You didn't tell anyone," I remarked.

"We blood bonded when Quinn's voice freed us from Gabriela," Josef admitted. "We sought to leave, and had plans to form our own clan. Erik had an idea to invite Lorenzo and Andreas to join us. But when Matteo turned Quinn, we were drawn to her."

I glanced at Erik, who was even older than me. The one vampire I'd known my entire existence other than Gabriela. "You would have made a great King," I told him.

He smiled. "I'm more suited to be the warrior of a great King."

"Alright, have you both fed? Perhaps we can hunt together tonight?" I offered.

Both their eyes lit up with joy.

"It would be an honour to hunt with you, Carlos," Josef said with a wide grin. "We invite you to join us in our territory. What are you in the mood for tonight?"

Chapter 31

The woman's lips were soft, and I sighed as I pressed in, kissing her with force. Her warm, naked body melted against mine, her hands roaming up my back and across my shoulders before tracing lines down my arms. I started to pull away and she clung to me, grasping the back of my head, my neck, holding me to her. Instead of overpowering her attempt, I gave in, letting her pull me into a deeper kiss. The hunger between us blazed; an inferno, and I growled, wanting her with every part of me.

When she let me go, I trailed my lips over her jaw, down to her throat. She shivered, and I smiled. Her body under mine stilled, waiting. As my fangs slid in, she moaned, then murmured in Castellano. I knew her voice and froze. This time I did pull out of her grasp.

Her brown eyes met mine, wide with shock.

"Huntress," I growled.

I woke up, hard and panting, the light brush of her lips still a whisper against mine. It took a while to clear the fog from my head. Troubled as to why I was dreaming about the Huntress in such an intimate way, I tightened my arms around Celeste, breathing in her scent.

"You're sticking that thing into my back, is that a good morning erection or did you just have a really good dream? I hope it was about me," Celeste whispered.

She leaned her head to the side, her body cool in my embrace. I accepted her invitation, biting into her throat. She squirmed, pressing her ass against me, her lust already strong. I reached down, rubbing my fingers against her, finding her wet. She sucked in a small breath, pushing into my fingers, breathing hard.

We lay like that for a time, my fingers circling her clit, then probing into her, while I ground myself into her back. Both of our breaths were ragged, equally aroused. I could feel when the pleasure heightened through her body, pushing her close to orgasm. I fed from her, growling, and she whimpered, coming on my fingers. She quivered against me, panting.

I needed to slide into her, and I was not in a gentle mood. I nuzzled the back of her neck, enjoying her desperation, growling softly. She loved to hear me growl and shivered.

"This is a nice way to wake up," she struggled to talk as my fingers continued their rhythm. "Carlos…"

I nibbled on her earlobe, my own need intensifying.

"Come for me again," I ordered. "Like a good girl. Please your King. Then you get more." She whimpered at my words, her movements against my fingers more erratic, her body squirming. I whispered to her, a combination of French and Castellano, biting her shoulder, releasing venom. "Come for me," I whispered again.

She came a second time.

"You know what your desperation does to me," I whispered, nipping her ear as my other hand caressed her breasts, pinching nipples between my fingers. "Keep begging, I might reward you. Tell me what you want."

She whimpered again. "Fuck me, my King. Please."

Being called King intensified my lust. I flipped her over, pinning her to the bed. Her eyes red with lust, her fangs on display. She was showing me herself, revealing her desire for me.

I ground my cock against her, wanting again to bury myself deep inside her. But I needed to hear her beg first. "Come on Celeste, use your words." I lowered my mouth to her throat, nipping her again, to lick the blood away. The sweet flavour of her desire was thick in her blood. Breathing in her scent deep, I growled again. "I can smell how much you want me inside you, your lust. What do you want from your King?"

She lifted her head, kissing my neck, jaw and lips. I knew what she liked, but this was the game we always played. She wanted to be mastered by her King.

"I want my King's hand around my throat as he takes me from behind against the wall." she rasped. "I want you to leave bruises and bite marks."

"What word?" I demanded with a grin.

"Please, my King."

I moved us from the bed, pushing her against the wall, sliding into her with force. As my fingers gripped her throat I pulled out and slid in again. Her entire body quivered. Erik's presence at the doorway drew my attention, but I didn't stop as I turned my head to find him watching us, desire in his eyes. Over the years, he had developed a liking for watching others in the throes of passion. I could already see the erection in his pants. But he didn't move. His presence was for another reason.

"What?" I demanded.

"An ambassador of Raphael has arrived from France," he said, panting. As I waited for more, his eyes didn't leave us as I thrust into Celeste. "He's waiting with Matteo."

"He can wait until I'm done." I smiled as he watched. "Do you want to watch us, Erik?" He licked his lips, eyes wide. "What do you think, Celeste? Is Erik worthy of watching us?"

She looked over her shoulder at him, her body pushing against me as I slid into her again. I eased my hand from her throat. She wasn't one who liked to share me when she was in my bed; preferring to have me to herself when I was fucking her. But she'd accepted Erik watching, as long as that's all he did. At times, he tended to get too close for her comfort.

"Kneel to our King," she commanded.

Again, I contemplated what a Queen she'd make. To lead the clan alongside me. But I'd offered her the title when we arrived in Venice, only to be turned down. She wanted to be mine, but didn't want to rule with me.

Hungry, Erik fell to his knees, without waiting for my command. I chuckled. "Shall we give him a show?" I asked in Celeste's ear. "He's already hard."

"Yesss…" Her reply got lost in her sounds of pleasure. A mixture of moans and growls.

I squeezed her throat tight again, pressing my hand on her hip strong enough to bruise. The bruises wouldn't last long, but she loved the pain as much as I liked to inflict it. I glanced down at Erik once. His eyes were bright red as he palmed himself through his pants. Breathing hard, he met my gaze, the glint of lust unmistakable.

"Take your pants off," I commanded. "Pleasure yourself, make yourself come while I finish her off."

He didn't question, didn't hesitate. I gave Celeste my full attention. Erik pumping himself, and his breathing quickening only added to my enjoyment.

"Do you hear him?" I whispered in Celeste's ear, thrusting deep into her. I bit her neck, her shoulders, kissing her jaw before biting that too.

She couldn't talk, her entire body tensed, back arching.

"I want you to be loud," I told her. "Make sure the ambassador of Raphael can hear you. He's waiting; give him a show." I glanced back at Erik. "You, too."

My own release rushed towards me, and I sped up my movement.

She came, moaning loudly, which in turn pushed me to my climax. I sensed Matteo's amusement. Erik groaned as he finished himself off. Celeste's legs gave out, and I carried her to my bed. I lay facing her, holding her in my arms.

She snuggled into my chest. "He's waiting," she whispered.

"He can wait," I told her. "You don't show up in another

man's territory unannounced." I tightened my arms around her. "Let me just hold you for now."

Her love of being held after sex gave me a chance to calm myself. I didn't like that the ambassador had shown up out of the blue. I would take my time. He was in my house now — I would not rush to see what he was here for. I could hear Matteo talking to him.

'*Is he annoyed yet?*' I asked Matteo.

'*That you've left him waiting while you have sex? Oh, yes, he's mad. He says it's an insult to Raphael, since he's here on his behalf.*'

I grinned, kissing Celeste. "I'm in no hurry," I told her and lifted my head. Erik was still on his knees, hand on his cock. "You may leave now. This is Celeste's time."

Erik quickly pulled on his trousers and left my room. Curiosity rose as to whether he would go to Josef.

"Let me run you a bath," I suggested to Celeste. "I'll wash you."

"Only if I can wash you, too," she offered.

An hour passed before I eventually headed towards the

lounge room, Celeste at my side. A tall vampire sat in the chair, frown lines embedded in his forehead.

"Finally!" he grumbled, standing when he saw me. Apart from his height, I noticed nothing special about him. Just a messenger.

I took a seat on the couch, and I met Annika's eyes, then Lorenzo's. They sat on either side of me. Matteo positioned himself behind the couch, Josef next to him. Erik squeezed the messenger's shoulder, forcing him to his knees, where he and Andreas stood over him. Quinn sat on a nearby chair, and Celeste took another.

"You will have manners in my house," I snapped. "Raphael gave me no warning that I was to receive you. You think I'm going to finish what I'm doing just because you got here? That would make me a poor lover, wouldn't it?"

I placed a hand over Lorenzo and Annika's laps, the messenger's eyes following the movement.

"He is generous in that department," Quinn said, as she and Celeste exchanged smiles.

The messenger's eyes shifted to Quinn. "You as well?"

I chuckled. "I hold a special bond with all of my clan. Now why are you here?"

"Raphael has Hunters in Marseille, Nice, and Montpellier," he informed me.

I frowned. "So? Why is that my problem?" I had my own Hunter to deal with.

"Two weeks ago, we welcomed the Elders into Paris. We know Italy was their next stop when they left France. The Hunters seem to be following the Elders."

I laughed. "Then they've fallen behind a little. The Elders were here over a week ago."

"Two weeks ago," Matteo corrected.

"Two," I said. "They'd be on their way down to Rome by now."

"They're assembling en masse." He glanced around at my clan. "I'm not talking about a small number. They're recruiting and putting a call out. There are already fifty Hunters gathering. Eva sent word that she had a similar amount in Zurich last week. Two days ago they were in Geneva."

Erik watched the messenger with narrowed eyes. My stomach churned. We only had one Hunter in Venice that we knew of. It seemed that they were on the move, towards Italy. At least a hundred Hunters — that was a problem. More than likely, it would be my problem, if I wasn't careful.

"He sent you here to warn us," I let my voice soften. Raphael had done us a generous favour.

The messenger nodded. "I could be on my way to San Marino. But you had to make me wait an hour."

For him to speak to a King that way, he was high up in Raphael's circle. But I couldn't deny his anger was justified. "My apologies, and sincerest gratitude," I said..

"How many of your clan were in the war?" the messenger asked me. "Other than you."

"Two. Erik and…" I paused, casting a look over my shoulder at Josef. He smirked at me. "Josef was a Hunter. He knows a lot of their ways."

I smiled at the memory. He'd been hunting us for three days, and I had someone turn him. His maker had awakened him as close to the Hunters' camp as we could get, and Josef massacred twenty Hunters before he remembered who he was. But he'd, returned to his maker's side and been a loyal soldier in our army, providing us with valuable information. He held no resentment, and still thanked me to this day for freeing him. A deadly warrior.

The messenger addressed Erik and Josef. "Then you'll remember what the war was like. How they targeted the Elders. They've already killed one."

I growled. "I was there when she was killed. King Luis decreed that no one is to mention her."

"Do the Elders know they have a horde of Hunters on their tail?" Josef asked.

"They said nothing to me," I replied.

"Did they share their blood with you?" The French vampire looked at me.

I nodded.

"Then they know."

I tuned out as he spoke, not hearing a thing. Then Matteo and Lorenzo escorted him from Venice.

Josef stood in front of me. "What is it?" he asked.

"It is no light action for Elders to share their blood in this manner. With that many Hunters gathering, and the Elders sharing blood with all the Kings and Queens, I would say they're building their own army. One with strength and hunger that rivals a normal vamp. The oldest, strongest of us, leading our own clans."

"War." Josef said with a hard glint in his eyes. "The Elders, and the Hunters are both preparing for war."

Chapter 32

He kissed me with force, and I melted against his body, wanting to touch him. I ran my hands down his back, and when he started to pull away, I pulled him back, yearning for more of his lips, his warmth. As my hands grasped the back of his head and his neck, small tremors ran down my spine. His naked body pinned mine to the bed, our lips crushing against one another.

His lips found their way down to my throat, and I shivered, closing my eyes. Fangs slid in, filling me with pleasure and desire. I had *never* wanted anyone as much as him.

"Don't stop," I murmured in Castellano.

His body stiffened against mine and he pulled out of my grasp.

Disappointment surged through me, and I opened my eyes. Carlos lay over me, red eyes, my blood on his lips.

I sat up gasping, my body still flooded with warmth, and my heart pounded.

"Fuck," I muttered. "Now I'm dreaming about him?!"

Wet and breathing hard, I tried to catch my breath. It disturbed me that I would have such a dream about a filthy bloodsucker. But in the dream, I'd wanted it. I would never want such a thing.

However, my body disagreed, and I was already worked up, needing release. My phone showed three am. I climbed from my bed and moved to the punching bag. I put everything into my punches and kicks. The bag swung as I moved, my breathing steady. I worked through every combo for what felt like hours. Sweat lined my skin, my muscles screaming.

When I finally stopped, only an hour had passed. My shoulders heaved and my fists clenched and unclenched. I turned the shower on, washing myself under the hot water. But it soon became apparent that my body only wanted one type of release. I ground my teeth together, my cheeks flaming. Bile rose at the very idea of the effect my dream was having on me. But the more I tried to deny it, the more I needed to give in to what my body wanted.

"Fuck it," I muttered, and reached down, pressing my fingers against my own clit as hot water cascaded down my back.

With one hand flat on the shower wall, I forced down my shame. The wrongness of why I was doing this wasn't enough to stop me. Envisioning a vampire. I had never been more disgusted and wet at the same time. I moved my fingers in a rhythm, finding the pace that I knew would get me off. This wasn't my first time I'd satisfied myself, but it was the first time a vampire had driven me to that state. Despite being uneasy about this, my body soon started to respond, that familiar pleasure rising within me.

My breathing picked up as warmth spread through me, taking me higher, closer to the climax that I sought. I moved my fingers faster, chasing it, almost desperate. The memory of him pressed against me when I'd danced at the bar flashed through my head, and I could almost feel him. The taste of his lips and the effect of his bite in my dream. I closed my eyes, but the images of him only became clearer. The slight curve of his lips, the intensity of his blue eyes. His kiss at the masquerade. I groaned, sickened.

I wanted it to stop. I didn't want to be standing in the shower imagining the things he'd do to me. To feel his hand around my throat, his tongue on me. To feel his fangs, his venom.

"No," a sob rose up. "Stop."

My orgasm rolled over me, crashing down hard, sounds escaping my mouth that would definitely bring me shame if anyone had heard me. My trembling legs gave out, and I dropped to the shower floor, pulling my knees to me, wrapping my arms around them. Hot water continued to fall as I bowed my head and sobbed, letting tears slide down my cheeks.

"I need to leave Venice." I mumbled as the tears fell.

He had warned me to leave. I considered telling my father I'd eliminated the vampire and searching the Hunter network for other jobs. Somewhere else in Italy would do, maybe even France.

I could find other Hunters and join their hunts, but it wouldn't be long before my father would start searching for me. He'd come to Venice and likely find vampires here. He'd probably assume I was dead and put it on the Hunter network. The only ones who would mourn me would be Sofia and Diego.

As the last tremors of my orgasm finished, I didn't move. Far from home, relieving myself to a dream of the damned vampire I was supposed to be killing, tears continued to fall. This was so far from the life I wanted, but it was all I had ever known. I didn't even know what I wanted. Maybe creative writing, or dress-making. The only things I was good at, other than making weapons, martial arts, and stitching up wounds.

"Maybe I should be a doctor," I muttered as I finally climbed to my feet and turned the water off.

I wrapped a towel around me and walked into my bed-room. My phone flashed and I picked it up.

A text from my sister, Sofia. *<I miss you, hope you're okay.>*

"No," I muttered. "I am *so* far from okay right now."

<I miss you too.> I replied quickly. We'd always been close. I had never felt so far from my family. Not just location, but I couldn't tell her anything. I didn't want to risk our father reading her phone.

Her response came through quickly *<Happy birthday, Millie. Me and Diego will have some cake for you.>*

The misery that I'd been holding off, flooded through me. I had forgotten that today was my birthday. I'd never felt so alone.

Chapter 33

I paced my bedroom, careful to keep my thoughts locked up. I didn't want Matteo or King Luis to catch anything. The meeting with the Elders made more sense now. Josef and Erik stood nearby, watching me. Matteo and Quinn's voices wafted through from the kitchen. I picked up the sweet aroma of chocolate, almost over powered by the strong smell of what I'd come to know as Vegemite. Her parents must have sent her another care package from Australia. Elsewhere, Lorenzo and Annika were having sex. Celeste had left, probably to go hunting. I wasn't sure where Andreas was.

"Carlos?" Josef spoke quietly.

"I always knew there'd be another war," I said, halting my pacing. "But the number of Hunters in the world today is far greater than seven hundred years ago. They have weapons that were never around back then."

Erik nodded. "We left behind the days of swords, shields, and archers a long time ago. Many of them do still prefer their crossbows and swords, but guns are a threat to us. Some countries, more so than others. Bullets of wood. All it would take is for a well-trained sniper to sit on a roof. They even have night vision now."

As a human, swords and axes had been Erik's speciality, so he'd kept up to date with the advancement of weapons. We'd seen it first hand while scavenging battlefields in human wars. We'd seen the effects of bombs, and learned of their most destructive weapon yet, the atomic bomb. I'd felt sorry for those in Japan. Human or not, that was a horrible way to die.

"You're scared," Josef said. "Carlos, you're The Killer. I recall you being fearless. You taunted the Hunters as you killed them. You even turned a few into ferals. You were never afraid."

"I'm scared for you, the others," I admitted. "They haven't faced Hunters to the level we have. I remember how many vampires we lost fighting them. How they burned through villages to take us down. I don't want to lose anyone."

"Matteo took down a few in Melbourne." Erik reminded me.

"He was wounded and starving," I recalled. "And trying to get to Quinn. He only tried to escape when she told him she loved him. After the torment they put him through, he'd all but given up." I shook my head. "If they come here, there's only nine of us."

"Then we call another clan for help," Erik suggested. "If they want a war, then perhaps we give them a war. Yes, there are more of them than there used to be, but there are more of us, too. One vampire is worth five humans at least. Probably more for those lucky enough to have Elder blood."

The last war, I did not have to make any decisions. That worried me the most. I'd been the weapon, and had led vampires into battle, but on the orders of Luis or Gabriela. I didn't want to make a decision that would get any of my clan killed. What if, by asking for help, it would only bring the Hunters here. Would they bother with such a small city, when there were larger areas with much bigger clans? I knew that *Famiglia di Sammarinese,* Giuseppe's clan, had fifty vampires. *Legione* in Rome at least a hundred. In the separation into clans, Luis had offered me the position to lead one, and I'd been unwilling to leave Gabriela at the time.

"Matteo is my second, but you were there. I want you both to advise me, should war break out. Anything war-related is your business. I was a personal guard and general to King Luis. That is what you both are to me."

"Yes, Carlos," they agreed.

I continued pacing. Again, I wondered if I should be reaching out to King Luis. Cowering to someone wasn't my way. I knew I'd speak to Matteo later.

"Then we keep ourselves alert," I spoke slowly, considering my actions. "You two will tell the rest of the clan. To be wary of anything that feels out of place. No one hunts alone. We watch each other's backs. Put Celeste and Andreas in the same territory." I glanced at Josef. "You once got into the

Hunter network, can you do it again to get more up-to-date information? Get a glimpse behind the curtain. See if we can find out where they're heading."

"I can try," Josef promised. "They tortured me for days before I managed to get free and take the laptop. I'm not doing that again."

The unmistakable fury glinted in Erik's eyes. He had raged over Josef's capture at the time.

"It won't come to that," I reassured them both. "If they're coming, I want to be ready."

"Should I arm us?" Erik asked. "I can get any weapon you want."

The idea of arming my clan with modern weapons made me uneasy. "No. *We* are the weapons. I wouldn't mind armour, though. See if you can get something to be used against bullets. Perhaps track down a Magic Wielder to enhance it." This whole thing was making me hungry. "Erik, bare your throat, I need to feed."

He obeyed, and I closed the gap between us, sinking my fangs in deep.

Chapter 34

Hungry, I stalked through the crowd. Humans moved around me, many glancing at me as they passed. Unsure what I was in the mood for, I stopped, scanning those around me. I caught the gaze of a man watching me. He smiled and quickly averted his eyes. I didn't move, focused on him. Slowly, he lifted his face towards me again, and my own smile widened.

Emboldened by my grin, he beamed. I approached him without hurry.

"Are you enjoying the sights?" I asked.

"I am now," he said.

I touched his arm. "Then perhaps you'd like to join me for a drink."

I led him to a bar, watching with amusement as he downed his beer quickly. He chatted to me about Venice and his time in Italy.

An hour later, he accepted my invitation to a gondola ride. I led him to Dante, a gondolier who's services I had paid for many times over the past five years. As I stepped onto the gondola, I handed Dante cash. It was more than the cost of the ride, and he knew what this meant. At the end, he'd leave us alone.

I sat down next to the human male. The alcohol had washed away his inhibitions, and he slid an arm around me.

I gave him a seductive smile as I shifted my own arm around him. I'd not met anyone who could resist my smile when I turned on the charm.

"Just sit back, and enjoy the ride." I told him, lowering my voice.

Desire flickered in his eyes.

Dante turned us down a narrow canal. My companion turned his body, his eyes on my face. I leaned forward but stopped, waiting. He bit his lower lip and closed in for the kiss. This close, his own lust coming off him in waves, combined with my hunger and the scent of his blood, I was already hard. I considered giving him a little bit more pleasure than just my bite.

There was a loud thud and the gondola rocked. A growl tore from me as I pulled away from the human. The Huntress stood facing me, sword drawn. I was on my feet in an instant, hissing, fangs bared.

"You!" I ground out, enraged that she'd interrupted my meal. "How is it everywhere I turn, there you are?"

The human stumbled away from us. Dante had enough of a mind to take us to the side of the canal, and quickly left, cursing in Italian. My meal quickly followed.

"That's what makes me a good Hunter," she shot back.

I glanced at the retreating back of what should have been my dinner, maybe more. "Damn, I really had a craving for him," I muttered before turning my attention back to the Huntress. "You don't have the Barones to protect you now."

She glared back. "We'll see how much I need them when I cut your damn head off, *diablo*."

I sighed. "Alright, but can I take my jacket off first?"

Without another word, she lunged forward. I moved out of the way of the arching sword. I took my jacket off, not wanting it to end up in ribbons. I threw it to the *fondamenta.*

The Huntress swung again. Impressed by her footing in the unstable surface beneath us, I ducked out of the way again and chuckled.

"You interrupted my meal," I told her. "So I'll have to make do with you."

I advanced on her, making a playful swipe to her left side. She countered me with her sword, blade swiping across my arm. I bared my fangs.

"This is just like the dance at the masquerade," I reminded her. "I do like to play with my food, and you'll likely tire before me."

"Or I'll kill you before you have to worry about that," she snapped.

Her entire body was tense, her focus never wavering as we moved around each other. I was playing with her stretching out our fight. She wouldn't have the strength to struggle by the time I sunk my fangs into her throat. The gondola rocked and shifted beneath us. Strike after strike, she always corrected her footing before preparing for the next attack. Each time I moved, she anticipated my attacks, meeting me with her blade.

So I focused on throwing her off-balance, by adding to the instability of the gondola beneath us.

We both went in, the water closing over our heads.

I resurfaced at the same time she did, right next to the gondola. She coughed and sputtered for air, no longer gripping her sword. Likely at the bottom of the canal by now. I powered through the water and wrapped my hand around her throat.

"Fucking Hunters, will I never be rid of your plague?" I growled.

Through her defiance, the glint of fear reflected in her eyes. She'd never looked at me that way, and in that moment she looked less like a Hunter, more like the young woman she was. Vulnerable. Terrified. *Good.* A look I'd take with me after I drowned her.

The sight of us naked, my lips pressed against hers, soft and warm slammed into me. Dreams that had no place haunting me now. I growled and shook my head as if to shake the vision away.

She lifted her chin, her attempt at courage not quite rising to the surface. She knew she was going to die.

"What are you waiting for?" she choked around my hand. "Kill me, more will come."

I tightened my grip to silence her.

Again, the memory of my dream washed over me, this time

with my cock responding. I could almost feel the warmth of her body in my embrace, the hunger of her kiss, the way she held on as I lowered my lips to her throat, moaning and squirming against me.

"Stop!" I grunted.

She frowned, her eyes clouded with confusion.

Now that it started, I couldn't stop it. She'd interrupted me in the middle of a kiss, and I was still heated from that. So my need shifted to her and my yearning to kiss her became too much.

"Fuck." I growled.

I lifted her from the water and into the gondola. She didn't move, sucking in air. Her shoulders heaved as I pulled myself from the canal. Dripping wet, I stood over her. She raised her head, meeting my eyes. There was a grim acceptance within their depths, as if she had accepted that she was about to die. Admiration stirred in my chest.

"Smile, Huntress, you live another day," I said.

I left the gondola and retrieved my jacket, turning once to look down at her.

"Why?" she asked, her voice raw.

Red marks were already showing around her throat.

I shrugged. "You look like a drowned rat. Pitiful. Go clean yourself up, face me as a warrior."

I left her there, still gasping and heaving to catch her breath. Hungry, hard, and annoyed that once again I'd failed to kill her, I made my way towards my den. I needed to shower before returning to the hunt. But above all, I was bothered by the dreams, and my mind's timing to relive them.

Chapter 35

Carlos stared down at me, his wet tee-shirt clinging to his body, hair dripping. I stared up at him, absolute fury that had glinted from his eyes, replaced by wariness and uncertainty. Confused by the change in him, I could only lie there, dripping wet, struggling to catch my breath. *How am I still alive?* One moment I was in the water, his hand around my throat, darkness closing in, and the next I found myself in the gondola.

I had never felt so vulnerable as I did then. I had no strength to fight him, and lay at his feet waiting for my inevitable death. *I tried.* My eyes welled up with tears but

I held them back. I would not die begging. His lips curved into a smile. Not the cold or savage glint of the vampire that I had come to know. His eye contact and tilted head confused me. *Is that admiration?*

"Smile, Huntress, you live another day," he said.

I watched in shock as he left the gondola, picking up his jacket. Was this a game, where he would return and tear out my throat, or throw me back in the canal where I would most likely drown? He stopped and turned around, his face in shadow.

"Why?" I croaked. The grip he'd had, left my throat feeling bruised, and it hurt to speak.

He shrugged. "You look like a drowned rat. Pitiful. Go clean yourself up, face me as a warrior."

Then he was gone. I didn't move, waiting for him to return. When it became apparent that maybe this wasn't some twisted cruelty, I pushed myself up. *I'm alive.* My legs shook and I almost collapsed as I left the gondola. I sucked in sweet air, never appreciating the ability to breathe as much as I did then. I slowly walked home, glad that it was late and barely anyone was around. Those who did walk by glanced at me with curiosity. Soaking wet, I wanted to get out of my clothes and dry off. The chill of the air soaked into the wet clothes, and I shivered.

I arrived back at my house and choked on a sob as the night's events washed over me. My muscles were fatigued as I stripped off my clothes and stepped into the hot shower. Once again, I'd survived another confrontation with one of history's most notoriously brutal vampires. I had been patrolling when I'd recognised him in the gondola with the man. It dawned on me that I had one chance to catch him by surprise, and instinct had kicked in. I'd found myself fighting him in the gondola. Then we ended up in the water.

By rights, I should be dead. I still couldn't believe what had happened. I closed my eyes, replaying every blow, every move, and my thoughts churned. The only way I could kill him would be to catch him by surprise. But even then, I'd have a split second to get the upper hand. He was too quick, too strong. Our first meeting, I'd been so close. The night of the gallery, he'd barely managed to stop me killing him. But tonight, as I leapt into the gondola, I'd let arrogance almost get me killed.

This sight of him standing over me flashed through my mind. The way his body showed through the soaked white tee-shirt. My dreams about him were starting to play tricks on me as lust coursed through me. His kisses, his bite. As we faced each other in the water, the vicious snarl had changed — and for a brief moment, *desire* had reflected through his red eyes. I shook my head. Surely lack of oxygen had caused me to see something that wasn't there. Then he lifted me from the water.

Confused, I finished my shower and wrapped a towel around myself. Staring in the mirror, I tenderly massaged my throat, the telltale signs of deep bruising already showing. I would need ice, and maybe painkillers. I wanted to talk to Sofia, to tell her that once again I'd survived. To share my relief. But when I returned to my bedroom and grabbed my phone, I saw an hour's old message from my father.

<Report.>

I sighed. Nothing like his demands to bring me back down to earth.

<Engaged with enemy. Failed to eliminate.> I responded

and threw my phone on my bed. I grew tired of his messages and requests. My time in Venice had given me freedom from him. I'd always obeyed and followed orders. But he'd sent me here for one reason, and I'd faced death more times than I wanted to think about.

"Fuck you!" My voice was hoarse, and I winced again at the pain in my throat.

The idea that I shouldn't have to follow his orders blossomed, and a lightness in my chest spread out. After my latest near-death experience, a new appreciation for life had awoken.

Carlos had warned me to leave. Once again, I considered doing just that. Torn between wanting to leave, and dismay at the idea of doing what a vampire told me to do, I lay back on my bed. I was tired of people making demands of me, enemies and family alike.

I had survived my father's attempt to kill me, and the vampire's. A slow smile spread across my face, and I started to laugh.

Chapter 36

Cold water dripped down my neck; my hair hung limply in my eyes. I contemplated returning to finish the Huntress off. But each time I stopped, I forced myself not to. I wasn't sure it was thoughts of her death that drew me towards her. My erection pushed against my jeans as I made my way towards the den. I couldn't keep out images of my dreams, nor the kiss at the masquerade, from my head. Nor the way she'd looked at me when my hand was wrapped around her throat. That resignation with a glint of defiance. She'd known she was about to die, and she had accepted it. There was fear, deep within her eyes as she faced her death, and me, head on.

She had a strength about her, a power that I didn't usually see in humans. To continuously face me, and get up with every defeat. To not crumble, but meet my eyes unflinchingly. Until I faced her in the water, she had shown a lack of fear. She had launched herself into battle, leaping into the gondola, and I couldn't lie: that impressed me.

"Damnit, her courage isn't supposed to have this kind of effect on me," I muttered. "She's a Hunter."

But I couldn't shake the look she'd given me. Not just the fear as we glared at each other in the water. I'd granted her a gift by allowing her to live, by pulling her from the canal. As she lay in the gondola, catching her breath, her eyes had clouded over. But the unmistakable relief shining through at me had set off a warmth within my chest. I smiled. It was likely that every breath she drew after that had never tasted so sweet.

Need burst through me, and I growled. As I reached the den, Josef and Andreas speaking in low voices, and the distinctive clicking of a mouse caught my attention. Looking through records as I had asked. I paused, listening.

"No, that family only has sons," Josef read. *Click.* "No, that's a solo hunter. Idiot." The pair laughed. *Click.* "No, they're too old." Josef growled in frustration."This is taking too long! I thought computers were supposed to be fast!" Footsteps indicated Josef was pacing. "We know nothing about her. We could have gone through her family record already without realising."

A chair scraped. "Your short temper isn't going to help," Andreas said. "Why don't you let me look for a while. Go hunting, Josef, you'll feel better."

I walked through the living room where Erik was watching TV. He glanced up at me, taking in my soaked appearance.

"Why are you wet?" Erik asked from the lounge chair. "Fall off a bridge, blood drunk again?"

"That happened *once*!" I declared. "I still maintain they need handrails to prevent people from walking right into the canal."

"They do have handrails; well, most of them do!" Erik laughed. "You just had to pick a bridge that didn't."

I glanced at the TV, grinning at him. On screen was a fight with swords and shields. An old TV show that had driven Erik into furious rants many times over the years. "Why are you watching that show again when the historical inaccuracies infuriate you so much?" I asked.

Matteo and Quinn walked in, the scent of blood indicating they'd just fed.

"Don't get me started on the idiocracy of making a historical show but getting so much wrong in it. As if they were too lazy to research how we actually looked and lived," Erik muttered. "This brings shame to my people." He glanced at Quinn. "Second-hand shame. I am ashamed for all those this is supposed to portray."

"I don't think they counted on real Vikings being around to watch and tear apart their show," Matteo quipped.

"Vikings!" Erik grumbled. "We didn't call ourselves that!"

"That main actor is hot," Quinn added. "Plus, he's Aussie."

"Why is he bald?" Erik raged. "Do they not realise how cold it was? In Norway and the North Sea! And those costumes." He shook his head in disbelief. A character appeared on screen wearing only trousers. "And why is he not fully clothed? No armour?"

I chuckled. "Yet, you still watch it."

Erik smirked. "It still reminds me of home. I can't help myself. It's not as if I can get on a plane and go home. Well, I can, but Norway isn't what it once was. I'm stuck watching TV for any ounce of a reminder." He muted the TV. "You deflected my question."

I groaned. "If you must know, I fell off a gondola." I decided not to tell them about the Huntress.

His laughter thundered from him. Matteo scoffed, but held back a laugh. Quinn stared at me, amusement dancing in her eyes.

"I need a shower," I said. and walked away.

"Something has him all hot and bothered," Quinn said. "Did you see the bulge in his jeans? He's probably going to jerk off in the shower."

"I heard that!" I called back.

"Love you!" she replied.

In my bathroom, I discarded my drenched clothes and stepped into the stream of hot water. Still hard, I gripped my own cock, giving it a few pumps in my hand. I'd had many dreams over the centuries that had left me needing relief. Never over a Hunter, though. I groaned as a new picture ran through my mind. She was on her knees before me, her lips stretched around my cock.

I caught the slow heartbeat close by.

"Erik," I whispered. "I know you're out there."

I needed to distract myself, fill my mind with other visualisations.

"I am," he spoke in a soft voice just outside my bedroom door.

"Would you like to watch?" I asked, pausing my pace.

"I would," he replied, his voice rough with want.

I considered dragging it out, teasing him.

"Then come in," I invited him.

He entered my bathroom, eyes red, filled with need.

"Remove your clothes," I commanded, still holding my cock. "Slowly. Give me a show."

He lifted his tee-shirt, revealing a hard abdomen and chest covered in Norse tattoos. Runes and symbols of gods. They each told stories, or represented a part of his life. The words 'La Voz' were over his heart, like everyone else in the clan. He paused, gazing at me. I started to stroke myself, yearning to touch him. Finally, he removed the tee-shirt and started on his belt. I continued my pace, watching Erik as he undid the buckle, pulling it off slowly.

A deep rumble rose from my chest. He quickened his movements, tearing at his jeans so hard the brass dome flew across the room. Then his jeans were off, showing Erik's long, hard erection.

I turned the water off and spat in my hand, before resuming my slow strokes, keeping my eyes on Erik. His gaze remained on my hand, and he licked his lips. My hand slid over my shaft, and my breathing hitched as warmth unfurled in me, spreading out. I groaned, speeding my strokes. Erik panted, his hand moving down to touch himself.

"Do you want to touch me, Erik?" I asked, needing hands on me. Needing to touch him.

His eyes lifted to mine, pupils dilated.

"Go on," I encouraged.

He moved closer, reaching for me. One warm hand

ran over my torso, the contact sending bursts of pleasure through me. His slender fingers slid over my body, and he panted. I lifted my free hand to trace fingers over his tattoos, starting at his chest, moving lower. Pressure built inside my groin. Erik's other hand pressed against my chest, and he leaned forward, nipping at my jaw. I moaned, the action adding to the orgasm rushing towards me. Our eyes locked as my palm continued to slide.

"Erik," I rasped, my body tensed. Tremors shot through me, and heat. My muscles began to pulse and tighten. "Erik!" I said again, adding a growl to my voice.

He whimpered, his hands pressing harder on my body.

"Finish me off," I commanded.

"Yes, my King." He didn't hesitate, and was on his knees before me.

His hand closed around my base and his lips over the tip of my cock, his mouth warm. I grasped his hair with both hands. His tongue swirled, and he bobbed his head. I thrust forward, pulling him towards me simultaneously, hitting the back of his throat. He slid his mouth over me again. My entire body spasmed, and a jolt passed through me just before I came. The sight of the Huntress on her knees in Erik's place filled my head.

"Fuuuuck," I growled in one long moan as bliss burst through me.

In mid-orgasm, I pulled Erik off me, and lifted him, sinking my fangs into his throat. His hand slid around my back as I drank from him.

Chapter 37

I stood on the roof of the casino, the blood of my recent feed still on my lips when I picked up *her* scent.

"Huntress," I growled.

It had been days since our fight. My dreams had not ceased, and I had woken many times with an erection. Betrayed by my own body, I'd sought to find pleasure in my clan, to replace the taste of her in my dreams with Annika and Lorenzo. Even Erik and Josef had finally opened their bed to me, the feast of humans a delight as we took pleasure from each other. The dreams worsened, and I attempted to drown out the sound of her moans with Celeste's, or even

Quinn's screams.

I had let her live, and I still wasn't sure why. But her nearby presence presented me with another opportunity. So, I followed her, keeping my distance. I would bide my time, waiting for the perfect moment. I wanted to torment her. After all, my madness was because of her. The dreams were an affliction I wanted to be rid of. Only her death would achieve that.

Humans often had the ability to sense danger, and she shivered as if sensing my presence. I backed off, allowing her to feel safe while I stalked her from the shadows.

Remembering what she tasted like, my fangs lengthened. Her heartbeat and the rush of her blood were music to my ears. Her attempts to kill me had come very close, so I needed to eliminate her before she did manage to kill me or those from my clan. So I tracked her, patiently, waiting for her to lead me to where she lived.

She finally reached a house in San Marco. Worried about the location being in Matteo and Quinn's feeding ground, I left the cover of shadows.

"Little *Cazadora,*" I called out softly.

She turned, firing her crossbow at me, but missed. Irritated at her continuously shooting at or stabbing me, I grabbed her by the throat, a deep growl erupting from me, and I knocked her crossbow to the ground.

Instead of anticipated fear, she glared, her fury so strong I could taste it.

"Are you going to kill me or just snarl?" she choked. "I'm starting to feel like you're all growl and no bite."

I frowned, loosening my grip, surprised again at her lack of fear. "Are you mocking me?" This human was strange.

"You're supposed to be this big, menacing vampire who terrorised Europe, and somehow I've survived you every time we cross paths. I think the history records exaggerated who you are," she scoffed.

Something had changed in her. She was emboldened, unafraid.

"You looked me up?" I gave her what I knew to be an arrogant smirk.

I had no doubt I'd come up once or twice in their records. They'd tried more than once to take me down over the centuries. "Have you been thinking about me, then? Looking up your Hunter records to find information on me?" I lowered my voice. "I've been thinking about you, too, sweet Huntress. The taste of your blood, your firm little body. It's enough to get me rock hard." Once again, the memory of my dreams washed over me, and my cock responded. I breathed in deep. "You smell delicious." I let out a low growl.

Her heart skipped and her eyes widened, but she hardened her gaze and forced a knife to my throat. "Do you ever shut up, or do I need to cut out your tongue?"

"Oh, keep going with the threats." I raised my hand, wrapping it around hers and the handle, interested to see if she'd cut my throat. "You know that won't kill me."

"No, but it'll hurt." There was a spark of glee in her eyes.

"Oh, you like causing pain, do you? A woman after my own heart." I applied just a little bit of pressure to the knife at my throat.

"Hold still so I can cut your dead heart out." She kicked me then. Creating distance in an attempt to escape inside. Likely to retrieve more weapons. I went with it.

Before she could open her door, I spun her around and

slammed her into the wall. She grunted in pain. Her eyes blazed with fury, and she glanced down at her crossbow. I kicked it away. "You were amusing at first, but now, you're just annoying." I eyed her throat and leaned forward, fangs lengthening. I was ready to finish her, already hungering for her blood. Too bad Matteo wasn't with me to hear her screams.

Her entire body stiffened. "Keep those things away from me!"

I smiled and snapped at her with my teeth. "It's alright, I'll make it good for you."

She sliced across with the knife, deep. As my blood gushed, she turned her face away to avoid the spray, closing her mouth tight. I grabbed her chin, pulling her face forward. For the first time I noticed gold flecks in her eyes.

"You should look at a man in the eye if you're going to slit his throat." I growled.

The wound in my throat closed, but she'd ruined another tee shirt. Her own clothes had also caught the spray.

She glared. "You're not a man."

I leaned in again, ready to kill. "I'm more man than you can handle."

She struggled uselessly against me as I licked her throat.

"Mmmm, I can taste how sweet you'll be already," I growled in her ear before my fangs slid into her throat.

I'd contemplated whether to make this hurt, and decided I would enjoy seeing her squirm under the effects of my venom. That she'd be too caught up in pleasure to fight her approaching death. Her struggle stopped, and she let out a long moan, the sound vibrating through me. Her knife slipped from her fingers, and instead of trying to push me away, she clutched at my jacket. I let out a moan myself, at the spice of fear in her blood, realising it was also filled with desire, and not from my venom.

I pulled away and met her eyes, our faces inches apart, gazes locked. Her pupils dilated and her heart pounded. Her hands were clutching at my jacket, her breathing ragged.

"You want me, sweet Huntress," I observed with amusement.

We didn't move. Her eyes dropped to my lips. Sheer lust rose up, then my mouth was on hers. She didn't resist me as my tongue slipped past her lips and a shudder passed through her. But then she stiffened, and I pulled back.

"Stop doing that," she snapped.

"You're still holding on to me." I said, nodding to her hands grasping my jacket.

She let go immediately, and I caught a flicker of confusion in her eyes. With a smile, I leaned in again, my hands on the wall on either side of her.

"Don't," she pleaded, sounding unsure.

With the idea to tease her, I planted light kisses across her jaw, trailing down to her neck. Fear flickered in her, and I resisted the urge to bite again, but I also sensed desire. She wanted me to kiss her. Even if she didn't quite know it yet. I barely touched her, my lips brushing lightly across the pulse in her throat. Her blood pulled at me. *What am I doing?*

"You smell so good, sweet *Cazadora*," I murmured, a growl rumbling deep in my chest.

I lifted my head, eyes on her lips. A deep shudder tore through her, and with both hands she grasped the front of my jacket again, pulling me forward. She met my lips with hunger, our kiss hard. This time her tongue pushed forward, not gentle as it met mine. I slid one arm around the small of her back, pulling her tight against my body. With my other hand I grasped the back of her neck.

The smell of her perfume, softness of her lips, flutter of her heart against my chest, all overpowered me at once and I groaned into her mouth, melting against her.

I dropped my hands, only to grab the backs of her thighs, and lifted. She wrapped her legs around my waist, her arms locking around my neck.

I withdrew first, her teeth pulling on my bottom lip. She panted, catching her breath, and the distinct scent of lust clung to her. My fully erect cock strained against my jeans. She moved slightly, grinding against me. Such a subtle movement, but it was enough for me to realise what I was about to do. With a Hunter. She was a beautiful woman, and I'd be blind not to notice that. But there was something more. She knew what I was and still wanted me, so it made me dizzy with need.

"I'm not gentle." I growled into her ear. "I don't know how to be."

Her heart thumped against my chest, its pace quickened. "Why do you talk so much?" she gasped. "Just fuck me."

"A bossy little Huntress, aren't you?" I flashed her a smile. With her legs still around my waist, she reached back with one hand, pulling the door open. I stepped inside, and she started to peel off my jacket. Shrugging it off, I let her strip off my tee-shirt. Her eyes widened at the sight of my tattoo. I tore her tee-shirt over her head. We both fumbled to unzip our jeans, pulling them down enough for what we needed. I pushed her up against the wall, hard, and entered her roughly. She gasped. She pulsed around me and I paused, meeting her eyes.

"Don't stop," she pleaded..

I held on to her gaze, and I thrust deep, rolling my hips. Her arms tightened around my neck as we moved, her motion sending waves of pleasure through me. We moved as one, our movements quick and rough.

Her eyes closed, and she threw her head back. My fangs ached as I stared at her throat. I licked her neck, and she froze, her entire body tensing. My fangs slid in, and she relaxed, the effect of my venom taking hold. As we moved our hips in rhythm, she moaned, and I quickened my pace as I rode closer to my own pleasure. Hers rose through her like waves of pleasure and desire. Warm and surging with need, I growled. I removed my fangs from her throat, licking her blood from the bite marks. The room was filled with thumping and slaps of our bodies and our breaths. Pressure welled up, and I soared higher on pleasure, my body wound tight. Small spasms jolted through me, and I grunted as I came. The sound that erupted from her was not quite a scream, and she clenched around me.

Her entire body was shaking, and I glanced around the room we were in. Her arm moved, and she pointed to a door. I pulled out, and moved through the door, before laying her on the bed, discarding my jeans. She tossed hers on the floor, followed by her shoes. I noticed the crossbow tattoo on her ankle. She lay on her stomach.

I followed her, taking my time to kiss a trail up her back. She shivered. I moved my hands over her, starting with the small of her back, moving up slowly. I dropped a kiss to her as I shifted. I wanted more. More sex, more blood. More of her. But I lay next to her, pulling her to me and wrapped my arms around her body. Warmth blazed from her, the skin-on-skin contact pleasant.

She didn't struggle or throw any looks of hatred at me. Instead, she leaned into my embrace, welcoming it. Her warm breath tickled my chest. I stroked the back of her head, glancing around the room. Nearby, leather padded restraints hung from the wall. A laptop sat on a desk, and suitcases rested in the corner. The bed was a lot smaller than my own. The Huntress's body heaved as she struggled to catch her breath. Her fingers slid back and forth over the wolf tattooed on my chest.

"I recognise your tattoo from one of the nude paintings at the gallery." She tilted her head to gaze into my eyes. "What's it mean?" she asked. "One of your names is The Immortal Wolf."

"Many thought I was a wolf," I replied. "So much so that a pack came looking for me. They made me an honorary member of their pack and named me The Immortal Wolf. The name stuck."

Her hands stilled as she settled into me again. Before long, her breaths became deep. I smiled.

"Have I worn you out?" I asked, not expecting an answer.

I took the time again to examine her bedroom. Mine was larger than her house, with art and items I'd collected over the years, including a portrait of me from Matteo. Hers was bare, reminding me of a cell. Curious at the restraints, I twisted my neck to look into her face. She looked relaxed, with a small smile. Satisfied, I closed my eyes, listening to the thud of her heart.

Chapter 38

Movement on the bed woke me. A human was present, and I resisted the instinct to growl or attack. I'd fallen asleep in the house of the hunter. I opened my eyes and caught her, still naked, typing into her phone. She let out a sigh. I played over what we had done, curious as to why I now lay in her bed instead of celebrating her death with my clan. *What has she done to me?*

"I'm sensing tension," I murmured. "And conflict."

She put down the phone and stared at me in shock.

"I just lied to my father," she said, her voice tight.

Her father, possibly another Hunter. As if I didn't have the threat of an army of Hunters approaching, now I worried that he was here too. "Where is he?"

She gave me a small laugh. "Back home in Spain. It's just me here. He won't come here."

I watched her. "So you didn't tell him that you let a vampire fuck you up against the wall?"

"No." Her voice was barely audible.

"And that's the conflict I sense," I said.

She nodded. "You're a vampire."

I smirked. "I am. Have been for a while. Are you just noticing this?"

"You're my enemy," she said. "I've hated your kind my entire life. This is unnatural."

I laughed. "I can assure you it is perfectly natural. Our desire to kill each other obviously became a desire for each other. It happens." Sitting up, I reached for her face, gripping her chin. "You're not as horrified by the deed as you're trying to show that you are."

"You fed off me. Not just before, but while we were . . ." she stopped, shaking her head.

That part did bother her. "You tilted back your head, baring your throat. To a vampire, that's an invitation. I thought you were indicating for me to bite, to drink."

She sighed again, her eyes darting over my chest, and down my body. "It felt…good," she admitted with reluctance. "The biting and the sex." Her hand rose to where I'd bitten her. My venom had already started to heal the wounds my fangs had left.

"In a day or so, it will be as if it were never there." I brushed my fingers down her throat. "You're surprised that you enjoyed it."

"You're a vampire," she said again.

"You said that," I laughed

With her gaze still on me, I stretched, letting her see every part of me, enjoying the slight intake of her breath.

"Like what you see, do you?" I challenged, and she averted her gaze. "Stare all you like. I don't mind."

"Were you this smug when you were human, or did that come when you were turned?" she blurted.

I lost my smile.

She lifted her eyes to my face. "Did I ask something wrong?"

"I never gave a thought to my life before I died," I admitted. "My life, this life started, and I didn't care about who I was before. The only thing I held onto was my name." It was a good name.

"So, when you woke up..." She stopped.

I gave her a hard look. "Are you sure you want to know this story?"

"Probably not," she said in a low voice. "But I'm curious."

I shrugged. "Alright then. When we wake up, the only thing we know is hunger, and the blood bond to the one who turned us."

I let the memory of my first night as a vampire rise up. It wasn't a bad memory, just not something I gave much thought to.

"Carlos, it's time to wake up." A voice called me from the dark. I opened my eyes to find Gabriela lying next to me, her eyes red. "Finally. Welcome to your new life, Little Killer."

I sat up. A deep hunger clawed at me from within. My mouth felt strange, and I ran my tongue over long, sharp fangs.

She stood and helped me to my feet. I glanced around; we were in a house. A man watched from a dark corner, saying nothing.

"That's Erik," she said.

My tunic was covered in blood. The whisper of a memory of pain rose inside me. I put my hand to my stomach, then my chest.

"You've healed," she told me. "No one can kill you now." She laughed. "But after we're done here, they will certainly try."

I couldn't concentrate on her words, as my attention was drawn elsewhere. My entire being focused on the thumping, and I followed the sound outside, finding myself in a forest.

"Eager to get started already?" She fell into step beside me, and Erik followed us. "Everyone in that village will be terrified when they see you. They already fear you, as it is, after what you did, but you took three arrows. Mortal wounds, and they all saw it."

"What did I do?" I asked. I couldn't remember anything before waking at her command. There was a connection between the two of us.

"You protected someone the villagers saw as an evil creature," she said. "So you got killed for it. The one whose arrows ended your life, I'll save him for you. I believe he was your father."

"Who did I protect?" I asked, the thumping louder, continuing to draw me forward, my fangs aching. I let out a growl.

"You protected me, Little Killer. You sliced someone's throat open, and you're still covered in their blood. I was impressed. So when you fell, I gave you a new life."

We stopped at the edge of the forest, the thumping coming from the village. I stepped forward, but Gabriela stopped me.

"He's already eager," Erik laughed. "Let him go."

"The moment they catch sight of you, they will run screaming," Gabriela said. "Let them run. Fear is intoxicating to us, and you will catch them easily. Make them suffer. Enjoy the kill." She took her hand from my shoulder. "Go, Carlos. Feed. Don't stop

until they're all dead. Then we will leave here, and you will turn your back on who you were as a human. Who you were doesn't matter any more. What matters is who you are now. What you are."

"What am I?" I asked, again running my tongue over the tips of my fangs.

She flashed her fangs at me. "You are a vampire. Only blood will satisfy your hunger, and you'll never again know their weakness. Your days of living among such creatures are over."

I gave in to my hunger, moving towards the village with surprising speed. Gabriela and Erik ran beside me.

"No venom," Gabriela instructed Erik. "These humans tried to kill me. I want them to suffer for it."

"Understood," Erik replied as we entered the village. "Let the screaming and panic begin!"

A woman was walking towards me and stopped in her tracks, looking at me, her mouth open.

"Carlos," she said, taking a step away from me.

"Oh, the lovely bride!" Gabriela laughed. "Take pleasure in the kill, Carlos,"

Gabriela and Erik left me. Something inside the human woman sang to me. Her blood and her fear. I leapt at her, and she let out a scream as I pinned her to the ground. Unable to hold back, I bit in deep, the taste of her blood a pleasure as it burst into my mouth. I nuzzled deeper. When her heart stopped, I released her, looking around. More villagers arrived. I moved fast, tearing into their throats, taking pleasure from the way their blood gushed into my mouth, down my chin. Many screamed. None could outrun me as I gave chase. The village was alive with fear and screams, and I enjoyed every moment of it.

Two men fell to their knees before me.

"Please Carlos, stop this madness," the younger one begged.

"Run," I told him. "Then I'll show you madness."

I was intoxicated on blood, fear, and the strength that came from drinking from them. I felt powerful. The older of the men grabbed the younger and pulled him to his feet. "That's not our brother any more. He has been cursed. Run, Jullian."

I laughed as he stood between me and his younger brother. "You want to die first, then?" I asked.

He shook his head. "I'm sorry for what our father did, Carlos. I'm sorry this happened to you."

In response, I moved past him, tearing into the younger human. Thrilled by the screams that rose from him, I stopped when a hand touched my back. I lifted my head, turning with a growl. The older human stood there, his hands trembling.

"Carlos, he was your brother," he told me. His eyes darted from me to the body beneath me. A tear slid down his cheek. "He was my brother," he whispered. "You killed our brother."

Silence passed between us, in which more screaming and the scent of blood filled the air.

"My brother? I don't know who you are," I said. "Nor him." I circled him and leaned in, breathing deep. "Mmmm, I know I'm going to enjoy feeding from you. She was right. That scent, it's intoxicating."

He tried to run, and a growl tore from me. I moved fast, taking us both to the ground. Something in me wanted to draw it out. To bring pleasure in the feed. I lowered my head, licking his throat as he struggled under my weight.

"Carlos," Gabriela said from behind me. "I have brought you a gift, as soon as you're done with that."

I glanced up. She and Erik were covered in blood, and I realised the screams had stopped. The village was silent. A human stood by her side, eyes vacant.

"Father! Run!" the human below me cried out.

"He can't," Gabriela laughed. "I've instructed him not to move unless I say so. I don't think you're going anywhere, either."

I lowered my head, meeting the human's eyes. The terror I saw there reached out to me. Without another word, I tore into his throat, groaning at the welcome blood.

"He's a real animal," Erik murmured to Gabriela. "I can't wait to see more. You were right about him."

I finished feeding and climbed to my feet, studying the man that Gabriela had brought me.

"Do you know him?" she asked me. "Is there any familiarity when you look upon him?"

I shook my head.

She grabbed him and turned him to face her. "On your knees," she said.

He knelt.

"Now, look upon your son. Look at what he has become."

The man looked up at me with disgust. "My son is dead. That thing is an animal with no spark of humanity in him."

"He's the one who killed you," Gabriela said to me. "He shot you with arrows. If I hadn't helped you, you'd be dead. Perhaps you'd like to repay the deed."

I approached the man. There was no fear, only contempt as he glared back.

"He's not afraid," I said to Gabriela.

"Then give him a reason to be afraid, Little Killer," she laughed. "Make it hurt, draw it out. He'll either scream, or beg you to kill him."

"I'll do neither, Demon," he argued.

"Oh, foolish human. You're already on your knees." She put

her hand on my shoulder. "Make him suffer. Then we'll leave here. I'll take you to see my King. I think he'll like you."

"Will we feed like this again?" I asked. "I never want this to end."

Erik chuckled.

"It's intoxicating, isn't it?" she turned her focus on the man kneeling before me. "Kill him, and we'll seek out the next village.

"So you slaughtered your entire village?" The Huntress asked in a quiet voice, bringing me back.

"I did," I confirmed.

"Your father? Do you regret killing him, and your brothers?" she asked.

The face flashed before me. A man I felt no connection to and whose death I had enjoyed. It had lasted for hours. "No. I was only doing what was in my nature to do. He killed me, and I'd be dead if it weren't for Gabriela."

She met my eyes, a look in their depths that I recognised. She was struggling to understand how I could kill my own blood.

I paused. "Even when I regained my human memories, I didn't grieve him, and I held no remorse for his death. For any of their deaths. After all, he'd killed me. So it was only natural that I be the one to end his life. And my brothers.'"

I didn't tell her that the moment I'd regained my memories, I'd grieved my brothers. The only good memories I had as a human were of the three of us.

She'd gone quiet, her mind churning, but I couldn't grasp any clear thoughts.

"I did warn you that you probably didn't want to hear it," I muttered.

"You did." She wouldn't meet my eyes.

The change in her mood reminded me of what we both were. Vampire and Huntress. I didn't belong in her bed. *What am I doing here?* Those damn dreams had created lust for her that I shouldn't have.

"What did you think, that you'd talk to a vampire about his past and it would be all sunshine and roses?" I snapped. "Don't try to humanise me to justify what happened tonight. You know what I am. This was a fun night, but I think it's time I left. Your humanity is suffocating."

I climbed around her, leaving the bed, asking myself why I wasn't just killing her. After all, the next time she saw me, she'd probably try to kill me again.

"It's a lot to get used to," she explained. "We're supposed to be enemies and I…It's a lot to get used to. I still don't know why…"

"Okay, so next time we cross paths, you tell me whether you want to kill me or kiss me." I flashed her a smile. "Although I wouldn't mind the kissing again." I cast my eyes over her naked body. "Or the fucking." I pulled on my jeans.

I walked into the other room where the rest of my clothes lay. My tee-shirt was blood-soaked, and I didn't feel like putting it back on. I left it on the floor. As I was pulling my leather jacket over my shoulders, she stood at the doorway, a bathrobe pulled around her.

"I read your record," she said. "You're among the most feared in the world."

I smiled in satisfaction. "Quite a colourful collection, I imagine."

"You're the reason we exist. Hunters," she said.

I stepped towards her, looking down. "Well, I suppose I

am." I laughed at the memory. "We were feared and lived for the kill. Not many survived me. It was the ferals we created that drew the attention of your ancestors. They had a savagery that we couldn't control." Our nature and blood thirst in creatures that killed all they came across. Beings that woke up, never to regain their human memories again. Nothing but bloodthirsty killers. I had turned many in my day, until their destruction.

I pulled her into a short kiss, again asking myself what I was doing. I wanted more of her. It was definitely time to leave before I gave in to my own lust again.

"Do you still kill?" she asked.

Her questions were starting to become annoying. I lost my smile as I turned around again. "Your interrogation is over, beautiful Huntress."

I left her there, shaking my head in disbelief. Instead of killing her as I had wanted to, I'd fucked and bared my dark soul to her.

"What are you doing, Carlos?" I grumbled.

Chapter 39

The vampire, Carlos, shut the door behind him. I glanced around the room, my cheeks hot as I stared at the dent in the wall where he'd slammed into me. My body ached both from the sex and the wall. I surprised myself that the pain was more pleasurable than painful. *What am I doing? I should go after him, finish what I'd been sent here for.* I opened the door, finding my crossbow on the ground where he'd kicked it, and my knife nearby.

I couldn't deny I'd been attracted to him since the first time I saw him, and being Spanish only added to his appeal. But a fucking vampire? As I picked up my weapons, I glanced around for him. There was no sign that he'd stuck around. Memory of it all washed over me. His lips were warm and soft, but his kiss was hungry, demanding. Just the memory of it and my pussy throbbed.

I'm not gentle. His red eyes had burned into mine as the both of us realised what was about to happen. *I don't know how to be.* A small voice inside me had whispered '*I don't want gentle.*' I shivered as the words replayed themselves in my mind, and what I'd said in response. I went back inside, exhausted. I had betrayed myself, my family and every human who had died at the hands of a vampire. Of *that* vampire. I dropped the crossbow and knife on the table.

Changing into training clothes, I prepared to have a workout and readied the punching bag. I needed to shift my focus from Carlos. I needed to push out the sight of his naked body in my bed. His lean body, hard against mine, his muscles, the feel of his cock inside me, driving deep as I moaned, my legs wrapped around him.

I let out a frustrated sound as I started to punch. I put all my strength into the blows. Left, right, jab, jab, uppercut. I went through every combo I could until my muscles burned. My heart raced, sweat lined my skin, and my breathing was fast. I stopped, staring at the bag as I caught my breath. I felt better and started to remove the gloves and wraps from my hands.

I made my way towards the bathroom, to shower.

Hot water cascaded down on me, and my muscles started to relax. I couldn't stop the vision of what we'd done replaying in my head. Each time I pushed one image out, the next forced its way in. My skin blazed where he'd touched me, his hands on my thighs, my ass, my hips. His mouth on mine, my throat as he —

"Stop!" I groaned, banging my head on the shower wall.

Fuck, I needed a drink. I needed to sleep so I wouldn't have to think about any of this.

I couldn't even blame him. I wanted it. *He must have compelled me.* I couldn't make myself believe that, though. *It was his venom; I would never want that.* I left the shower, wincing as I walked back to my bedroom. Bruises were starting to form on my back, as well as where he'd gripped me.

He'd wanted to kill me, there was no doubt about that. I'd seen the dangerous glint in his eyes, the bloodlust as he'd bitten into me. In that instant, I'd thought I was about to die and knew I could do nothing to stop it. But instead of the expected pain he'd promised me, desire and pleasure had overwhelmed me.

"Stop thinking about it," I muttered to myself.

Finally, too exhausted to do anything else, I fell onto my bed. It was cold, but *his* scent lingered. I breathed in leather and cinnamon. Not what I expected a vampire to smell like. I stared at the ceiling, his scent still overwhelming. I hadn't wanted him to leave and had actually felt disappointed when he walked through the door.

"Fuck."

I started to wish I hadn't been sent here. But it was my own fault. I closed my eyes as the memory of being sent to Venice played itself again.

My father paced in front of me, and his fury was unmistakable. "Your hesitation got your mother killed. Explain to me what was going through your head. Only those on their first hunt hesitate."

I could only look at the ground as he reprimanded me. Anything

I said would only enrage him further. He wasn't really interested in any answer I'd give, anyway. He was grieving and angry. My guilt was already crushing. The entire family had been tracking a vampire, and she got through our defences because of me. I still didn't know what had happened.

"Are you going to answer me, or are you just going to stare at the floor?" He'd stopped pacing and ranting and was glaring at me.

"I don't know how it happened," I mumbled.

"I'm sending you away," he informed me.

Panic swept through me. "What?"

"You have to hunt alone, to learn not to hesitate," he said.

Hunt alone? We never hunted alone. Vampires were too strong for us. Dread turned my blood to ice. He was sending me away to die. There was no way I'd survive a solo hunt.

"But —"

"I don't want to hear it. I have an easy job for you, I've received word that there might be a vampire in Venice, and another one near Athens. I'll give you the choice."

He was letting me choose where to die. I fought back tears.

"Padre, no." My sister Sofia's eyes were wide, fearful. "That's not a punishment; that's a death sentence."

"Silence.," he snapped. "Unless you have anything useful to add."

Sofia stared at me. "There's no way the vampire near Athens is by itself. That's where Dimitrios and his clan hunt."

Dimitrios was a brutal vampire who was very territorial and didn't take kindly to Hunters. He killed his own kind when they angered him. Sofia was right. "Venice," I agreed with a heavy heart.

"Fine. You leave in the morning. Pack your things." He didn't

wait for my reply and left.

"You'll be okay. I'm certain it's only one," Sofia said. "Get the lay of the land, try to catch the vamp in mid-hunt."

"If I don't?" My hands shook.

"Diego is working on something new that may incapacitate them momentarily. Once he's got it worked out, I'll make sure to send you any updates." She wrapped me in a hug. Three years older than me, she'd taken a beating from vamps and survived. I could only hope I would, too.

"Sof?"

"Yeah."

"Do you blame me?" This time I didn't hold the tears back, letting them slide down my cheeks.

She took a minute to answer. "No," she said finally. "We die in hunts all the time; it's just your bad luck that it happened today."

"I can't even be here for her funeral," I almost sobbed.

She lay her hand over my heart. "She knows you'll be here in spirit. May she watch over you for your hunt. Be careful, Millie. They're starting to get aggressive. Diego thinks something is building." She tightened her hug as if it were the last time we would see each other. Maybe it was. Then without a word, she left me alone.

Alone. I would spend the rest of my days alone. I would probably die alone, with a vampire ripping out my throat. I braced myself as I started to pack clothes, weapons, and my laptop. Now was not the time to focus on such things. Such thoughts would get me killed. I took a deep breath. Maybe I could somehow succeed in the hunt, but would my father let me come home? I wondered if I should try to complete the job and just stay in Venice. Or go somewhere else, start afresh.

Chapter 40

I rubbed the dried blood on my throat from where the Hunter had slit it. My bare chest under my jacket would have drawn a few stares if people had been awake so early. Not far from the Huntress's house, I came across Quinn feeding. Hearing my approach, she turned, not letting go of the human, one eye on me. Her gaze darted over my jacket, taking in the missing tee-shirt. She let her meal go, giving him a seductive smile.

"Thank you," she said. "You can go now. You went for a walk and got lost. You never saw me." The man walked away as if nothing happened, already forgetting Quinn.

"I still don't understand why you thank them." I muttered. "It's not like they know what you're thanking them for. You don't see humans thanking cows or sheep."

"I like to have good manners," she said, wiping away the blood from the corner of her mouth, licking it from her fingers. "Something left over from when I was human, I suppose." She pointed at my chest and neck. "So, what happened? Did you forget to put on a tee-shirt when you left the den? You look like someone slit your throat, and you smell like sex."

"You should be careful feeding in this area." I warned, avoiding her question.

She tilted her head and moved quickly towards me, placing a hand on my chest. Pressing her nose to my abdomen, she breathed in, moving up to my chest, lifting her eyes to mine, her lips lifting into a small smile.

"I know that scent," she said. "She's the one who slit your throat, isn't she."

I couldn't contain my smile. "She is."

Quinn grabbed my chin, sniffing my breath. "You tasted her." She frowned. "Is she dead?"

I'd been dreading this. "No."

Her eyes narrowed. "You promised us, Carlos. That you would drain her dry, and Matteo would be present for her screams." She breathed in again. "What are you doing? This is a dangerous game, even for you."

My hand struck fast, fingers gripping her throat. "Do not challenge me," I roared. "Let me worry about the Huntress. I'll do what I need to."

Her eyes widened. I'd never shown her my rage before, and although her fear did satisfy, shame came with it. I'd seen enough of Gabriela's rage to know what kind of King I didn't want to be. But I needed to remind her that while she and Matteo often shared my bed, I was still her King. I released her.

"Yes, my King," she replied and dropped to her knee, head bowed. "Forgive me. We saw her come close to killing you. I'm scared for you. We can't lose you, Carlos."

Her voice cracked on my name.

I grabbed her chin, roughly pulling it up to bring her eyes to mine. "Hunters have tried for centuries to put me in the ground. I promised you all I'd take care of it, and I will. Don't question me again."

She gazed up at me. Had it not been for me raising my voice and choking her, I would have pulled her to her feet. But after my time in the Huntress's bed, I wasn't in the mood to be tender. I'd given in to a lust that had been building, which I'd tried to deny. To ignore. The dreams, waking up hard, trying to distract myself, only to fuck the Huntress up against the wall, almost desperately. Now I just wanted to walk, to clear my mind. To be rid of such desires. Yet a small part of me wanted it again. The temptation to march back to her house and fill her as I pressed her against the wall again. Or use those restraints on her.

I released Quinn, turning away. Damnit, I was hard again. I growled.

"I need you to leave this feeding ground for a while. You and Matteo must go to Castello," I ordered, adjusting myself through the jeans.

"That's Lorenzo and Annika's feeding ground," she complained as she rose to her feet. "I don't like sharing territory, and I know Matteo won't be a fan of that either."

"Just do what I ask," I warned, turning to give her a hard stare.

She bowed her head again, submitting to my order. "Yes, Carlos."

She walked beside me in silence.

"Where's Matteo?" I asked. "Don't the two of you usually feed together?"

"Not always," she said. "He's at the gallery."

"Go home, the sun will be up soon," I instructed, and I left her.

I headed towards the gallery. It was a warm night, but I zipped up my jacket.

I found Matteo on the roof opposite his gallery, arms folded as he frowned.

"You smell like sex," he commented, not bothering to look up at me. "At least someone's had a good night."

We stood in silence watching the gallery. There were now guards at the locked doors. I recognised their faces: they were local humans who knew of us, worked for us. We paid them a lot of money for their silence, with the promise that they, and their families would never be fed on.

"You didn't clear that with me," I muttered.

"It's my gallery," he replied. "I needed security." Finally he turned to meet my eyes. "She walked right in. She knows it's mine, so I'm sorry, but I wanted to protect it. And anyone inside. This damn war is about to spill over onto the streets. They're supposed to keep hidden, as we are."

I glared. "You're the one who almost exposed us all, Matteo. You let her provoke you. You're smarter than that."

His jaw was tight, and his eyes turned red. "I can smell her on you. Is that your way of trying to kill her?"

"It was an unforeseen weakness," I admitted. "Things got a little heated."

His grin was savage. "If it were me, I would have drained her dry during the act." He crossed his arms. "If you were in need of sex, you could have come to us. But to be with a Hunter…" His lip curled in disgust.

I couldn't blame him. If he were the one standing before me smelling like sex, with the scent of a Hunter on him, I would have reacted far worse.

"I found this. by the way." He held up what looked like a speaker. "There were ten in total spread around the gallery. Andreas said it's likely what she used that night."

I took it from him. "Where are the rest?"

"At the bottom of the canal. Andreas asked that we keep one so he could have a look at it."

Andreas was a four-hundred-year-old Austrian who had taken an interest in studying technology and had created security systems for us at the villa.

I sat down on the edge of the building, Matteo taking his place next to me. "I know your opening was ruined, and for that I'm sorry," I said.

"Actually, I had some large donations and impressive reviews." He smiled. "And my anonymity has only added more interest." His smile widened. "Also, there are humans from outside Venice who are offering to pay a lot of money for the private viewing of the nude exhibition. It won't be long before vampires from other clans start to ask me to paint them to set up their own variations of what we've done."

I watched him, his joy. "Do you regret that you have to remain in the shadows?"

He shook his head. "No, because in twenty, fifty, even a hundred years' time, I'll be able to stand here as we are now and look down on a gallery with my art in it, alongside artists who hopefully would have gone on to live their dreams." He turned back to the gallery. "I've been contacted by other vampires who want private midnight showings, some who want their own art in it." He laughed. "Not bad for a feral."

"You have to stop doing that," I told him. "Stop referring to yourself as a feral."

"Am I not? Even Nico called me a feral," he pointed out.

"I think you've lived in the shadow of what ferals were far too long." I pointed to the gallery. "Ferals didn't paint magnificent works of art, nor own galleries. They were not the second in command to vampire clans. Look at how the others trust you, and that you haven't killed in years."

"Because of Quinn," he muttered.

"I think if you were truly perceived as a feral, like the ones I created, the Elders would have killed you. Ferals had no control and lacked the awareness to maintain any. If they were around today, vampires would have been exposed with the technology humans have." I said. "You have a feral nature, but you're not *a feral*. There is a difference."

We sat in silence, listening to the city as it woke up.

"Let's go home," I said. "I need a shower to get the smell of Huntress off me."

He glanced at me. "Did you taste her?"

I leapt from the building, absorbing the impact, Matteo landing beside me a second later.

I laughed. "Of course I did."

His eyes blazed, crimson and smug. "Then don't be surprised if she comes looking for you, wanting more. Your venom is potent right now. Chances are, she's already addicted."

I said nothing as we walked. It wasn't the idea of the Huntress seeking me out that kept me silent. It was that I wanted her to.

Chapter 41

Another King was coming to visit. I sent Lorenzo, Annika, and Matteo to meet King Giuseppe and escort him into my city. I'd known him from the vampire war, so we were on friendly terms, but it was still difficult to let someone into my territory. It wasn't just Venice I felt protective over, it was the humans. I had rules to maintain and didn't want Giuseppe feeding off locals.

"Carlos!" Giuseppe's voice boomed across the villa. "I'm hurt that you didn't meet me yourself!"

I grinned. "Why do what my clan can do for me? You should know, I have rules here."

He eyed Matteo. "No feeding off the locals. Your second has already given me a hard word about that. Do we at least get to enjoy a drink? We came a long way."

I motioned for him to lead the way. "How about we get down to business first."

We moved into a meeting room, his second with him, and Matteo at my side. Our clan watched us as we walked past.

"So, what brings you here?" I asked.

He took his time to answer, and I figured he and his second were bonded, probably talking in private.

"Have you seen the Elders recently?" he asked.

I stiffened. "Yes. What about them?"

"Sia's as seductive as ever." The scent of desire rose off him. "That woman can do whatever she wants to me, and I'd just lay back and let her."

I'd seen first-hand what her habits were like in bed and smirked. "She is something." I motioned at Matteo with my thumb. "She had her eye on him. Turns out he's from her bloodline."

Giuseppe shot a glance at Matteo. "Lucky man." He returned his attention to me. "The Hunters are gathering, and I believe the Elders are trying to start another war."

I leaned forward. "What happened when they were in San Marino?"

"I got blood drunk." He pressed his hands together. "Nico offered a blood bond."

"And?" I prompted.

His eyes darted to Matteo and then towards the door, his heartbeat erratic. "Can your clan hear us?"

"Don't worry about my clan, worry about me," I stated. "What happened?"

He frowned. "Why do I get the feeling you already know? Venom, frenzy, and a dead human. Yet here I sit, still alive."

"Here you sit," I agreed.

"Would you join them if a war did break out?" Giuseppe's eyes were watchful now.

He'd been a General to Nico in the war and was a cunning vampire, often fishing for loyalty.

I didn't hesitate. "Of course I would"

He lowered his voice. "They did say that they'd have the Killer, the Feral and The Siren soon enough, and that they can't lose."

Matteo growled, and I held up my hand to silence him. "What did you say?" I demanded.

Giuseppe pointed at me. "The Killer." He pointed to Matteo. "The Feral. And the Siren. Whoever that is. Didn't sirens die out?"

'They know?' Matteo roared through our bond *'How do they know?'*

I turned to Giuseppe. "Leave, now."

His smile faded. "Excuse me?"

I stood. "Why did you come here, old friend? To test my loyalty?"

He looked offended. "I came to see if we would be brothers in arms again. I heard you have a bit of a Hunter problem at the moment. I took one down just last week. Olivia finished one off a few months ago. An entire family was tracking her, and she managed to compel one of them just enough to escape. Took one of them out when she did."

I frowned. "Olivia doesn't kill, neither does her clan; so, why were Hunters after her?"

"This is war, old friend. It will be bloody, it will be glorious.

This time, we won't lose." He shot a smile at me, and it faded quickly. "So?"

I could feel Matteo's eyes on me as I sat down again, leaning forward. "They killed Gabriela, and her entire clan in Australia," I growled. "If it comes to war, I will relish the chance to kill Hunters again."

He nodded. "Good. Let me know if you need help with your Hunter problem. I can help."

"That won't be necessary. Now leave," I ordered.

His eyes hardened. "Not without a drink. We travelled all this way."

I nodded to Matteo, and he left.

Giuseppe eyed me. "So, do I get to meet this siren of yours? She must be really something as a vampire. The Elders seemed to think the three of you would be a powerful trio."

"How do they know about her?" I demanded.

He had lost all traces of a smile as he met my hard stare. "They've known for a while. They aren't happy that you've tried to hide her from them."

My chest tightened. I'd put my entire clan, especially Quinn, at risk by not telling the Elders about her. "How?" I repeated.

"Gabriela told them when you left Australia. You've had twenty years to tell the Elders about who was in your clan. You have someone powerful enough to take down an Elder. I'd be careful, if I were you."

"But you said they *want* her," I reminded him.

"They want all three of you." He smiled at me. "Don't you remember how it was before? No laws. How feared we were? The thrill of the kill." Pure glee shone through his eyes.

"I remember. I remember you were the most bloodthirsty of us all. You were magnificent."

Matteo returned with humans that we'd taken for the meeting. Giuseppe was on his feet in an instant with a savage growl. His second didn't hesitate. I grabbed a human and grinned at Matteo before letting my fangs sink into her throat. She didn't have the spice of fear, but she'd do. Her reaction to my venom was almost immediate, the humans around us moaning, mine grinding against me.

The Hunter flashed before my eyes, moaning in ecstasy as I slammed her against the wall. I pulled away from the human, frowning. I could almost feel her against my body. I let the human go, and she watched me. Compelled, she wouldn't leave until released.

Giuseppe finished and met my eyes. "Here's to the Elders," he said.

I couldn't smile after what my mind had just pulled on me. "You've had your drink, now leave."

He smirked. "You always were territorial." His eyes took a faraway expression. "Do you ever wonder, if you hadn't met Gabriela…"

"No," I cut him off, confused by his change in subject. "What-ifs are for humans, not us."

He moved with speed and pushed Matteo against the wall, his second moving with him. I reacted fast, trying to pull him away, but he simply held his hand out, grabbing me by the throat.

"Do you realise how much stronger vampire blood makes us?" he challenged in a savage voice. Matteo struggled, growling. "Stop struggling," Giuseppe ordered.

When Matteo stopped, Giuseppe leaned forward. *He can*

compel other vampires not of his clan? I glared.

'Call Quinn in here now.' I told Matteo. *'He wants to meet the siren; get her in here.'*

It wasn't long before the door opened, and her song filled the room. A humming that I'd heard from her mother when Gabriela had attacked. I'd experienced the effects myself. Her vampirism strengthened her abilities as a siren. And as expected, Giuseppe and his second fell to their knees, hands pressed to their ears.

"Did he drink?" I asked Matteo.

He nodded, eyes flashing red.

I stood over Giuseppe. "You think you can attack my second? On my territory? I ought to kill you right now!" Fury lashed through me, dark and overpowering. I resisted the urge to tear out his throat. "You want a war, but are you sure you want to start one with *me*?! *I am* The Killer, and for that, your second will pay with his life."

Giuseppe's eyes moved towards the vampire that knelt beside him before returning to mine. He sneered. "You wouldn't dare."

"Every vampire in Venice is under my protection. To attack a member of my clan, is an attack on me. Therefore, I am within my rights to retaliate," I declared.

I knew I'd be starting something, but anger wrapped around me, and all I cared about in that moment was to protect my clan. He'd attacked Matteo and fed from him without my approval. I punched into Marco's chest, bones cracking. A howl rose from Giuseppe, one of pain and sorrow. Since Marco couldn't move while my hand was wrapped around his heart, fear flickered through his eyes.

"Giuseppe," Marco pleaded.

"Carlos, please." Giuseppe had desperation in his eyes.

I tore out Marco's heart, and a roar rose from Giuseppe, his eyes crimson, fangs bared as he tried to attack me. Once again, Quinn brought him to his knees.

"She can kill you." I growled. "Test it if you will. You're lucky I don't."

He whimpered. "Stop, please."

I nodded to Quinn who stopped, then turned to Matteo. "Your enemy fell by my hand, do what you want with his heart." I threw the heart at Matteo, and he caught it.

He grinned at me. "I think we should give it to Giuseppe as a reminder of what his arrogance cost him today."

I knelt and grabbed Giuseppe by the chin. "I welcomed you into my territory, I was a gracious host. You abused that. The only one who can feed from any of my clan is me. You are no longer welcome here."

"If you have any thoughts to bring your clan here to retaliate, you will be met with force." Matteo said, and the rest of the clan arrived, surrounding him. "We may be a small clan, but remember who makes up one third of us." He gave Giuseppe the heart I had torn from Marco's chest. "Lorenzo, Andreas, Annika, help me escort our *guests* from the territory."

"I'm coming, too," Quinn said. "In case he tries anything again."

As they led him past, I grabbed his arm. "You brought this on yourself, Giuseppe. I showed mercy today by not killing you. Insult me again and I'll remove your head and send it back to your clan."

He glared as he left the room, and I wondered if I'd made a mistake. It was likely he'd want retaliation.

"Celeste, Erik, clean up this mess," I commanded.

Chapter 42

I watched the Huntress from the shadows. She returned to my territory, as she had the last few nights, but it merely looked like she was trying to *find* me, not hunt me. Her walk took her past many of my favourite feeding spots, but she barely looked. I was unsettled that I had taken to following her, watching from the shadows, yet I couldn't resist.

"I know you're there," she muttered under her breath in Castellano. "Show yourself."

I fought the urge to step forward, to reveal myself to her. I wasn't sure if I was in the mood to fight her or fuck her.

Maybe both. There was nothing quite like working through aggression with aggressive sex. I would need to be careful if I ended up down that road again. I'd been foolish to let myself fall asleep in her bed when she could have easily killed me.

She turned around, and it almost looked as if she were disappointed as she searched the shadows for me.

"Stop it, Camila; the only reason you should be hoping to find a vampire is to kill it," she said to herself.

Camila. Her name itself had an allure to it. Elegant. Her words resonated with me. She was as at odds as I was with our encounter. Again, the temptation to leave behind my place in the shadows battled against the impulse to rip her throat out. Thoughts of a war between our people should have filled me with joy. Instead, I found myself watching her, entranced. She didn't just have beauty, she had an inner strength, and underneath her hatred of vampires, there was a guilt, a pain that she struggled to keep at bay.

I wanted to strike down whatever caused her pain. To hold her in my arms and whisper her name. For her to moan mine. I growled when my fangs extended, the combination of desires to kill or fuck her were clearly affecting me in a way that awakened my hunger. She twirled the knife in her hand, and her eyes widened.

"I can't see you, but growling from the dark is a certain way to tell me you are there." The hope in her voice almost won me over. Almost pulled me towards her. "Carlos," she whispered my name. "What have you done to me?"

I couldn't stay. The way she spoke my name, and longing in her question set off an ache in my chest I was unaccustomed to. I left her behind, returning to the villa. If the clan knew what I'd done, they'd deem me a failure. *Why couldn't*

I kill the Huntress?

"What have you done to me?" I murmured, repeating her words.

"Carlos, we have a problem." Annika approached with urgency.

"Calm down, take a breath. Then tell me," I requested.

"There's a fight. Lorenzo and Matteo," she informed me.

"What the hell could they be fighting over?" I demanded.

"Matteo and Quinn have moved into our territory,"she said.

Shit! I forgot to tell them that I'd moved Quinn and Matteo.

"Show me where they are." I sighed.

Annika led me through the city to where Lorenzo and Matteo were locked in a fight, deep growls rose from them. They were both bleeding, and Matteo tore into Lorenzo's shoulder before being thrown. He barely hit the ground before he was on his feet, charging at Lorenzo again. He snapped his teeth, a warning, right before he tried to rip out Lorenzo's throat.

"Stop." I commanded.

They couldn't disobey my voice. I hated using it, as Gabriela had abused it often. The two of them stopped immediately.

"Come here." They were in front of me glaring at each other. Quinn stood nearby. "You, too." I told her, and she obeyed. "Kneel." The three of them knelt at my feet. "Lorenzo, I told them to come here. Their territory is not safe right now." I turned my gaze to Matteo. "While I have done so, you two will respect Lorenzo. This is his and Annika's territory. I did not send you here for you to claim their territory as your own. Am I understood?"

"Yes, Carlos," Matteo and Quinn chorused.

Lorenzo scowled.

"Lorenzo, I should have told you. But I need to know everyone is safe, especially my second. Break your territory in half if you have to, just figure it out. No fighting. Do you understand me?" I glared down at him.

"Yes, Carlos." Lorenzo said.

"All three of you are bound to the den tonight." I decided. "Fighting in the open like that? You risked exposing us. Have you forgotten we have a Hunter in Venice? She's already invaded Matteo's, and my territory; don't give her a reason to come here, too."

Quinn frowned then, and I glared. Her eyes lowered and she submitted, recognising my authority with a bowed head.

"Go home, now," I told them.

They left, Annika with them. I focused my senses for any human heartbeat to ensure they hadn't been seen. A gasping breath not far away caught my attention. I sought out the human, finding a woman hiding. She caught sight of me as I advanced towards her, and the scent of fear rose from her.

"Please don't hurt me," she begged. "I won't tell anyone."

"Shhhh, I know you won't." I used a gentle voice on her to calm her. The last thing I needed was for her to scream and draw attention. I slowed my movements to not startle her. I caught her eye. "Come here. You're okay."

Her gaze was on me, unable to look away as she moved towards me, her fear fading. I held my arms out, and she walked into my embrace, her body small in my arms. I caged her in, waiting for her to calm down.

"No one will hurt you," I soothed. "You were just in the

wrong place at the wrong time."

"Vampires are real," she whispered to me. "They're real."

"Yes, we are," I agreed.

She started to tremble. "Are you going to kill me?" Her fear spiked again.

I was focusing on her throat, my fangs lengthening. "No, I'm just going to make it all go away."

She took in a deep breath. "You smell good."

I grinned against her neck. "So do you." I licked her throat.

She gasped a little as my fangs pierced her flesh, until my venom released into her veins. The delicious sound she made vibrated against my chest, and I fought back the need to tear so her blood would gush. She started to unbuckle my belt, and again, Camila's face flashed before me.

I tensed, releasing the human and lifting her chin to pull her mind into mine. "Go home," I instructed her. "Forget what you saw here. Vampires don't exist, we're nothing more than monsters in books and movies."

"Vampires don't exist," she repeated my words and turned away.

As I watched her, frustration surged in me. Twice now I had been interrupted in feeding by that damn Hunter. My mind was betraying me, as was my body.

Chapter 43

I woke up from another dream about Carlos, wet and panting. Always the same, every night, him pinning me against the wall, his fangs sinking into my throat as he slid into me. I had never imagined that the effects of his bite, his venom would be this powerful. Not just the bite, but the memory of the sex itself sent ripples of desire through my body. Always leaving me wanting the real thing.

"Goddammit." I muttered, climbing out of bed. "Fucking vampire."

I needed fresh air, to clear my head, to move. What I'd done…what I'd allowed to happen went against everything

I had been taught. I wanted more, and I shouldn't have been obsessing over such a creature. In the last week, my patrols were only for the sake of being honest with my father about doing so. My reports weren't as routine as they should be, and my father's annoyance showed through in his messages. As I walked, I somehow knew Carlos was in the dark, following me. Watching me. But he never showed himself, leaving me disappointed and confused.

I walked for half an hour, the air cool against my hot skin. My spine tingled, but I didn't look around for him. I would only see him if he wanted me to. I was being stalked by a vampire King, and I appreciated that he only watched me, and hadn't tried to kill me. I could only hope he was as obsessed as I was over our tryst.

I stopped near the Grand Canal. Most of the gondolas were empty, the canal eerily silent. I stared out over the water, not really seeing anything. Finally, I gave up, and turned around to go home. There he was, watching me under a street lamp, his usual smirk in place.

"Do you wear anything else?" I asked, my mind mush.

His eyes searched my hands. "I don't see any weapons, what are you doing?"

"I needed to go for a walk. I couldn't sleep. Why were you following me?" I wasn't ready to tell him he was the reason I couldn't sleep.

In an instant, he stood in front of me, and I had to tilt my head slightly to meet his eyes. I forced down the urge to recoil, to step away from him. The speed of a vampire unnerved me. His eyes razed down my body, stopping between my legs.

"You smell aroused." His smug grin was unmistakable. As

if he knew the cause of it.

"You didn't answer my question," I replied, hoping to deter that topic.

"I've been following you for the last week," he confirmed my suspicion. "Your attempts to actually find me have been noticeably pathetic. Surely you were trained better than that. I have to admit I'm somewhat disappointed."

"You and my father have something in common," I grumbled.

His smirk disappeared then, his eyes on mine with an intensity that sent flutters to my stomach. I couldn't move as he reached a hand out towards my face, then pulled it back and frowned. Damn, if he were to kiss me, I wouldn't fight it. I held my breath, but he didn't move, his eyes boring deep into mine. I needed to say something.

"Kiss," I whispered.

"What?" His eyebrows raised.

"You told me the next time we crossed paths, to let you know if I wanted to kiss you or kill —" My words were cut off by his mouth crushing against mine. *Oh!*

He smelled like leather and cinnamon, and his body was warmer than the last time. He grasped the back of my head, his other arm wrapping around my lower back, pulling my body hard against his. He'd caged me in, and I couldn't break free if I wanted to. I cradled both sides of his face and gave myself into the kiss, closing my eyes.

He pulled away, looking as shaken as I felt.

"What am I doing?" I muttered.

My heart and mind raced.

He let out a sound that may have been a laugh. "I ask myself the same thing, every time I follow you," he murmured. "I can't seem to stop myself, though."

"That's stalker-like behaviour," I told him. "Although I appreciate that you didn't kill me."

He chuckled, his body shaking. I couldn't hold back my own laughter.

"My sweet *Cazadora*, I don't think I can stay away," he declared.

My sweet Cazadora. My heart fluttered at those words.

"It's Camila," I said.

"I know." His eyes glinted. "Camila." When he spoke it, a slight Spanish accent came forward in his voice.

Again, we didn't move, our gazes locked. The way he looked at me was a mixture of interest, wonder, and puzzlement.

"What do we do now?" I asked. "It's clear we can't stay away from each other, and we've failed at killing one another."

It took him a while to voice his thoughts, his breathing ragged.

"I know what I *want* to do." His voice dropped. "But I'll leave this up to you. Can my sweet *Cazadora* get past what I am?"

Can I? My brain was telling me to end him, to drive an arrow through his chest. But my heart and body were screaming for me to fall into his arms. "I don't know." I admitted. "But I also don't want you to let me go."

He lifted me in his arms easily. "Then I won't."

I gazed up at his face as Venice blurred around us. We reached my front door in about five minutes.

"That took me half an hour to walk." I commented.

He flashed me his smile that made my heart skip again. "I

know. You were painfully slow."

"We can't all have supernatural speed," I joked as I opened the door.

His eyes locked onto mine. "Can't we?" There was no hint of amusement in his intense gaze, and I stiffened when his fingers brushed my throat, his eyes turning red, fangs on display.

What he was suggesting sent ice through my blood. That he could say such a thing and mean it only served as a reminder that I was fucking a vampire. I glanced away, unable to look him in the eye, suddenly afraid that he would try to turn me. I started to pull away from him. His hand tightened on my arm, and strong fingers grasped my chin, forcing me to look at him.

The red in his eyes faded, and his fangs retracted. "I made you uncomfortable. I'm sorry. Let me make it up to you." He leaned forward, his teeth grazed my earlobe, and his hands moved under my tee-shirt, firm against my body, caressing me. "Let me," he whispered, almost pleading.

I got the feeling he didn't apologise all that often. With his touch blazing across my skin, discomfort was quickly replaced by an aching want. I whimpered when he pushed me up against the wall, pinning me with his body. His lips trailed across my jaw and I turned my head, our kiss fierce.

"Do you want me to take you against the wall again, or do you prefer the bed?" he asked, his fingers digging into my hip painfully. His breathing had changed, and his erection pressed against me through his jeans.

I didn't know how such words could send my desire higher. He'd left bruises last time, and my body had ached for days afterwards. I wanted more. More pain, more of him; I even wanted him to bite me. The yearning left me breathless.

"Bed," I managed.

In my bedroom, he lowered me to the bed. I watched him strip, and he sat on the bed in front of me, pulling my tee-shirt over my head. He then removed my jeans, and we simply sat facing each other. His hands caressed my legs, and he pulled me into his lap. I wrapped my legs around him. I yearned to touch him, and I ran my hands from his abs to his chest, over his wolf tattoo. He was lean, and his firm body moved under my touch, warm, inviting. The urge to lick him rose in me, so I dragged my tongue over his chest. Carlos sighed.

"Don't stop that," he growled, his own fingers tracing over my body, and I shivered, sensitive to his touch.

We didn't move from that position, simply exploring each other with our fingers, our breathing the only sound in the room. I leaned forward, our bodies touching, kissing his shoulder. Slowly, I trailed my kisses across towards his neck, up to his jaw. His lips met mine, and he wrapped his arms around me. Fire blazed through my entire being with that kiss. I grasped his hair with one hand, wrapping my other arm around his back. I soared.

When we finally broke apart, he pressed his hand to my chest, gently pushing me away from his body. His face lowered, nuzzling between my breasts. I squirmed, need tightening my core muscles. Unable to hold back, I ground myself against him, rocking. His tongue swirled over my nipple, fangs scraping my skin. His lips moved from my breast, upward. He licked my throat, slowly, as if he were tasting me. I could feel his fangs pressed against my neck.

"Not yet," I whispered. "I want you inside me first."

He growled, and for a moment, I worried he was going to disregard what I'd said. His arms tightened around me. With a fistful of his hair, I pulled his head back, surprised when he didn't resist. His red eyes bored into mine with an inhuman glint.

"Not yet," he finally agreed, and lowered a hand between us, fingers sliding through my pussy. Wet with need, I ground myself against his fingers. "Oh, it feels like you're ready for me," he said and lifted his hand, putting his fingers into his mouth.

"More than ready," I breathed, and our gazes locked.

He touched my cheek with the back of his fingers. Heat flooded me. My mind still questioned what we were doing, my body pleading for him to fill me. I caught his unrestrained lust deep in his eyes, and a savageness that exhilarated me. I closed my fingers around his cock, guiding it into my opening. He slid in deep, filling me. He held me in place with one hand pressed against my back.

I couldn't hold back the moan. He didn't thrust, we just rocked, and he hit places that sent waves of bliss and a strong surge of pleasure.

"Carlos," I gasped, overcome by the urge to say his name.

I clung to him, his body against mine, our hips rolling in rhythm with one another. His breath hitched in my ear.

"Fuck," he growled. "The way you say my name."

His eyes held me in place, and I couldn't look away. I pulsed around him, and another wave of pleasure coursed through me. Heat wound tight around my spine, taking me higher.

"Carlos." This time it came out in a long moan. A growl tore from him, primal and unrestrained. The glint in his eyes returned. "Immortal Wolf," I said, unsure why I'd said that. I rested my hand over his wolf tattoo.

"Lean back," he instructed.

I leaned back.

"Further. Don't worry about falling, I've got you," he promised.

I leaned back further, and he was now supporting me entirely, our eyes still locked. I shifted myself, allowing him deeper. Our rocking became quicker movements, rougher. He had one hand on my back, the other pressing into my hip, fingers digging in. Pain and pleasure became the same thing.

"Bare your throat, my sweet *Cazadora*," he ordered. "Let me bite you...I need..." He hissed, flashing his fangs, eyes crimson. "Bare your fucking throat. NOW!" His last words came out a growl.

I didn't argue, just tilted my head to the side. He pulled me to him again, his warm mouth on my neck. The sharp sting of his fangs was replaced almost immediately by pleasure as his venom surged through me. I'd needed this since the last time he bit me, yearned for it. I lost myself to the effects of his bite, closing my eyes as pure euphoria engulfed me. My entire body tensed, and my orgasm hit me hard and his followed immediately as he let out a roar, releasing my throat.

Tremors shook my body while I tried to catch my breath. He lifted me off him.

"Lie back," he murmured.

As I complied, he lay beside me. We continued facing each other. He grabbed my chin, tilting it to examine my throat. "Did I hurt you?"

"No." I replied, still in a fog from his bite. "You did that pleasure thing, with your venom, and that's all I felt." I grinned. "That, and your cock."

He smiled and examined my throat. "I bit deep; it will leave a scar." There was a strange tone to his voice, almost like he was proud.

I put my hand to where he'd bitten me. They weren't small punctures this time. "You really nipped hard, didn't you?"

"I told you I wasn't gentle." Amusement danced in his eyes.

I cradled his cheek. "I'd be disappointed if you were."

He flashed a smirk at me. "Come here."

I moved towards him, and his arms wrapped around me. With my face pressed into his chest, I breathed in his scent of leather and cinnamon. "You smell nice," I murmured.

"So do you," he said.

I rolled my eyes. "You mean my blood?"

He shook his head. "Like apples and vanilla."

I snuggled into him. "We have an orchard back in Spain."

His embrace tightened at the mention of Spain. "Tell me about your home. What do you miss the most?"

"In the summers, during the hottest time of day, we were excused from training. I'd go to the beach with my sister, Sofia. I would live for those moments. To feel the warmth of the sun on my skin, and the refreshing water, or eating *helado*." I sighed. Just talking about it, I could almost smell the beach, feel the warmth of the sun.

"I prefer to avoid the sun," he said. "I don't remember what it feels like, to enjoy that warmth."

I shifted myself so I could see his face. "Even Hunters know the sun doesn't hurt you. Do you take the creatures of the night thing so seriously that you avoid it completely?"

His eyes lit up with amusement. "Creatures of the night?" His body shook as he tried to suppress laughter. "I'll have to use that line." He flashed his eyes at me, lowering his voice. "I'm a creature of the night. Bend to my will; let me seduce you so I can drink from your throat." He shook his head.

I couldn't help but smile. "I'm serious, though; you really don't go outside during the day?"

"We can go out during the day," he affirmed. "I just prefer not to. I think I've lived so long in the shadows, that I prefer it." He kissed my forehead. "Do you miss Spain?"

I nodded. "Do you?"

His eyes widened, and he contemplated my question. "That's not something I've considered," he admitted thoughtfully. "I've lived in many countries, and haven't thought of Spain in a very long time."

"Have you not considered going back?" I pushed. I couldn't imagine just turning my back on my home.

"I can't say I have," he said. "But yes, in a way, I think I do miss Spain. It has a certain… feel to it that I sometimes dream about. A feeling of…" he paused. "I don't know. Something familiar?"

I smiled. "Home," I finished for him.

Shock flared in his eyes. "Yes, I suppose it does."

Chapter 44

With Camila asleep in my arms, I listened to her breathing and the beat of her heart. Once again, I lifted my hand to brush my fingers over her neck. I'd bitten hard while caught up in my own lust. The venom in my saliva would help quicken the healing process, yet she would still have a scar. I held back a smile.

"Why do you keep doing that?" she asked in Castellano, half asleep. "Do you need blood again?"

In her state, she probably didn't know what she was offering. I nuzzled her. "No, just examining my handiwork." I whispered next to her ear, also in Castellano. "I marked you, and I'm feeling rather proud right now."

"Marked?" She was awake now, and sat up, putting her hand to where I'd bitten her. "What do you mean, marked?"

"Often, when a vampire bites during sex, we can bite hard. There is no real feeding that takes place, just the impulse to bite. Often the sign of deep feel —" I stopped. "The vampire bites deep enough to leave a mark that doesn't heal completely. If any other vampire were to see that, they would leave you alone to avoid risking the wrath of the one who marked you."

"Deep feelings?" she pushed.

"Deep feelings of lust." I frowned at what I'd been about to say. Surely it was pure lust that had driven me to bite her. I'd *never* marked a human before. Her disappointment was visible. I kissed her cheek. "It means you have my protection," I told her. "Are you okay with that?"

She mulled over my words. "Protected by a vampire," she said, taking her time. "Years of hatred for your kind are hard to overcome, so there's resistance over the very idea. But I kind of like it. I like waking up with you. I never imagined I'd hear myself say that of a vampire." She brushed her fingers over her neck again, the movement mesmerising me. "Or that I would feel special over being marked by one."

"Oh, you are special," I reassured her. "I've *never* marked a human before. This is only the second time I've softened towards one." I pushed her to lie back and tilted her chin with my fingers.

"The second?" she asked. The sharp scent of jealousy rose from her.

"Is that jealousy I can smell?" I licked the mark on her throat.

"No." Her heart pounded.

I pressed my lips to her neck, fangs scraping flesh. Camila sucked in a breath, her fingers shifting through my hair.

"She belongs to another, so you have nothing to be jealous of," I told her.

"Are you going to bite me again?" she whispered.

I wanted to, and I had never fought against doing what I wanted as much as that moment. I kissed the mark and lifted my head instead. "Not tonight," I said. "Maybe I'll let you get used to the idea that you've taken a vampire to your bed before I do that again."

Her heart skipped at 'taken a vampire to your bed.' I lay down beside her.

"This will take some getting used to," she murmured, facing me.

"Take all the time you need," I said. "I have patience. I've had nothing but time; I'm sure I can manage however long you take." I smirked. "As long as we can still have sex, though; a vampire has needs, you know. I can always go to my clan I suppose."

She laughed. "You're a lot less intimidating like this."

"Intimidating?" I bared my fangs and hissed. "My sweet *Cazadora*, you should be terrified!" I snapped at her with a playful growl, her smile widening. I gazed into her eyes, loving the way they lit up.

Her hand reached towards me, cupping my face, intense heat in her eyes. "I like you like this," she stated simply. "You do have a charm."

I found myself wanting to be tender with her. I raised my own hand, cradling her cheek.

"So beautiful," I murmured. "I'm in the bed of a Huntress,

and she's not trying to kill me. The wonders of this life never cease to amaze me." Warmth and joy burst through my chest.

Her lips parted and we kissed. There was no urgency, no hunger, just a sweetness that I never wanted to end. She moved her hand around, sifting through my hair again, a motion that I enjoyed. We pulled apart, just staring at each other. My need to touch her won out, and I laid my hand over her chest. She, in turn, pressed hers against my wolf tattoo.

"You can be gentle when you want to be," she said.

"Well, gentleness is needed sometimes. You humans are delicate," I said.

"Can I ask you something?" she said.

"You just did," I responded, smirking at her again.

She rolled her eyes. "I'm serious."

I wasn't sure what she wanted to ask, but I was caught up in the moment, unable to take my eyes from her. I would have agreed to anything. "Ask away."

"Tonight, can we not be vampire and human? Or Hunter? Just two people. Wrapped in each other's presence. I want to enjoy this without the constant reminder of what we are," she asserted.

I brushed hair from her forehead. "Anything you want."

Wrapping my arms around her, gentle with my embrace, I felt it. We were just two people, and I certainly appreciated her presence.

Contentment rumbled deep in my chest.

"Except for that," she murmured, closing her eyes, and I could tell she was drifting closer to sleep again. "Keep making that sound. It does something to me." I let out a growl, and a shiver passed through her, bringing a smile to her face. "It sounds like you're purring."

She'd likened me to a cat. "Purring?" I asked, raising my eyebrow at her. "I am the King of La Voz, to be revered, not compared to such an inferior creature."

Laughter reflected in her eyes. "Not even a tiger? The largest, strongest, and most fierce of all cats." She kissed me hard.

I stroked her face. "I could accept that, I suppose."

Her smile showed a glint of mischievousness. "I have a tiger vamp in my bed. *Mi Tigre.*" She stroked my face. "Please don't leave in anger this time."

I kissed her cheek. "I'm not going anywhere."

We gazed at each other, not moving. She fought to keep her eyes open, but it wasn't long until she lost that fight. Her eyes closed, and her breathing indicated she'd already fallen asleep.

Chapter 45

I awoke to Camila in my arms, trying to snuggle into me for warmth, while pulling her quilt tighter around her. It had been hours since I'd fed, so it was likely my body temperature had dropped. I found myself wrapping her in an embrace, and I kissed the back of her neck, basking in the heat of her body against mine.

"Mmmm, keep doing that and you're going to awaken a different hunger." I growled in her ear.

"*Buenas Días, Mi Tigre*," she said.

I took pleasure in the pet name she'd given me. Those in my clan usually just used my title, King.

Her words sank in slowly. *Morning.* I lifted my head,

turning my attention to the window. Daylight streamed around the curtains. I had no way to get home, my sunglasses useless in my bedroom at the den. I cursed under my breath.

"What is it?" Her tone indicated worry.

"I fell asleep." I grumbled. "I got too comfortable."

"Why is that such a bad thing?" she challenged.

I almost laughed at her question. Humans! "I don't have my sunglasses, and it doesn't look like there's any cloud cover. I won't be able to leave until the sun sets." It wouldn't be lethal, I just didn't like travelling in the sunlight.

"I have sunglasses," she offered.

I did laugh then. "Ours are magically enhanced. Normal sunglasses are useless for our light sensitivity."

She turned to face me. "Magically enhanced sunglasses? That's something we don't have in the records." Her fingers touched my face, caressing my cheek with wonder. "I still can't believe…" She trailed off, her eyes lifting to meet mine. "I have a vampire in my bed. And he can't leave until the sun sets. I have you all to myself for the day."

"A greedy little human, aren't you?" I kissed her. "It's not a bad bed to be stuck in for the day. Somewhat smaller than what I'm used to. But my clan will…" I stopped talking. To speak about my clan to a Hunter, it was on me to protect them.

I needed to let Matteo know not to worry. *'Matteo, I'm safe.'*

'Where are you?' came his response, concern echoing through our connection.

'Staying put until the sun goes down. I'll see you tonight,' I replied.

His silence indicated he was still worried but accepted my

words.

"You still don't trust me, do you?" she asked. There was no hurt, she was just stating a fact.

"You said so yourself, there's years of animosity to overcome." I told her. "Only a couple of decades for you, centuries for me. I am a little protective."

"I won't hurt them," she promised with an earnest tone to her voice.

I hesitated. "My instinct is to protect my clan. You did attack us at the gallery." Not to mention that she'd almost killed me, again.

"I did." She wore a pained expression. "I'm sorry. I was sent here; there were reports of a vampire."

"Who would send you to hunt a vampire *alone*?" I asked. "You hunters work in numbers. You're not strong enough to take us alone. You clearly weren't expecting a clan to be here. Even as small as we are, we're still too much for a solo hunter."

She sat up and turned away from me. I sat myself up, pulling her face towards me. A tear slid down her cheek, pain visible in her eyes. I brushed her tear away and waited, unsure what to say.

"My father sent me here as punishment," her voice broke. "My mother got killed in a hunt, because of me. I'm certain he sent me here in the hopes that I'd..."

I understood then. "He sent you here to die," I finished, my chest aching at the thought that her father had served such a punishment. In all my experience with Hunters, I had never heard of such cruelty. They protected their own, as vampires did. They did not send them to die. "Even in anger, I would never do that to my clan. My second, Matteo, he would challenge me if I did. Despite the blood bond. What kind of father sends his child to die?"

"Blood bond? You're his maker?" she asked in surprise.

Her change in topic told me she didn't want to talk about her father, so I didn't push.

I shook my head. "No, but his maker was dead. He needed a blood bond. He was practically a feral when he came to us. At the time, I didn't know why Gabriela would want him to join us, as ferals were not known for…well, any resemblance to anything remotely reasonable. Not like us. Plus, in the accords we'd agreed not to make any. But she forced me to share my blood with him in an attempt to stabilise his nature."

"I get the feeling you didn't like that. Or him," she noted.

I laughed. "At the time, I didn't. I used my power over him to torment him, in the hopes he'd attack me so I could kill him. He did a few times. But after a few years, our bond changed us. We became close."

"Is he still a feral?" she asked.

I was telling her a story that wasn't mine to tell.

"Perhaps this is a story for another time," I said.

"The first time we met, you said you lived in Australia. I saw in the records what happened with Quinn Bailey," she said.

Curious little human.

"She goes by Quinn Barone these days." I said. "She and Matteo couldn't stay away from each other. Although for a time, she did try."

"What about you? You left Gabriela," she pointed out.

I noted the jealousy in her voice and couldn't help but laugh. "Gabriela was my maker. Nothing more. I stayed with her out of loyalty over the life she gave me. We were never beloved." I chuckled again. "Is that what's in the records about us?" Amused, I kissed her again. "I cared greatly for her, and mourned her death, but only in the same way a human would for their mother."

Relief crossed over her features.

"Don't worry," I reassured her. "You don't have to compare yourself to her."

She lay down again, pressing her body against mine.

"You won't get warmth from me." I told her. "I'm sorry. I need to have freshly fed for that."

"You're not cold, just a little cool," she said. "How often do you have to feed?"

"It seems that while you have access to a lot of information about us through your Hunters' records, there's also a lot that you don't have access to." I rubbed my thumb over her eyebrow. "I can't say I've ever been this open with a human before. Not even Quinn before she turned."

"I get the feeling that scares you," she noted.

I paused. Fear wasn't something I was accustomed to. "What scares me is how close you came to killing me," I confessed. "That first night we met. I've never run from a human before," I admitted. "Then the night of the opening. You came so close to —"

Her hand covered my mouth. "I know. Let's not focus on that."

"You're right. Let's sleep." I pulled her in tight.

She squirmed. "You just slept."

"While the sun is up, I can't go anywhere, so it's either that, or…" I gave her a small smile. "I can think of another activity we can do while I'm stuck here."

"You are such a…" She stopped, wincing.

"Vampire?" I grinned. "We do tend to sleep during the day. Or fuck."

Her phone pinged.

"I have to send my father a report," she said, reaching for her phone.

I tightened my arms around her. "He sent you here to die, and he's all the way in Spain. You owe him nothing." I nuzzled her neck with a soft growl. "Me, on the other hand." I moved, pinning her beneath my body, the quilt falling on the floor. "I'm here, and I wouldn't mind some attention." I pointed at the shackles. "I want to use *those,* this time."

Chapter 46

Carlos pushed me into the wall, hard. His body pressed in behind me and he reached around, grabbing my throat. Fingers of his other hand grasped my arm. He lowered his face, breathing in deep.

"Mmmm, Camila, I can smell how much you want me," he said close to my ear.

We had both given up English, falling into a comfortable habit of speaking Castellano. His voice was low and guttural, and it spoke to a deep part of me that screamed for more. Heat flooded through me, and I pushed against his erection. I leaned my head against his shoulder. He removed his hand

and peppered kisses over my throat. I moaned, his lips setting fire to my skin.

"Are you baring your throat to me?" he whispered.

"Yes," I breathed, reaching up to grab the back of his head.

His tongue slid over my neck, sending a shiver through me. The moment his fangs pierced my throat, I couldn't hold back the moan, long and lustful. The grip on my arm tightened, becoming almost painful. Euphoria coursed through my veins, and heat spread in its wake. I ground myself against him again, a low grumble vibrating through him, which I felt in my bones. When he pulled back, he spun me around to face him, his eyes gazing into mine. He released my arm.

"Sorry," he whispered. "I tend to get a little rough."

"You don't know how to be gentle. I remember." I smiled. "Then don't."

He smirked. "You like rough?"

I nodded. "And pain, it seems."

A spark of raw lust reflected from his red eyes.

"You surprise me, sweet Huntress," he said, his voice smug.

"I surprise *myself*," I admitted. "That first time, my body ached for days, and you left some bruises, but I liked it. I wanted more."

He raised his hand, stroking my neck "Tell me if you want me to stop. My clan can take a lot more than you can, so I need you to tell me if I'm too rough."

I nodded again.

His fingers squeezed lightly around the sides of my throat, careful to not use too much strength in his grip. His eyes burned into mine. Giddy, I let out a soft whimper. His lips crushed against mine, his kiss hard, aggressive. I closed my eyes. He released my throat, and the rattle of chains brought my eyes open again.

"I told you I wanted to use these," he murmured, a wicked glint in his eyes as he held the shackles up. "Now be a good little Huntress and let me put these on you. Kneel for your King."

A glint of command reflected in his eyes. He was a King, and used to being obeyed. Part of me wanted to kneel for him, but part of me wanted to defy his command.

"What will you do if I disobey you?" I asked.

Challenge flickered in his eyes. "*No one* disobeys me."

I couldn't help myself. "Well, you're not *my* King. You don't have the command here that you would with your clan."

His eyes flashed. "You dare?"

Unsure where my desire to challenge him came from, I grinned. "I dare."

He growled, pushing me until my back hit the wall. Fingers closed around the sides of my throat again, which only added to my need. "How about now?"

I smiled in response, lifting my chin to meet his eyes, and pointed to the cuffs. "I think those would look better on you. Perhaps the King needs to be put in his place, told he's a bad boy."

He started to laugh, but stopped, looking down at me. While pinned to the wall, I reached for a knife on the table next to my bed. As if realising what I was doing, he let me go. I grabbed the knife.

"Out there, with your clan, you're King. But this is *my* domain. In here, I'm Queen." I pressed the blade to his throat. "Or shall I slit your throat again?" Once again, I wasn't sure what I was doing.

His smirk returned, and raw lust glinted in his eyes. "Oh, please do."

I hesitated. "You want me to?"

He chuckled. "Like you, I do have a fondness for pain, especially with knives." He stepped closer to me, and my blade pressed harder into his throat. "Don't stop now, Huntress." His eyes darted down the length of my body. "You were saying in here, you're Queen? What a Queen you'd make."

An idea took root in my mind, one that made me ache. Feeling brave, I put command into my tone. "Then kneel," I ordered, thrilled by the thought of him kneeling to me. Intensity glinted in his eyes, smouldering as he looked down at me.

"Say that again!" he demanded.

"Kneel," I whispered, suddenly afraid. I'd just told a vampire King to kneel to me. *What am I doing?*

He tilted his head, eyes narrowed. The moment stretched out, and he didn't say anything, or move. Then without a word, he dropped to his knees. Deep within, a joy lit up at seeing him kneel. Yet I was baffled that he'd done so.

"What are you doing?" I asked.

He lifted his chin to meet my gaze. "There's some authority in you, I like it." He held the shackles out to me. "If you want me in these, you'll have to put them on."

"You'd let me restrain you?" I asked.

"You don't want to?" He grabbed my hand that still held the knife, bringing it to his chest. "You like pain, and you like to inflict it. So let's play. Let's find what else is buried inside this hot little package of Huntress."

I stared at him, confused.

"Oh, I see." Understanding filtered through his eyes then. "Don't question it. If this is what wets your pussy, then this is what we'll do. There is a vixen in you that wants to break free. It looks like I'm to be the one to help her find herself." He held the shackles up again. "Now put these on me." His voice sent a shiver through me.

This time I did as he said. He watched me as I closed the cuff over his wrists. The sight of him in restraints and on his knees before me sparked an inferno.

He took in a deep breath, burying his face between my legs. "Oh, delicious." A growl rumbled from him. He tore himself away and gazed up at me. "Tell me what you want, Huntress," he said. "I'm yours to command."

I leaned down to kiss him. He grasped my hips as he lifted himself, head tilted back to meet my lips. One hand slid around, squeezing my ass cheek, the other inching up my body.

"No," I instructed, pushing him down.

I circled him, running my fingers over his chest and back as I did. I noticed another tattoo I hadn't seen before. The words La Voz, with a crown across the centre of his upper back. He didn't move. "Stay," I commanded.

I grabbed the chains, lifting them up towards the hook on the wall, forcing his hands up over his head. I pulled the chains taut, restricting the length. Restricting his movement. Sheer panic crossed his features as he turned his face up to where I'd hooked the chain. But before I could ask if I'd done something wrong, he turned his attention to me, his eyes heated as he raked them down my body. His lips curved, his slow smile spreading across his face.

"Now," I smiled down at him. "Back to that kiss."

I stood over him and grabbed a fistful of his hair at the back of his head. He tried to reach for me with his hands, the chains stopping him. He started to rise again, but with my fingers still in his hair, I pulled him back. He possessed the strength to resist, but he chose to just go with it. Finally, I bent forward, our lips brushing. He tried to press his lips harder against mine, but I moved around him, away from the wall, and out of his reach. He turned, watching me. I moved my hand over my own breast.

A groan escaped from him and he tried to move forward, restricted again by the chains.

"No hands." I said. "No touching."

He let out a frustrated growl. "Camila…"

The pleading tone in his voice was unexpected, but not as much as my own body's reaction. Filled with pleasure, I wanted more. I took another step away from him. He pulled on the chains, a wild glint in his eyes.

I smiled. "The more you try to reach for me, the longer I'll stand here, beyond your reach. Be a good King and look, but don't touch."

I could have sworn his cock moved and the intensity of his gaze surged. He breathed hard, as if panting. "Camila…"

Finally, I stepped forward. "I told you before, in here I'm Queen. Acknowledge that."

He opened his mouth, his chin raised. But he hesitated. His hesitance worried me. Had I gone too far? For a vampire King to call a human-

"Queen," he said, finally, desperation flickering in his face. "Please, my Queen Huntress. Let me touch you. Let me kiss you."

My stomach fluttered. "Then kiss me," I whispered, and reached down, pressing my fingers into my own wetness. His eyes dropped to my hand and he licked his lips as he realised what I was asking. I probed my fingers into his mouth. "Kiss me," I repeated. "And I may let you touch me." I pulled my fingers free.

The wild glint returned, his eyes and smile almost feral. "As you command, My Queen." Instinctively he reached for me again and growled. The sound reverberated through me. "Maybe you should hold on to something."

I laughed. He leaned forward, his lips kissing me softly. I didn't have to see his mouth to know he was smiling.

"Is this okay?" I whispered.

"Mmm," he said against my pussy and lifted his mouth. "Let yourself go, Camila. Don't worry about me, I'm not doing anything I don't want to do. I am at your command; appreciate it."

Then he pushed his tongue into me and all doubt vanished. He licked slowly, tasting me. He couldn't touch me, but his face pressed forward, hard, almost burying it in me. I suppressed a laugh as the term 'eating me out' ran through my mind. He really was feasting, his tongue unrelenting. I couldn't resist pushing hard against his mouth. His eyes didn't leave my face, as if he wanted to watch me reach the point of bliss.

My hands grasped the back of his head as if holding him there. Not that I needed to. His tongue glued me to the spot, flicking, swirling and lapping through my centre. Waves of pleasure rose, igniting little tremors within me.

He paused, lifting his mouth from my clit. "Put your leg over my shoulder," he murmured.

I was willing to try whatever he suggested. I lifted one leg, hooking it over his shoulder, leaning against him for balance. My fingers ran through his hair as he returned to sucking and licking. Only this time, I was more open, giving him more access, and his tongue probed deep. He set more quivers off as he touched sensitive nerves, and I moaned, grinding into his face, wanting more. It dawned on me that he was holding back, being gentle.

"Please, be rough," I instructed. I was no longer commanding, but pleading with him.

He did as I asked, his tongue movements ferocious, speeding up. His chains rattled again as he moved forward. He started to growl, the sound piercing me. His growls turned to satisfied grunts. I let out a gasp, then a moan. His name became one long sound as I let the pleasure wash over me. I squirmed, my skin hot and ripples of electricity spreading out.

"Oh fuck!" I groaned, my entire body tensing.

The pressure built to a crescendo, my orgasm like a lightning bolt.

My legs turned to jelly, and I leaned heavily on Carlos.

He moved himself underneath me, and I was actually riding his face. I groaned; my clit was ultra-sensitive and his tongue didn't stop. I gasped for breath, squeezing his shoulders as the pressure started to build again.

"Stop," I rasped out. "Carlos, I can't."

Fine quivers ran through my body, and I couldn't hold back the second orgasm.

I couldn't stand, and Carlos moved, taking the shackles from the wall and catching me in one swift motion.

Before I knew it, we were on the bed.

"You weren't supposed to touch me," I managed, still jolting.

"You couldn't stand." He laughed. "But if you want to continue…"

He moved from the bed fast, retrieving the knife I'd dropped, and pushed the blade into the wooden headboard. I flinched; the blade would be unusable. Ruined.

He lay on his back, offering me his arms. I realised what he'd done and pushed his hands over his head, linking the chain around the knife, and climbed on top of him.

"Ready to continue whenever you are…My Queen." His voice was rough. "Just tell me what you want."

With my hands on his chest, I leaned down and kissed him, hard. His mouth and chin were wet, and he groaned into my kiss. When I pulled away, he lifted his head. I lowered my mouth to whisper in his ear. "While I ride your cock, I want you to bite me."

His fangs emerged, and he waited, hunger glinting in his eyes. "Then what are you waiting for?"

I lowered myself onto him, and with my hands on his abs, pushed myself up and down, Carlos's cock sliding in and out of me, filling and stretching me.

"Camila, this look suits you." Carlos growled. "I want to touch you. You're driving me mad."

"*Queen* Camila," I reminded him, high from the feeling of having authority over him. I'd never behaved like this in the bedroom before. He'd awoken a part of me that yearned to exercise dominance. His willingness to go with it only made me eager to learn more about this side of myself.

"Queen Camila," he panted.

The uncertainty from earlier was gone. I was in charge,

and it was powerful. I'd had a vampire King kneel to me, and obey me. "Good boy," I grunted, and his cock hit a spot that elicited a long moan from me.

Carlos's breathing changed, and under me he drove his hips to match my movements. As pleasure surged through me, I lowered myself, my body flush against his, and pressed our lips together.

Sweat lined my skin, and my face heated. Every movement felt like I was flying. Every nerve felt exposed, and jolts of pleasure left me breathless. His body moved against mine, his breathing as ragged as mine. Our gazes locked. His irises were bright red, and his pupils were dilated. Lust flared in his eyes, and my stomach knotted. But I glimpsed something more in his eyes, something deeper. It was as if I were staring into his very soul and seeing who he was for the first time. Each movement of our hips, each time his cock slid through me, sending bursts of pleasure, I wanted him more. I'd never known such a need for someone.

The room faded, and I only saw him, only wanted what he could give me. Longing and hunger sparked in his eyes, a reflection of my own feelings. He lifted his head to kiss me.

"You're close," he growled. "Bare your throat."

Instead, I pushed myself up. "Beg me for it," I whispered.

I was soaring, my orgasm close. But I wanted to hear him beg. I wanted to show my control again. A spark of surprise flickered in those red eyes.

"Please," his voice came out almost a growl.

"Please what?" I prompted.

His raw desperation only added to the heat curling around me. "Please, my Queen, bare your throat."

Complete bliss created a storm deep inside me.

I lowered my mouth to whisper in his ear. "I like hearing you beg. Do it again."

He didn't hesitate. "Please let me bite you. I need to bite!" A growl tore from him. "Camila, fuck!"

I offered my throat, and his fangs sunk into my flesh, his venom bringing the familiar euphoria. I held on to him as the pressure exploded. He grunted against my throat as we came together.

I was limbless, and I lay on top of him not moving, catching my breath.

He withdrew his fangs from me. "Can I take the chains down?" he asked.

I hummed in agreement, and his arms were around me. "You did well," he whispered in my ear. "It's powerful, isn't it?" He pulled out of me.

"What?" I asked into his chest.

"Having authority in the bedroom. You're a natural. I could see how much it exhilarated you. Next time you'll have no hesitance."

I said nothing, and he stroked my back, the movement calming.

"You accomplished something that no one else *ever* has before," he murmured, his own voice coming out lazily.

I didn't even have the ability to form words.

"I relinquished my power to you in the bedroom," he continued. "*No one* has achieved that before. That, in itself, is a deed you should be proud of."

I did move then, lifting myself up to look at him. "I did enjoy being the one to make the all mighty King Carlos kneel," I laughed.

"That clearly had an intoxicating effect on you," he said.

There was amusement in his eyes. "Now let me take care of you. You look a little worn out."

I reached a hand towards his face, just wanting to touch. He kissed my hand, his embrace around me tight.

I had no strength, no energy as I came down from the high of my orgasms.

"I am," I agreed.

I relaxed into his arms, strong and comforting. He kissed my neck and stroked the back of my head. It occurred to me that the day would be over soon, and he would return to his den. I didn't want him to go.

I realised then that this was no longer about just sex. *Real feelings* were developing in me. What had started as cold hatred was becoming something warm, wrapping around my heart. Fear pulsed, and a tear slid down my cheek. He would live forever and would probably forget me in his life.

"I do love the scent of fear, but this is a strange time for such emotions," he said.

"Don't leave me," I whispered.

"I'll never leave you," he promised.

Drowsiness closed in, and I let it. Just before I fell asleep, he whispered, more to himself than to me.

"You really would make an impressive Queen, my beautiful sweet Huntress. I'd be more than willing to kneel to you beyond the bedroom."

My heart pounded, and he could probably feel it in his own chest. I didn't have energy to pull myself from the pleasant sleep that pulled me under.

Chapter 47

It was just before sunset when Camila woke up. Her movement pulled me from my own sleep.

"Are you okay?" I asked her. "Do you need some water? You should probably eat."

"Water would be nice," she commented.

I reached for the glass of water on the bedside table, passing it to her. She gulped back greedily. I took the glass back from her, setting it aside.

"Lie back," I told her. "Let me hold you."

She did as I asked, gazing into my face.

"Let's talk about what we did," I suggested with a gentle

tone.

Her eyes lit up. "You want to talk about it?"

I cradled her face. "I do. I want to know how you feel about the things we did. Playing rough, and taking control, are new to you. I've always been this way, especially when I'm in the heat of my own pleasure. Was I too rough? Was there anything that you were worried or unsure about?"

She took a little while to reply. "I was a little scared when I told you to kneel. I didn't know where that came from, and I worried that I'd gone too far," she admitted. "A human telling a vampire king to kneel? I didn't know how you'd react."

I gave her a smile. "That surprised me, too. Even more so when I realised that I *wanted* to kneel to you, and again when you said you were the Queen."

"Was it okay that I did all that?" she asked.

I nodded, stroking her cheek with my thumb. "More than okay. Is there anything that made you uncomfortable? If there was, I'll make sure not to do it again."

Again she seemed to think about my question before answering. "When you held out the restraints, I didn't want to be cuffed. I spent three days in those cuffs after you gave me your blood. I suppose I relate being cuffed to that, now."

I understood. I'd felt panic when she'd lifted my hands over my head, connecting the chain to the wall. The number of times being shackled had come with starvation was difficult to overlook. But I'd pushed through it, for her. "That's okay. If you ever do want me to restrain you, there are other ways I can do so that don't involve cuffs. You can explore that when you're ready."

"Okay," she said.

I sat up. "Let's have a shower, then get some food into you. The sun sets in an hour, and I have to return to my den. I don't want to leave you alone; however, my clan will be worried. We don't usually spend the day away from the safety of our den. Then I need to feed properly. But if you want me to, I can come back around midnight."

Delight filled her face. "I do want that."

I led her to the bathroom and turned on the shower. When the water was hot, we stepped in. I gently washed her, taking mental note of the discolouration of bruises already showing against her warm brown skin. I kissed each bruise, giving small massages to help ease her aching muscles. With her taken care of, she started to wash me, so I let her. We finished showering, and as she dried off, I looked around for food, finding none.

"Anyone would think a vampire lived here, with the lack of food," I remarked.

Now, fully dressed, she entered the kitchen, and let out a giggle. "I haven't had a chance to shop for food in the last few days, so I've picked up meals as I need them. I'll go shopping while you're at your den." She lowered her eyes to the towel around my waist. I smirked at her and returned to her bedroom pulling my clothes on. "You need to eat," I called out to her.

"I ordered food," she called back. "Please don't eat the delivery person."

I chuckled. "No promises."

Night fell, and I reluctantly left Camila. I kissed her forehead and wrapped my arms around her.

"I'll come back," I reminded her.

Outside, the sky was clear, the air cold. I found a tourist, drinking from him before making my way towards my den. After a day of sleeping with Camila in my arms and fucking her when we awoke, I reflected on what had occurred. I'd knelt to her and obeyed her commands instead of giving them. That alone had impacted me more than I would have guessed. To relinquish my power to someone, I would have thought unthinkable. But it had been almost liberating, to let another take that control. Of course, taking control was so new to my sweet little *Cazadora* that I'd had to provide some instruction — topping from the bottom — but once guided, she took to the roleplay like a pro. Her hesitance and uncertainty suggested that I had witnessed some self-discovery in her, and it was enchanting to see her give herself to something that clearly stirred an excitement in her.

Thoughts turned to those in my clan. I could never allow that with other vampires. To give up my power in the bedroom, with one of my kind, would mean to give it up completely. It would be seen as a weakness. The moment my knees hit the ground would be acceptance of a new King. Or Queen. I'd accepted my role twenty years ago, and all that came with it. None could know what had happened in the bedroom of a human. Not even Matteo.

When I did finally get home, Quinn and Matteo were in the kitchen.

"You smell like sex." Matteo said, glancing up. *'And like Hunter.'* He frowned. "Why didn't you come home last night? I was worried. *We* were worried."

"I told you I was safe and not to worry." I motioned to the mess in the kitchen. Flour lined the counter, and spaghetti filled a bowl. "What are you doing?"

His eyes remained on me a moment longer.

Josef walked through the kitchen and glanced at the food. "Well, I use that counter to eat my food, too. At least my meals don't make that much of a mess. Although she may have left behind a little after I was done fucking her."

"Josef, that's gross!" Quinn said, rolling her eyes. "I hope you cleaned up. I don't want your human's juices in my food. A bench is not for fucking on."

"I didn't hear you complaining last week when you claimed Matteo on it," Josef grinned at her, and left the room.

"He had us make pasta from scratch, now he's showing me his way of doing spag bol." Quinn explained after glaring in the direction Josef had left.

"It's not my way, it's the right way…and stop calling it that." Matteo grumbled.

Quinn grinned, reaching for his face. "My sweet Italian vampire, I'm winding you up. You'd think you would be used to that by now."

"You don't need human food, why do you still eat it?" I asked. "It's not like you gain anything from it. It doesn't sustain us."

"We can still enjoy it," Quinn said. "The taste, the aroma, the texture, the nostalgia or the novelty," she explained. "All the grief I give him, I have to admit I enjoy the flavour of Italian food." She winked at him. "Including you, my sweet."

By our standards, she was a young vampire and yet to let go of her desire to consume human food and drink. To maintain a human appearance that most vampires ceased to care about after a century. I figured when her parents were gone, her need to do so would go, too. Her last attachment to her human life would be gone. I couldn't blame Matteo for playing along. The way his face lit up as he gazed at her was answer enough. He would do anything to make her happy. If that meant enjoying human food, he would. We could still eat food, and taste it, but I saw no purpose in it.

He laughed. "Your parents still send you Vegemite, so your taste for human food is questionable."

"They also send Tim Tams; I don't see you complaining about that." She crossed her arms. "I have to hold most of the clan at bay when Mum and Dad send those. They've now started to send extra packets. My parents are now sending Tim Tams to my clan." She glanced over at me and a smirk crossed her face before she returned her gaze to Matteo. "You're questioning my taste? Perhaps I should try something else. I hear Spanish food is good." He growled at her, his eyes changing colour, and she only widened her grin. "I love when you get all possessive." She leaned in to kiss him and he wrapped his arms around her, pulling her hard against him. Their kiss was long, the scent of desire strong. When they finally pulled apart, she murmured to him in Italian.

He beamed at her. "I love when you speak Italian, you should do that more often."

Lorenzo entered the kitchen then, and Matteo's head jerked around, watching him. A glare of hostility passed between the two. That was on me for forcing them into the same feeding ground.

"You two stop it." I grumbled. "I will not have you fight."

Matteo glared. "If the Hunter were dead, we could go back to our —"

I cut him off with a menacing growl. My reaction surprised me as I realised it was his threat to Camila that had set me off. *Am I possessive? Over a human?* I pushed the thought down.

"He's right," Lorenzo said. "I know you're trying to protect them, but you must know how to find her, so why not take care of it now? Just wait until she's asleep."

'You could have taken care of her when you were in her bed,' Matteo accused through our bond.

I felt the heat of both their glares. They'd gone from hostile at each other, to pushing me. "Give me time," I said. "Everything will be as it was soon enough."

Even Quinn's eyes were narrowed as the three of them watched me. Angered by their scrutiny, I closed my fist and slammed it down, cracking the countertop.

"Do not question me," I ordered. "I gave you my word that I would take care of the problem, and you will trust me to do so without question. Am I understood?"

The three of them nodded. "Yes, my King," they said in unison.

I walked to my bedroom without another word.

I paced my bedroom. I was betraying my clan, by sleeping with the enemy. How could I tell them she was no longer a danger to them? Could I believe that she wasn't? With the threat of a brewing war, uncertainty bore down on me. I clenched my fists and jaw, holding back a growl as I stared at my reflection. Unaccustomed to such conflicting feelings, the urge to smash the mirror surged. *What's wrong with me?*

My entire existence revolved around being a vampire. In all my years, I yearned for nothing. Camila had created a rift within me. My clan should come first, before all else. I nodded to myself, and it took a while to realise someone was standing in my doorway. Celeste. Her dark hair hung past her shoulders, deep brown eyes dancing with desire.

"I thought you might be hungry," she offered.

I had fed, but the craving for vampire blood overwhelmed me. "Come here," I commanded.

She stood before me, baring her throat. I grabbed a fist full of her hair, pulling her head back more, roughly. Her gaze burned into mine.

She breathed in deep. "You've taken a human to bed." She stared at me. "Perhaps you'd consider sharing her next time?"

"Not this one." I said and forced her around, so she had her back pressed to me.

My fangs pierced her flesh, and she relaxed against me. She leaned her head against my chest, her breathing ragged. Vampire blood had never fulfilled me before, so it was an adjustment to not only hunger for it but be sated. It burned through me, and I released her.

She turned around and reached for my jacket, her lust-filled eyes red. I had never resisted my clan's sexual needs. Especially not Celeste's. I had a great amount of affection for her. I had never turned her away. I had never resisted the urge to strip her bare and slam her against the wall before thrusting deep into her. But I'd spent the day having my needs taken care of, and for once, I just wanted to be left in peace.

Reluctantly, I gripped her hands, pulling them away. She tried again, sliding her hands under my tee-shirt.

"No." I told her. "You gave me what I hungered for, now go." I turned away from her.

"You've never denied me." Hurt echoed in her voice.

"I said go," I told her and took off my jacket, hanging it over the back of a chair. I swiftly took my tee-shirt off next, needing to change my clothes.

"Is it the human?" she asked. "You got your fill from a human, and you turn your clan down?"

I sighed as I faced her, gripping her throat tight. "If you disobey me again, you will not enjoy the consequences," I hissed, showing her my red eyes.

She whimpered, and I let her go. She remained, staring at me. I undid my belt and dropped my jeans, picking out fresh clothes. I knew Celeste was hurt that I was not paying her the attention she wanted, and deserved. Yet I found my mind wandering back to Camila. It was *her* touch I wanted, to hold her in my arms. To guide her in exploring her desire to dominate. As King, I had responsibility to my clan, before I could return to my bedroom Queen, my *Cazadora*.

Chapter 48

My body ached. Aside from Carlos's mark, I also had bruises around my throat, hips, biceps and wrists. Not that I was complaining. He'd put shackles on, for me. He'd bitten me, bruised me, and the pain had only added to the pleasure. Just thinking about it made me wet.

After the day I'd had, I stared at the weapons on my table. The desire to keep these out held no appeal — I didn't want any part of them, nor what came with them. I picked up the crossbow and put it in the case, packing the arrows around it. I packed away the wooden stakes, and I picked up a knife.

Maybe I should keep that, just in case.

My phone buzzed, and I put down my knife, reading the message.

<*I'm in Venice, I'll be there soon.*> From Sofia.

Sofia was coming here? *Shit!* I glanced around my living room, relieved to find nothing she should worry about. Just the bruises and bite marks. I pulled on my jacket, zipping it up. The knock at my door made me gasp. What if it was Carlos? With my sister in town, I didn't want any overlapping of the two being in each other's presence. It dawned on me that Carlos probably wouldn't knock, he'd just walk in as if he owned the place.

"Millie? Are you home? It's me!" Sofia called from the other side of the door.

I opened the door. "Sof, does Father know you're here? How did you get him to accept that?"

Her eyes widened. "Please don't tell him!"

I let her in, "Of course I won't. What are you doing here?"

My sister and I looked alike. Long, curly, black hair, the same brown eyes and brown skin, but she was slightly taller than me. A scar on her neck showed the fight from her first hunt, where she'd almost died before I'd managed to kill the vampire who was trying to kill her.

"Remember how we learned when we were young what our family did, and you cried?" She stared at me with wide eyes.

Taken aback by her question, I nodded. "Yeah, being told our family were killers was horrifying. Even if it was the murder of monsters. I didn't want anything to do with it."

That had never changed, but I'd had no choice. My father had turned me into a killer.

"I never said it at the time, but I was just as scared. Because Mama told me that one day we'd be married to other Hunters to continue our family lines. I hated the idea that we would have to marry a killer."

Her conversation was unexpected. She'd fallen into training and everything a lot quicker than I had. I realised what she was trying to tell me. "Who?" I asked.

"Alejandro Delgado." Tears slid down her cheek.

I flinched, recognising the name. Unlike our family, who were descended from the First Hunters, they were new to the business. Alejandro's mother had been killed when he was only two, pushing his father to become a Hunter. Alejandro had willingly followed in his father's footsteps.

"Why anyone would choose this life is something I'll never understand," I muttered. "So you ran?"

"I can't put this on children," she said. "I want out. I can't do this any more. We've already lost our mother, and I still bear the scars from the worst day of my life. I can't remember the number of times I've almost died." She sat at my table.

I took a seat, grasping her hand. "At least he hasn't sent you away to die," I muttered, unable to hold back my bitterness.

She bowed her head. "It's as if you're already dead. No one talks about you. He caught me and Diego talking, and he demanded we stop. He was furious when he found out Diego sent you the audio weapon."

I could only imagine his reaction upon finding out that they'd helped me.

"How have you gotten by? You've been here almost six months, and you told me it's Carlos Rivera that you face." She frowned. "How has he not killed, or seriously hurt you?"

My cheeks were warm, and I stood up. "Why don't we go for a walk?"

She eyed me suspiciously but followed me out the door. The cold air made me glad I'd worn my jacket. Our breath was white. We walked in silence, stopping to watch a gondola. "Have you been in one yet?" she asked.

"No, I haven't had a chance. I felt guilty every time I considered it," I told her.

She laughed. "Yeah, everything we do that isn't related to hunting, our father's voice is right there."

I grasped her hand. "The guilt is less than it was when I first got here. Maybe one day I'll feel normal. What are you going to do?"

We stopped on the Rialto Bridge, and she looked out over the canal. There was a crowd on the bridge, everyone eager to watch the gondolas. Someone bumped past me and didn't look back. "I don't know. I wish I could just go somewhere and live a quiet life. Work in a bookstore, or a museum or something."

I glanced at her. "He's going to look for you."

She nodded. "That's why I thought I'd stay here for a few days. He won't think to look for me here."

I froze. "What? Here?" The vampires here would see her, probably mistake her for me.

"I knew it!" She turned to face me. "What aren't you telling me, Camila? There's something *off* about you."

I shrugged. "I'm just used to being on my own. Father did me a favour by sending me away. It's given me a chance to think about what I want from life. I don't *have* to live by his rules. I feel *free*."

Her eyes narrowed as she studied me. "There is something

different about you." She grinned. "Have you found any hot Italian men to sweep you off your feet?"

"He's not Italian," I said without thinking, and winced.

Her smile widened. "Camila! Tell me everything!" She laughed. "How do you find the time while taking on one of the deadliest vampires in history?"

I contemplated telling her everything. "Why don't we go somewhere to eat?" I suggested instead.

She walked beside me in silence as I led her to a Spanish restaurant I'd found.

"You live in Venice and still manage to find a Spanish restaurant!" Sofia laughed.

I grinned. "It reminds me of home. We can go to an Italian restaurant if you prefer."

She glanced around. "I'd like that. I didn't come to Italy for a taste of home."

We found a restaurant that overlooked the canal.

A waiter seated us near the window and gave us menus. I smiled at him. "*Grazie.*"

"You're speaking Italian now?" Sofia rolled her eyes. "It's like I don't know you."

I laughed. "Relax, Sof, I only know basic words."

"Is this mystery man teaching you? Oh, but he's not Italian." Her excitement was starting to bubble up.

I watched her. She wanted out of the life of Hunters as much as I did. I could never keep secrets from her, and she'd eventually find out anyway. One way or another. "He's Spanish," I said at last.

Her smile faltered. "Spanish?"

I could see it in her eyes that she knew exactly who I was talking about. "Yes, Spanish." I fought the urge to avert my gaze.

Shock, disgust, horror, and fear crossed her face. "Well, I guess that explains why he hasn't killed you."

I scoffed. "Oh, believe me, he tried. We both did."

The waiter arrived to take our orders and left again quickly.

"So, what, you stopped trying to kill him and just climbed into his bed instead?" she asked.

"Actually, I haven't seen his bed," I admitted. "And yes."

"Millie, I hope you know what you're doing. I researched him. You really want to allow such a monster to touch you? You know what he is, and you still did that?"

I sighed. Now that I had nothing to hide, I took my jacket off. "I know exactly what he is."

I caught the fury as she stared at the bruises on my arms. Her eyes lifted to my throat. "You let him bite you?" She rose from her chair. "I'm going to kill him myself."

I stood and grabbed her arm. *"Please don't.* Sof, I told you because I trust you. I didn't have to. He hasn't done anything I don't want."

She sat down. "You *want* this? Bite marks and bruises?" She leaned back in her chair. "Who are you?"

"I'm still your little sister." I put a hand on her wrist. She wasn't happy with the news that I'd been with a vampire. It went against everything we'd been taught. Even after that first time, I hadn't thought it natural. But we'd returned to each other, and I'd learned a great deal about myself. "I like it," I admitted. "I like pain." We'd always been open with each other, but admitting this to her was difficult. Her expression of horror only added to it.

"Pain?" She lowered her voice into a whisper. "You mean

it turns you on?"

I lifted my hand off her arm, uncomfortable, and hurt at the way she was looking at me. "It does," I said defensively. "Just be my sister and be glad that I found some sort of happiness in our shitty lives."

"I'm sorry," she said. "This is just a lot to take, Millie. Everything we were taught…"

"Exactly." I interrupted her. "*Taught*. We were taught to hate them. Things can be unlearned."

She leaned on the table. "Is he going to turn you? Is that what you want?"

"NO!" The very idea made me shudder. "I may be okay with what he is, but I would never let him do that to me."

Her eyes dropped to my neck again. "Then what hope do you have for any kind of future with him? We're their food source, and the occasional fuck. They'd never see us as anything else. Is this just a fling, or are you going to keep going until he drains you dry, or accidentally tears out your throat? What about when he gets bored with you?"

Her questions left me winded. She had voiced the same warnings I had been desperately trying to ignore. I wanted to believe Carlos wouldn't do that to me, but how well did I really know him?

"This isn't the end of this discussion," my sister asserted as our food arrived.

I was about to face a Sofia Martinez interrogation.

Chapter 49

I almost grabbed her from behind. Almost. Camila would have known my touch and melted against me as I kissed her neck. But the breeze changed direction, and her scent was *wrong*. Before she realised I was behind her, I returned to the shadows, watching.

She knocked. "Millie? Are you home? It's me!"

Curious, I waited.

After dead silence, Camila opened the door. "Sof, does Father know you're here? How did you get him to accept that?"

Her sister. I bit back a growl. Another Hunter, that's

all I needed. They went inside, and I listened to their conversation for a few minutes before relaxing. She wasn't here for any of my clan. Just a sister needing to talk. I walked away, a little disappointed.

'Carlos, we have a problem.' Matteo's voice through our bond surprised me. He was tense, and I could sense anger.

'Where are you?' I asked.

'The den. We need you. Now.' There was desperation in his voice.

I didn't waste any time, and it took me three minutes to get there. I arrived to find my entire clan facing off against Giuseppe and ten other vampires.

"Giuseppe, I warned you not to make a move against me," I growled. "Did you bring more people for me to tear their hearts from their chests?"

"I challenge you," he said. "You killed —"

"I don't care." I stepped towards him, and we were inches apart, our fangs bared. "You brought your men to a slaughter. You're on my territory, which King Luis granted to me. I am bonded with him. What do you think he would do to you?" I glanced at his men. "Giuseppe is bonded with Nico. Me, I was chosen by Luis. The Bloodking himself! You have one minute to make your decision. Stand against me and my clan, or leave." I glanced at Quinn, whose eyes were red, her anger shining through. Next to her, Matteo was focused on Giuseppe. "Quinn, show them what it is they face." I pointed to one of Giuseppe's clan. "That one."

Before she could use her power, Giuseppe moved fast for her. Only to find himself face to face with an enraged Matteo. Erik and Josef had also stepped in, putting themselves between Giuseppe and Quinn, standing on either side of

Matteo.

"I will rip out your heart if you don't move," Matteo warned. "Your last visit here, you provoked Carlos, but now it's *me* you're provoking." He bared fangs with a deep growl.

Giuseppe grabbed him by the throat. "I am a King, and you will show me respect."

"But you're not my King." Matteo stated. "I will defend what is mine."

I moved up behind Giuseppe, wrapping my arm around his neck. "Stand down," I warned in his ear. "You've not faced him when he goes feral. You have one chance to show your clan who you are. Don't be foolish. Leave here in peace, or in pieces. It's your choice."

I stepped back, releasing him. Giuseppe growled, and his closed fist connected with Matteo's chest. A loud crack sounded, and Matteo was on the ground. Then Quinn was singing, her eyes glowing green. Giuseppe fell to his knees, hands over his ears. In her anger, Quinn put extra strength into her siren power, and I struggled against the sound. Despite her attempt to control where she directed it, the clan still felt the strength, everyone wincing. Its effects were painful, similar to the audio weapon my Huntress had used, and I used my own anger to battle through it.

I turned to the rest of Giuseppe's clan, who were also on their knees. "Your king has fallen. It would be in your best interest to find a new one who will not lead you to your slaughter. What will it be? Share his fate, or leave here to live another day?"

They stared at their leader in shock. Matteo, on his feet again, punched hard into Giuseppe's chest, pulling out his heart, and Quinn stopped singing. Giuseppe's body crumpled and Matteo turned around, offering Quinn the heart. She took it without hesitation, and my clan faced the remaining vampires.

"I am his second," someone spoke up. "I will take his mantle. We will not challenge you."

"What's your name?" I asked.

"I'm Luca," he replied, his eyes on Quinn. "She's a siren."

"I would be very careful if I were you, Luca. My second is rather protective of her," I warned him.

His eyes darted from me to Matteo, then Erik and Josef. "I can see he's not the only one. Nico will not take this well."

I reached out to Luis. *Giuseppe is dead. Matteo killed him. He sought to quarrel with my clan.*

His mind in mine was uncomfortable as he found what he needed. *It is done, don't fret. Nico is angry, but the fault was not yours.* He withdrew from my mind quickly.

"Luis does not hold me responsible for Giuseppe's death," I said to Luca.

"And neither do we," Luca cast a look to the others. "I'm sorry this happened, King Carlos. I know of you by reputation. No one from my clan will challenge you, or enter your territory without your knowledge."

Another vampire stepped forward. "We did not know the reason Giuseppe wanted to challenge you. Just that he returned without Marco, and he wanted retribution. You have shown us mercy, and we thank you."

I motioned to Quinn. "Just know, anyone who challenges me, she has the power to bring a King to his knees." I pointed to Matteo. "You anger him, I will let him go feral."

The vampires knelt to me, including Luca.

Matteo met my eyes. *'Does he not know what he's doing?'*

'I want you and Josef with me when he learns what he's done,' I commanded him.

I turned to my clan. "Celeste, Andreas, Quinn, escort our guests out of Venice. Erik, too. I wish to speak with Luca alone. Josef and Matteo will escort him out when I am done." I caught the worried expressions of his clan. "I mean your King no harm," I reassured them.

They left, and I walked from the den with Luca.

"How long have you been a vampire, Luca?" I asked.

"Three centuries," he said. "Am I too young to be a King?"

I laughed, casting a glance at Matteo and Josef as they followed us. "Not at all. My clan once chose Quinn for their Queen, only days after she turned. She knelt to me, and they accepted her choice. Is your maker still alive?"

He paused. "No. She died a century ago."

His pain was unmistakable. "I know that sorrow; I lost mine about fifteen years ago."

We walked in silence, Matteo and Josef shadowing us. Humans around us moved out of our way, our presence making them uneasy. Glances towards us showed their apprehension.

"Did Giuseppe teach you much about what it means to be a King?" I asked.

"I know nothing about being a King," he admitted.

I laughed. "None of us do when we're forced into the role. It was trial and error for me. When we first arrived here, I had to figure out what kind of King I wanted to be. Some rule by fear, others with compassion. That is something you will work out."

He nodded thoughtfully as we led him into a dark alleyway.

I stopped. Matteo and Josef closed in.

"You are young, Luca. I am surprised that he would have named you his second without teaching you the basics," I said.

He eyed Matteo and Josef. "The basics? What am I missing?"

"Kings never kneel to other Kings or Queens," Matteo said. "To do so is to submit."

"You offered yourself, and your entire clan to Carlos." Josef smiled. "You may not have known what you were doing at the time, but it still stands."

Luca frowned. "This is why you separated me from my clan."

I gave him my biggest smile. "I'd be stupid not to take the opportunity. You have a large clan, and we have Hunters heading our way."

He visibly gave up, his shoulders slumped. "What do I do, then?" he asked, the defeat clear in his voice.

"Kneel to your King," Matteo commanded.

The three of us stood around him, our eyes red, fangs bared.

Luca didn't hesitate, and dropped to his knees.

"Bare your throat." I said.

He tilted his head to the side, and I slid my fangs into the exposed flesh. Luca groaned in pain, as I hadn't released any venom into my bite. I took only a little blood, then released him.

"Of course, I'll need someone I trust to make sure you don't plan to disobey me," I said.

"You would send a member of your clan to ensure I follow your commands?" he asked.

I lifted my head, meeting Josef's eyes. "No. I would bond you to Josef. He will be your advisor, and he will open communication between me and you. Any command he gives you will be mine."

Josef smiled, baring fangs, and lowered his mouth to Luca's throat.

Chapter 50

I waited for Camila's sister to leave before returning to my Queen's bed. She had me in restraints again. I had been chained many times after the war, when my hunger and lack of control got the best of me. I had used cuffs many times for sexual satisfaction, but I had *never* allowed anyone to shackle *me* for sex. When it came to matters of the bedroom, even before becoming a King, I had always taken charge.

But from the first time Camila had said 'kneel,' I had dropped to my knees, willing and eager. I found a certain gratification in yielding to her, and I had witnessed Camila finding what brought her pleasure. I could not have guessed there was such a beast beneath her surface. If only her bed weren't so small.

She lay in my arms gazing into my eyes with a smile. I leaned forward and nuzzled her throat. She shifted her head slightly, exposing her neck. I ran my tongue slowly over skin and growled before sinking my fangs in, letting the taste of her blood fill me with satisfaction. She let out a deep sigh of contentment, her hand on the back of my head. Her sigh turned into a moan, the sound piercing me. I groaned into her throat, and her grasp tightened.

I tore myself from her, so as not to take too much, and I pulled back to look at her. Red fingerprints lined her throat and arms, over the top of older, purple bruising from days before. She had demanded that I bruise her, hurt her, and it filled me with joy to do so. I ran my thumb over the mark, and the bruises.

"My filthy little Huntress," I remarked with a smile. "There's no hiding what you are now. What you do in the bedroom. These are there for all to see."

"My sister saw," she murmured. "I told her, about you. About us."

I met her gaze. "Should I be concerned?"

"No." She placed her hand on my arm. "She wasn't exactly thrilled by the idea that I had taken you to my bed, and she is worried that you'll accidentally kill me, but she would never do anything to hurt me."

I kissed her forehead. "I would never hurt you."

Her phone beeped. With a groan, she reached for the phone and threw it.

"Is that not important?" I asked.

"It's just my father, with his usual message of 'Report.'" She put on a deep voice as if imitating her father. "Seeing as I'm currently in bed with a vampire, he can wait."

I lifted my head to see where the phone had landed. "Maybe you should answer him. I don't want your silence to give him any reason to come here. I won't hurt you, or your sister. Or allow my clan to. But I have no intention of extending that courtesy to him."

"You would kill him?" A dark look crossed over her face, and I wondered if she hated her father that much.

"I would protect my clan, and all those important to me, including you, if he threatened you," I told her, surprising myself at the change in who I would protect.

She gazed into my eyes for a moment longer and then climbed from her bed to fetch the phone she'd thrown. As she picked it up, her laptop beeped. I sat up, watching while she took a seat in front of the computer, reading.

She glanced over at me, shock across her features. "There's a lot of Hunter activity at the moment. I've never seen anything like it. I would say they're tracking something, to gather like that." She frowned. "I saw the call go out, but that's an unusual number of Hunters answering it."

"How many?" I asked.

She typed into her phone and returned to me. "Hundreds. Are they following something? Do your people have something happening?"

I pulled her to me. "They haven't got it in your records, what they're doing?"

She shook her head. "There are different levels in our security. General information that we all have access to for updates, Hunter movements, etcetera. But more in-depth details are only for the heads of families."

"Hunters are protecting their reason for being on the move?" I asked.

She turned her phone around to show me. "I can communicate with other Hunters, update Hunting logs and see call outs for help. Even put one out myself. There has been a call to travel to Italy and move South. But I don't know the reason, or the target."

I looked at the screen, reading. I knew what their target was. "Why the extra caution?" I asked. "Wouldn't they want all Hunters to know?"

She gave me a tight smile. "We used to. Everything was open to all until a few years ago, until we picked up a login from a Hunter who missed his check-in and was later found dead. We realised it had been compromised. The entire system underwent an upgrade for security."

I couldn't hold back the grin. "That was Josef."

She sat up. "He hacked into the Hunter network? Did he kill the Hunter?"

"He was captured and tortured. What he did was in retaliation after five days of starvation,' I explained. "He saw an opportunity and took it. Andreas downloaded everything, but we were locked out quickly. So we don't have anything up-to-date."

"Josef is the reason our entire security system got upgraded?" She laughed. "He's one of the most sought-after vampires because he was a former Hunter. If only people knew that."

I shrugged. "He went to represent me to a Queen in Spain for a few days. A Hunter recognised him. Many do rather quickly. He told me you looked him up on your phone. Your technology really has advanced over the years."

"He looked familiar, but I couldn't place him. We learn about him very early on in our training." She grinned at me. "How did he accept becoming the very thing he'd once hunted?"

I caressed her face. "He woke up a vampire and killed his entire camp. Once he regained his memories, he gave himself fully to being a vampire."

"He was okay with that? He didn't feel guilty?" she asked.

Her curiosity made me wonder what was behind her questions. "When we first awaken, our hunger is extremely powerful. He held no desire to fight what he'd become. We don't. It's all part of being turned. We're completely remade; our nature and instinct become a deep part of us. We don't completely lose humanity, but we do lose touch with our human selves. We still love, feel loss, and have compassion. But how we view humans changes. Human frailties are gone, human sentiments diminish."

She absorbed my words. "So, no one tries to fight the new nature?"

I shook my head. "Very few resist it. Those who do, aren't usually accepted into clans."

"Did you turn him?" she asked me. "I feel like that's something you'd do."

I gave her a tight smile. "It *was* my idea to turn a Hunter, but not my blood that flows through him. The only vampires I ever made were ferals. I never considered turning anyone with the blood bond." I paused. I'd marked Camila, and she was a Hunter, so I wasn't sure our path would ever go that way. I had never thought about the future, and for the first time I wondered what lay in ours. "Josef was delighted to find himself in the records. He remembers the day the artist drew his picture. You really chronicle everything?"

She nodded. "Our ancestors kept journals for centuries. We still have them. The computer age had us uploading everything online. It makes it easier for us to share information. Kills, vampire sightings, suspicious deaths. You name it."

Curiosity got the better of me. "So, did you read all the records of me?"

She met my eyes. "No Hunter has anything good to say about you. I saw your name before I knew who you were. I was trying to work out who it was I was up against. But I dismissed it." She leaned in for a brief kiss. "None of them talked about how attractive and charming you are. Or how easy it would be to get you in chains on your knees."

My body shook from laughter. "You dismissed it?" I pressed. "You didn't believe I was me?" The chains rattled as I wrapped my arms around her.

She chuckled. "You were smug and arrogant, and terrifying, but I didn't see how you could be who the records described."

"Smug and arrogant?" I asked, feigning offence.

She pulled back, gazing into my eyes. "You are too beautiful to be alone; please honour me with your company," she quoted me. "Do you honestly lure in people with such a line?"

"Ouch," I pressed my lips to hers. Our kiss was long, hungry. The quickening of her heart vibrated through my chest. Wrapped in warmth, I let go with reluctance, and ran my fingers over her mark. "I was hungry, and my charm had never failed me. I didn't lie, though; you are beautiful."

Her eyes lit up. Then she gave me a serious look. "Your charm is a little old-fashioned. If I hadn't been hunting you, too, I would have rolled my eyes and written you off as a creepy red flag."

"A creepy red flag? Well, that hurts," I laughed. "Okay then, my little Huntress, teach me the ways of how to lure the modern woman."

A strange expression passed over her face. "Well, for starters, eww, that's creepy. Also, no."

"No?" I kissed her throat. "You've called me creepy, not once but twice, yet here you are, your throat beneath my fangs." I kissed her throat again. "You lie next to me naked. Have my attempts to lure you been a complete failure?"

She bared her throat then, tilting her head enough to let me know what she wanted. Not willing to deny her, I sunk my fangs in again. Her blood hit my tongue, and I groaned, fighting the desire to bite again, harder. Drinking from her had ceased to become a normal feeding. There was something deeper, almost binding me to her, an intensity of yearning that I didn't understand. I was the one with the power over people, yet her power over me was becoming more and more noticeable.

I didn't take much from her, despite wanting to. Next to the bed was a bottle of water, and I let her go to drink. She swallowed a couple of iron tablets.

"I'm not going to help you lure other women," she said at last, returning to my embrace.

"Ohh, possessive. I like it." I grinned. "Your Hunter records are right, you know."

"About what?" she asked.

"I have no doubt what Hunters of the past say about me.

That I'm a killer. *The* Killer. I earned that name. Father of Ferals. The Immortal Wolf. That I'm dangerous. I've been a vampire so long, I know no other way. I live for it. Many Hunters have tried to take me out, but only two have come remotely close to succeeding." I wondered how it had come to pass that I was in the bed of a Hunter. "And one of those two now lies next to me in bed, naked."

"You don't scare me, Carlos," she murmured. "Yes, I've seen that side of you. I've also seen the side of you where your touch is so gentle, even though you said you're not. But it's your rougher touch that lights a fire in me. You make me feel things." She paused. "I never imagined it would be a vampire that awoke this."

"Awoke what?" I pressed. I knew the answer, but I wanted to hear the words.

"This hunger for pain with pleasure," she touched the leather cuff around my wrist. "To do this and take such pleasure from it. I never imagined—" she stopped and shook her head.

"You've discovered your kinks. You've found who you are." I said. "You like to be in control as much as you like to be controlled. Don't be afraid of that." I lifted my arm, letting the chains rattle. "Know that you are the first person, *ever,* who I have willingly let put these on me. That is no small feat."

She snuggled into me then, and I wrapped both arms around her. She had awoken something in me, too, and she made me feel things. I just didn't understand exactly what.

Chapter 51

My obsession with Camila had taken over my entire life. I was like a man possessed, unable to stay away. Every night that week, I sought her out. This night was no different. After feeding, I caught her scent and found her outside a cafe with a coffee in front of her. She glanced up with a smile, and she kicked the chair out for me, when I stepped from the shadows. Her eyes fell to my mouth.

"Maybe you shouldn't be in public like that," she whispered and held out a napkin.

In my haste to find her, I had walked right into a very

public square, filled with humans. I wiped the blood from my chin and sat down opposite her.

"I got home today in time to have a new bed delivered," she revealed. "I've never had such a large bed."

"Oh good, you got it," I said with a smile.

"You really bought me a new bed?" Her voice was almost a whisper.

I reached across the table, stroking her arm. "I marked you, I wanted to do something nice for you. So I thought buying a gift would be —"

I stopped talking when she burst out laughing. I watched in silence.

"I'm sorry," she said through laughter. "Now I know you haven't been human in a long time."

Her reaction was not what I had expected. "Was I not supposed to get you a bed?"

Her laughter died. "Oh, no, I love that you bought that. It's just not the norm for a gift. Especially these days." She shook her head. "Your gift was touching, Carlos, just unusual."

My own uncertainty surprised me. "What is normal for a gift?" I asked. Perhaps I should have asked Matteo, as he was always being romantic with Quinn. Although that conversation would not have been a good idea.

She reached her hand towards me. "It doesn't matter what's normal. We're not exactly a normal pair." She gave me a small smile. "But I wouldn't complain if you wanted to get me flowers. Or even jewellery."

"Noted," I said.

She gave me a joyful grin. "I got you something, too. I ordered it online especially."

Surprised, I watched her as she pulled a small box from

her bag, pushing it across the table at me. Delight shone through her eyes. Quinn, Annika and Celeste had bought me gifts, but this was a surprise. Warmth spread across my chest as I grabbed the box.

"Open it," she said.

I lifted the box, removing the top. Inside sat a leather bracelet. It was wide with a silver buckle.

"Will you allow me to put it on?" she asked.

I knew exactly what it was. She wanted to take our games beyond the bedroom. To put it on display. "You're asking me?" I challenged her.

Understanding filled her eyes and she lifted the bracelet, grabbing my wrist. As she closed the buckle, her eyes met mine. "You can't take it off," she told me.

I fought down the urge to growl and take her right there. "No…my Queen," I replied.

The glee that shone through her eyes warmed me again.

"You've been doing your research," I said with pride.

She ducked her head. "After discovering this side to myself, I wanted to understand it more. There's a whole world that I never knew about. Maybe we can try blindfolds, or… oh! A whip!" Her entire face lit up.

I reached a hand towards her, loving her eagerness. "We can try whatever you want. There is more that I would like to show you." I dropped my voice. "I do have toys I can bring with me."

"Tell me!" she encouraged. "Will it hurt?" Lust glinted in her eyes, and I picked up her sweet scent of arousal. "Whatever you want to bring, I want to try." She gave me a wide smile.

She was not shying away from my suggestion. Celeste

favoured pain, being mastered, and being watched. Quinn had accepted knife play, and she loved to be punished, not to mention her 'vampire orgies'. Annika had a preference for anal and for being tied up. But the woman in front of me displayed such enthusiasm to explore. A willingness, even a hunger for it. As I gazed across the table at her, it struck me that I may have met my match, in every way.

"Why are you so perfect?" I asked in wonder.

"Because you needed to be put in your place and told you're a good boy," she said with a sly smile.

Heat unfurled in my groin. "Maybe my sweet *Cazadora* needs to be told she's a good girl, marked, and spanked," I blurted out.

Her lips parted, her intake of air showed I'd struck a nerve. Her eyes blazed, her scent washing over me again.

A waitress interrupted us. Camila ordered an espresso for me. I couldn't remember the last time I'd had coffee, but I wanted to enjoy her presence a little while longer. The waitress hurried away again. I smiled. We'd been speaking in English, and she had obviously heard more of our conversation than she wanted to.

As if to deliberately tempt me, Camila tilted her head to the side, her fingers brushing over my mark. I couldn't look away. She gave a small smile and turned her head to the side.

My fangs lengthened as I stared, a low growl rumbling from me. "Temptress, " I said, in Castellano.

"Carlos!" She glanced around to make sure no one had seen my fangs or heard my growl, also speaking in Castellano. "I don't want anyone to scream 'vampire' in the middle of the square. There are people who may not be Hunters but do communicate with us. They report sightings to us."

A different waitress brought my coffee. "*Grazie*," I said, catching her eyes to put her at ease. She beamed back at me and blushed before walking away.

"What did you do?" Camila asked.

I took a sip of the coffee, careful to not take too much of a mouthful. It was a hot liquid and humans would notice if I drank it too quickly. "I compelled her a little, to put her at ease." I said. "Some humans tend to sense there's something…not right, with me. Especially when I'm not hunting." I didn't need to tell her that when I was hunting, humans couldn't stay away.

Camila nodded. "Your presence definitely sets off alarms. I get the feeling you enjoy that, though."

"Oh I do," I laughed. "When I put effort in, they see just a man. When I don't, some people tend to keep a wide berth around me."

"So, you're just a vampire and nothing else?" she asked.

I nodded. "What else is there?" My words shocked her, I could tell by the way she stared into her coffee. "I've existed as a vampire since the eleven hundreds. It's all I've ever been since Gabriela pulled me from slumber."

She eyed me. "That's a little sad."

Sad? "How can it be sad? I'm happy with what I am."

"Don't you get lonely?" There was sympathy in her gaze.

Her words were starting to make me uncomfortable. I didn't understand her sympathy, nor why she was so concerned. "Why would I be lonely? I have my clan. I take the occasional human to my bed when I feel the need, but mostly I pick someone from my clan to enjoy."

Shock widened her eyes. "You have more than one sexual

partner from your clan? Is that a vampire thing?"

I laughed then, relieved that she was following a new path with our conversation. Looks of sympathy and talk of loneliness set a tightness in my chest I didn't like. "We do have increased sexual…appetites. Especially when we feed. But I'm intimate with multiple men and women. Although we only have three women in my clan."

Understanding filtered through her gaze. "Oh, you're polyamorous. And bisexual."

Quinn had said the same once. "You humans have words for everything now," I murmured. "I never needed to explain my…" I lifted my hand, shrugging.

"Orientation." She finished for me. "They're okay that you share them all?"

I leaned forward, stroking the back of her hand with my thumb. "They are. They know I share affection for each of them equally. Does that bother you? Are you okay to share me?"

She took a minute to answer, her eyes on my face. "I can't imagine they'd be happy sharing you with a Hunter," she said. "I would rather have you to myself, but I will not tell you who you can and can't be intimate with."

"Are you still a Hunter?" I asked with a grin. "If you're fucking a vampire."

Her face darkened, and she tried to hide it behind sipping her coffee and looking around the square. "If my father knew…" Her fingers brushed my mark. "If he saw this, he'd tell everyone I had been compromised. I'd be exiled."

I drank from my own cup. "Is that so bad, to be excluded from a community that kills my kind? That would try to kill my clan, or me?"

She frowned. "I hadn't thought about it. I guess I'm still getting used to the idea."

I couldn't blame her. We were from opposite sides of a war that had existed for centuries. Despite the peace, and accords, it hadn't really ended; both our peoples still hated one another. She had grown up in a world where I was her enemy, and she had been taught that her entire purpose was to kill me. I had fought in the very war that had made us enemies. I'd probably fought her ancestors. Now it looked like we would soon be fighting again. I had told my clan I wouldn't hesitate to join the Elders, but now, with her in front of me, something had changed. I didn't want her to get caught up in the coming war.

"There's something brewing," I warned her. "You should be careful. Perhaps you should leave Venice. Hide."

Alarm flickered across her face. "My sister said the same thing. You think it'll come to another war?"

"I know it will." I glanced around the square and finished my coffee. So many humans at surrounding tables, shopping, taking photos. Excited to be in Venice. Many different languages, most of which I spoke. As we sat amongst them, speaking in our mother tongue, listening to them speak in theirs, it occurred to me what was at stake. "This time the Elders will not back down. Humans are likely to get caught in the crossfire." I didn't add that the only human I gave a damn about getting caught in the war, was the one in front of me.

She watched those around us. "I've often been envious of them," she said in a low voice. "Oblivious to it all. Even though I'm supposed to be like them, I never felt like I fit in. One foot in their world, one in yours."

I understood then her earlier talk of loneliness and sadness with a clarity that I felt deep within. "It's *you* who's lonely," I acknowledged, squeezing her hand. "And sad. Your ancestors put a burden on you, and your father sent you to die." I recalled the guilt and pain I'd sensed in her the first time I lay in her bed. "Why did he seek to punish you over your mother's death?"

It took a long time for her to answer. Pain and guilt crossed over her face. "It hurts," she said. "To speak the words, I'm not sure I can, not here."

I reached for her face. "Then show me." I brushed against her mind, waiting for her permission. Usually I wouldn't hesitate, but something told me to wait. She nodded, and I pushed in, searching her memories. The hunt in which her mother got killed. Her grief surrounded me, but I dug deeper, caressing her face to comfort her. I caught only a glimpse of the vampire who'd done it, but I saw enough to recognise Olivia.

'*I hesitated.*' She was considering what she wanted to say to me, and I heard it as clearly as if she'd spoken aloud.

I watched as Olivia, cornered, sought out her escape. The youngest of the family, her hesitance wasn't in killing, but in being there in the first place. I could feel it from Camila, like a mark that Olivia had left in her mind.

Olivia pushed her will on Camila. '*Young Huntress, let me go; give me my freedom. Perhaps then you can gain your own.*'

"You *didn't* hesitate. She *compelled* you," I clarified, pulling from Camila's mind. "It's not your fault. You don't have to feel guilty. No human can fight the will of a vampire." It was unlike Olivia to take a human life; she must have felt threatened, to do so. Being cornered by a family of Hunters wouldn't be enough. "You were possibly close to her den; she would have been protecting her clan. I would have done the same. Only, I would have torn every last Hunter apart."

"She compelled me?" Camila stared. "So, when I thought I was hesitating…"

"You were giving her a chance to escape, just as she told you to." I had seen something else in her mind that made me curious. Olivia had likely found it within seconds. "Do you want to be a Hunter?" I asked.

Her face crumbled, and I thought she was about to cry. But it passed, and she forced a smile instead.

"Can we just sit and be?" she asked in an attempt to avoid my question. "I want to feel like I'm one of *them*. Normal. Happy. No looming war, no Hunters or vampires."

It wasn't the first time she had asked something similar, to ignore what we were. What she was.

I lifted her hand, kissing it softly. "Okay. For now, I'll pretend that I'm human with you. Two people taking in the sights of Venice." I smiled. "Show me your world, Camila." I pointed to her empty cup. "You've finished your coffee, what do you want to do?"

Her face lit up, and I couldn't help but smile back. "I always wanted to go for a gondola ride!" she exclaimed.

I stood and held my hand out. "What my Queen wants, she shall have."

Chapter 52

To my surprise, Carlos led me away from the Grand Canal.

"Aren't we going the wrong way?" I asked.

He chuckled. "Only if you want to pay more, and face bigger crowds. This way you can enjoy the allure of Venice without all the tourists."

We walked to a smaller, quieter street, where a few gondolas waited. He approached a gondolier I recognised from our fight. The man looked me over with a frown. The two spoke in Italian, and Carlos handed over cash.

With a small bow, Carlos gave me a wide smile and held a

hand out. "My Queen, your chariot awaits!"

My heart fluttered as I took his hand, allowing him to guide me into the gondola. He sat down beside me, pulling me close.

"How many languages do you speak?" I asked in Castellano. There was a level of privacy when we didn't speak in English. Especially particular topics. After the waitress overheard our very kinky conversation, I realised it was safer to converse in our native language.

He grinned. "Other than Castellano, English, and Italian you mean?" I nodded. "I can speak fluent French, Latin, German, Old Norse, Portuguese, Arabic, and Japanese. I've been learning to speak Quinn's native language, Te Reo Māori," he informed me.

My mouth hung open. That was a lot of languages.

His laughter vibrated through me. "Don't look so impressed. I've had a *long* time on this planet. I'll always prefer Castellano, although the dialect of that has somewhat changed over the centuries, too. I quite enjoy learning other languages."

I leaned into him, savouring the warmth of his embrace. As we started to move, I took in our surroundings. I had not come here for such things, but having the chance to see Venice from this angle was something I knew I'd never forget. Water lapped at the side of our gondola.

"Old Norse?" I asked.

"I learned that just after the war, when we became clans. A vampire who was there when I awoke was once what society calls a Viking," he explained. "Just don't ever call *him* that. Erik hates the term. He is a couple of centuries older than me, and he delighted in teaching me his language."

I didn't say anything about the fact that he'd just named one of his clan members.

The city by night was something to marvel at, with a magical feeling to it. I took notice of the different types of buildings. I realised that my time here had been wasted, hunting, when I could have been learning about Venice and its history and beautiful architecture.

"This is the older part of Venice," Carlos said.

"My own personal tour guide," I laughed, filled with wonder.

I'd always watched gondolas in the Grand Canal where it was crowded, with people eager for rides. By bringing me to a quieter part of the city, Carlos had shown me another world, one of beauty and serenity. Not the hustle and bustle I'd come to know.

"That's where Lenora Barone lives," he pointed. "Well, her name may be different now, but she's still a Barone by blood. She's descended from Matteo."

He was pointing to a villa. As we passed, Lenora walked outside and watched us as we passed her. He called out to her in Italian. She responded. I assumed he was telling her she had nothing to worry about.

"She told me the Barones have an agreement with you and your clan," I said.

He smiled down at me. "They let us feed, look the other way, as long as we leave the locals alone." He chuckled. "We took back Matteo's family home, the largest of their properties. Even after all this time, he still prefers a lavish lifestyle. Not that I blame him."

"The gallery?" I asked.

"That's to fund the life he prefers. He's always spoiling

Quinn. Buying her gifts." He smirked. "Perhaps I should have taken inspiration from him."

"What about the other one?" I pressed. "With the nudes, and the 'private showings.' Are people honestly paying you to be fed on?"

'Posing for that was fun. And yes, that private exhibition is popular. Matteo really outdid himself painting those."

The way he talked about Quinn and Matteo suggested affection. "You care deeply for them," I murmured.

He gave me a slight squeeze. "Jealous?"

I *was* a little jealous. I was a one-man woman, but I couldn't tell him not to be who he was. It would take some time to get used to the idea that he was intimate with others, but at least he was open about it. "I am," I said. "I've never known anyone before who's polyamorous. If I have to share you, at least I know about it."

"Oh yes, you can call me many things, but a cheater I am not," he whispered in my ear.

I started to relax, resting my head on his shoulder. His arm tightened around me.

"Are you having fun?" he asked. "Feeling normal?"

"I am," I agreed. "This is very romantic. Are you sure this is what you want to do? You don't strike me as the romantic type."

His fingers lifted my chin, forcing me to look at him. Then leaning in, he kissed me, his lips soft as they brushed mine. My stomach flipped, and I yielded to him. I didn't care what he was; all that mattered was how I felt. His kiss was all-consuming, engulfing me in flames. I was disappointed when the kiss ended. But he remained close, our faces inches apart, his eyes gazing deep into mine. His lips curved into a small smile.

Then he started to sing in Castellano, his voice deep and captivating. A hypnotic sound; words that I'd heard before. Entranced by his voice, I couldn't move. He sang a story of two lovers meant for each other, who, despite their families trying to keep them apart, overcame all obstacles. That they found great happiness in each other, until the woman died, leaving the man alone to grieve her.

The song resembled the love story of Romeo and Juliet. I couldn't help but notice the similarities to our own story.

Tears sprung to my eyes as I listened. People turned to stare as we drifted past. He stopped short of her death, though.

"How's that for romantic?" he asked when he finished.

I couldn't speak. He brushed tears away with his thumbs and pressed his lips against mine again. I soared.

"That was beautiful," I whispered.

"A beautiful song for a beautiful woman," he murmured.

My heart ached from the song, from the beauty of his voice. "How do you know that song?" I asked.

"I haven't heard or sung it since I was human." He explained with a faraway look in his eyes. "The men in my village would sing to woo women."

He'd told me he'd turned his back on his human life, so for him to sing a song from then left me breathless. As I cradled his face, the world faded away. I wondered if he remembered how it ended, or if that was a more modern addition. "If I had lived in your village, and heard you sing, I wouldn't have been able to resist you."

His face lit up, not an expression I'd seen on him before, pure and open delight. I couldn't help but wonder if it was a human part of him that he'd buried shining through. Unguarded, not smug. Just a man, who'd serenaded me in a gondola, with a song from his youth. I kissed him, filled with tenderness and warmth.

He moved his hand under my jacket, sliding under my tee-shirt. Warm fingers brushed against my breast, and a low rumble vibrated from him. His other hand slid round, resting on my bare back. Consumed by desire, I moved my hand under his tee-shirt, wanting to touch him, to caress him. But I yearned for more than what we could do on the gondola, or in public.

His fangs extended, and we pulled apart. Disappointed, I gazed into his red eyes, my breathing ragged.

"Sorry," he rasped. "You make me lose control, Camila." A wild glint reflected in his eyes, and he licked his lips.

The way he said my name. I could barely contain myself. "We need to get out," I whispered, groping him through his jeans. He was hard, and I wanted to climb on top of him.

He smirked. "No, sweet Huntress, we're not done being human." His voice had dropped. He was as aroused as I was. "The ride isn't over yet."

He caressed my neck, his fingers light, sending tingles through me, before his lips brushed the mark. I let out a shaky breath.

"You're not very good at self-control," I whispered.

He laughed. "I will not deny that. You make it that much harder." His breath was hot on my throat. "Your self-control is not much better right now."

He licked the scar and a full body quiver tore through me, my muscles tightening. His fangs grazed my flesh.

"The gondolier," I whispered.

"He's extremely well paid to not see anything," Carlos murmured. "I've hired him before, he knows about us."

Lenora had told me people worked for the vampires. There were probably a few gondoliers like this one. The thought occurred to me that Carlos had brought women, even men, into a gondola to feed on. I recalled the man who had been in his arms when I'd interrupted them.

I realised that we were alone. The gondolier had left us in a water level entrance to a house. Carlos's hands moved across my body, leaving me yearning for more, my skin hot where he touched me.

"I want to devour you," his voice rumbled as he growled. "Bare your throat, Camila. Now."

So much for behaving human. My entire body tensed. I wanted his bite. I needed it. I tilted my head to the side, and when his fangs slid in, it took everything not to cry out. I clutched at him, whimpering in an effort to not moan. I soared, loving the effects of his venom. It was just him and me, in a gondola.

He released me, and I climbed on top of him, grinding against his erection. Breathing hard, and already wet, I pulled at his belt.

"Slow down, my lovely Huntress," he grunted. "What were you saying about self-control?"

"Fuck self control," I said, unzipping his jeans and stroked his erection. "I need you to fuck me. Right now."

A trace of amusement came through the heavy longing in his eyes. I pulled at his tee-shirt, and he removed it for me, followed by mine. I pressed my hands against his chest, and down his abs, yearning for the warmth of his firm body against mine. He removed the rest of our clothes.

I shifted myself, kissing his chest. His low rumbles only encouraged me as I trailed down. I ran my tongue over him, and he took in a deep breath, letting it go slowly. Then I moved further down, grabbing his cock. I started with small, delicate licks and then teased him with kisses down his shaft. Lifting my eyes, I caught him looking at me, his fangs out, mouth open. I licked up his precum, and a ferocious growl rose from him. I smiled up at him.

"Mmmm, don't stop now," he said, almost pained at my teasing.

I bobbed my head, down his length.

"Take all of me," he ordered, his hand wrapping in my hair. "Keep going."

I pushed further, suppressing my gag reflexes.

"Good girl," his voice was more beast than man as he teetered on the edge of a primal nature that glinted from his eyes.

His words sent a thrill through me.

He gripped the side of the gondola with his other hand, I swirled my tongue and took his whole length again. His breathing was ragged, and he threw his head back, thrusting into my mouth.

A crunch drew my attention — he'd crushed the side of the gondola. I laughed, the sound vibrating through him. He leaned back, his head against the seat. I reached up, tapping him on his ribs. When he lowered his face, I pointed to my eyes with two fingers. He hissed at me, but did as I was asking, our eyes locking.

His stare always made me feel like I was the only one in his world. I knew that wasn't the case, but he never rushed through our time together; he always made sure

I was satisfied. At that moment, I never wanted to be apart from him.

Carlos thrust into my mouth again. His hand was on the back of my head, pushing me down as his hips rose up. I knew he was close when he tensed, his movements faster.

"Camila, don't stop," he pleaded breathlessly. He let out a soft moan, which became louder. "Fuck," he grunted. "Take me deep, Huntress.'

I almost gagged again as his cock slid in. I cupped his balls as I took him deeper and his sounds became animalistic. His whole body strained, and he roared. Warm liquid sprayed the back of my throat. I swallowed it down and licked his head before releasing him.

As he spasmed, I moved, kissing trails up his body, stopping at his collarbone, pressing myself against him. I moved up his neck towards his lips, but he stopped me.

"Bite my throat," he gasped out.

I stared at him in shock. "What?"

"Your teeth aren't sharp enough to draw blood. Bite, my Huntress." His neck was exposed, and I hesitated. "It's all right. I won't Bestow you this time."

I had no idea what he meant with bestow, and realised he was likely accustomed to being bitten when he lay with those in his clan. He was asking me for something he liked. I forced down my uncertainty, meeting his heated gaze before pressing my teeth against his neck.

"Harder," he commanded me.

I shuddered but did as he asked, pressing my teeth in, hoping that I wouldn't draw blood. Even just a taste would have effects on me. I'd already been through that. His hand stroked my hair as he made a sound of contentment.

"Stop," he said.

I lifted my head, to check that I hadn't bitten too deep. My teeth left indentations in his flesh.

"See, no blood." He smiled, his eyes flashing at me.

"My teeth marks are…never mind." They smoothed over before my eyes. "I don't think I'll ever get used to that."

"You've marked me, then, my lovely Huntress." His voice had a huskiness to it. "It doesn't matter that it's gone."

Feeling braver, I licked where I'd bitten him, then pressed my mouth to his. Then I was on my back, the full moon behind him as he stared hungrily down at me. That look was enough to sweep everything else from my mind. I craved him. I had never met a man who'd had this effect on me.

His cock slid into me, and I stretched around him as he filled me. The gondola rocked under us, and I reached for the side, glancing around.

"No one can see us. There's no one here. If anyone does catch us, I'll just growl at them until they go away." He pulled my hand from the side, guiding it to his abs. "If you're going to hold on to something, hold on to me."

Surprised to find myself exhilarated by the idea of someone catching us in the act, and of Carlos growling, I smiled at him with excitement. Then I grabbed his ass as he drove into me, pushing me into a pleasure-filled haze. He chuckled down at me before kissing my neck. "You like that?" he asked, against my throat. "You want someone to catch us? Pain isn't enough, you want someone to watch us?" I let out a moan around the word yes.

"There is more to you than meets the eye, my filthy little Huntress," he whispered. "I think you and Erik would have a lot to talk about."

With his lips on my throat, the anticipation of his bite spread through me as his cock hit deep, eliciting a whimper from me.

"Oh god, bite me, Carlos," I begged.

Far away, I observed I was begging a vampire to bite me, while he was inside me, in a gondola. A vampire I was here to kill. But as his fangs entered me, and his venom flooded my senses, I dismissed the observation. I didn't want to kill vampires, I just wanted to enjoy Carlos. Nothing else. I let out a long moan, almost screaming as I came. His rougher tendencies and inhuman sexual appetite had awoken my own desires. I wanted pain with the pleasure. To be bitten and marked, bruised and sore, in his arms while he fed from me.

Chapter 53

"We sat in your world," I told Camila. "I had coffee with you. I serenaded you. I played the part of a human. Which I don't do very well. Now come and see mine."

Her arousal clung to her, a scent that made my canines ache. I was aware that I'd been losing control with her and needed to be careful. But her scent, that scent, drove me wild. I wanted to take her, again and again. I wanted to hear her begging me to hurt her as I buried myself deep in her again. I was barely holding myself back.

She gave me an uncertain smile.

I held my hand out, and she took it. "Don't worry, I think you'll enjoy this."

I led her away from the gondola, and down an alley.

"Where are we going?" she asked.

"What, don't tell me you're scared of me dragging you into the dark and feeding from you," I joked.

"You already did that," she pointed out.

Her voice, begging me to bite her, echoed in my mind. The very memory sent delicious shivers through me. Humans had been known to become addicted to the effects of our venom, and mine was stronger now. I needed to be careful.

I picked her up in my arms. "You're safe, sweet *Cazadora*."

Before she could say anything, I leapt to the top of the building. Her heart pounded, her eyes closed tight.

"Don't be afraid." I told her. "You're on steady ground." I let her stand. "Well, as much as you can be, in a city on water."

She laughed, relaxing. I led her to the other side of the building, which looked over *Ponte di Rialto*. I stood behind her, my arms wrapped around her waist. She placed her hands over mine.

"It's beautiful," she murmured, leaning against me. "So, this is what you mean by your world? You stand on rooftops?"

"Look how peaceful it is when all the tourists aren't packed in, taking photos," I said. "This is where I come to watch over the city. To make sure no one tries to enter my territory."

The Elders had declared this my territory, so it was unlikely other vampires would try to challenge me now. Even less likely after Giuseppe's failed attempt. Word would spread as to what had happened. But there were other creatures out there, many of which had tried to take Venice. Their attempts had been short-lived.

Camila relaxed, leaning her head back against my shoulder. "How do you feed if you're always up so late?" she asked. "You don't feed from locals, but the visitors usually go home at night."

I lowered my head, kissing her neck. "We don't need to be invited in," I reminded her. "Hunting can easily be walking into a hotel. All it takes is knocking, or scratching on the door. Plus, there's always someone who can't sleep, drawn to go for a walk. You never know what's in the dark, waiting." I yearned to bite her again. I growled softly, letting my fangs lengthen.

"Do it," she whispered and moved her head to the side, baring her throat to me again. All thoughts of being careful were swept away by my desire for her. I licked her throat before sinking my fangs in. A gentle nip. I fought back the urge to bite deep and tear as I did with my clan, reminding myself she didn't have our healing abilities. Camila moaned and her knees gave out, so I supported her completely. I retracted my fangs, kissing her throat again.

"I do believe you're beginning to want it." I whispered into her ear. "Do you yearn for my vampire's kiss, little Huntress?"

"I do." Her voice was barely audible.

Her admission made me grin. and I bit her again, this time her wrist. When I straightened, I made sure she could stand. She turned to face me, eyes burning.

"Did I hurt you?" I asked, glancing at where my fangs had marked her again. "I have a tendency to bite deep at times." I had tried to be careful.

"No, I'm okay," she said, and stretched up to kiss me.

She didn't react to her blood being on my lips. No shudder of revulsion this time. Wrapping my arms around her, I pulled her tight against me, aware that I was hard. Damn, this woman. I'd taken humans to bed as I fed on them, but never more than once with the same one. None of them had the effect that this one did. It was too late to run; she had her claws in me. A human. I wanted her, I wanted to claim her, but I held back. Deep down, she was still a Hunter. It was common knowledge, even to her people, what that meant.

We pulled apart, watching the city from the edge of the rooftop.

"Can we walk across the Rialto Bridge?" she asked.

I lifted her in my arms again, returning to the ground. *"Ponte de Rialto,"* I said. 'We can do anything that you want." She was stalling going home. I knew what she was doing, because I was doing the same. I would walk with her all night if I could.

"Do you all hunt wherever you want?" she asked.

I glanced down, her questions getting a bit more into natural human curiosity, less that of a Hunter. "We have territories. Venice has been divided into six neighbourhoods, or sestieri. Castello, Cannaregio, San Polo, San Marco, Santa Croce, and Dorsoduro. San Polo is my territory."

She repeated each territory. "I'm in San Marco. Who hunts there?"

She clung to my arm as we walked.

"Matteo and Quinn. I moved them to another territory when I realised where you live. Perhaps you should try to stay in mine if you go anywhere at night without me," I suggested. 'I cannot protect you if you stray into another vampire's feeding ground. Other vampires will not be so welcoming if they come across a Hunter. They know your face."

"Even with your mark?" she asked.

"You're a Hunter. That's the first thing they'll see. They've seen you come very close to killing their King; they will not stop to ask questions. I fear they might be more interested in dropping your body at my feet."

She absorbed my words slowly. "They won't care that I've been marked by a vampire. Or who marked me." Her eyes lost their light. "Would you feel sorrow if that happened?"

Pain stabbed at my chest, surprising me. The idea that the loss of a human life would have such an impact was foreign to me. A Hunter, no less. But I'd come to see her less and less as a Huntress.

"I would feel something," I admitted. "It would also put me in a difficult situation with my clan. They are and always will be my first priority. But for them to kill one I'd marked, it would be punishable. The clan may not appreciate me taking such action. You are a Hunter, and they may challenge me."

Her fingers caressed the leather bracelet on my wrist. "Then show me your territory," she murmured. "I will not stray from it. Especially at night."

I took her on the boundaries of my hunting ground. Of San Polo. "I don't kill," I told her. "I take only enough to keep me satisfied, and I feed daily to avoid taking too much. I follow the accords, and I enforce them within my clan."

"Six months ago, a floater was found with knife wounds in her throat. My family suspected a vampire trying to cover their tracks," she explained.

I frowned. "If someone in my clan has killed, I did not know of it." I would need to investigate that. She stifled a yawn. "I should take you home," I said. "I still have to be a King, you still have to be a human. You need sleep. And food. Make sure to drink plenty of fluids after what I took from you tonight."

We turned in the direction of where she lived. "I wish we could just stay in bed and not worry about anything else," she sighed.

I stopped walking. "Are you saying you enjoy my company? Or is it my cock?"

She grinned, continuing walking. I growled at her silence. "Your cock certainly hits all the right places,' she said slowly as I caught up to her.

"You shouldn't tease a vampire," I threatened.

"I'm not teasing a vampire," she laughed. "I'm teasing a man who needs to be reminded who his Queen is." Her words took me by surprise, and I stopped midstep. This time she stopped, too, turning to face me. "You caught that?"

"You called me 'a man'," I stated in shock before giving her a smirk. "What happened to 'You're not a man'?"

She pressed her body against me, cradling my cock through the jeans. "What happened to 'I'm more man than you can handle?'"

"I suppose I was wrong about what you could or couldn't handle," I admitted. "Perhaps you'd like to handle me again before I return to my den." We turned the corner and I stopped, staring at her door. A heart beat on the other side of the door, a man pacing, the strange presence disturbing me. I bit back a growl, I moved fast, taking her with me, away from the door.

"What are you doing?" she asked.

"Someone is in your house," I told her.

"What?" Her voice rose in panic. "Can you tell who it is? Human or vampire?"

"Human." I leaned into my senses to get an impression of who was in her house. "It's a male. It smells like he eats a lot of garlic."

She swore in Castellano. "It's my father."

Her fear crashed over me in sweet, mouth-watering waves, awakening the part of me that lived for that scent. That longed to give chase.

I nuzzled her, breathing her in. "Your fear is intoxicating." I growled. With difficulty, I forced down the urge to tell her to run. "You're afraid of your father."

"Well, it can't be good if he's here. He sent me here to die; there's no reason for him to be here." She stared at her house. "Is he with anyone else, or is it just him?"

"Just him," I said. "Could he be here because of what you told your sister?"

"No!" she glared. "Sof would never share that. Besides, she's hiding from him, anyway, so she's unlikely to contact him for any reason. It could be that he's looking for her, though." Panic glinted in her eyes. "I can't go in there. He'll see that I've been marked by a vampire. It's the first thing he'll notice, and he'll accuse me of being compromised." Her hands trembled. "Carlos, what do I do?"

I did like her using my name in that way, the pleading, desperate tone. It was, however, not within my abilities to know any more than she did. "What will he do if you don't go home?" I considered taking her to the den, demanding that my clan offer her protection.

"He'll wait. The longer he waits, the worse it will be. If he considers me dead, he'll bring someone else in," she said.

I didn't like having another Hunter in Venice, nor the effect his presence was having on Camila. A growl bubbled up, and I pulled her close to me. She leaned into my body, her head resting on my chest.

"I have to go in," she realised. I held her as she fought against her own fear.

"What will he do?" I asked. "If he deems you compromised?"

She lifted her head, meeting my eyes. "I'll be exiled from my family, probably from Spain. It will go on my file in the records, so all Hunters will know. I'd be recognised as a vampire sympathiser."

I frowned. "You're fucking a vampire; would you really continue to hunt my kind?"

Her eyes widened, and she jerked as if I'd slapped her. "You know I wouldn't. But being exiled isn't exactly something I want either, though."

I pulled her out of my embrace. "I have an idea, but I don't know if you'll like it."

"Will it hurt?" she asked.

"Yes, in fact quite a lot." I caressed her cheek. "Not in the enjoyable way either."

She met my gaze. "I already don't like it. Will it help, though?"

"I would say so. Hopefully enough to get your father off your back and go home." I growled again. "I don't like him here. He needs to leave."

"What are you going to do?" she asked warily.

I grinned. "I wouldn't object to scaring him at least. But

that's not what I have in mind."

She sighed. "What's your idea?"

"That you show up with clear signs of being attacked by a vampire," I said.

Her silence stretched out and I wondered if I'd gone too far.

"It might work," she said slowly, thinking it over. "A bite to hide the mark that's already there."

"It will scar, and it will be a lot more noticeable than the mark you already have," I warned her. "It will also hurt. A lot." I shifted my hand to her hip where I knew she kept her knife. "If it helps, this will hurt me, too." I pulled her weapon out, wrapping her fingers around the handle.

Her eyes darted from the knife, to my face. "You want me to stab you?"

I smirked. "I do like to play with knives, but this is not going to be a pleasant pain. Whether I can heal or not, being stabbed in the gut is excruciating. So no, I don't want you to stab me, but if it's to help your situation, I'll let you, just this once. Just please avoid the leather. I'll never hear the end of it if Quinn has to buy another jacket for me."

I held the front of my jacket out of the way as she stared at me. "You're serious." She frowned. "Why am I stabbing you?"

"Because you'll have a knife covered in blood to show you fought back," I said.

She lifted the knife with hesitance. "They're right about you when they say you're cunning."

I kissed her. "I can also be incredibly stupid. Getting involved with a Huntress is not smart whatsoever. Go."

I braced myself as the blade pierced my abdomen. She

pulled it out, the blade red with my blood. My wound closed.

"Damn, you heal quickly," she acknowledged.

I was well fed. But I would need to feed again soon after being stabbed. I gave her a small smile. "Ready? I'm not going to use my venom."

Her eyes widened. "I really don't know if this is a good idea."

"It will only hurt for a moment. You don't want to stand before your father looking like you enjoyed it, do you?" I pulled back. "I won't push you into it. If you know of another way…"

She lifted her chin. "Okay. No. You're right."

Baring her throat to me, a spike of fear fluttered within her.

"Relax." I murmured as I leaned in. "When he's gone, I can make sure you enjoy my bite again. This is all for show, my sweet Huntress."

My fangs sunk in, and she started to cry out and pull away. I pressed one hand over her mouth, the other around her waist, holding her to me. My chest tightened as she tried to push me, tense and sobbing. A strange sensation swept over me: my throat closed, and a single tear fell from my eye. I didn't like hurting her in this way. I resisted the urge to put venom into my bite. I released her, wrapping my arms around her, stroking her hair.

"I'm sorry," I whispered.

She whimpered and let out a shuddering breath into my chest, not moving. I held her, offering her what comfort I could.

When she stepped back, her eyelashes were wet. She looked up at me with misery.

"I'm sorry," I said again, wiping away her tears with my thumbs. "Camila—"

"I'm okay," she cut me off. "Just please, *never* do that again."

I lifted her chin brushing my lips against hers softly before pulling back. "You have my word," I promised.

Her body was still tense, and a spark of fear lit up in her eyes. I wasn't sure it came from my bite, or from the idea of facing her father.

Blood spilled from where I'd bitten her, staining her tee-shirt. I lifted her hand to the wound. "Make sure to get your hand nice and bloody."

"Stay." She pressed her hand to her throat. "Not to do anything, just so I know you're here."

My heart melted at her wide eyes and downturned mouth.

She'd faced me without fear but was afraid of her father. I fought down the urge to march into her house and rip him apart, letting his warm blood gush onto my face.

"I'll be here," I agreed. "If he tries to hurt you, I can't promise I won't do anything."

Chapter 54

I waited, listening as she went inside, her heart pounding like a jackhammer. The strong scent of her blood in the air pulled at me. I'd hurt her, and my own reaction of protectiveness was unexpected. I had never felt so defensive over a human.

"What are you doing, Carlos?" I grumbled to myself. These were human matters, not something I should be bothering with.

But I'd promised Camila I would stay. I pressed my fingers to the leather wrapped around my wrist, smiling in the dark. The first gift from a human, the second, her trust. She trusted me. The realisation sent a wave of shock through me. I wanted to be worthy of her. Of her trust. Matteo had said the same of Quinn once, and standing outside the house of a Huntress, I finally understood.

"Padre." Her voice shook.

A long silence stretched out between the two of them.

"Camila, clean yourself up. I'll stitch it." The male had a deep voice, full of condescension as he spoke to her. I forced back a growl, not understanding my possessiveness over her. Something else I could now begin to comprehend about Matteo.

"I can do it," she said firmly. "I've done it before."

He hadn't bothered to ask if she was okay. The bite in his daughter's throat should be enough for any human parent to worry. Hunters considered themselves soldiers and raised their children as such. I smiled. When war broke out, he'd be the first one I'd kill, and while he gurgled in his own blood, the sight of my kissing Camila over him would be the last thing he saw.

The sound of running water indicated she was cleaning up.

"Where's your sister?" he demanded.

Her heart skipped. "I don't know."

"She didn't come here?" He clearly didn't believe her.

"No, why? Has something happened?" Even from where I stood, it was obvious she was lying.

There was another long silence.

"Report," he said at last, no softening of tone in his voice at all.

Metal hit the floor. Her knife. "He came at me and tore into my throat before I had a chance to react. I lost my crossbow in the canal and managed to stick the knife in him. I stabbed him in the gut. Filthy bloodsucker ran before I could stab him again."

She sounded like the Huntress she was, but her words were like an arrow through my heart. I'd heard Hunters call me that many times, but from her, the words felt like a curse.

"Who was he? The one you fought before?" The older Hunter asked. He was starting to piss me off. "Have you identified him yet?"

"He's the only one I've seen," her voice shook.

She grunted in pain, and I allowed myself into her mind. She was stitching her own throat. Guilt pierced me, cold and unfamiliar. She seemed to sense my presence in her mind, taking comfort from it.

'Don't leave me,' her thoughts were loud.

'I'm not going anywhere,' I promised, unsure if she could hear me.

"I don't believe he's here alone." Her father's footsteps indicated he was pacing again.

"Why are you here?" she demanded. "What brought you here *now*?" The unmistakable tone of anger seeped into her rising voice. "I know you sent me here to die. Why are you here? Do you not trust me to finish the job, or were you here to see if I was dead yet? Were you hoping to find my body somewhere, throat torn out?"

Pride swelled in my chest for her. She'd surpassed her fear and challenged him.

"Your time alone has made you careless with your tongue," he snapped. "Remember who you're talking to."

"Sorry, sir." Sarcasm dripped from her voice. "I guess being sent to Venice to die gave me a different perspective on life."

Still in her mind, I could see he towered over her. I was surprised that he was somewhat paler than Camila and her sister, suggesting that it was their mother from whom they had inherited their bronzed skin. She faced him, standing her ground. Her shock at doing so indicated this was her first time ever standing up to her father. Likely, her time away from him had given her courage she'd never had before. I'd felt the same after months away from Gabriela, when we first parted from her. I'd claimed my clan, starting with Matteo and Quinn, and the others had joined us. But it had taken me a while to feel like I deserved to be their leader. Their King.

"I'm here because you haven't been reporting in," the Hunter said. "You ignored the schedule, and I worried that you'd been compromised."

"Don't pretend that you were worried about me." Her anger set off my own, and I held myself very still. "It's *your own* reputation that concerns you. I wonder what other Hunters would say if they knew you sent your own child *to die*. What would that do to your reputation?"

"Your ancestor was there at the end of the war. We are known to be descendants from a man who almost decapitated The Immortal Wolf himself. Your ancestor survived almost having his throat torn by the very same vampire. He killed an original vampire. If one of us became compromised, our reputation amongst Hunters would die."

The face of the man who'd almost decapitated me flashed before me. I'd come so close to killing him during the war. A growl tore from my throat. To have his descendant be the one I would mark, I'd want to claim. Some old gods somewhere had placed a cruel fate on the two of us. To know I'd come so close to killing him. To never having met Camila centuries later. The one who'd killed Amara, and I'd failed.

"You mean *your* reputation," she muttered. "I'd be exiled, so it wouldn't be my reputation you were worried about; it'd be your own."

Pride swelled in me, and I hoped this damn Hunter would leave soon. If he didn't, I'd kill him myself.

'Kill them both.' Luis whispered in my mind. *'The descendants of Amara's killer, you must kill them both, now.'* His fury was so strong I could taste it. *'I want their whole bloodline eliminated.'*

Up until then, I'd ignored his presence in my mind. In my anger, I had shown him everything. He'd discovered the identity of the murderer of his Beloved. His pain and fury became my own.

I could not kill Camila, and as long as she asked me not to hurt her father, I wouldn't.

'What is she to you?' Luis demanded. *'She's a Hunter. It should not be difficult to tear into her throat and let her blood wash down yours. Remember...'*

Images passed through my mind, swift, but clear. His own memories of me. Of the killer that I was. The desire, the hunger surged. The bloodlust. To kill as I once had. But not if it meant hurting Camila. My sweet Huntress whom I'd marked.

'You marked a Hunter?' Luis's voice reflected disbelief. *'Then you must claim her. If you will not kill her, you must make her yours.'*

Camila and her father continued to speak, but I'd tuned

them out when Luis invaded my mind.

'I cannot do that.' I replied.

'The great Carlos Rivera, whom I once proudly called my personal guard, my general, terrorising humanity since the day he woke up. Now refusing to kill a human.' The disappointment in his voice was unmistakable. Painful. *'You have three days to kill them. If you fail, you will not like the consequences. This is how we start the war, Carlos. You can feed all you like without restraint. Remember how that felt. End the line that killed Amara. Let us be what we once were.'*

His presence left me. But his words remained. *What we once were.* Feared. Powerful. Not hiding in the shadows. Feeding until we couldn't see straight. Letting our true nature show. My fangs lengthened. Luis's words had an effect on me. Partly Luis's power over me through our bond, partly my own primal beast wanting to be free. I cast a glance over towards Camila's house. I needed to leave. Before I gave in to the command surging through my body.

Chapter 55

"You mean *your* reputation," I snapped. "I'd be exiled, so it wouldn't be my reputation you were worried about; it'd be your own."

Surprised by my own boldness, I caught the glint of fury in his eyes and wondered if one of his famous beatings was coming. Instead of fear, all I felt was rage.

"Explain yourself," his voice boomed. "Why did you slack on your reports? You were to report daily."

I struggled against my own anger. He had sent me to Venice to die after my mother's death. And in the time I'd been here, away from his influence, I'd learned to survive on my own. I didn't want him here.

He didn't wait for me to answer. "The reports you do send are vague, without detail on your hunt. Are you to tell me that, after finding clear signs of feeding, you've seen nothing in the last month? No vampire can resist; there would have been someone roaming around, loss of memory. You hunt every night, but find no sign of the bloodsucker? There are rumours circulating about vampires fighting, but you insist there is only one here."

He had no idea that the descendants of a very well-known vampire covered up all traces of their presence. Worried that Carlos was hearing all of this, I hesitated. That was a mistake. My father grabbed my chin and lifted it, his eyes on the savage bite that I'd just finished stitching. With his fingers tight around my arm, he pulled me over towards the light.

"What are you doing?" I demanded, wondering if Carlos was going to come barging in. "Let go of me!" I almost hoped he would. I'd asked him not to hurt my father, but at that moment, I was too angry. I pushed at him. "Get your hands off me! How dare you come here and..."

"Silence!" his own anger bounced off the walls. He picked up the knife still wet with Carlos's blood, examining it before returning his hardened gaze to my throat. "Do you take me for a fool?"

Shit. "I don't know what you're talking about." Even through my anger, I could hear the tremor in my own voice.

Again, he lifted my chin, this time his fingers tracing over the stitching. I flinched at the pain. He was not gentle. My mind was screaming that Carlos should have pushed his way through the door by now. As my father's fingers traced over my throat, they stopped. "You let a vampire mark you." The fury and disgust in his voice made me want to curl up. "Vampire's whore! I should have known. You protect vampires?! I sent you here to *kill* him, not let him mark you! Did you open your legs for him, too?"

Without a word, he dragged me into my bedroom. I struggled against him uselessly. The need for Carlos became too much that I whimpered for him to help as my father pulled me to the leather restraints that hung from the wall. I fought against him as he closed them around my wrists.

"Who are you calling to? Vampires don't care about humans. Only themselves. You stupid little idiot. After I track down your vampire, I will make it known that you were compromised and ensure that you are exiled. No Hunter will help you. You'll be branded a traitor to all."

It hurt that Carlos had not come to help me. That he had not busted through the door and torn out my father's throat. Surprised at my own vehement thoughts, I struggled to push them down. I let out a long cry of pain and rage, trying to lunge at my father, only to be pulled back by the restraints.

"Almost as animalistic as one of them. I will finish your job for you before I let you go. Stay here, or go, I don't care. Do *not* try to return to Spain. *You are dead to me.*"

I wanted to plead with him, to beg him to let me go. But my voice would only fall on deaf ears. Instead, I turned to threats. "There's a war coming," I snapped. "One that we will lose. Your presence here will only contribute to that. You will not survive, Father." I snarled the last word, unsure why I was speaking in such a way.

He glared down at me, his arms folded. "Marked by a vampire, already displaying the need to protect it. Which one was it? Tell me!"

"Carlos Rivera!" I grunted and started laughing. "You'll die, The Immortal Wolf will see you coming and tear out your throat." I couldn't stop laughing and wondered if I was hysterical. "If not him, his clan —" I cut myself off. *Shit.*

"Then I'll have to make sure I take as many out with me as I can. There are other Hunters gathering, heading towards Rome. Perhaps I should summon them here, first." His mouth was set in a hard line. "Maybe I'll take out Carlos himself. Finish what you could not. Do what our ancestor hoped we'd do." He glared. "I had no idea a child of mine would be so weak. Did you fuck him, too? You let a vampire turn you against what you are."

"What I am?" I muttered. "A killer? I never asked for this. You *forced* this on me, on us. You turned your own children into killers." I pulled on the chains. "Now you chain me to a wall because I didn't kill? We're no better than those we hunt." I'd flipped a switch, and everything was falling from my tongue. "You know, he asked if I wanted to be a Hunter, and my first thought was no. I want a normal life, to love and be loved, and to not fear for my life. When I was a child, I wished many times that I'd been born into any other family. One that didn't force me to train when other girls my age were giggling about crushes and trying on makeup. Not me, I was firing crossbows at targets and learning about a war that no one else knows about. Forced into all those martial arts classes when all I wanted was to be like everyone else." I stopped. I'd feared my father my whole life, but now I just hated him. "Go." I said. "I hope you get yourself killed."

"You are no daughter of mine," he spat, and walked out.

In the next room, weapons shifted from my table. My

sword. He was going to try to decapitate Carlos. My anger crumbled and I sobbed. Everything was over.

"Carlos, where are you?" I whispered. "You have to go, he's coming for you."

Only silence greeted me.

Chapter 56

King Luis's words coursed through me. As I walked through the empty streets of Venice, hunger and the desire to kill blazed within. Every human heartbeat around me sounded like war drums, beating against my skull. The urge to break into the nearest house overwhelmed me. With a groan, I stumbled towards my den. Bloodlust held me in its grip, and I fought against the command that pushed its way through me.

Kill.

King Luis had demanded I kill the descendants of his Beloved's murderer. He had awoken the beast that had slumbered for centuries. A nature that I had struggled to contain when the accords had been created. He had reminded me of who I was. I growled as I forced down that part of me. If I let go now, much of Venice would suffer, tourists and locals alike, since every time I lost control of my nature, I'd been caged and starved. I had gone from feeding freely, to facing punishment for doing what came natural to me.

The Hunter who'd almost decapitated me all those years ago should have died. I hadn't known at the time I had come so close to eliminating Amara's killer. Our Queen of all vampires, whose death had been the cause of King Luis's fight. He'd lost his beloved the night the war began, and we rained destruction on the Hunters in return. I had failed her. I had failed King Luis. But I *couldn't* hurt Camila. I *wouldn't*.

Another Hunter was in my city. I needed to be rid of him. War really was about to break out, and the descendant of the Hunter who'd once come close to killing me as I tried to tear out his throat would feel my fangs as his ancestor had. Just as I had promised. But unlike his ancestor, he wouldn't survive. He would die choking on his own blood.

I found myself in *Piazza San Marco* and froze. *Humans!* I felt my control slipping. I was either about to kill everyone in that square, or march back and kill Camila's father. I had to protect my clan, and Camila.

"Carlos," a familiar voice from behind me pulled me back.

I spun around, meeting concerned brown eyes. Matteo stepped towards me and glanced around the square.

"Matteo, get me back to the den," I growled. "Now."

He didn't ask any questions. Without hesitation he wrapped an arm around me and moved fast. I slid my arm around his back, holding on.

We got back to the den.

"Shackles," I growled.

On our arrival in Venice, we had turned a bedroom into a holding room. It wasn't like the cell that Gabriela had once made. It was not a threat that hung over my clans' heads. It was merely a precaution. One that was needed now. The red haze rose up, and I fell into the past.

Six years had passed since the war ended. With seven other vampires who didn't care for our new laws, I attempted to draw out Hunters to kill them. Our killing spree drew the attention of the Bloodking. Gabriela took me before King Luis. Overfed and blood drunk, I could barely stand. Gabriela's vice-like grip was the only thing that held me up. Nearby, three humans watched, a witness to our punishments. The three Hunters who had forced the accords on us.

"Carlos, you have broken the accords...again," King Luis declared.

Nico and Sia stood on either side of him.

"The accords!" I scoffed. "Why does the Bloodking kneel to the demands of humans?"

He moved fast, his fist connecting with my chest. The impact flung me through the air. When I landed, I didn't move. I couldn't move in my current state of intoxication. Certain that he'd cracked my chest, I stared up at the night sky as I healed.

"Get him up!" King Luis commanded.

'Carlos, what's gotten into you?' Gabriela asked through our bond.

"Blood, and lots of it." I had meant to reply silently but realised I had said that out loud. Laughter thundered from me as vampires pulled me to my feet.

"Gabriela, you named him your second," King Luis reminded her. "Do you not think someone with more respect and more control of themselves should have had that role?" He shook his head. "He's such a disappointment to the general that fought by my side."

I swayed as Gabriela knelt at King Luis's feet, her head bowed. "Please forgive him, my King. The new existence we find ourselves in has been difficult for many of us. He was forced to watch as those he'd turned were destroyed. He mourns his feral fledglings just as one would mourn a child. Give him time." She grabbed my arm and pulled me down. I fell to my knees. "The humans have bound us to their rules. We have never had to control our natures as we do now."

"We all lost someone!" Nico pointed out. "Amara was the first of our losses. Yet you don't see King Luis unable to stand after a feeding frenzy, leaving dead in his wake. Your second is a disgrace."

A growl ripped from King Luis. "Do not speak her name," he commanded. "I forbid her name from being spoken. By any vampire."

"What punishment do you serve?" Gabriela asked.

I held my breath as King Luis contemplated her question. I had already been shackled and starved for my inability to resist killing. Starvation was painful, but the moment they freed me, my hunger would likely drive me into another feeding frenzy. I lifted my head, glaring at the Hunters.

"These vampires follow your example," King Luis said to me, pointing at the others also facing his judgment. "You lead them?"

I glanced at them. "I am no King," I said. "They joined me freely, in protest of the accords. We were trying to draw the Hunters out, so we could show them what we thought of their accords."

"We will claim one of these followers to ensure no one joins him in his continued rebellion," one of the Hunters said. "That one." He pointed.

King Luis nodded. The vampire in question was dragged to the humans. Animal sounds filled the night as he struggled. The woman Hunter pulled out a sword, and the vampire's head hit the ground. I howled in rage. His death was on me.

"I'll kill you and every one of your descendants!" I promised the Hunters.

The one who bore my scars on his throat smiled at me. "Perhaps it will be my descendants who bring you to your knees. Father of Ferals, The Killer, The Immortal Wolf, you are a threat to our peace. I should ask King Luis for your head."

"That won't be necessary," King Luis spoke up. "I will not permit that."

"Do you protect him because he was your general?" the woman Hunter with white- blonde hair asked. "Make an example out of him. The killing of humans must end. It has been six years. If you cannot bring your vampires to heel, we have rights to their lives. You agreed to that."

King Luis glared down at me. "Starving you is having no effect. Perhaps it's time to rethink my punishments," he muttered. "Something that will hurt you enough to put fear into you. Worse than starvation."

No one moved. Worse than starvation? It occurred to me that he was about to make an example out of me. Just as the Hunters told him to. Whatever punishment he deemed as fitting would be horrific.

"Starvation only lasts a few days. Vampires sink into madness, but can quickly recover. There is a form of discipline that you *will not soon forget. In my world, it was outlawed. Of course, we are not in my world any more," King Luis said. "You will face starvation. But you will also be de-fanged. It will take months for your fangs to grow back. You can't go ripping out human throats, and will rely on your clan to bring you food."*

Horror swept through me, and I was on my feet and making a run for it. I wouldn't allow them to rip out my fangs. Gabriela's shock flooded me.

I didn't get far. Hunters drew their weapons.

"Stop him. Bring him to me," King Luis commanded.

Vampires blocked my escape. Growling and hissing, I fought against those who returned me to the Bloodking. My attempts to break free were hopeless.

"Shackle him," King Luis ordered.

Nico brought shackles towards me. "The Father of Ferals is accurate; he's no better than they were," he commented.

The restraints closed around my wrists, only encouraging me to fight harder. King Luis had formed an alliance with wielders of magic, and there was no escape from the enhanced shackles. The cold energy of magic closed around my wrists as the shackles did.

"Please," I pleaded as I was forced to my knees before King Luis.

There was no sign of feeling in him as he stared down at me. "Bare your fangs," he said in a low voice.

I shook my head, turning to Gabriela for help. She wouldn't meet my eyes. 'Gabriela, please. You will feel this. Don't let him de-fang me.' Through our bond I could feel her horror over what was about to happen. Once again, I tried to wrench free of my captors, without success.

"Please," I pleaded again. "King Luis, don't take my fangs. I'll obey the accords."

"Yes, you will," he agreed. "Now bare your fangs."

His voice held me captive. Only the beginning of my bloodline, and first-generation vampires, held power in their voices over me. I fought his words, but his command boomed through me. Against my will, I hissed, my fangs lengthening. Sia stepped forward then, her strong fingers gripping my chin. As King Luis approached, I was already screaming.

I woke up screaming. Shackles around my wrists set off panic, and I snarled, rising to my feet in a crouch.

"Carlos, let me remove them," a voice echoed around the room.

I growled, and I lifted my hands, heart racing, to my mouth, checking that my fangs were still there. Relief washed over me, the pain still deep within.

"Stop," a vampire nearby spoke. "Carlos, we won't hurt you."

"Something's wrong. He's hungry." a figure knelt down before me. "Have you not fed? Why are you on the verge of bloodlust like this? Has something happened?"

King Luis had reminded me of who I was before and during the war. Of my hatred for Hunters. But it was the hunger I needed to deal with now. I focused on those around me. Matteo, right in front of me, the others behind him. All with concern in their eyes.

"Need…blood," I croaked. "Now."

Matteo rose to his feet, glancing around the room. "You heard him. Feed our King."

Annika was the first to step forward. She smiled at me, baring her throat. I gave in to the need to sink my fangs into soft flesh, caging her to me with an unbreakable grip. I tore into her neck, and her fiery blood filled my mouth. I groaned as I fed, her moans making me hard. I tightened my grip, biting deeper into her throat, needing the blood to flow. She started to struggle in my embrace.

A hand touched my back. I growled.

"It's okay, my King. Let me feed you. You can bite as deep as you want. Don't hurt Annika," Lorenzo pleaded.

I lifted my head, meeting his worried eyes. Annika's blood dripped from my mouth.

"It's okay, Carlos. Just please, let her go." Lorenzo bared his throat.

Chapter 57

Once I got myself back under control, I returned to Camila's house, finding only her presence inside. Scanning the surroundings, I found no one around, so I let myself in. Chains rattled in the bedroom.

"Hello?" Her voice shook. "Father? Please let me out. I'll leave, you'll never see me again. Carlos…" Her words ended in a sob.

I wanted to tear the place apart at the pain and surrender in her voice. Instead, I opened the door to her bedroom. "Carlos what?" I asked.

She was chained to the wall, and a growl erupted from

my chest. She lifted her head, staring at me with puffy eyes, red from crying. Her mouth hung open. "Carlos? You came back? I thought you left me."

"I'm sorry, my beautiful Huntress, I had to leave. But you didn't think I'd abandon you, did you?" A flash of pain in her eyes drove straight to my chest. I brushed a tear away with my thumb. "I'm sorry," I murmured, pressing my forehead to hers, before kissing her on the cheek. "Did he hurt you?"

"You have to go." Her gaze hardened, urgent. "Before he comes back. Please. He has my sword."

Sword. I had a Hunter on the loose with a sword, intending to decapitate vampires. In my territory.

"I thought you dropped your sword in the canal," I commented.

She gazed up at me. "I had another one. Hunters tend to have a lot of weapons. Not just one of each."

I put a sense of urgency into a command upon my clan. They couldn't hear words as Matteo would, but they'd feel what I was urging them to do. *Return to the den, immediately.*

Matteo's mind was alert. *'What is it?'* he asked.

'Hunter.'

'The girl?'

I glanced down at Camila. *'The girl is no threat. But her father is. He's armed with a sword.'*

"Please, Carlos, leave," Camila said again. "If he finds you here, he'll kill you."

"He can try," I muttered, and I pulled apart a cuff at her wrist, then the other. "I want you to leave Venice." I told her.

Camila's hands reached for me, and I wrapped her in an embrace, kissing the top of her head. She trembled, trying to burrow deeper into my arms.

"Camila, my lovely Huntress. I cannot protect you from my clan. I will protect them above all, and if you remain in Venice, they will find you." I pulled back. "You cannot save your father, but you can save yourself. I need you to leave. *Now.* I *need* you to be *safe,* and far from what's about to happen."

If she was still here when the Elders arrived, they'd find her. They'd probably make me kill her to start the war.

"War?" she asked.

I nodded. "The Elders want me to lead it with them. They've shared their blood with clan leaders to connect us, so they can have the strongest of the vampires with them. They want Hunters dead. To be able to feed freely again."

"Is this what you want?" she asked.

If she had asked me a month ago, I would have said yes. Without hesitation. But as I stood in her bedroom, with a human in my arms, a Hunter, no less, I wasn't so sure any more. I'd never been so torn, and it confused me. I had fought against the Bloodking's command, and against my own bloodlust, because of her. Because of my clan.

"You asked me if I wanted to be a Hunter," she reminded me. "I never did. All the training, I hated that I was born into this family. When I met you, Carlos, you freed me."

Warmth spread across my chest. I smiled at her. "No, I didn't. *You* did that. You discovered yourself, my Queen, and I am so proud of you."

The words 'my Queen' had slipped out. But she smiled back. A tentative smile at first. Then I could see my words sink in, and she beamed at me.

I willed her to listen to me. "Please Camila, leave Venice. I need you to be safe."

She shook her head. "I won't. I'm not going to stop you from killing him, but you cannot ask me to leave."

I glared at her. "I can make you."

She glared back. "You can, but you won't."

'Carlos.' Matteo's pain through our bond pulled me out of our stand-off. 'Carlos, please come. We need you.' He shut himself off from me, but not before I sensed agony. Something had happened, and the warmth in my chest turned to ice.

"I have to go," I said.

Before I turned to leave, I reached for Camila's chin, forcing her to look at me. Anger blazed in her beautiful eyes. I gazed deep into them until they softened, then I kissed her, long and hard with all the affection I could. Her heart fluttered and she finally kissed back, grasping my leather jacket.

"Go, please," I whispered again, and left her there.

With the blood bond, I tracked Matteo to Lorenzo's territory. Annoyed, I hoped they hadn't been fighting again. Watchful of the Hunter, I found no sign of him. I finally caught sight of Matteo, his arm around Quinn. They turned as I approached, their eyes wide with horror. Her eyelashes were wet, his mouth in a hard line. His anguish flooded through me, and rage that burned bright.

"What is it?" I demanded. "Why did you call me here?"

I picked up the scent of blood. They stepped aside, showing Annika on the ground, her back to me, head bowed. A body lay across her lap, and she whispered in Italian. Her words were soft, but she was pleading, urging. I stepped forward and Matteo came with me, his hand on my arm. His need to touch me was enough to make me pause. The rest of the clan arrived.

"He showed me his face," Annika revealed without looking up. "I saw the Hunter attack, I felt his death. He died, alone." Her voice was rough with emotion.

Grief gripped my chest the split second before I saw Lorenzo's head in her lap, eyes open, staring into mine. Pain blazed in my chest, and a guttural scream tore from me, deep sorrow clawing into my heart. Erik, Josef, Andreas, and Celeste's cries were full of anguish. My knees gave out. Matteo held me up, him and Quinn pressing in on either side of me, the others sliding in around us.

"Move!" I commanded. "Andreas, Celeste, help Annika and Lorenzo back to the den." My voice broke on Lorenzo's name. The pain in my chest was beyond anything I'd experienced. To lose someone in my clan, tears welled in my eyes.

They were gone in an instant. All but Matteo.

"You too," I growled.

"I'm not leaving you. I know what you're going to try to do. As your second, I will be by your side when you tear his heart from his body."

Shaking, I bared my fangs at him. "I told you to go," I hissed.

I would find the Hunter, and unleash The Killer. I would become what King Luis wanted me to. But first I needed to feed.

Chapter 58

I was packing a backpack when my father returned. I tucked my knife into the sheath at my hip, then took it out, laying it on the table. The sound of the door opening chilled me to the bone. I hurried from my bedroom to find him cleaning the sword. My sword. There was blood on it. Carlos had left quickly; was it a member of his clan, or had my father found him? The idea of Carlos's death hurt more than I would have thought. *No, not him.* Surely my father wouldn't be able to get the better of a vampire King. I was surprised he'd killed a vampire so quickly.

"What have you done?" I gasped.

"What I'm supposed to," came his curt reply without looking up from the sword. "I don't need to ask how you got out of those restraints. Is he still here?"

I laughed, hysteria bubbling up. "If he was, you'd be dead."

He did look up then, giving me the once-over, the disappointment clear on his face. "Where did I go so wrong with you?"

Not so long ago, those words would have crushed me. Now, I glared. "You're going to die here," I told him, and pointed to the bloody sword. "Whoever's blood that is, you've started something that will only end in *your* death." *And probably mine.*

I finished packing my bag, with no idea where I was going to go. This house had been secured through the Hunter network, so I would either have to find a hotel, or seek out Carlos for help. Not that his den would be an option, the way his clan probably currently felt about me.

"A dead bloodsucker is a good thing," he said. "One less killer in the world. I'm not finished here. I'll have to finish what you couldn't."

"They're not the animals you told us they were," I said, lifting the bag to my shoulder. "Goodbye, Father."

Before I could leave, he lifted his phone, turning it towards me. "Is that him?"

I stared at the phone in mute horror. On the screen, a photo of me sitting opposite Carlos earlier that night, putting the leather bracelet cuff on his wrist. The look Carlos was giving me was one of adoration, melting my heart.

Fuck.

"Were you…were you spying on me?" I demanded, my

face hot.

"Is that him?" he repeated. "Is he the one who defiled my daughter?"

"Your daughter?!" I scoffed. "*Now* I'm your daughter?!" I shook my head. "Did you confirm that the vampire you beheaded had broken the accords?"

"I don't care about the accords!" His voice boomed, making me jump. "It's *never* been about the accords. We are weapons, Camila, to protect humanity. These things are monsters, feeding off human blood, living forever. We need to eliminate every single one of them. Why else do you think Hunters are on the move?"

Carlos had been sure that a war was on its way. A storm raged inside, urgency. I needed to warn Carlos.

"You know he's going to come for you," I warned.

"Let him come. I'll be prepared." He opened my weapons bags. "Why are these still in the bags?" He started to unload the weapons that I'd packed away after Carlos had spent the day in my bed.

I turned, opening the door.

His voice called me back. "You're not going anywhere."

"Is that an order?" I challenged. I'd taken orders from him my entire life, living in fear of letting him down. "I'm *done* taking your orders. You say I've been compromised, but you've completely gone off the rails. To not care about the accords, you yourself are breaking them! This isn't the legacy the First Hunters left us with."

I walked through the door, closing it behind me. He called out my name and cursed, throwing something. Relief flooded me over my new-found freedom. I no longer had to take orders from him and hoped to never see him again.

Carlos had told me to leave, but I needed to know he was alright. If he'd found whoever my father had killed, he'd be with his clan. The urge to see him overwhelmed me. Instead of leaving, I wandered the streets, hoping to find him, or any one of his clan. They'd know me by sight from the gallery. Hopefully I could convince them, before they tore my throat out, to take me to him. For the first time in my life, I was not carrying any weapons, and the feeling was liberating. I hoped that was not a mistake.

The night had grown cold and silent. It was well past midnight. No one remained on the streets. As if they could sense what was coming. I made my way to the gallery, knowing it was not Carlos's territory. Maybe I could find Matteo or Quinn. I hoped I'd at least have a chance to speak before they decided to tear me apart. I broke into a cold sweat at the idea that I'd never see my death coming if any vampire did decide to kill me where I stood. Quinn might be more sympathetic with me, having been turned only twenty years ago.

As I approached the gallery, I searched my surroundings. If vampires were around, they could move without sound, and fast. I recalled the last time I'd been here, comparing the crowd from that night to the dead silence now. My phone pinged. A message through the Hunter network.

<Landed, on my way to your location.> I frowned. *Another* Hunter here? That couldn't be good.

Shit. I'd called her here. Lilith. I'd completely forgotten. I started to type out a reply.

<Be careful. Camila has been compromised. May have alliance with vamps. I look forward to hunting with the legend that took down Gabriela.> My father's response sent anger surging

through me. He was already telling Hunters not to trust me.

I changed what I'd been about to type, feeling spiteful.

<War is coming.> I wrote. *<I hope you're ready.>*

Access revoked.

I threw my phone, taking joy from hearing it smash on the ground. I never wanted to be a Hunter, but to be exiled still hurt. I had never felt so alone.

"You're not the Hunter he told us to find, but you'll do." A voice made me spin around. Quinn, fangs bared, stood so close I took a step back. I hadn't heard her at all. "I'll drop your broken body at your father's feet. Right before I tear out his throat."

I glanced over Quinn's face. There was pain there. Grief. *Oh no.* I didn't know her, but with my own loss still a shadow over my heart, it hurt for the pain Quinn would be feeling.

"I'm sorry you lost a member of your clan," I said.

Her fangs retracted. "You almost sound like you mean it."

"I didn't do this. Please, take me to Carlos," I pleaded. "Let me see him." I dropped my bag at her feet, and lifted my hands. "I carry no weapons."

Confusion passed over her face. "You think you can make demands of me? Lorenzo is dead because of you."

I recognised the name Lorenzo. He had been mentioned in the records. Frustration surged that I no longer had access to them. She took a step towards me, baring her fangs.

I showed her my throat. "I am marked by Carlos. You cannot hurt me." My bravado didn't stop the pit of fear in my stomach. I softened my voice. "My father's presence was not something I wanted." I told her honestly, and held my wrists out, showing her the red from the restraints. "He had me chained up. Please, take me to Carlos. If he tells you to kill me, I will not fight." I was playing a dangerous game, hoping Carlos didn't want me dead in his grief. "I'm not a Hunter any more. I care about Carlos. I know you don't trust me, you have no reason to." I watched her, hoping to appeal to anything in her that would hear me. "You should know, a friend of yours is on her way."

Her eyes widened. "Lilith?"

I nodded.

The cold glint in her eyes thawed a little as she smiled. "Thank you. You actually seem genuine, so I'm going to be real with you. Carlos might not recognise you right now." She paused and met my eyes. "I know he's been with you, I suspect more than once. Your presence isn't going to soothe him. For a King to lose a member of his clan, it's more painful than you can imagine. He is mourning someone he's known for hundreds of years, and you can't help that."

I nodded again. "He told me he takes others to his bed, was Lorenzo one of them?" I knew Quinn herself also had a place in Carlos's bed, and heart. But instead of the expected jealousy, I felt that we both understood each other's feelings for him.

She took a while to answer. "He has told you a lot, hasn't he? Yes, Lorenzo was among his lovers. We're all feeling that loss, but Carlos is really hurting."

The need to see Carlos grew. I wanted to comfort him. But going into a vampire's den was risky, and likely the last thing I ever did.

"I'm sorry," I said. "I'm sorry that you all lost him."

Her watchful gaze gave me hope. She wasn't trying to kill me. "Okay," she said at last, giving in. "I'll take you to him. Just be prepared for what you might find. He's on the verge of a feeding frenzy, and he has ordered the entire clan to find your father. He wasn't at your house, so he's being hunted."

"Lead the way," I replied.

Chapter 59

I watched the *Ponte di Rialto* from my usual place, not hearing anything. Fury and a deep anguish blazed inside of me; my heart turned to ice. I planned my next move. I wanted revenge. Camila's father had started a war, and I would not let him remain in my territory without consequence. A deep growl rumbled in my chest. This was my fault. A hot tear left a trail down my cheek. I was suffocating, drowning in grief and anger. A crushing weight pushed against my chest, and I fought against the rising red haze.

"Carlos." The voice calling my name sounded far away.

I didn't move.

A hand touched my shoulder, and I spun around, baring my fangs with a hiss. Quinn stood before me, her eyes empty.

"She wanted to see you," she said, "She *begged* me to bring her to you." She stepped aside to reveal Camila.

I stared at the Huntress, numb. "What are you doing here?"

"I hoped I'd find you, Carlos, I'm sorry." She ran to me, her arms wrapping around me.

"I told you to leave," I said, not returning the embrace.

She pulled away, tears streaming down her face. I resisted the urge to brush them away.

"I was packing to leave, but my father returned before I could. When I realised what he'd done, I had to see you," she told me. "Carlos, I'm so sorry. You know I didn't want this."

I glanced over at Quinn. "You listened to her?"

Quinn gave me a sad smile. I saw pain in her own eyes. The whole clan was feeling Lorenzo's loss, but they'd put their grief aside. For me. "Her words appealed to me. She genuinely seemed to care about what happened," she said. "Otherwise, I would have left her body for her father to find."

I'd sent the entire clan out to find him, with the command to drop him bleeding at my feet so I could finish him off. I planned to make it hurt, for days.

The two women before me both had strength, and in another life they might have formed a strong friendship. But as I stared down at Camila, the splinter of pain in my heart only grew. *Her* father had done this.

Camila turned to face Quinn. "He wouldn't care. I let a vampire feed from and mark me. I shared my bed with him. In my world that's unforgivable. He's already announced that I've been compromised."

Surprise flickered through Quinn's eyes. Then she turned her gaze to me. Waiting.

"The only one we're killing is her father," I said to Quinn before meeting Camila's eyes. "You need to leave."

Camila's hand touched my wrist, tracing over the leather bracelet. "Carlos—"

"I said leave!" I growled, pulling my hand away, and her eyes widened. She took a step back from me. I forced myself to calm down. "You won't want to be here for what's about to happen."

"You're going to kill him." Hope filtered through her eyes.

"What did you expect was going to happen?" Quinn demanded. "If he exiled you, why do you care?"

"I don't," Camila admitted.

I could sense Matteo's approach. His growl echoed across the rooftop, and he had his hand wrapped around Camila's throat. "Scream for me," he said. "I'm going to tear you apart, and you'll be awake through all of it."

"Let her go." I sighed. "She's not the one we want to kill."

"What?" Matteo's eyes flashed, his voice heavy with fury. He released Camila and glared at me. "She's a Hunter. You allow her to live, after what happened?"

"She didn't do this. She's not a threat to us." I glanced down at Camila. "Is he at your house?"

Camila swallowed heavily, rubbing her throat, and nodded. "He's likely waiting for the arrival of another Hunter." She lifted her eyes to Quinn, understanding passing between the two.

Quinn nodded, and touched Matteo's arm. He looked down at her, to Camila, then to me.

"Then we hunt the Hunter who did this," he said.

"We hunt the Hunter," I agreed. I moved away from Camila. "Leave Venice, like I told you," I said over my shoulder. "I can't protect you in what's to come." I shot Matteo and Quinn a look for them to follow and leapt off the side.

They landed next to me a moment later, and we moved silently. I knew where he was. We stopped at the house, where I could smell him inside. The loss of Lorenzo burrowed deep inside of me, and I could only focus on killing his murderer. I would unleash The Killer. Annika joined us. Then Andreas.

"Where are the others?" I was emotionally empty.

"We're here," Erik said, Celeste and Josef behind him. "We're ready, Carlos. What are your orders?"

"We should have killed his daughter and dumped her here," Matteo grumbled. "I don't understand why you won't."

"You let his daughter go?" Annika demanded, her eyes hardening.

"His daughter didn't kill Lorenzo," I shot back.

"Lorenzo would still be alive if you had killed her when you were supposed to." Annika's grief over her maker's death was making her speak to me in a way she never had dared before.

"Do you love her?" Matteo asked in a quiet voice.

"Don't be stupid," I scoffed.

"It's a reasonable question." Quinn said. Her and Matteo's hands were intertwined. "We need to know that you will do what's best for the clan."

I grit my teeth together, struggling to contain my fury. They were challenging me, and I couldn't blame them. My anger was at myself, because they were right. I had failed time and time again to kill Camila, only to protect her from

Matteo.

"Stop," I used my command over them. "Let's just kill him before anything else." I glanced at Annika. "For Lorenzo."

They had no ability to fight me.

As we watched, a woman arrived and knocked on the door once. An older woman who had to be close to fifty. She had long, white-blonde hair tied into a braid that hung down her back. She glanced around once as she waited, a jagged white scar across her neck, clear signs of a vampire attack. Another Hunter. She didn't look Spanish, though.

Quinn gasped. I cast her a look, and she was staring at the new arrival with horror and recognition. I glanced at the woman again, recognising her this time. She'd aged somewhat, but I'd seen her when she took Matteo, and other times when Quinn was human. Twenty years ago, her hair had been shorter, and the hardened glint currently in her eyes hadn't been there. I knew that glint. She was a killer. Of my kind. Still a Hunter.

The door opened, and a large, blond, bearded man with blue eyes opened it, letting her in. I recognised Camila's father from her mind.

"It's him," Annika whispered. "Lorenzo showed me his face before he died. It was brief, but enough."

"Lilith," Quinn whispered.

Matteo's arms were around her, holding her up. He murmured to her, words of comfort.

A growl rumbled from me. There were two Hunters, now, who had taken from me. Lorenzo's killer, and Gabriela's.

"We'll kill them both," I declared.

Chapter 60

The Hunters talked inside as I worked out what to do.

"Antonio, it's an honour to work with you, but where is your daughter? She called me here." Lilith sounded the same as she had twenty years ago.

Hurt reverberated through me. Betrayal. Camila had called Gabriela's killer here.

"My daughter won't be with us," Antonio said. "She was compromised. She took a bloodsucker to her bed, let it mark her."

"I see." A chair scraped, and footsteps indicated pacing.

"Which one?" Her Australian accent was harsher than Quinn's. I realised that twenty years in Italy had softened the siren's accent.

"Carlos Rivera." His voice was heavy with disgust.

I would rip his tongue out for daring to speak my name.

"I met him a couple of times twenty years ago. Evil seeps from his very presence," she said.

Evil? I'd never considered myself good, but evil? I smirked. They had no idea what was coming for them. If they wanted to call me evil, I would show them who I was.

"Why was she here alone? One Hunter is not going to do much against one vampire, let alone a clan. How many hunts does she have under her belt?" Lilith's pacing stopped, her tone hard. *"You sent her here to die. Your own daughter?!"* Shock sounded in her voice.

"Why aren't we going in there and ripping them apart?" Annika demanded. "Then finding his daughter and tearing out her throat?"

"Not Lilith," Quinn pleaded. "Please, Carlos. Last time she was here, you promised you wouldn't hurt her."

"That was before I knew she'd killed Gabriela," I grumbled. She whimpered.

"Go home," I told them all. "Matteo, you stay with me. We'll bring them to you."

No one moved.

"Do not disobey me," I raised my voice.

"Go," Matteo agreed. "We'll watch them. I can reach out to Quinn when it's time for the killing."

They left, and I fumed that they'd listened to Matteo and not me.

"To use the Hunter's word, have you been compromised?"

he asked. "You put her before your clan, and Lorenzo is dead. Can you blame them for their anger and mistrust?" He lifted his eyes to the door. " I'll ask you again. Do you love her?"

"What difference will that make?" I asked. "Either way, these two will die. I know Quinn still cares, but her friend has a lot to answer for. That will not go without consequences."

"Her family tortured me for hours," Matteo raged. "She tried to kill me and succeeded in killing Quinn. I want to show her the same courtesy." His wrath was unmistakable. "Antonio took from the entire clan. They deserve for us to make them suffer."

I nodded. "We will have all of that. You'll have his screams." A low growl rumbled from me. "I will feed him to the clan, and Annika will have his heart."

Matteo grinned at me, his teeth flashing in the moonlight. "Then let's lead them to the villa. Perhaps we should bring Quinn back. Use her siren voice on them and lead them to their death. We can trap them in the courtyard, cut off any exit."

I put a hand on his shoulder. "It was well before your time, but you would have made a terrific soldier in the vampire war. I'm honoured to have you as my second."

He grinned again. "Perhaps when this is over, we can cover ourselves in their blood and have Quinn lick us clean."

"I will fuck you both in a pool of their blood." I snapped at his jaw with my teeth before turning towards the house. "Alright. Get Quinn here. She will lead them to the den. To the clan."

Quinn arrived within minutes. She stared at the door. "I

can't do that to Lilith. No matter what happened between us, I *won't.*"

Before I could say anything, Matteo spoke up. "Do you think she'd have the same values? She came to Venice looking for you, Quinn. I don't think it was to have a chat. She came armed, and prepared for the both of us."

The two of them stared at each other until her shoulders slumped. "You're right," she agreed. "It doesn't make it any easier. We were friends for our whole lives. It's not easy to forget that."

"I want to draw them out first," Matteo said. "Then we lead them to the den with your voice."

Finally.

"How do you propose we do that?" I asked.

"Why, we knock of course." He was advancing before I could say anything and banging on the door. "Hunters! I know you're in there. I am Matteo Barone, and I'm out here with Carlos Rivera and Quinn Barone. You want us, come get us."

Well, that was one way to get their attention. I joined him at the door. Matteo's eyes were red, his fangs glinted. Quinn followed us.

The conversation inside stopped, and weapons shifted. Someone loaded a crossbow. The pair whispered to each other. I laughed. They were arming themselves.

Good. This was going to be fun. "You know, I remember your ancestor," I said through the door to Antonio. "He did come close to decapitating me, but I left my mark on him. He didn't enjoy it nearly as much as your daughter, when I fucked her in that very house." I couldn't hold back. "Up against the wall. I believe there might still be a dent from it. And in her bed. We even used those restraints. She's irresistible. She was begging me to bite her."

I was taunting him, but I didn't like talking about Camila in that way. Matteo frowned at me.

I could smell Antonio's fury, a sharp scent that rolled off him. Lilith murmured to calm him.

"You, little Australian Hunter, you've aged. We have special plans for you. After what you did to Matteo and Quinn, I am going to make you feel all of their pain before I hand you over to the Bloodking. He is hungry for your death. You did, after all, kill his daughter. My maker. I am going to enjoy this."

"Quinn," Lilith whispered through the door. "You're here, too?"

"I'm here," Quinn said. "Lil…"

"Enough!" I stopped their conversation.

Their heartbeats were calm and steady. They were ready for war. *Good,* so was I.

'*Be ready,*' I commanded Matteo.

I smashed through the door with my fists and kicked it off the hinges. Enraged, they aimed their weapons at us. I gave them my most savage smile, revealing my fangs. Lilith fired first, and I leaned to my right slightly so it sailed past me.

"You missed!" I laughed. "Welcome to the second vampire war."

"Where's my daughter?" Antonio demanded.

"Hopefully, far from here," I replied. "Quinn."

She started to hum, the sound rising from inside her. The effect of her voice was instant. Antonio's face went blank, eyes on her. Lilith, too. Quinn's eyes glowed green as she let her power rise from her, and if I concentrated enough, I could *see* the energy of her voice.

"Good, let's go." I said, and turned around, Matteo and Quinn beside me.

The walk to the den was not far, but the humans were unbearably slow, and it tested my patience.

"She's dropped back," Matteo observed.

"She struggled against me," Quinn said. "I couldn't hold on to her. She has a strong love that a siren's voice can't overcome.

I glanced at Quinn with curiosity. She gazed back at me, unflinching.

"It doesn't matter," I added. "We're almost there, and I've worked up a hunger." We'd get her soon enough.

"I'm going to enjoy this," Matteo said.

"Not more than I," I replied.

I sent the call to the clan. We were close enough, and I didn't want to wait any more.

"The hunt is on," I declared. "Release him."

Quinn stopped humming. I knew exactly where each of my vampires were as they spread out. Antonio blinked and took in his surroundings.

I grabbed Quinn's chin. "Is your past friendship with the Australian Huntress going to be a problem?" I asked. "Did you release her?"

She'd been here once, years before, and couldn't find us on account of Matteo picking up her scent. We'd been very careful in feeding, to avoid her detection. It had been painful for Quinn, watching her former friend from the shadows.

"No more than your affection for Camila," she growled and pulled her chin from my grasp. "I will do what I must for the clan. Will you? If it were her we were hunting, who would you put first?"

I'd never seen Quinn this angry before, nor had she challenged me in such a manner.

"Go," Matteo instructed her. "We're hungry; join the others. He's about to run. Close him in."

She disappeared into the night.

"We need to talk about your obsession with the Huntress," Matteo said. "Everyone has noticed. You've come home smelling like her, and you spent a day away from the safety of the villa. It's a concern. You keep avoiding talking about it, or how you feel for her, but it's obvious you have deep affection for her. Please, Carlos, I've known you a long time, and I've never seen you behave this way. Over *any* human. What you said to her father was cruel, intended to anger him, but it hurt you."

I didn't want to speak to Matteo about Camila. I didn't want to feel what his words were doing to me. The feelings churning inside my chest.

"Let's worry about killing the Hunters for now," I instructed him.

I sensed an uneasiness coming from Matteo, and fear. He was afraid for me, and for the clan. But he pushed it down as we waited for Antonio to notice us. With Matteo, I circled him, both of us growling. Antonio aimed his crossbow at me.

Josef moved from the dark. The Hunter turned around, finding himself face to face with Josef.

"Hello," Josef smiled. "Did I startle you? I thought we'd have a little chat. Hunter to...well, former Hunter."

"You're Josef Alfaro," Antonio confirmed.

Josef laughed. "I am."

"You turned on your own people. Traitor." Antonio spat, turning the crossbow to Josef.

"We're going to kill you, and that's what you're worried about? Yes, I slaughtered fellow Hunters. I was hungry. I have no remorse for doing so." Josef lifted his gaze to meet my eyes. "He's stalling. Where's the other one? She'll be close by, probably already aiming at one of us."

As he'd been speaking, the rest of my vampires had closed in, their growls feral-like.

"He won't be around long enough," I said, and moved too fast for the Hunter to see. "You killed one of my clan; you will pay with your life," I declared.

"Then you are breaking the accords." He put contempt into the word accords.

"You don't care about the accords," Josef laughed. "But you think reminding us not to break them will mean anything."

I grabbed the front of Antonio's jacket, pulling him towards me. Our faces were inches apart. "Good. I don't care about the accords either. You're by yourself, Hunter. I will make this hurt. My second would like to hear you scream."

"He will not have the satisfaction to hear my screams," Antonio declared with a steady voice.

My clan were so close we were almost touching. But they wouldn't move until I gave them permission. This was my kill. Without wasting more time, I buried my fangs deep in his throat, shivering as flesh gave way beneath my teeth. I groaned against his neck as hot blood spurted into my mouth, spilling down my throat. His ability to control his fear didn't change that he was afraid. The spice of fear hit me, and I gave in to the red haze. Beside me, Matteo took the other side of his throat, a deep rumbling coming from his chest.

Antonio did scream then, struggling against us. Resisting the pain of our bite was one thing, but we were ripping into his throat. My bite had never been gentle, and Matteo had let his feral nature drive his. Matteo's pleasure surged through me, the sounds of screams something he'd always enjoyed. I couldn't blame him; they were music to my ears.

I lifted my mouth from the Hunter enough to speak to my clan. "Feed. Do not use your venom, let him feel the pain as eight vampires tear him apart like wolves in the wild."

I opened the vein in his throat, my face wet, dripping with his blood. Beside me, Quinn tore into his wrist, with Annika taking his forearm. The growls around me really did sound like a pack of wolves. We lowered to the ground as we finished him off. I didn't notice when his screams stopped. A faint drum of his heart became fainter. Without moving from his throat, I punched into his chest, removing his still-twitching heart.

No more blood pumped through his body. I lifted my head, only to have Matteo nuzzle at me, then Quinn. I placed the heart into Annika's hand and coated blood over her face. Matteo smeared his hand across my cheek, covering every part of my face in the blood of our enemy. He did the same to Quinn while I painted his face. Josef and Erik surrounded Annika, while Andreas and Celeste pressed themselves hard against each other.

Quinn rubbed her cheek against mine, and then Matteo's. Every inch of all our faces was covered in blood. Matteo started to lick my chin. I was still wrapped in bloodlust as I moved my tongue across Quinn's jaw. Footsteps behind us made us all turn as one, snarling in warning. A human couple froze, their fear sending me into a frenzy.

I couldn't have stopped my clan if I'd tried. We were all frenzied and intoxicated. I didn't want to stop them.

I wanted to feed.

Chapter 61

Crouched over the human woman, I watched my clan. Their satisfied growls as they cleaned blood off each other's faces made me smile. Three dead humans lay around us. I could sense that King Luis was close; his pride surged through me. I had spent too long suppressing my nature and enforcing laws to follow the accords. Even as Gabriela's second. As Matteo crouched down in front of me, a feral gleam shone through his eyes.

"Matteo?" I asked. "Are you with us?"

He'd given in to his nature, and it was hard to tell if he was still buried within the bloodlust.

Quinn dropped down beside him. "My sweet feral, do you want me to sing to you?"

"That's not needed." His voice was rough, primal. He grinned at me. "I like this look on you. I can't say I've ever seen you look so..." he paused, as if searching for the word.

"Feral." Quinn finished for him.

They started to lick my face. I wanted to take them both there in the street. The rest of the clan surrounded us then, each wanting to clean me, so I rose to my feet, taking them with me. Matteo and Quinn stepped back, focusing on each other. Need arose in me, and I didn't know what I wanted more. My red haze started to fade, and an image of Camila flashed before me.

An arrow hit Matteo in the throat. Then another, in his shoulder and a third in his chest. Matteo dropped to one knee in front of me, choking.

"Matteo?" Quinn's voice was filled with panic as she crouched over him.

He tore the arrow from his throat. "I'm okay; it missed my heart," he grunted. "It still hurts, though."

I lifted my head, searching in the direction the arrows had come from. The Hunter from Australia smiled at me from a rooftop. Something covered her eyes, with a glint of green.

"Night goggles," Erik said as the clan closed in around Matteo.

Her crossbow shifted, as if she were finding her next target. She stopped, and I followed the line of her aim.

"Quinn," I warned with urgency.

The Hunter lifted her crossbow again and fired. The arrow moved fast, the advancement of weaponry. It was aimed at me, and should have pierced my heart. With Matteo still on his knees, pulling the other arrows out, Quinn stood up in response to me. Her eyes reflected questions.

Matteo had told me what it felt like the split-second before the arrow hit her chest all those years ago. That he'd been slower, weak because of what the Hunters had done to him. He'd been helpless to stop it from happening. Blood drunk and sluggish, I stepped forward, reaching for her. She started to turn around to see what I was staring at. She had unknowingly put herself between me and the arrow. The arrow aimed at my heart entered her chest. Anguish and fury burst from me. Matteo's own reaction echoed mine. I wrapped my arms around her before she fell.

"Did it pierce her heart?" Matteo asked, panic radiating from him. He stared at both of us, fear glinting in his eyes, unsure what to do. "Carlos, can you tell if…Quinn?"

"Protect Carlos," Josef shouted, and my clan were around us. Erik moved towards the Australian Hunter.

Quinn's mouth opened and closed in surprise, her eyes on Matteo's. I clung to her, not holding back my own anguish. Her eyes closed. We were crouched, holding her.

"No, no no no." Matteo whispered. "Quinn, keep your eyes open. Please. My love, my siren."

Two more arrows rained down on us, missing. Then Lilith was fighting Erik, his growls savage as he went in for the kill.

"We need to take the arrow out," I said. "Matteo, if it's not in her heart, it is close — get it out, *now!*"

He shook his head. "If it's missed, doing so could kill her. It could still pierce her heart on the way out."

'Carlos,' A familiar voice boomed through our blood bond. *'I feel your anguish. I'm on my way.'*

'*King Luis?*' I reached out to him, letting him in. '*King Luis, I have to help her, she's hurt. If she dies, Matteo will lose himself completely.*' I lost control of my ability to hold back my grief, overwhelmed at the idea of losing Quinn and Matteo on the same night I had already lost Lorenzo.

I felt him in my mind, looking through my eyes. Gabriela had done that many times. '*She needs blood.*'

Quinn's eyes opened and closed again, as Matteo's words to her faded around me. A strange sound inside her rasped as she breathed.

I choked back on grief. '*How will that help if she's dying?*'

'*She needs her maker's blood...and yours.*' King Luis advised me. '*His gave her life, and yours is stronger than normal vampire blood now. You have Elder blood in you. We are immune to wood. Only our children have a vulnerability to it. She'll also need your strength. You must bond with her.*' His presence was gone from my mind.

I frowned. To bond with her would mean I'd be bonded with three. The Elders had always told us we could only bond with two. But in that moment, I didn't care. If it would help Quinn, I would do what I needed to.

"She needs blood." I murmured, dreading what I was about to do. Bonding with another vampire was one thing, but with an already bonded vampire who belonged to another was not going to be welcomed.

Matteo growled as I lifted my wrist to my mouth. He grabbed my arm.

"Matteo, please trust me. Trust King Luis. Maker *and Elder* blood will help her." *I hope.*

The moment felt like an eternity. Finally, he released me. "Mine first." He tore into his wrist, pressing it against her mouth. "Quinn, drink. Please."

I lifted her arm to my mouth, biting in, taking her blood. Matteo growled, but did nothing, his eyes on her.

'She's not drinking.' Panic came through his voice.

'Take the arrow out,' I told him. I held her shoulder to steady her as Matteo used his free hand to snap the arrow in half and push it through.

Quinn screamed, her body arching and eyes opening again. She focused on me, eyes pleading, and they darted toward Matteo before returning to my face. My own heart broke as it hit me: she believed she was about to die. Matteo had gone on a rampage once when he thought he'd lost Quinn. Her fear of what her death would do to him showed, and she was asking me to look after him. To not kill him.

"Drink." Matteo murmured. "Please, Quinn. *Mi amore,* drink."

"Drink," I told her. "Trust him. Trust me."

The growls of Erik and grunts of the Hunter nearby as they fought, were background noise, the rest of our clan crowding around.

"Drink," they murmured, stroking her face, holding her up.

Finally, the sound of her swallowing his blood sent relief rushing through me.

'I really hope you're right.' I wasn't sure if King Luis would be paying attention.

Matteo caressed her cheek, and she reached up, cupping his face with one hand.

After a time, he pulled his arm away. "Carlos is going to give you his blood now," he whispered. "It's stronger than mine."

He gazed at me. "I trust you."

My chest ached, and I threw my trust into what King Luis had told me. I tore deep into my wrist, letting the blood gush, and I held it to her mouth. I'd once told her she must never drink from me. Now I was going against everything I had ever been taught, everything I knew.

The connection opened between us as soon as my blood entered her system. She was talking to Matteo.

'*Hold on,*' he told her.

"*Please, my Matteo...*" she stopped. "*Carlos, I can hear you.*" She frowned. '*Why are you doing this to yourselves? Now you'll both feel my death.*'

'*Shhhh, please, have trust in me, young siren,*' I murmured through our link.

The connection had opened up the pain she was feeling, and I resisted the urge to clutch at my own chest.

Tears were falling from her eyes as she whimpered. '*Look after him. Please.*'

'*It won't come to that,*' I promised.

'*How are you so sure this will work?*' she asked, but she swallowed my blood.

I had to believe King Luis knew what he was talking about. "Just drink."

Chapter 62

The Australian Hunter injured Erik enough for her to escape. Josef hunted with Erik, while I carried Quinn back to the den, surrounded by the clan. I carried her to my bed, and we curled around her. Josef and Erik joined us when they returned, bringing nourishment for Quinn. She clutched at Matteo, falling asleep as he whispered to her in Italian. She was weakened, but alive, and we all rejoiced.

As I lay in my bed, my thoughts thundered around my head, too many to grasp at once. Lorenzo: dead. The sorrow over his death crushed me. I recalled the day Gabriela had found him, bringing him into our clan. He had been a vampire for only a century, and his maker had been killed, his clan scattered. As he recovered from the death of his maker, he had asked me to help him track down the Hunters responsible. I'd been more than willing to do so. That had been mere days before Matteo's arrival within our clan.

Lorenzo had met Annika only a couple of centuries ago, and he had confessed to me he'd found a woman that he wanted to share with me. She had become a vampire only a few days later, after begging him to turn her so she could be with him for eternity. I grieved his death in silence.

Quinn herself had come close to dying, too. Had she died, I would have lost Matteo. Quinn had helped calm his feral side, and in her absence, he would have given in completely. I took Annika in my arms to offer her solace over the loss of her maker, her beloved.

We spent the entire day in my bed, caring for Quinn, comforting Annika. We encouraged Quinn to feed, but she wouldn't drink, which only worried me more. I shared more blood with her, as did Matteo.

When the sun set, I left them in my bed, and I walked through the streets of Venice. I felt nothing as I hunted, no pleasure in the feed, only a deep wound in my heart.

"Where did I go wrong?" I demanded towards the sky. Dark clouds threatening rain had closed over.

Humans hurried past, either away from me, or to get home before the rain. I didn't care.

"Carlos." I turned at the voice, finding myself face to face with King Luis. His eyes were full of sympathy. "You're in pain," he said. "You're tormenting yourself. I've never known you to behave in such a way. Torment is something for humans." He grinned. "It's more fun when it's us doing the tormenting, too."

I fell to my knees at his feet, bowing my head. Had he heard what had happened? "I've failed." I murmured. "I've failed my clan, I've failed you."

His silence was broken only by the thunder. I raised my head, unsure he had heard.

"You've had a Hunter infestation," he said finally.

I nodded. Too many Hunters had come into my territory.

"I always hated what the Hunters did to us," his tone was low, dark. "We surpass them in strength, power, and more. But we submitted to them, let them dictate to us how to live. I was forced to punish vampires with whom I agreed."

His words sunk in. "You de-fanged me," I reminded him. "You starved me."

He nodded. "And for that, I'm sorry. I needed you to get in line, I needed time. To strike back. I have put so much into place, over the centuries, in preparation for this war. I've bided my time, and I've been patient. I punished many, so that the Hunters believed I was in agreement with the accords. Amara would have done the same, if I had died."

He had not spoken of his Beloved since her death.

"You planned this," I realised. "You let them kill vampires. Half of them kill us for what we are, whether we take lives or not. We should have ended them centuries ago. You forced me to comply with the accords." I half-understood him, yet remained unwilling to let go of my growing anger. "Gabriela died. Her whole clan died." Every vampire who I had seen die over time flashed through my mind. "Their deaths are on your hands. All of them. You betrayed us." I had been convinced that I had failed him. "It is you who has failed us,"

I growled.

He took a deep breath, letting it out. "I'm sorry, my son. You have suffered greatly. More than anyone else. I want you as my general. You have more reason than anyone to want Hunters dead." He offered a smile. "Come, I have something for you. You can redeem yourself to your clan. Then we can talk about war."

I followed him back to my den. Sia and Nico waited for us in the courtyard. My clan watched us from the door, their eyes wary as we stood in the courtyard. Nearby, two human heartbeats echoed through my head.

Nico brought the pale-haired Hunter forward, forcing her to her knees. Surprised that they'd found her, I glanced at Quinn. She was still weak, and leaning on Matteo. Lilith had once been a friend to Quinn, but now, she had almost killed her a second time. More than anything, I wanted to kill her, and I hoped they'd let me do it. But if anyone deserved that privilege, it was Quinn. Lilith raised her eyes to Quinn, but quickly glanced away again.

Sia circled Lilith with a slow smile on her face, fangs bared. My clan were watching in silence. King Luis's eyes were on me but shifted to Quinn.

"That must be the siren," he stated. "It's a pleasure to meet you, my dear. I'm glad to see you survived."

She gave him a hesitant smile, still leaning on Matteo. King Luis addressed all of us.

"With my general at my side, and the clan La Voz as witnesses, I declare war on every Hunter," he said. "The accords were their way to muzzle us, hidden under deceit with the lie of peace. No more. Blood will run in the streets. Humans will run screaming. I have chosen my champions.

The Immortal Wolf, the Feral, and the Siren." He turned to Lilith. "Antonio Martinez was the first casualty. Now, I want to send a message to all Hunters with her death."

Lilith glared up around us, more angry than afraid.

"This one led the assassination of La Primera Familia," King Luis said. "She declared war on them, and after they were dead, she took it upon herself to travel the world to help Hunters do the same in their territories. She helped them track down dens, leaving many in ash." He turned to Sia and Nico, and a look passed between them. He stood over Lilith. "Hunter, Lilith De Micheli, you are responsible for killing many of our children. We have felt their pain over the years. You killed my first daughter, Gabriela, and I hoped I would one day meet her murderer."

Hatred shone through Lilith's eyes as she glowered at King Luis. "She was killing humans, a violation of the accords. So I did my duty. I put her down." Lilith grunted in pain when Nico's hand tightened on her shoulder. "The way you're talking about your children, am I to assume I'm in the presence of the Original Three?"

"The very same," Sia boasted.

"You signed the accords but forgot to enforce them on 'your children.' Those who have died, did so because they broke them. Too bloodthirsty to care. So, yeah, I declared war on them for having broken the accords." She glared at those around us, her stare finishing on me. "He has a feral in his clan responsible for many deaths across Europe and Melbourne. You allow him to live, knowing that! Then you're as responsible as he is." Her eyes darted to Quinn. "And that one killed when she first turned, so she by rights should be dead, too. But you allow her to live?"

Quinn made a small sound, turning her head into Matteo's chest. Lilith noticed, and for a moment, her expression softened, but it was gone, her hardened mask in place again.

King Luis growled. "You *dare* to tell us that our children deserve to die?! You arrogant human, we've enforced the laws. We travel to each of the clans to remind their leaders of the consequences if they break them. We've tried the guilty and starved them as discipline."

Lilith laughed. "Then you're a bigger idiot than I thought. Did you fail to see, or just believe the lies they told you to avoid such discipline?"

Sia hit Lilith and it would have knocked her to the ground had Nico not been holding her. My clan took a step forward, as Lilith spat out blood.

"Truth hurts, bitch," Lilith said.

Sia hissed.

"As Gabriela's maker, I would very much like to be the one to end your miserable life," King Luis said, and turned to me. "Carlos, she killed your maker. She tried to kill one from your clan, so I turn her over to you."

Rage burned through me as I considered all the things I could do to her. Drain her slowly, let my clan feed from her, torment her for days, turn her and leave her for Hunters to find. I could even do as the Elders did and give her my blood to make the torture last longer, years. But instead, I met Matteo's gaze, then Quinn's.

"My clan are important to me," I said. "I know of many ways to punish my maker's killer. But the one person who deserves that right is one who has now taken an arrow from her twice, and almost died this very day."

Lilith's eyes lifted as Quinn left Matteo's arms, stepping

into the courtyard. I could feel Matteo's concern as he watched. Quinn was still weak, and I moved forward to steady her. We stopped over Lilith.

"You've shot me — twice," Quinn's voice was quiet.

"You got in the way, twice, when I was aiming for others," Lilith snapped, shooting an icy look at me, and at Matteo.

Quinn gripped my arm in anger, trying to control herself. "You declared us enemies twenty years ago, and you're right, we are enemies. But we didn't *have* to be. I mourned Mia just as you did."

"Don't you dare speak her name," Lilith spat, her eyes glinting. "I was going to marry her. You knew that. You murdered her, and you showed no remorse as you stood over her body with *him*." She lifted her chin in the direction of Matteo.

Quinn knelt in front of Lilith. "Lil, look at me. Have you forgotten the friendship between us? Twenty years. You were there when my sister died, and when Steven left me in pieces. Talk to me, please."

"Just kill me, get it over with," Lilith said. "Maybe I can join Mia."

Instead, Quinn hummed, and Lilith winced. The humming became louder, more powerful, and Lilith pressed her hand to her ears.

"It's been so long since I've heard a siren's voice," Sia murmured. "Beautiful."

"Talk to me," Quinn said again.

"I mourned you when I mourned Mia. I missed you both every day." A tear slid down Lilth's face.

I could feel Quinn's relief through our bond. "I missed you, too," she admitted.

'What is she doing?' King Luis asked me silently. *'This is a waste of time. Kill her and be done with it.'*

'Trust her,' I replied to him, but was just as uncertain as he was about what Quinn was doing.

"But Mia and Quinn died. Twenty years ago." Anger and pain mixed in Lilith's voice. "You died. Because of me." Her eyes darted to Matteo. "But of course, you wouldn't let her die in peace. You had to make her like you. A monster."

"You still carry that guilt, don't you?" Quinn asked.

More tears streamed down Lilith's cheeks. It was as if a dam broke. Tears she'd been holding onto for two decades.

"Same," Quinn whispered. "I'm sorry, Lilith. For all we both lost." Quinn stood up and faced us. I held out my arm again to support her, but she shook her head. "I saw her memories. I saw our friendship. That she cried when I left. She still carries a photo of the three of us. She declared us enemies, but as she said, she mourned me. You don't do that for your enemies." She turned back to Lilith. "I also saw Mia's ghost. And your daughters. So in honour of the friendship we once had, I'm letting you go."

I groaned inwardly. This would cause disagreement among my clan later, and with the Elders. I could already feel King Luis's annoyance.

"You're letting her go?" I repeated.

Even Lilith seemed surprised. Quinn smiled down at her.

"On the condition that you *retire from hunting.* For the sake of your daughters. You do not kill *any* more vampires. If you do, then I will kill you myself. I've shown you the power of my voice. You'll feel it on a greater scale."

Lilith shook her head. "To give up hunting means to be defenceless. Every vampire who knows who I am will try to kill me."

"Then take your family and go into hiding. Disappear, Lilith, and hope that no vampire finds you," Quinn said.

King Luis chuckled. *'She has a most delightful sense of cruelty.'* His approval flooded through our bond. I wasn't sure Quinn was doing it to be cruel. "I accept her punishment," he said out loud. "If I receive word of any De Micheli still hunting, I will drag you before the siren. Whether now, or in a hundred years, the punishment will stand."

Lilith stared at Quinn with a line in her forehead, and mouthed 'siren?'

Nico took his hand from Lilith's shoulder.

"Go home, Hunter. Get your family, and run," King Luis ordered. "We know your scent now, and should we find you, we'll end your entire bloodline."

She rose to her feet and faced Quinn. I recognised the look that passed between the two. *Understanding.* Quinn had set her free instead of killing her, proving herself to the Hunter. She reached into her jacket and pulled out a photo, held it out to Quinn. When Quinn didn't take it, I grabbed it, and the Hunter walked away.

I studied the photo. A very human and happy-looking Quinn stood alongside Lilith and the other woman who I had seen with them a few times. The one she'd killed the day she awoke as a vampire.

Quinn had not brought any photos of her human life with her. She still spoke to her parents, and they visited often, but she refused any photos.

I held the photo out to Matteo. He smiled. "The siren who Called me," he recalled. "The human I fell in love with."

"Please get rid of it," Quinn pleaded, refusing to look at the photo.

I placed my hand on her shoulder. "You may not want it now, but one day, you will. I will hold it until then."

"You're the only one who has a photo of when they were human," Matteo said.

She glared at him. "You were all vampires before the camera was invented." She turned her eyes to me.

"It's okay," I encouraged her. "I'll put it away. I won't talk about it, no one else will see it. You'll want to see it one day. When everyone you know is gone, it will be a reminder of who you were."

"What if I don't want to remember who I was?" she asked.

"Give it a century or two, and you'll be glad I kept it," I promised.

Her parents had given me photos on their last visit, asking that I hold on to them for her. I'd told them that their death would most likely be the day she'd want to see them. After twenty years, they were very aware of their own mortality, and worried for their daughter. I'd promised them I would protect her. That Matteo made her happy, which they'd seen a long time ago.

King Luis put his hand on my shoulder. "Now for the main event," he said. "You said you failed your clan, this is your chance to show them that you haven't."

Sia laughed joyfully. "Finally, I've been waiting for this part."

Nico disappeared, and returned with a human woman. Her brown eyes met mine as he led her forward. He forced her to her knees in front of me. I stared down at Camila, my heart pounding. I'd told her to leave, to prevent this.

Thunder rumbled overhead again.

"Before your Elders, and your clan you have a chance to repay what was done, to show us where your loyalty is," King Luis said. "Kill her, Carlos, and all will be forgiven."

Chapter 63

The vampire Elders, whom I recognised from the descriptions in the Hunter records, had found me on the roof where Carlos had left me. They'd taken me, telling me not to scream, struggle, or move, and all fight had left me. Somehow, I knew I'd see Carlos again, but I didn't think that he'd be the one to kill me. His eyes darkened as he stared at me in silence, lacking the warmth he'd shown me in the days before my father had ruined everything. There was no sign of that Carlos. Only the vampire who I'd glimpsed all the times we'd tried to kill each other. His face, and the faces of those around the courtyard were red, except for where it looked like the blood had been cleaned off.

"Carlos," I whispered.

If he was to be the one to kill me, I hoped it wouldn't hurt. He looked every part the bloodthirsty vampire I'd imagined when I first read the records about him.

"Kill her," the female vampire Elder, who could only be Sia, told him. "What are you waiting for? In the eyes of your clan, there is only one choice."

His eyes shifted to the mark on my throat, the one he'd left, and his face softened. He held me frozen in place with that intense gaze of his, deep into my eyes. The look that made my stomach flutter. I couldn't look away

"You should have run," he said harshly.

Sia laughed. "You left her on a roof that she couldn't get down from."

"Kill her." The Elder who spoke had long, black hair and red eyes. I wondered if he was The Bloodking. "Your clan is watching."

Carlos glanced back over his shoulder at Matteo. Meanwhile, my heart was pounding hard, and I braced myself.

"No," Carlos said so quietly I wasn't sure I heard him.

Matteo stepped forward. "Carlos, she is the reason Lorenzo is dead. Quinn almost died because she called Lilith here. What are you doing?"

"Her father killed Lorenzo, and we killed him," Carlos said. Calm washed over me when I realised it was my father's blood on his face. "Lilith shot Quinn, not Camila. I will not kill her. I cannot."

"You are not fit to be our King," Josef declared. "Your refusal to kill her is a betrayal. I challenge you. I put my support behind Matteo."

The clan moved to stand behind Matteo, showing their support for him. All but Quinn, her eyes darting between the two of us, watchful. Carlos and Matteo's eyes locked. I held on to hope that Matteo wouldn't kill me.

"If you do not kill her, I will," the male Elder said. "Why do you hesitate to kill her? Where is The Killer that Gabriela brought to us? Where is the Immortal Wolf, who tore his enemies apart?"

Carlos turned his gaze to me, his face unreadable. I didn't move. I couldn't move. My heart thundered, and I knew they could all hear it.

Matteo put his hand on Carlos's arm. "Quinn thinks you feel more than just affection for her. Is that true?"

Carlos turned his eyes to Quinn.

Quinn smiled up at Matteo. "Not so long ago, I was the one struggling to accept what my heart wanted. I know that look anywhere. She feels the same way."

Carlos glanced at Matteo, who nodded in encouragement.

"I…" Carlos seemed to struggle, as if the words wanted to tumble out but he tried to hold them back. "I love her," he said, and my heart skipped. "I will kill anyone who tries to harm her."

The vampire that held me shook his head in disbelief. "The great Carlos Rivera loves a human." The others snickered.

Matteo frowned, his dark brown eyes softening as he shifted his gaze from Quinn, to me, and back to Carlos. "You love her?" he repeated.

Carlos's eyes were on me again as if he were confused, and he crossed his arms. "I do. I want to take her in my arms and protect her. I marked her. You do not need to challenge me, Matteo; I release my role to you. I have failed you all."

Something passed between the two, and I couldn't help but wonder if they were having their own conversation, privately. A heated discussion, their eyes narrowed as they glared at each other. Finally, Matteo let out a breath.

"If you love her, you have not failed us, Carlos." He reached for Quinn, pulling her towards him. "We cannot help who our hearts choose. Although I never thought I'd see the day that yours chose a human's. Or that of a Hunter."

Did Carlos really hate Hunters that much, that loving one seemed impossible to those who knew him?

"I ask you what you once asked me," Matteo said. "Do you claim this human?"

I froze, ice creeping through my veins. If Carlos claimed me, there was only one fate for me, and I did not want that. I would never want that. Taking a vampire to my bed, letting him confess his love for me was one thing, but I had been raised to hate vampires, how could I accept being turned as a fate?

The time it took Carlos to answer the question felt like hours. It could have been. I held my breath.

"I do," Carlos said.

I whimpered.

"The human has something to say to that," Matteo said, and all eyes were on me.

"You claim that you love me, yet you sentence me to…" I couldn't finish.

"A monstrous existence?" Quinn said with amusement in her eyes.

I nodded, feeling an appreciation for her. The vampires laughed.

Quinn crouched in front of me. "I once thought the same. I'd fallen in love with a vampire, but he wanted this life for me, and it hurt more than anything that he would, knowing that I didn't want it."

"Yet you're okay that he took that choice away from you?" I asked.

Carlos's eyes bored into me. I could feel them. The weight of the stare sent chills down my spine, and I avoided looking at him.

"It wasn't. I *chose* this. I wanted this," Quinn told me.

I frowned. "Only because you were dying."

Quinn shook her head. "Those Hunter records of yours don't include the whole story. I'd asked Matteo to turn me, before I got hit by an arrow." She glanced over at him, and his smile lit up his whole face. "But once you awaken as a vampire, all human fears of such things are gone. You'll be a vampire, and that's all that will matter. Because you'll have the one you love, by your side forever."

Carlos had said something similar.

Matteo pulled Quinn into his arms, and they murmured to each other in low voices.

Finally, I looked at Carlos. "I will never make that choice. I can't."

A heavy silence followed as Carlos considered my words.

"I claim her. She is mine. But I will only turn her when she *asks* me to." Carlos said. "If you want me exiled from the clan, I will leave, with what is mine."

Matteo faced the vampire clan. "I loved a human once, and you all accepted her." He nuzzled Quinn's throat with a soft growl. "Lorenzo loved a human, too. We welcomed Annika and Quinn into our clan without question. I will do the same for Camila. Carlos has marked her and claims her as his. She has been exiled from the Hunter community, so I accept her presence among us, whether as human or vampire."

"I accept her," Quinn said.

"Well, this is disappointing," Sia muttered.

Carlos watched me. I tried to push aside everything I'd felt for vampires, to understand my own feelings.

One by one, the vampires voiced their acceptance. All that remained was a blonde vampire who didn't look happy about what had just happened.

"How can you accept her?" she demanded of the clan. "Her father killed Lorenzo." She snarled, and then she was in front of me, sharp fangs bared, eyes red as she grabbed me by the shoulders. Her grip hurt and she leaned in, her teeth on my throat. I closed my eyes. *This is it.*

Her mouth and hands were pulled from me, and I opened my eyes to find Carlos between us, with her on her back on the ground. She was on her feet in an instant, growling. He returned the growl, a deep sound that rattled me down to my bones.

"Annika, he has *claimed* her. You *cannot* hurt a human claimed by a vampire," Matteo said, trying to intervene. He stepped between the two.

"Get out of my way." She glared at Matteo. "I'll kill both of them. Carlos is as responsible as she is." She focused on Carlos. "You felt the pain of your maker's death, so you of all people should understand my rage."

Carlos had his back to me, so I couldn't see his face as he confronted her.

"I faced Gabriela's killer and let another decide her fate.

Killing her would not bring Gabriela back, just like this will not bring Lorenzo back," Carlos told her. "Annika, please. To hurt her, is to hurt me."

"No." Annika cut him off. "Stand aside." She moved fast, and I knew my death was coming for me.

Matteo flew through the air as she shoved him aside, but Carlos stopped her reaching me. I gasped, choking down a scream. His hand was inside her chest.

"She. Is. Mine." Carlos's voice jarred me, a deep guttural sound. Unrecognisable. "This is your last chance. Please, Annika, stop."

Hands were pulling at me, away from the fight to my feet. I shivered, letting myself be moved. Annika's cold, hateful stare followed me.

"This is fascinating." King Luis said from behind me. "Cold-hearted Carlos, threatening another vampire to protect a human. I never thought I'd see the day."

"You might want to look away." Quinn, the one who'd pulled me away, whispered in my ear.

Annika hissed, still watching me. She looked like she was in pain, and I wondered how she was not screaming while Carlos had his hand in her chest.

"I cannot. I will not. Lorenzo is dead! You'll have to kill me if you want to protect her." She turned her glare to Carlos, letting a deep, low growl. "Because if you don't, I will kill her."

Carlos pulled his hand from her chest, his fist bloody, gripping her heart. I did scream then as Annika crumbled to the ground. Other vampires wailed, but remained where they were. Carlos stood over Annika's body for a long time, not moving. I realised he was speaking, but too low for me to hear. Matteo dropped to his knees, and the rest of the clan followed, their heads bowed.

Carlos turned around, an inhuman look in his eyes. Tears slid down his cheeks. He approached me, and my stomach churned. *What is he about to do?* I took a step back, only for Quinn to stop me by placing a hand flat against my back.

"Don't move," she whispered. "Trust me, Camila."

She had shown me kindness, and right now she seemed to be my biggest supporter, so I did as she said. Carlos growled and stopped just in front of me. He looked at me, his eyes glinting.

"Claim what is yours." Matteo said to Carlos. "Then take your place as our King once more."

"You are mine," he declared, and the entire clan closed in.

I forced down my fear, trying not to look at the bloody heart still gripped in his hand.

Each of the vampires took turns in sniffing me, including Matteo and Quinn. They leaned towards me and breathed in deep. Their fingers caressed my throat, and I flinched as they touched the stitches. I didn't know what to expect, and when Carlos held out the dead vampire's heart to me I almost gagged.

"He has marked you, and he has claimed you as his." Matteo's voice rang out, as thunder grumbled overhead. I stared in shock at Carlos, the urge to vomit rising. "He killed for you, and now he brings you the heart of the fallen. Of your enemy."

I couldn't move. *My enemy?*

"Think carefully about how to respond," Quinn said. "I know you feel the same. Accept that you are his; accept the heart. If you do not accept his gift, it will mean you reject him."

There was a spark of hope in his eyes as he waited. Those beautiful eyes that were currently red. The very first thing I'd noticed about him was his smirk, but it wasn't on show now. Instead, I beheld a mixture of hope, fear, love, and longing. From a vampire. I worried about what would happen if I rejected him. Whether they'd kill me or let me walk. Another rumble of thunder vibrated through me, and it started to rain. Hard.

I was drenched within seconds, cold water dripping down my face and neck. Carlos remained still, his dark, curly hair plastered to his head. I knew then that I *couldn't* walk away from him. I took a deep breath, still afraid I'd vomit, and I accepted the heart from him.

"I'm yours." My words came out hoarse, and his face lit up, the joy I'd seen in the gondola.

I started to shiver and returned his smile. Carlos pointed to the heart, losing his smile. "Now eat it," he commanded.

"W-what?" My teeth were chattering, and darkness danced up before me.

"Carlos, now you're just being cruel," Matteo said. "Maybe we should get her out of the rain. She's shivering. She doesn't have the same tolerance we have."

Carlos tilted my chin up, with the hand that hadn't just been holding onto a heart, and he lowered his head. Our lips met in a fiery kiss, his mouth warm, his tongue pushing forward. There was blood still on his face. My father's. I shuddered, but I wrapped my arms around him, the heart falling to the ground. I didn't know what to expect from belonging to a vampire, but I never wanted to let him go.

Chapter 64

I had my arms wrapped around a shivering Camila as the Elders approached me before I could take her inside.

"Will you come to Rome?" King Luis asked, speaking in Italian. "The Hunters are moving; they've bypassed your city for bigger prey. I've sent many clans there. I want my Killer there too. The Immortal Wolf."

I wanted to join him, to be there when war broke out. To let blood run, to watch humans run. To smell and taste their fear. I wanted to see an end to the accords I'd fought so hard to destroy centuries ago. But after just having claimed Camila, I didn't want to leave her. I wanted to nest, to spend days in my bed with her in my arms, to claim her, to mark her. She didn't want to be a vampire, so I wanted to make the most out of the time I had with her. I wanted to protect her, and my clan. I'd never had such an internal battle as I did at that moment.

"I cannot fight while I have a human with me," I said, also in Italian. "But soon. I will join when I can. Humans have technology now that will expose us. It will not just be Hunters that we face this time."

Camila's arms slid around me, trying to get warm. I'd certainly fed enough to give her that warmth.

"I care little about whether or not humanity knows of our existence," King Luis said. "Let them discover us. I will declare war on every single one of them." He turned towards Nico and Sia. "It will be as it was. As it should be."

It dawned on me then what King Luis really wanted. "You want control of them. All of humanity."

He smiled in answer. "We'd have free rein over how we feed."

"That's why you need me. That's why you want Matteo and Quinn." A siren's voice with vampire strength could bring all of humanity to its knees.

"Is it not what you want?" King Luis demanded. "I know what you are, Carlos. I've seen the joy in you from giving in to your nature. Tonight, I felt it when you killed her father."

Camila laid her head on my chest.

"She and my clan are my first priorities. They will follow me into battle. Give me a few years," I requested.

"I have already declared war. It will not wait," he replied.

I nodded and met the eyes of each member of my clan. "War will last for many years. My clan and I will remain in the shadows until we are ready."

King Luis glanced down at Camila. "It would be useful to have a Hunter in our army," he said. "Even exiled, she'd have valuable information. This is not the only Hunter in your clan; you do have a way with Hunters. Perhaps we should name you the Hunter Whisperer." He chuckled. "I'm disappointed that we are going to war without you. But you are correct. This war will be bloody, and last many years. We will welcome you when you are ready. Will any of your clan come with us?"

"We go where Carlos goes," Matteo said, and the others agreed.

Camila's shivering became uncontrollable.

"Please allow me to take her inside to warm up," I asked King Luis. "Matteo can bring you an offering. I'll be out to finish this conversation soon, once she's comfortable."

King Luis nodded.

"Matteo, I leave the funeral in your hands. I will attend if you allow me. Josef, Erik, prepare Annika and Lorenzo for their farewell," I ordered. "We burn them at sunset tomorrow."

I picked Camila up in my arms and carried her to my bedroom. She looked around in awe. Her gaze shifted around the room, taking in the bed, the art, and the toys I'd once offered to take to her.

"You need to warm up in the shower," I told her. "It'll stop the shivering. Take your clothes off."

I stripped off my own clothes, and once she'd done the same, I led her to the bathroom, turning the water on in the shower. As it heated up, I ran my hands over her body. She was mine, and she had publicly accepted it. In a daze that

I had realised I loved her, I couldn't keep my eyes, or my hands to myself. I pushed her into the hot water, and she tilted her head back to let the water run through her hair.

I growled, my eyes on her throat. She knew what that did to me. She lowered her chin, but I pushed her against the wall of the shower.

"Bare your throat," I commanded her.

She did as ordered, and I ran my tongue over the stitches, trying to be gentle. My mark. I trailed kisses across her throat, enjoying the shiver that passed through her.

"Are you going to bite me?" she asked.

I lifted my head, recalling the last time I'd bitten her. "Do you want me to?"

Her eyes were on mine, hungry, full of desire. "I do."

I licked the unmarked side of her throat and pressed her naked body to mine. As my fangs sunk into her throat, she relaxed against me, a moan escaping her lips. Her blood was sweet, without fear.

I washed, the water turned red at our feet. The blood of her father, and the humans that followed.

"You killed him," she asked as she assisted in cleaning the blood off my face with a face cloth.

I nodded. "He killed Lorenzo. I could not let that go. I'm sorry." Her silence bothered me. I lifted her chin. "I'm sorry," I said again, softer.

"He died on the job," she said with a strange calmness. "I'll have to contact my brother and sister to let them know. Diego will take his place as head of the family."

I stiffened. "Will they come here?"

She frowned. "Sofia has already abandoned the Hunter lifestyle. Diego will not do anything against either of us;

he's nothing like our father. Now that I've been claimed by a vampire, it will take them both a while to accept that, but they will want nothing but peace with you. Real peace."

"They both felt as you did? About hunting?" I asked.

"Sofia and I hated it. Diego may take some convincing. If they ask, will you allow them entry here?"

I ran my hands over her body, slippery with soap. "I cannot deny you anything."

Loss and regret filled me. Both Lorenzo and Annika were gone. Everyone had felt Lorenzo's death, and would have felt that of Annika, too. I'd had no choice but to protect Camila, but Annika's death had pierced my heart as much as Lorenzo's had.

It delighted me that Camila had accepted the heart I'd offered her. There had been a moment where I had feared she would reject it. Reject me. I could feel her thoughts dwelling on the heart I'd given her.

"I'll offer you flowers next time," I promised, pulling her mouth to mine for a quick kiss. "Or chocolate. Or jewellery."

Her fingers traced over the leather bracelet. "You still have it, you didn't take it off."

"You told me not to," I reminded her.

Her hand cupped my cheek. "I don't know what I've gotten myself into. Loving a vampire?"

I gave her a smile, pulling her hand to my lips. "I promise to behave. Maybe I'll let you teach me human ways. It's been awhile, so I'm a little out of practise."

I would follow her anywhere. If that meant sitting down in public over a coffee, so be it. As long as I was near her.

"You won't try to turn me?" she asked.

I put my hand to my heart. "You have my word. Only if

you ask me to." The silence that passed between us filled my chest with an ache. If she never asked me, I would watch her grow old and eventually die. "I will love you until your last breath." Grateful for the shower, I was able to hide the tears. To lose her would be unbearable.

We finished in the shower, and after drying off, I led her to my bedroom. I lay her on my bed, pinning her under my body. "I am King of this clan," I told her, trailing kisses from her soft throat to her navel. "Of this territory." I shifted myself, grabbing her hips with enough pressure to bruise, knowing that she liked the pain. "That makes you my Queen. I intend to treat you like the Queen you are." I kissed her inner thigh and met her eyes. Propped up by my pillows, she watched me, waiting. "Let me worship you, *mi Reina*."

She sucked in a breath at my words. Her fingers threaded through my hair. I couldn't shift my gaze from her eyes. I wanted to please her, to satisfy her before all else. I kissed her clit, and she shivered slightly, smiling. I sucked on her, swirling my tongue, and licking.

"Don't be gentle," she whispered. "Please, be as rough as you need."

I couldn't hold back the grin. I bit her inner thigh, releasing venom into her veins. Her eyes rolled back, and she moaned, long and lustful.

"Keep your eyes on me," I commanded. I wanted to watch her as she came apart, and I wanted her to watch me as I gave her an orgasm she would remember. I could not use my full strength or be as rough as I was with my clan, but I added a little more as I returned to her wet centre.

She gripped the sheet with one hand as I pressed my tongue into her, lapping up the seam. I gazed deep into her eyes, loving the way they dilated, and she started to pant and squirm. Her hips rose off the bed as she pressed herself into my face. Her moans rose in pitch, and elsewhere in the villa, my clan and the Elders went silent. I didn't care that they were listening. *Let them.* All I cared about was that she was tense, her hand pulling at my hair.

Come for me. I willed the command into her. *Be as loud as you need.* Her eyes widened as she heard my voice in her mind. Her whole body tensed, her eyes still on mine. With her arousal on my face, I sped up, pressing in harder. *Mi Reina.*

Her climax hit her hard. My name fell from her lips in one beautiful long moan that surged through me. Her hand became a fist in my hair. But she could pull as hard as she needed to.

She lay breathing hard as I crawled up her body, planting soft kisses, pleased with the tremors that still ran through her. I pulled her nipple into my mouth, letting my fangs scrape against the soft flesh of her breast. I ground my cock against her opening as I reached her mouth, pressing in for a hard kiss. Her lips parted, allowing me in. I pushed my tongue in, overcome by a warmth and an ache in my chest.

"You're so beautiful," I murmured. "I don't think I've ever seen or noticed any human like this until I met you." I stroked her cheek with the back of my fingers.

"Even though we were trying to kill each other?" She smirked.

I claimed her soft lips again, and she grabbed the back of my neck, holding me down hard.

"Even then, I saw what a beauty you were. If only I'd known you would be the one to —" my words cut off as she pulled me down to her mouth again, while her other hand reached for my cock.

"I'd be the one to melt your dead, vampire heart?" she laughed.

"My heart's not dead, but you've given it a reason to beat," I told her.

On the other side of the den, Quinn complained about me being cheesy, followed by Matteo's low rumble of a laugh. Their minds pressed against mine, along with Luis's. The moment I thought of him, he forced his way in. *'We make our leave,'* he said through our bond. *'Enjoy your time with your young Queen. We will call upon you, very soon. All of you. We finally have our war.'* I could sense his disappointment that while he had declared war, the champions he wanted at his side would not be with him. That Matteo and Quinn would only follow me into battle. I wanted to be with Camila as long as I could before we went up against the Hunters.

"Come back to me, my King," Camila whispered. I grinned. I liked her calling me King. "When you are in my bed, you are with me, so pay attention."

I growled. "I do like when you speak that way." I kissed her neck. "But let me correct you. You're in *my* bed now. this is *my* domain."

She laughed. "Well, you can't think I'm going back to where I was before after seeing this bedroom. No, this is my home now, with you. Therefore, this bed is mine."

I snapped at her with my teeth, and she laughed again.

"Now stop talking, and fuck me," she said. "I need you inside me."

I pushed into her, slowly, stretching her. "As my Queen commands," I agreed. "Just know, the entire clan can hear you."

Chapter 65

Five years later - 2050

War broke out. Humans learned of the existence of vampires. The Bloodking captured Rome, claiming it as his territory, and he sent vampire armies around the world, claiming Moscow, Beijing, Paris, and London, and replacing their human governmental infrastructures with ones run by vampires. At the Barones' insistence, the locals of Venice took care to keep my clan in the dark. We'd not fed from them, and our presence meant they were protected from other vampires, so they showed us their appreciation.

I yearned to join the Elders but remained with Camila, to my own surprise as much as everyone else's. Antonio's death had come after he'd uploaded a photo of Camila and myself, into the Hunter records. Hunters had come, seeking me out unsuccessfully. Matteo had declared I had to have an escort whenever I left the den. It made hunting more of a challenge when people recognised what we were.

Camila took a job at Matteo's gallery, where she and Quinn ran it, while Matteo remained the mysterious artist in the shadows. What had begun as a dream when he was human had finally come to fruition, this time not being burned down as had his first attempt. It pleased me to see him happy, his feral side no longer the problem it once was. I wondered if the gallery and Quinn had finally helped him accept himself. An unexpected arrival from his past was a surprise to us all.

My Queen had agreed to us posing naked for Matteo. Sitting still next to her for such a long time became impossible. The way he had us posed while he painted, all I could see was my mark and purple bruises from my fingers around her throat and arms. With her body on display for me, I sat in a state of want and need, which I knew Matteo could not only smell, but feel. Naturally, I couldn't resist biting her. Which led to the two of us giving in to our desire for each other while our artist looked on with red eyes. Having someone watch only added to her arousal, so the two of us gave my second a show all three of us enjoyed. Erik had been unimpressed that we hadn't invited him beforehand.

While she wouldn't partake when I bedded the others, telling me I was enough for her, she did allow others in to watch when I took her. Often Erik would push his limits and touch me, or even her, but that was the most I allowed. She was understanding of my affection and the connection I had with my clan, often encouraging me to another's bed, so as to not neglect anyone.

Camila and Josef built a strong friendship, the both of them being former Hunters, and found a lot in common. I was aware that Josef intended to do so, to ease her exile. Her brother and sister were welcome, and Diego always informed us of potential problems from other Hunters. She formed close bonds with Quinn and Celeste. That all three of my women were so close filled me with joy. Each member of my clan had an equal place in my heart. It made me happy that they had welcomed Camila into the clan, despite her being human.

Having a blood bond with King Luis, Matteo, and Quinn led to the discovery that it wasn't as dangerous as we'd been led to believe, but added to my own strengths. I tested my theory by bonding to Erik and Josef. King Luis warned me only once, to stop, and to keep my discovery to myself, which I was more than happy to do. I would not give up my advantage.

I finally gave in to Quinn's pleas to play the piano with her on the nights she sang at the bar. I had to admit that I found it pleasing to have an audience, revelling in their wonder as they listened to the two of us. I surprised Quinn when I sang along with her. I'd heard her songs enough to know the words. She adapted a couple of songs to allow for me to sing solo, in Castellano at Camila's suggestion. We became known as The King and The Siren. I may have had something to do with that name.

Camila adapted to living with vampires. None of us were

accustomed to having a human in our home, so there was an adjustment period for all of us. Especially when she bled. During that time, she stayed with Lenora, and I eagerly welcomed her back upon her return. She did, however, need days away from my den, away from vampires, to just be human. This usually involved the two of us doing very human things. Meeting on *Ponte di Rialto*, sitting down for coffee, and the occasional gondola ride. She accepted our habits for *Carnevale,* but demanded I dance with her before my main meal.

Camila explored her inclinations, learning more about the world of pain, and BDSM. We often left Venice to take part in clubs in which she delved into her fantasies. Vampires from other clans soon learned to respect my Queen as they would me, and she became recognised as the human Queen of La Voz, visitors bowing to both of us. She named Josef her second.

She taught me how to fit into human society, to walk among them. A slow process for me, which she took great pride in teaching me "humanisms".

I had my Queen, and I could not say no to her.

I lay on my back, one hand behind my head, the other on Camila's shoulder as she rested on my chest. Her fingers traced over the arrow tattooed over my heart. Her mark on me, with the assistance of Famiglia di Sammarinese's Magic Wielder. She in turn had received a La Voz tattoo on her back, with a crown.

We were both naked and sweaty, and the sweet smell of her orgasm still clung to her.

"I love the sound of your heart," she murmured and tapped her fingers on me in time with my pulse.

I gave her a squeeze. "I love the sound of yours."

She was uncharacteristically quiet. Josef had told me Camila had been asking questions recently. Usually on the subject of how he had adjusted to becoming what he'd once hunted, the hunger, having to drink blood, and how long he could go without. I'd begun to wonder if she was changing her mind about becoming a vampire. I hoped she would raise her questions with me, but I wouldn't pressure her. It was unnatural to claim a human and not turn them, and I didn't want to push her away. I didn't care if it would take ten years or twenty; I'd wait.

"You're cold," she murmured. "You haven't fed."

I grinned. "Are you offering?"

She lifted her head, and I showed fang, laughing when she rolled her eyes.

"Hey, you knew what you were in for, loving a vampire," I told her. "You can't blame a man for trying." I was as hooked on her blood as she was on my venom.

I reached up, brushing my fingers over the twin scars on her throat. My mark. Still there for all to see. I still loved to look at it, to touch it. As she tilted her head back, stroking her own neck teasingly, my canines ached. I wrapped my hand around the side of her throat, careful to not be rough against her windpipe as I flipped us over, pushing her to the bed. I kissed the mark, delighting in the way her heartbeat skipped.

"You're so perfect for me," I said against her throat. "And you're mine."

She grabbed my hand, her fingers tracing over the leather bracelet. "I am yours," she said. "Just like you're mine."

I pulled back, searching her face. She'd told me she loved me, but she had never officially claimed me as hers the vampire way. I never thought such simple words would have such an effect on me. I gave her my widest grin. "Is that you claiming me, *mi Reina*?"

"It is," she confirmed. "I claim you as mine. But you know you've been mine since the day I gave you this." She touched the leather bracelet again.

"She claimed me!" I declared to the den. The clan's joy for me echoed through the villa.

Her words exhilarated me, and I pulled her into a kiss, unable to hold back. We pulled apart. "I'm yours," I agreed. "As long as you live."

Her energy changed and she buried her face in my chest. I stroked the back of her head.

"You don't know what your words mean to me," I told her.

She pulled out of my embrace, sitting up, resolution glinting in her eyes. "Carlos?"

"Mmmm." It dawned on me slowly that I was hungry. She was right, I hadn't fed.

"Turn me," she whispered.

I stilled. "What?"

"I mean it. It's been five years, I'm older than you now —"

I laughed. "You'll never be older than me."

Her fingers pressed against my mouth to silence me. "You know what I mean. I'm almost thirty, While you're permanently twenty-three."

I wanted to turn her. I wanted her to be with me forever, and I didn't want her to age. But to hear her say this was more than I could hope for.

"What changed your mind?" I asked.

"Well, it might have something to do with the fact that I've lived with vampires the last five years," she said. "I'm the only human in a vampire clan. I've picked up habits from living with you all. I actually growled at Josef last week, which he took great delight in."

I laughed; the thought of her growling was appealing. "You do spend a lot of time with vampires; I suppose it was only natural that you started to behave like us. Although I would have liked to have heard that growl." I kissed her cheek. "Care to give me a rendition of it?"

She reached a hand up to my face instead. "The years with you have made me happier than I've ever been. I want the rest of my life to be with you. Forever. I've spoken to Diego and Sofia. They don't like my decision, but they will support me in whatever I do within my chosen family."

So she had decided already and had even shared it with her brother and sister.

"I'll turn you. Bare your throat to me," I commanded.

She did as I told her, and I kissed the mark again. It would be the last time I would see those scars. With my blood in her, they would fade away from existence. "I'm going to miss these," I murmured.

"You can bite, mark, bruise me as much as you want, and you won't have to hold back," she said.

"Oh, trust me, *mi Reina*, I intend to," I whispered next to her ear, and gave her a growl, loving the shiver that went through her. I opened my mouth and sunk my fangs into her throat.

I took my time, wanting to stretch out this moment. She grew weaker, and I supported her completely, lowering her back onto the bed. Her body squirmed from the effects of my venom.

'Matteo, can you bring me a knife? She's ready.' I didn't shift my attention from her, not even when Matteo entered my bedroom, with Quinn behind him.

I pulled back when I had taken enough that she would die if I didn't return it soon. Her heartbeat was already erratic. Without a word, Matteo gave me his knife, and the two of them climbed onto the bed, curling up next to her. I sliced the blade across my neck before lowering myself over her. Her mouth opened against my throat, her tongue sending a deep shiver through me. "That's it, drink." I soothed her.

I stroked her neck with my thumb as she took my blood. The mark I'd made smoothed over. I would have eternity to mark her, over and over again, just as she'd said.

'I'm proud of you, Carlos,' Matteo whispered in my mind. *'You were so patient.'*

As Camila drank from me, our minds opened to each other, that initial rush of our blood bond that would soon become quieter. With it, I could feel her love for me, so strong it hurt my own heart. I showed her mine. The cut on my throat closed, and she growled. The muscles in my chest tightened, the very sound reverberating through not just my body, but my entire being.

She bit me, hard. I could feel fangs, but not yet long enough. Baby fangs, the sign that my blood was starting to change her already.

"You do not have a gentle bite," I told Camila, unable to hold back the grin. She was going to make a magnificent vampire, and I couldn't wait to take her hunting.

I made another cut, enjoying the feel of her mouth on my throat, especially when her teeth clamped down. Her instinct to sink fangs into flesh was already awakening. Once I was sure she'd taken enough of my blood, I pulled away from her mouth. "You will experience a mortal death. Your heart will stop. But you won't truly be dead. You will merely slumber while your body makes the changes it needs for you to become like me."

Quinn and Matteo caressed her face. "Like us," Matteo said. "You have nothing to fear, Camila. We will *all* ease you into your new life."

The rest of the clan walked in, and they crawled onto my bed, curling around Camila. By now she was used to our ways, so it didn't alarm her that seven vampires were surrounding her, pressed into her. Not even that she was naked. Josef lay over Matteo to lick Camila's throat, before nuzzling his head under her chin. Erik stroked her face, Celeste squeezed her hand, and Andreas wrapped himself around her leg. She smiled, as her eyelids grew heavy and started to flutter.

I cleaned my blood from her chin. The sound of her heartbeat was deafening. It started to slow down.

"I'll wake you when it's time," I told her. "We'll be here when you awaken, and then we'll hunt."

She clung to me, whimpering. Her body was shutting down, and she could feel her death approaching. "I don't want to die," she pleaded.

"This is part of it," I whispered to her in Castellano. Words meant to soothe, with my arms around her. "You'll be okay. Don't be afraid, Camila. I'm here."

'Don't leave me,' she begged.

'I'll never leave you," I promised.

Her heart stopped. Her breathing stopped. But her mind remained strong, connected to mine as she fell into slumber. She would rest as her body made the change. It would replace human frailty and fears with strength and the mind of a predator. Her weak hearing and vision would be magnified, designed for hunting in the dark.

"Now we wait," I said, knowing I probably wouldn't leave her side while she slumbered.

"It will be a long wait." Matteo reached across to Quinn, the love that passed between them clear on their faces. "But look at her. Your Queen. She will awaken to your voice, and she will be yours, forever."

Camila had died at four o'clock in the morning. I had to wait twenty-four hours, to let her body complete the change. I lay with my arms wrapped around her, unmoving, unable to tear myself away from her. The ache of hunger started to spread through me.

"You're hungry," Erik said, and placed himself beside me, baring his throat. "Drink, my King."

I lifted my head and turned, feeding from him but not letting go of Camila. Then I returned to watching her face, waiting for the right time to awaken her. Technically, she was dead, deep in her slumber of transformation. Yet she appeared to only be asleep.

As we waited, the clan spoke of how they'd died, some of them unaware of what awaited them. Of their slumber, and awakening as vampires. I'd been there for both Quinn's and Josef's death's. The memory of my own rose up.

"I died at the hands of my father, for killing to protect Gabriela," I told my clan around me, aware that, across all our centuries together, I had *never* spoken to them about this. Only Erik knew this story. "My entire village wanted me dead. I felt betrayed, and I turned my back on humanity and who I had been because of it. When I awoke, I slaughtered them all, enjoying every moment of it. I didn't have my human memories at the time, but I think that betrayal was with me even then. For me to take such joy, it had to have been." Everyone's eyes were on me. "As my death closed in, I saw what I would become. I embraced it before I took my last breath as a human. The darkness that surrounded me while I slumbered, I welcomed it. An eternity passed before Gabriela's voice called me forth. She called me Little Killer, because that's what I was, before I was turned. As a vampire,

I revelled in that title. And all others that were given to me. Humans rarely survived me back then. I made ferals, not realising I needed to create a bond. Their creation delighted the Bloodking, so I made more. My bloodthirsty nature was what created the Hunters." I glanced at Josef with a smile. "To have Camila here, in her slumber, I would never have imagined a Huntress would be the Queen I took."

They said nothing, absorbing my words. Understanding flickered in Matteo's eyes. He finally understood then, why Gabriela had forced the bond on us. Equally as brutal as one another, we were a good match. I wondered if she had known the retaliation that Luis had planned.

"Carlos!" Celeste drew my attention, her voice heavy with excitement. "Look at her fangs."

Pointed tips showed between Camila's lips. I pulled back her upper lip, revealing long, sharp fangs. The sight of them filled me with joy. I let my own fangs descend, wanting to be me when she awoke. The first thing she would see would be my red eyes, looking into hers.

"She's ready." Matteo grinned at me. "Can you feel it?"

I stared at the man who'd been bonded to me for six centuries. He had become a maker and knew exactly what I was experiencing. "Turn out the lights," I told Celeste. "Light the candles."

Candles were spread around the room, the tiny flames casting a soft glow. I'd wanted to be romantic. I took a moment, stroking Camila's hair. I kissed her cheek, her forehead and the tip of her nose. She was as cold as the dead and would awaken hungry. My chest swelled, and it felt like my heart would burst. Celeste handed me the red carnation she'd retrieved for me while we waited for Camila.

Finally, I reached into her mind. An inferno blazed within her, brighter than the ember that I'd come to know. She was surrounded by the dark, in a state of calm. Resting. but ready.

"She's magnificent," I said to my clan, pride and warmth taking root deep within me.

"Call her from her slumber," Josef said. "Your Queen awaits."

"Our King's Queen," Celeste affirmed.

My clan dropped to their knees, waiting with their heads bowed.

"Camila, my Queen, it's time to wake up." I pushed the command into her, urging her to wake up. I'd turned and awoken ferals before, but this was the first time I was a maker, a true maker.

My command took effect. She responded to my voice, a spark of her presence reaching for me before she was ablaze with life. Her heart kicked, once, then a second time, and it started to beat again. The strong, slow pace of a vampire heart. Her red eyes opened, gazing into mine, and she smiled, showing me her fangs. She was still her, but the human memories would take a while to return. I'd seen it many times over the centuries. All she knew at that moment was vampire instinct. And me, her maker. I held out the flower.

She reached for my face, recognition flickering in her eyes, before accepting my gift.

Not only was I her maker, but also, I was her King. She pressed her thumb to my fang. Blood welled up, and I licked it away. Her eyes glinted, and she pushed at her own fang with her tongue.

She was absolutely stunning as a vampire, and I couldn't

keep my eyes off her. My chest ached. I'd dreamed of this moment for years, and I couldn't believe it was finally here. I cupped her face, and she leaned into my touch.

"I'm hungry." Her eyes darted to the others, still on their knees.

"You can't feed from them. They're your clan," I whispered to her. "My clan. Ours." I rose from the bed, pulling her with me. "They're here to welcome you, as one of us. As their Queen."

At my nod, they rose. Each of them nuzzled at Camila, and a growl of contentment rose from her. Damn, that sound. She nuzzled them back, and licked Josef's throat. She wouldn't know them yet, but she recognised they were the same as her. She reached a hand for Erik's face, then Celeste's, watching them.

I had not left her side while she slumbered, and I was glad we would be going hunting together, as I had always dreamed.

She turned her eyes to me, her fingers caressing my cheek again.

"Camila." I drew her to me, unable to resist. "My little *Cazadora. Mi Reina.* Time to hunt."

Bonus Chapter

an Marino, Italy - 2045

S Of the vampires who had followed King Giuseppe into Venice, two were missing. Including our King. The entire clan crowded around them.

"Where is King Giuseppe?" I asked. I wished he had taken me with him. I'd been trying to get into Venice for twenty years. Frustration surged through me that I had missed an opportunity.

"King Giuseppe is dead," Ricardo declared. "He challenged King Carlos and lost. The feral killed him."

The feral! I wanted to ask more questions.

"Are we at war with them?" another vampire, Carmen, asked.

War? I hoped not.

"King Luca swore we had no quarrel with them," Ricardo said.

Giuseppe had recently taken Luca to be his second, after Marco's death. It had been unexpected; many vampires in the clan were older than Luca, more suited to the position. Many questioned the decision. I suspected Giuseppe's grief had affected his choice.

"Where is he?" I asked.

Pierre met my eyes. "He remained back to speak with Carlos. He will return soon." He addressed the clan. All fifty of us. "They have a siren. Her voice was incredibly powerful and had us all on our knees. Giuseppe did not care to warn us before he led us to what could have been our end. His death was deserved. As was Marco's. To not only challenge The Killer, but The Feral and a siren, too."

I fought down the urge to growl. Rage burst through me at his talk of my maker. Dead or not, I was still loyal to Marco. Pierre had been in our clan for at least a hundred years, but he was a vampire without loyalty.

A smirk crossed his face. "Luca has not yet taken a second. Who will challenge me?"

I knew why he wanted the role.

"Is it the role you want, or the clan?" I challenged.

He flashed his fangs at me. I laughed. Stupid child. He was not that much older than Luca. As a six-hundred-year-old vampire, *I* was among the eldest in the clan. I wasn't certain Luca as a King would make us the strong clan we should be.

But neither would Pierre.

I stepped forward. *"I challenge you,"* I spoke out, showing him my fangs.

Pierre tilted his head as he eyed me. "You are more suited for a King's Queen."

A shudder tore through me as I absorbed his words.

"No," I argued. "I challenge you for becoming *second*."

"There will be no challenge," Luca said. "I pick Aria for my second."

The clan knelt before Luca. I joined them. "Thank you, my King," I said, shooting a triumphant look at Pierre. He glared back. I would have to be careful with him.

Luca looked over the clan, and he let out a sigh. He hesitated, and uncertainty crossed his face. "King Carlos has taken control of our clan. He will allow me to be King, but I answer to him. To ensure loyalty, I am bonded to Josef Alfaro."

Everyone reacted in shock, their voices filling the den. This had been my clan since Marco turned me. It was not unheard of that Kings or Queens who were challenged would absorb the clan of the loser. But no one wanted to belong to a new King. I could see that in their faces.

"Why did he not send anyone here to oversee his new clan?" I asked. "Are we to expect Josef to join us?"

I knew exactly who Josef was. Every time I had tried to enter Venice, it was Josef Alfaro and Erik Haraldson who stopped me. They always called King Carlos, who had forced me out. The idea of Josef arriving in San Marino filled me with excitement, but I wasn't sure why.

"King Carlos will not absorb us," Luca said. "The rest of you can go. I will talk with my second." He waited for everyone to leave, then turned to me. "I want you to go to Venice in a few days. I will let Josef know to expect you. I hope to please Carlos. Make sure to appeal to him and the feral. There is no reason we cannot maintain a close friendship with his clan."

I forced down the grin that would have given me away. No one in the clan knew that I'd tried to get into Venice for the last twenty years. Nor could they know why. Only Marco knew. Venice had been my home, and over the centuries I had returned many times, to maintain a close connection with my descendants, and those of my uncle's. They knew what I was, and the day I received a message from Lenora of my father's return had been the best day of my existence.

"I will do what must be done," I agreed. "Will I be expected to take an offering with me?"

Luca considered this. "Perhaps. I'll think about that."

It occurred to me that Luca was in over his head. He was so young, and there could potentially be a challenge to his rule. Pierre or Ricardo were the most likely candidates. *Wouldn't it anger Pierre if I beat him to that, too?* I almost laughed at the idea.

Luca grabbed my arm. "Marco was your maker, wasn't he?" he asked, his voice gentle.

I nodded. "He was. I'm still feeling the effects of his death." It was as if it were *my* heart that had been ripped out, and now an emptiness filled me.

He gave me a sad smile. "I know what it feels like. I want to make sure you are not going to go to Venice for revenge. Carlos is very old and strong. His clan are loyal to him. They will tear you apart if you try anything." He closed his eyes and sighed. "Giuseppe didn't stand a chance. I don't want to see that happen to anyone else in my clan."

The idea of revenge hadn't occurred to me. "I will be there to represent our clan," I promised. "I will meet with King Carlos, and with his second, in peace."

His eyes narrowed. "Be careful. Matteo Barone is as feral as they say he is. He tore out our former king's heart before any of us could move to protect him."

I smelled fear. "You have nothing to worry about, Luca. We will give them no reason to attempt to kill any more in our clan."

I had lived six hundred years, but the next few days were the longest in my life. I approached Venice in what had once been King Giuseppe's boat. As expected, Josef and Erik met me. Josef laughed.

"How many times will it take for you to learn?" he demanded.

"You're expecting me." I told him. "I am King Luca's second. He sent me to meet with your King, and *his* second."

The pair of them exchanged a look filled with amusement.

"An interesting turn of events that no one could have foreseen," Erik said. "He will not be happy to see you. Does Luca know he sent the *one* person whose presence would anger our King?"

I remained silent, my heart pounding. This was the moment of truth. Whether they would send me back, or take me to their den.

"Surely Luca wouldn't be stupid enough to do anything to deliberately anger King Carlos," Erik said to Josef.

I watched them both. Erik was clearly from the days of the Vikings. His long, blond hair was tied back, and he still maintained a long but neat beard. His grey eyes focused on me with interest. Josef's blue eyes held the same interest, his dark hair shorter. They towered over me, and I decided that they were likely an intimidating duo. But instead of the expected fear, I found myself overcome by pure lust. I'd always been drawn to men like this.

They both breathed in deep, their eyes turning red as they closed in. They could smell my lust. I held still, waiting.

Erik leaned in, taking in my scent. Their own arousal spiked. "Well, don't you smell delicious," he said with a fanged smile.

There was silence for a moment, and I suspected they were talking through a blood bond. Both of them ran their eyes down my body. Josef moved around behind me, and he breathed in again.

Erik placing his hands on my hip was unexpected, and he pulled me towards him. Josef wrapped his arm around my stomach, and moved forward. I was locked in tight between them.

"You'll have to excuse us," Josef said, his breath tickling my ear. "It's been awhile since we've had a woman that our King didn't claim as his. We only have two females in our clan. Now he has the young Huntress, too."

I had a good idea what they were talking about, but I held my breath. The thought of fighting them occurred to me. To make them work for it.

"Ours," Josef declared, his hand grasping my chin to lift it, to expose my throat.

Exhilaration surged through me, and I decided against the traditional fight. I was from another clan, and not a new vampire. It was likely they expected me to make them work for it. Instead, I lifted my head high, inviting them to bite.

The two of them struck fast, sinking their fangs into my throat. Their venom flooded me and I let out a moan, my knees suddenly weak. Erik pressed himself against me. I could feel his erection through his trousers and ground myself against him. Josef's hand slid down into my jeans, pushing aside my panties. His fingers slid through my wetness, and a growl rose from him. I let out my own growl.

They removed their fangs, but their lips remained on my throat, their soft kisses sending a deep shiver through me. Their tongues slid over my skin, cleaning away blood. They had marked and claimed me, and I wanted it. I wanted them. I yearned to claim them, but this wasn't my territory. I would have to wait.

"Ours," Erik agreed when they released me. He gazed deep into my eyes. "That is just a taste of the pleasure we will give you. Voice your thoughts."

I grabbed a fistful of hair on the back of Erik's head and pulled him into a deep kiss. Then I turned, and with the same fervour, I kissed Josef. I pulled away from Josef, Erik's hands still on me, Josef's fingers still inside me. Their lips trailed hungrily across my mouth, meeting each other's before their teeth scraped over my jaw.

Josef lifted the fingers he had slid into me, towards his mouth. I grabbed his hand, pulling his fingers into *my* mouth.

His breathing changed as I sucked on his fingers, and he groaned.

"You cannot taste me yet," I declared, releasing his hand. "This is a business trip. Perhaps later we'll have time for pleasure."

I wanted these men to take me, and I struggled in turning

down their advances. I would have let them both fuck me in the very place we stood. But I had something else I needed to do first. Someone else I wanted to see. A reunion that was long overdue.

I gave them each a soft kiss again. They were so close to me, wanting more. And I stepped out from between them.

They both growled, and moved forward. I held my hands up to stop them. Raw desire glinted in their eyes.

"Business," I said again, my hands pressed against their chests.

I saw their internal struggle as they forced back their nature, their eyes returning to the normal colour.

"Oh, I love a determined woman," Erik's voice grumbled from him. He groaned. "You're *ours*, but we'll wait. You'll be worth the wait."

The smile he gave me sent a flutter through my stomach. Damn, I hungered for him. For both of them.

I snapped at his jaw playfully. "Perhaps when your King isn't waiting on me," I reminded them.

I had a villa, the very one that I had lived in with my parents. I could take them to that, let them claim me all they wanted. I hoped they played rough.

Josef lifted my hand, pressing his lips to my fingers.

"Come on then, I suppose we should present you to our King," Josef finally said. "At least now, you'll have protection."

To be claimed was an honour. I'd been claimed by two incredibly hot men, to whom I'd been attracted the first time I lay eyes on them. It meant that if Pierre tried anything, he had no right to me. It also meant I was tied to these men, and they would likely expect me to join *their* clan. With Marco dead, and Pierre closing in, I wondered if I should.

We approached the villa that I knew all too well. Lenora had told me they'd removed Pietro and his family and taken over what had once been my family home.

They stood in front of me as King Carlos entered the room with a human woman. The scent of her made my canines ache. Clearly, my arrival had interrupted his meal. I had fed before arriving in Venice, but to have a human right there, still warm from desire for the men before me, it was a struggle to keep my fangs from emerging.

"My King," Josef said. "Luca has sent a representative."

I realised they had not referred to Luca as 'King'.

"Then present her." Carlos demanded. I couldn't see him with the two men blocking me, but he sounded irritated. "Standing in front of her does not hide her scent. You know the warnings I have given her."

"We ask that you not harm her," Erik added. "She is Luca's second."

"Why does it matter?" A new voice had entered the conversation. One I knew. *He's here!* "Carlos clearly doesn't like her presence. Why would you bring her here and make such a plea?"

"Because they claimed her," Carlos said with laughter. "Alright, step aside, let me officially receive her, then."

They moved to the side, and I dropped to my knee immediately. I bowed my head. He wore only jeans, and I'd caught sight of a wolf tattoo on his bare chest. The Immortal Wolf was only one of many names he was known by.

King Carlos spoke to the human woman in another language. Likely Spanish. She replied. He pulled her to him for a kiss before releasing her, and then he spoke again.

The distinct scent of lust rose from her.

I lifted my eyes up slightly, glancing at the human woman. There was no glazed-over expression of a trance, and she'd been marked. King Carlos had claimed a human.

"Lower your gaze," the King's second commanded.

I dropped my eyes immediately. It stung to have him speak to me in such a formal way. That he hadn't recognised me. I reminded myself I'd been twelve, and human. Centuries ago. He would not be expecting me.

The King chuckled. "Matteo, I think you enjoy this too much."

The laughter that boomed from him set off memories of a human girl. She had died centuries ago, but she was still here.

"King Carlos," I said. "My King's second." I could have sworn my voice cracked.

I wanted to turn my head. To meet the eyes of the man to his right. But suddenly I was nervous. I'd dreamed about this reunion for centuries. Only Marco had known, and he had helped me try to find him.

"On your feet," King Carlos commanded.

I rose, careful to keep my eyes down.

"You've finally found your way into Venice, then." King Carlos chuckled.

"I was named as King Luca's second, and he wanted to send me here to meet with you." I informed him.

King Carlos moved away from me and sat in a large chair. The human woman took one beside him. I stared at the woman.

"Are we to discuss matters in front of her?" I asked as I took a seat.

A growl broke from King Carlos. "You will show my Queen the same respect you show me." He leaned forward. "Now tell me your name. And why you have been so determined to enter my domain."

Queen? A human? This did not match anything I had heard of King Carlos.

Finally, I lifted my eyes to the man who stood next to King Carlos.

He looked exactly as he had the last time I'd seen him. Over six hundred years ago, crouched on the ground, anguish in his face as he held her body in his arms. He'd told me to run to my uncle, and never return. Now, he met my gaze without recognition, curiosity glinting in his eyes.

"My name is Aria *Barone*," I emphasised, not looking away. Vampires around us gasped. Erik and Josef swore. I'd used the name he'd recognise instead of the name of the human I'd married before my mortal death. His eyes widened with shock, and he shook his head in disbelief. King Carlos turned his head, eyes darting between the two of us.

"I have been trying to find you for a very long time, *Father*."

Stay tuned for more on Aria, Erik and Josef.

Epilogue to follow

Epilogue

Venice 2050

Before my father had died, he'd added the photo of Carlos and me onto the Hunter records. In doing so, he had shone a light on the shadows Carlos preferred. The first photo of Carlos in history. Hunters finally knew what The Immortal Wolf looked like. He became a hot subject on the Hunter network, and everyone wanted the reputation that would come from being the one to kill him.

Hunters had descended on Venice in the hopes of taking out what their records referred to as the most brutal vampire in history. Luckily for us, Diego had warned us in advance, and the Barones and Venetians had covered for the clan. That had led to the clan becoming very hungry as they hid from the Hunters, and the Barones had sent them humans to feed from until it was safe to leave the den again.

The night Carlos had claimed me, I'd insisted on not being turned. But the next morning, waking up in his arms, realising I was now part of a vampire clan, I'd known it would be a decision I would eventually have to make. I had spent five years with that knowledge. Every year that passed, as I got older, I had known the day was coming. Carlos never pushed the matter, but I knew my ageing weighed on him. It took me five years to get used to the idea.

After I could no longer deny that the idea of becoming a vampire didn't terrify me as it once had, I'd started to ask Josef questions. He had answered them with patience and understanding. I had tried to frame them in such a way as to sound like curiosity, but I was sure he knew the reason. Then I had spoken to Diego and Sofia, and finally, I had asked Carlos to turn me.

I stared at my reflection, studying my red eyes, and baring

my fangs. Carlos's laughter boomed from him, and his arms slid around my waist. I leaned into him.

"I had no idea how difficult this would be," I said. "Why didn't you tell me?"

He kissed the back of my neck, and met my eyes in the mirror. "This is who you are now, Camila. It's not natural for us to hide our true face. Newer vampires take awhile to learn to hide their vampirism. You'll get used to it in your own time."

"This is why you encourage everyone to be themselves in the den," I commented.

He nodded. "We have to hide who we are from humans; there is no reason to hide from each other." He turned me around to face him. "It's okay, it just takes time. No one in the clan will fault you for not looking human. We're not human," he reminded me.

Frustration surged. I had only regained my human memories a day ago, and I had yet to learn control of my vampirism. Diego and Sofia were arriving the next morning, so I would rather put on a human face for them when they arrived. Carlos caressed my cheek, and I sighed, melting against him.

"Don't rush this," he whispered. "No vampire has learned this overnight." He dropped his voice. "I went three years before I even bothered trying to shift between faces." He cradled my cheek. "You're beautiful the way you are, and a Queen. *My* Queen. You can take all the time you need to look human, and I will still kneel at your feet, mark you, and claim you in our bed." He smiled down at me. "I still love you, whether you look human or not. Since the war began, some Kings and Queens have refused to show anything but their vampirism. Such worries are beneath you. Be who you are."

His words turned my insides to jelly.

"I can't face Diego or Sof like this," I complained.

Carlos kissed my forehead. "They're your brother and sister. Josef has already prepared them for what to expect."

I let out a sigh. "Why do you always have an answer for everything?"

He grinned at me. "Because, my beautiful Queen should not worry about what is beyond her control. This is normal." He tilted my chin up and lowered his head. Our lips met, and his arms closed around me.

When we finally pulled apart, his eyes gazed into mine. "Are you hungry?"

The question reminded me of the ever-present hunger since his voice had pulled me from slumber. I nodded, fighting back my desire to push him against the wall and show him what else I was hungry for. A rumble rose from him, and I realised he sensed my need through our blood bond.

"We have all night for that. Let's eat first. I'm taking you out for dinner." He turned towards the door. "Matteo! Josef! We're going hunting!

It didn't take long before Matteo and Josef stood at the door to our bedroom, ready. Our escorts. Because of the photo my father had uploaded to the Hunter records, Matteo had advised Carlos to have an escort whenever he left the den. For any reason. Since I was also in the photo, Josef, my second, had agreed.

Josef smiled at me as Matteo and Carlos led us out. "Are you excited to see Sofia and Diego?" he asked.

"A little," I said. "I'm also nervous. I'm the very thing that the three of us were taught to hunt. They accepted my decision, but for them to come here, and see the change in me, it's probably going to be awkward. I'm afraid that I won't know what to say."

"They wanted to come here, to see you. If they didn't, they would have turned down your invitation. They've agreed to adhere to our ways when they arrive," he told me. "They will address you as the Queen of La Voz, and they will kneel to you as any visiting vampire would. Carlos will sit beside you, and I'll be standing behind you."

It surprised me that Josef had already spoken to them in such depth. "Thank you," I said. "Will you stop me from attacking them if I fail in containing my nature?"

His hand squeezed my arm. "You have nothing to worry about, Camila. Let's just enjoy the hunt tonight. A cruise ship docked today. So you have plenty to choose from. It's a real smorgasbord! A special treat."

Carlos laughed from ahead of us. "Just don't drink too much and get so blood drunk that you find yourself still on the cruise ship after they've left," he called back to us.

"Who did that?" I asked Josef.

He grinned. "Erik and me, a few years before you came to us."

I shook my head in amusement, then focused on my surroundings. As a human, I had always loved the heat of the sun on my skin, and the noise of everyone going about their day. But I hadn't been out during the day since becoming a vampire. The idea just had no appeal to it. Carlos was still waiting for my enhanced sunglasses to arrive from the Magic Wielder in San Marino. Now, it was the night that had become a comfort. The silence, and the cool breeze against my skin, were pure bliss. I could hear the heartbeats of humans around us, smell coffee and blood, and see into the dark. The four of us ran through the streets, unseen.

We stopped in front of the cruise ship. I marvelled at the size of it, a literal hotel. I stared up. "How do we get onto it?" I asked.

Josef, Matteo, and Carlos all laughed.

"I love new vampires," Matteo said. "Their minds are still so limited."

Carlos grabbed one hand, and Josef grabbed the other. "Jump," Carlos instructed.

I launched myself into the darkness above and burst with glee as I realised a new vampire ability. Laughter erupted from me as we landed on the ship's top deck.

"Shhh!" Carlos said, covering my mouth. "Humans will hear you."

"Oh my god! That was awesome!" I declared.

I'd never been on a cruise ship before. Josef and Carlos quietly explained that the top deck was a romantic spot for quiet, mostly private stargazing at night. Lounge chairs were seated around the swimming pool, with a refreshment stand nearby, the smell of alcohol strong.

Matteo chuckled. "Okay, what's your plan, Carlos?"

Carlos started walking. "I was always a sucker for first-class."

Carlos led us down to the deck below, the sounds of human heartbeats closer, their deep breaths indicating many were asleep.

"These cabins have the best views," Josef told me.

"How do we get into the rooms? Don't they lock them?" I

asked

Carlos wrapped one arm around me. "We knock. Humans on a ship are more trusting. They open their door to anyone, since they're usually expecting staff. Then, with a little compulsion of course, they invite us in. Uninterrupted feeding. I do prefer the cabins that have couples, as we can drink more, without hurting anyone."

We stopped at a door. I stood behind Matteo and Carlos, Josef next to me. Carlos knocked. I listened to the people in the room whispering to each other. A minute later, steps approached, and the lock clicked. The door swung open, and it took everything in me to not leap at the human man that stood before us. Josef gripped my wrist tight, a reminder that he was there to stop me if needed. The sound of the humans' heartbeats echoed through my head, and I could already taste their blood. A growl rose up in my chest, but I held it back.

"Yes? Can I help you?" the human asked in an English accent.

"Actually, you can," Carlos replied, putting on an accent that matched theirs. "We're a little hungry. Can we come in?"

The human hesitated. "Don't you have food in your room?"

"We had an issue with our fridge, and they can't fix it until the morning," Carlos said.

The human stepped aside, and I kept my eyes down as I walked past. The deluxe cabin was equipped with a queen-sized bed, a bedside table, a fridge and microwave, a TV, two windows with fabulous views across the water, and an en suite full bathroom with a shower, over which the humans had hung their bathing suits to dry. The delicious scent of the humans enveloped me. Once the door closed, Carlos moved fast to silence the woman. Josef and Matteo held the man.

"Don't scream," Matteo said. "Don't fight us."

"Camila," Carlos called me over.

I approached him, smiling at the human woman.

"Vampire!" she whispered, her eyes wide as she took me in.

"Shhh, we won't hurt you," Carlos soothed her. "We're just going to feed, and leave the both of you. You'll wake up in the morning, and you won't remember anything."

The scent of blood filled the room. Josef and Matteo had already started feeding. Impatient, I licked the woman's throat, as Carlos had shown me, and I sunk my fangs in. Carlos took her a moment later. I soared. I drank from the woman. Her blood was rich and sweet. She whimpered softly from the effects of our venom.

'Stop,' Carlos pulled me out of the red haze with one word.

I let go and licked my lips. I wanted more, and I growled, but he held me back. "Shhh, Camila, we can find another room if you want more. Any more from her, and she'll need medical help. That would bring unwanted attention."

We left the room, and found another, feeding off the couple there, and a third room.

"Carlos," Josef sounded strained as we left the last room. "The Queen of Famiglia di Sammarinese has requested entrance to Venice."

"Is she alright?" Matteo had deep concern in his voice for his daughter.

Josef took awhile to answer as he spoke through a blood

bond. "She is. Erik's with her. Hunters have raided San Marino. They burned down her den. She has five vampires with her."

"The whole clan's gone?" Matteo asked.

Josef shook his head. "No, most of them were in Rome with the Bloodking. Ricardo was sent to join those in Washington, D.C. Aria got everyone out unharmed. Mostly. A couple of humans died in the fire."

Carlos cursed in Castellano. "Tell her to go to her villa. We have Diego and Sofia arriving at the den in a few hours. Remind her: no killing, and no locals."

Carlos stopped me to clean the blood from my chin. "Did you have enough?" he asked me.

I laughed, a little intoxicated, and licked his chin. "I had no idea how sexually arousing this is." I told him. "I could just lick you all over."

"Oh, I'd say she's had enough," Josef commented. "Maybe that third room wasn't necessary."

"She's new; her hunger hasn't settled down yet." Carlos pulled me to him, wrapping one arm around me. "When her brother and sister arrive, she'll be well-fed."

"And I thought you were trying to get me drunk," I joked.

"Well, that, too. I was waiting until we got home, so I can get you naked, and into my bed." Carlos said, and I realised he was also blood drunk. Heat and need surged between the two of us through our blood bond.

I turned towards Josef. "Will Erik be coming home? We have a new chair he can sit in to watch."

"Probably not tonight," Josef admitted. "The moment I get you home, I'll be joining him and Aria."

"Escort," Carlos said.

"Andreas will be with me," Josef added.

"La Voz, the celebrity clan," I added. "So many of us needing escorts."

"Unfortunately, that's the world we live in," Carlos said. "I think I actually miss the shadows."

"Wow, after all those years of missing the feeding in the open, and leading the rebellion against the accords, I could not have predicted that," Josef stated.

Carlos cast him a sad look. "Things change. I suppose I got used to living in the shadows. The Bloodking always wanted this, and there's no going back now. He has taken major cities in Europe; we'd have to compel every last human for them to forget, but there are very public records of vampires existing now. It won't be long before Hunters leak their records publicly. I'm surprised they haven't done that already."

I didn't want to think about the war, or Hunters. I'd spent most of my life as a Hunter; it had been an adjustment to shift my mindset. Now that I was a vampire, Hunters were my enemy.

"Let's get you home," Carlos said. "Seeing you feed has me a little heated."

I had to admit my sex drive had somewhat increased since my turning. "You're always a little heated," I replied.

We made our way through quiet streets, back to the den. Carlos rushed me to our bedroom.

"What are you in the mood for?" he asked.

As I gazed into his eyes, the strong scent of his arousal overpowered me. I didn't realise I'd moved until his back hit the wall, hard. A deep growl burst from me.

"Bare your throat," I ordered.

His eyes turned red, smouldering, as he gazed back at me. He tilted his head, baring the curve of his throat to me. I buried my fangs in his neck, marking him as he had once marked me. I let go, licking over where I'd bitten.

"You're mine," I declared.

"I am," he acknowledged. "Do you want me on my knees? I can get the shackles."

I took a deep breath, and I lowered myself to my knees before him, my chin raised to gauge his reaction. Surprise flickered across his face, a smile widening, showing fangs.

"*Mi Rey*, I want *you* to restrain *me*," I said in a soft voice.

In all we had tried in the bedroom, I had never let him restrain me before. I was always the one who put cuffs on him.

The sheer hunger that surged from him through our blood bond sent my mind reeling. I panted with need, for Carlos.

"Would you like to select a safe word?" he asked.

Now that I was a vampire, I didn't see the need for it. I shook my head.

"Very well. I have something special that I've been waiting to try," he informed me. "Take your clothes off. Get on the bed, and close your eyes.

I did as he demanded, already wet. On my back, with my eyes closed, I leaned into my other senses. Wood scraped as he pulled a drawer open, and the soft brush of silk rustled. His footsteps padded across the carpet, and our bed shifted under his weight.

"Do you trust me?" His breath brushed against my ear.

I couldn't speak, could only nod.

"Use your words, Camila." His voice had taken on a commanding tone, sending heat through me again.

"Yes," I whispered.

Soft material pressed over my eyes, as he tied a scarf behind my head. His touch moved to my hand, lifting it to rest above my head. He trailed kisses over my arm before tying another silk scarf around my wrist, securing it to the headboard. He repeated the motion with my other arm.

"Are you comfortable?" he asked.

"Yes," I confirmed.

He kissed my lips softly, then the heat of his body was gone. I listened, but only his heartbeat made a sound. Still adjusting to my new hearing, I didn't know if that meant he was right next to me, or on the other side of the room. I whimpered. The bed shifted again. Warm breath caressed the hot skin of my navel. It shifted down to my pussy.

"What do you want?" His voice had become rough, guttural.

"You," I could barely get the word out. "My King, I want you."

He didn't move. His breath was soft against my clit, and I squirmed, arching my back, hoping for something. He was sending me into desperation. I wanted his mouth on me.

"Please," I begged. "Carlos."

"You're ready for me," he growled. "I can smell how wet you are. I can see how eager you are for me. But we're going to stretch this out a little bit. You have no idea how much more heated you can get. You're going to enjoy my touch first. You're going to be begging me before I give you what you want. Understand?"

I whimpered again.

"Use your words," he reminded me.

"I understand," I stated, my muscles clenching.

"Good girl," he murmured.

I waited. Nothing happened. I turned my head, trying to sense him. "Carlos?"

Something touched me. Soft and feathery, sliding over my breasts and down to trace a circle over my navel. I let out a small gasp, a warm shiver running through me as the movement continued. Then it was gone, replaced by breath. Starting on my ankle, he moved up. Once he reached my thighs, the breaths turned to light kisses. I yearned to wrap my legs around his body. He paused, and kissed my clit. Heat roared through me, the need for him intensifying. I groaned, lifting my hips again, only to find him gone.

His fingers pinched one of my nipples, and his mouth closed on the other one, fangs scraping over my flesh. His tongue swirled, and he growled softly. A rumble rose up in my own chest in response. I moved my arms, wanting to touch him. His mouth left my breast, and my arms were pinned down.

"Try not to tear these," he warned.

"I just want to touch you," I pleaded, my body still squirming.

"Be patient," he instructed.

I said nothing, and once again, I waited for what was next. His hands moved over my body, massaging me, then tracing patterns with his fingers. All movement stopped again, except his breath, which was on my neck. I forced myself to wait. Warm and wet, his tongue slid over my throat. I threw my head back, baring my throat to him, wanting him to bite.

His lips trailed painstakingly slowly, down the length of my body. Each kiss was soft, barely touching my skin, yet it set me alight. His hands caressed me as he moved, the touch igniting a fire. Blazing with need, panting, and moaning, I couldn't escape his torment. I shivered, pulsing and squirming more. Pleasure was becoming a new pain I hadn't experienced as I yearned for him to bury himself inside me. For something to help me reach the orgasm that was rippling through me, like slow waves.

"Please,' I begged, and a growl tore from me. "I'm going to explode!"

He stopped, and his fingers slid through my wet pussy. "Oh, you are close, aren't you?" Finally, his body pressed against mine, the head of his cock pressed to my opening. He paused, stopping himself from entering all the way.

I groaned in frustration. Then to my relief, he slid inside me. I pulsed and stretched around him. Warmth and pleasure took hold, and small tremors started deep inside me.

"Fuck,' I gasped, as his cock moved through me. "I'm close to coming already."

"Don't come," he growled.

"What?" I asked in disbelief.

"You don't come, until *I say* you can. Now, wrap your legs around me," Carlos demanded.

I did as he commanded, as the urge to embrace him became too much. "Please let me touch you?" I pleaded.

He stopped in mid-thrust. "Is that what you want? Do you want me to remove the scarves?"

I did want to touch him, but he had never asked for restraints to be removed. "No," I admitted.

"No, what?" he pressed.

"No, my King,"

He resumed his movements, and his tongue slid over my throat again. The pressure of my orgasm started to rise through me. I threw my head back, waves of pleasure fogging my mind. Carlos stopped, removing himself, leaving me empty and throbbing.

"Don't come," he reminded me.

I writhed under him, pulling on the scarves. He pinned my arms down again.

"Oh fuck," I groaned, my entire body straining.

"Look at my beautiful sub, so close to the edge," he whispered, and nibbled on my ear. "Just looking at you like this drives me crazy."

His lips pressed hard against mine, and he ran his tongue over my fang. His blood added to the heat ravaging me.

"Do you want to come? Shall I give you what you want?" he said.

"Please! My King!" I roared, unable to control myself. My heated skin and quivering body were almost painful on the cusp of the orgasm I so desperately wanted.

He kissed the side of my throat, and I shivered, the touch so gentle. *Fuck*, What his lips were doing to me was almost enough to push me to my much-needed release. *Almost.* I had never been blindfolded before, and having my sight taken from me was really adding to all I could smell, feel and hear.

"Okay, I will give you what you want. Are you okay?" he asked. "Rough, or gentle?"

"Rough!" I murmured. "Please, all the roughness, don't hold back!" I yearned to be just as rough with him.

"I want you against the wall!" his voice dropped, the guttural tone that told me he was close.

"Do it!"

The scarves were untied from the bed, but he used them to bind my hands together.

"Put your arms over my head," he said. "Hold on to me."

I did, and the blindfold was removed. He took us from the bed and slammed me against the wall. That section of the wall was harder than the rest. He slid into me again, and I cried out with relief. His hips collided with mine. He was moving faster than before, rougher, growling as he did. I met his vigour with my own. Our breaths were ragged, both of us grunting. Elsewhere in the den, I heard Matteo and Quinn also having sex, the sound driving through me as his cock did.

A bellow burst from my mouth that was almost a scream. Long and animal-like.

"Come," Carlos ordered before biting me.

The pressure reached a crescendo, and I lost control. My back arched. Wave after wave of pure pleasure ripped through my entire being, my toes curling, and the need to bite down had me sinking my fangs into Carlos's shoulder. Against my body, Carlos tensed. His own release echoed mine, gratification surging through our blood bond.

Finally, I lifted my head. I had torn into his shoulder, ripping flesh, leaving behind a gaping wound. I licked at the blood as his body stitched itself together.

"I knew there was a beast inside you," he said, and pulled out of me.

I couldn't speak, still breathing hard, trembling. My knees gave out. Carlos lifted me in his arms, carrying me back to our bed.

"I didn't mean to bite so hard," I finally said when I caught my breath.

"You don't have to apologise for mauling me during the height of your orgasm," he laughed. "In fact, I hope you do that again." He untied my hands, and kissed me softly. "Are you alright? Anything that you didn't like?"

I grinned at him. "More than alright, and once I've recovered from that, I'll be ready for round two."

I sat in what I referred to as a throne, tapping my foot. It was a large wooden chair with a high back, on a slightly raised platform, with cushions. Carlos sat in one just like it next to me. We waited for Diego and Sofia to arrive. Erik and Aria had gone to bring them into the city.

"Relax," Josef said from behind me.

I forced myself to stop tapping my foot. Quinn, Celeste, and Andreas were seated nearby. Matteo stood on the other side of Carlos.

I could smell them the moment they entered the den, hear their hearts beating rapidly, and hear their footsteps. Erik and Aria made no sound as they entered the room, my brother and sister following. Sofia's eyes sought me out immediately, and she gave me an uncertain smile. I smiled back, sure I wore the same expression she did. I then shifted my gaze to Diego. He approached us, eyes on Carlos. It hurt that he hadn't looked at me yet.

Diego had shaved his hair off, and he had put on bulk since the war began. He usually didn't go anywhere unarmed; he always had knives, wooden stakes, and a mini-crossbow on him. But Erik carried a bag, which I assumed held any weapons Diego had arrived with. The two of them stopped in front of us and knelt immediately.

"King Carlos, of La Voz, I thank you for entry into your territory. I arrived armed, as I do not travel without weapons. But I surrendered all weapons to the vampires you sent to grant us entry," Diego said in a formal tone, still not looking at me.

"King of La Voz…King Carlos," Sofia said, her voice heavy with nerves. "Thank you for allowing us entry."

Finally, Diego turned his gaze on me. He stared for a long time, and I realised he was taking in the changes in me. I wanted to know his thoughts, but I resisted the urge to look into his mind. He started to stand, but he stopped. "Queen Camila of La Voz," he said, his voice still formal. "Thank you for the invitation, and for receiving us."

He was not looking at me as my brother, but as a Hunter to a vampire, and my heart broke a little. I'd hoped I would avoid this. I gave him a small smile.

"Queen Camila," Sofia started and broke into a wide grin.

Beside me, Carlos chuckled. "Enough formalities; relax. I welcome you both. While I appreciate your respect for the way we do things, you're family. You can stand."

Diego and Sofia rose to their feet.

"Can I…" Sofia turned towards Carlos. "Am I allowed to hug her?"

Carlos smiled. "That's something to ask her. Sofia, she's still your sister, you can talk to her."

Sofia moved towards me, and I stood. Her arms wrapped around me, her scent enveloping me. I pulled her into a hug, careful to not squeeze too tight.

"Sof," I whispered. "I'm so glad you're here."

Her arms tightened. "So am I."

We broke apart and grinned at each other. Relief engulfed me. She said nothing about my red eyes, or my fangs. She stepped away, and I looked at Diego, wondering if he would hug me. His face was expressionless, something he was good at, to hide his emotions from people.

"Diego?" My voice shook.

His mask fell, and he gave me his wide smile, eyes lighting up. "Do I still have to refer to you as Queen, or can I address my sister now?"

I let out a growl of frustration and he stepped forward, hugging me tight.

"Still the prankster," Sofia laughed, and wrapped her arms around us both.

I realised the clan had left the room, leaving the three of us alone. Except for Carlos.

"I know you've both had a long journey, and you are probably hungry," Carlos said. "Matteo and Quinn prepared a meal."

"Vampires can cook?" Sofia asked in shock.

Carlos grinned at her. "Matteo and Quinn love to cook. Please, come join us. My clan will eat with us. Aria had to leave, though; she has other matters to attend to."

Diego glanced at him. "I heard what happened in San Marino, is she okay?"

Carlos nodded. "Everyone in her clan who was there got out. There were a couple of humans in that fire, though. Do you know who it was who burned the den? They should answer for the human deaths before we get blamed for that."

Diego and Carlos walked ahead, talking, while Sofia stuck to my side.

"How is he?" I asked my sister.

She pressed her lips together. "It's been difficult. He wants peace, but in doing so, many have labelled him a vampire sympathiser. It's widely known that one of his sisters abandoned her post, and the other let a vampire mark her. He has managed to pull some into his way of thinking, though. But it's hard, when vampires are back to killing people."

We entered the dining room, a large, round table covered in dishes with hot food. I smiled at the sight of paella and lasagna in the centre of the table. I hoped Matteo and Quinn had cooked the paella correctly. The clan were already seated. I took a seat, Sofia and Diego taking place on either side of me.

Diego elbowed me. "No weapons at the table," he whispered, quoting something our mother had told us for years.

Confused, I looked up at him. Amusement danced in his eyes. He pointed to his mouth, and it dawned on me he was calling my fangs *weapons*.

"Diego! Don't talk about her fangs!" Sofia said with a little anger in her voice. "Josef told us she can't help it."

Despite my own frustration at my inability to put on a human face for my brother and sister, I couldn't help but smile. "It's okay, Sof."

My smile widened when around the table, every vampire bared their own fangs.

"Who's hungry?" Carlos asked with a growl.

Diego's eyes widened, then visibly relaxed. We started to eat.

I glanced across at Carlos, my heart full. My family, and my clan were eating at the same table. Diego and Sofia had accepted my decision and embraced the new me. I burst with happiness.

Diego's phone beeped and he glanced at it, swearing.

"What is it?" I asked.

"All Hunter records have been made public," he said, reading whatever was on his screen. "Histories, pictures, The War, everything."

Dread felt like a punch to my chest. That meant we'd all be publicly recognised.

Carlos's eyes glazed over then, his smile fading. I didn't like the look of that. "Carlos?"

He put down his fork, looking around the table at each of us.

"The Bloodking has summoned me to Rome," he announced. "He calls upon his generals."

THE END

King Luis's story will continue in Bloodking.

Acknowledgements

Jess, once again I cannot go without acknowledging you. You're the first to read everything I write, and I absolutely love it when you analyse my characters and bring up aspects of them that I never even thought of.

To all my alpha, beta, and ARC readers. Your encouragement, and your enthusiasm for my books, have kept me going in difficult times.

Alicia, I thank you for the inspiration of the *Carnevale di Venezia* scenes. I don't know if I would have thought that up if you hadn't told me all about your experience. I was able to create a scene that really added some tension between Carlos and Camila, hinting into the shift from enemies to lovers. This became one of my favourite scenes.

Tracey, you have been an incredible source of encouragement with your support. I am grateful to have you on this journey with me. Thank you so much for your excitement for the stories I write. You've helped me feel more like an author.

Ellen, I appreciate your input in being able to add to the

Dom/sub aspect of Carlos and Camila's relationship. Rep is important, and so is making sure it plays out the right way. I feel like what I finished with here is a healthy rep of this.

About the Author

Serra is an author of dark historical fantasy and paranormal romance books with stories that draw you in from page one. Within these worlds that she created, you will find unbreakable family bonds, darker aspects to humanity, shadow realms as well as passion, lust, strong FMC's and men who would risk anything for the women they love.

Serra's journey to becoming an author started from a young age, when her first creative writing attempt —a poem titled 'The Mighty Oak Tree,' —was published in her primary school newsletter. An avid reader with a vivid imagination, her Mum always encouraged her to keep writing. She proceeded to write poetry and short stories before discovering a deeper passion for novel writing and screenplays.

In 2021, she adapted a screenplay she'd been working on, into her debut novel 'The Shadow Within,' which was published in November 2023.

Serra is a Melbourne-based author from New Zealand. As a reader and a writer, she's drawn into the dark fantasy and paranormal romance genres. Like many authors, she balances her writing alongside a day job in which she works in the communications part of a marketing and digital team; by night, she's a weaver of words, creator of worlds bringing forth stories that hold readers captive.

If you wish to subscribe, please visit:

www.serrarosewrites.com

Be the first to receive updates and sneak peeks at character art, quotes, chapters, next projects and early access to pre-orders.

Also by Serra Rose

The Horsemen Chronicles:
The Shadow Within
Death's Shadow

Upcoming Titles in The Horsemen Chronicles:
The Whispers of War
The Echoes of War
The Scourge of Famine
The Plague of Humanity

The Bloodsong Series:
Bloodsong
Consumed

Upcoming Titles in The Bloodsong Series:
Bloodking

The Bloodsong Series Spin-offs:
Eternity
Lovestruck
Lovesong

www.ingramcontent.com/pod-product-compliance
Lightning Source LLC
Chambersburg PA
CBHW051307190726
48290CB00001B/39